ENDORSEMENTS

"Rich Adams has very neatly merged a wonderful view of West Point just before the Civil War with the national turmoil of that time, and in the process shown the impact of that turmoil on individuals from all sections of our country. Well done! My heartiest congratulations!

—Dave R. Palmer, Lieutenant General, U.S. Army (Ret.), former superintendent of West Point, historian, Distinguished Graduate of West Point, and author of *The Summons of the Trumpet, The Way of the Fox, and George Washington and Benedict Arnold.*

"…All of my life I have appreciated the privilege of developing great friendships…united behind America's freedom and liberty. But it was not always this way. During the Civil War, such friendships were ripped apart due to cadets' Southern or Northern home places. There was a "parting" of the ways, which led to fighting and killing one another. Thanks to the great work of Rich Adams in *The Parting*, such a terrible period in America's history is presented in a most profound and riveting fashion. There is a truth on these pages we can all benefit from. A great read."

—Hal Moore, Lieutenant General, U.S. Army (Ret.), Distinguished Graduate of West Point, and co-author of *We Were Soldiers Once…And Young.*

"*The Parting* is an authentic period-piece story and a gift for the ages to the Long Gray Line, and to all who embrace America's rich and sometimes heartbreaking history."

—Thomas B. Dyer III, president of the West Point Class of 1967, Distinguished Graduate of West Point, and chairman emeritus of the West Point Association of Graduates.

"*The Parting* is a captivating story about how the officers and cadets of West Point, especially those from the cotton and border states, confronted profound and divisive national political issues on the eve of the Civil War. The resolution of these issues would guide their allegiance in the national crisis. Having entered West Point from Tuscaloosa, Alabama, only a century later, I identified on the most personal level with the main character, John Pelham, native son of Alabama, who during the Civil War would be lauded as 'Gallant Pelham' by many, including Generals Robert E. Lee and J. E. B. Stuart."

—John S. Caldwell, Jr., Lieutenant General U.S. Army, (Ret.).

*—Adapted from the oil painting, Encampment
on the Plain, by William Guy Wall, 1862,
courtesy of the personal art collection of
Thomas Petrie, West Point Class of 1967—*

THE PARTING

A STORY OF WEST POINT
ON THE EVE OF THE CIVIL WAR

To Dr Bob,

With my very best wishes
and thanks for "looking
after me"!

Richard Adams

March 4, 2015

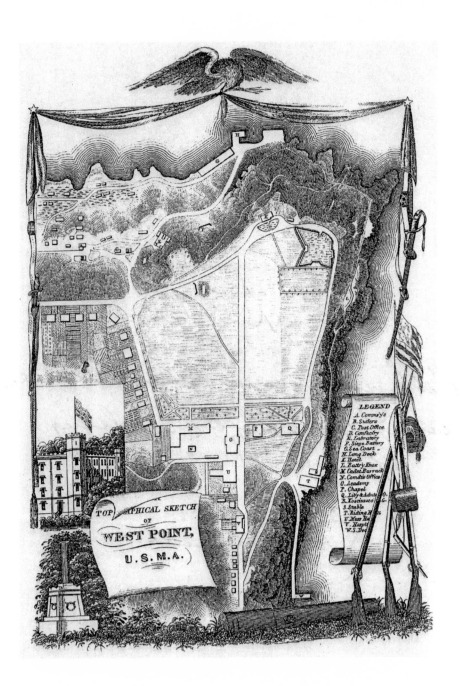

LEGEND

A. Comm'sy's
B. Sutlers
C. Post Office
D. Confectry
E. Labratory
F. Siege Battery
G. Sea Coast
H. Long Dock
K. Hotel
L. Batt'ry Knox
M. Cadet Barrack
N. Comd'ts Office
O. Academy
P. Chapel
Q. Lib'y & Adut't O.
R. Kosciusco G.
S. Stable
T. Riding Hall
V. Mess Ha
Y. Hospt'l
W. S. Dock

TOPOGRAPHICAL SKETCH
OF
WEST POINT,
U. S. M. A.

THE PARTING

A STORY OF WEST POINT
ON THE EVE OF THE CIVIL WAR

RICHARD BARLOW ADAMS
UNITED STATES MILITARY ACADEMY
AT WEST POINT, CLASS OF 1967

ISBN: Hardcover   978-1-4836-0231-8
             Softcover   978-1-4836-0225-7
             Ebook   978-1-4836-0226-4

Rev. date: 03/08/2013

To order additional copies of this book, contact:
Xlibris Corporation
1-888-795-4274
www.Xlibris.com
Orders@Xlibris.com
130288

To Debbie, the love of my life

From mid-April to mid-July 1861, the mood across the Union and the Confederacy was a paradox of fear and righteous indignation.

FOREWORD

When the author, Rich Adams, was a cadet, I returned to West Point to teach in the Department of Social Science. One of the courses I taught was the National Security Seminar. In it, we touched on the self-determination of nations—specifically how, through the years, the self-determination process influenced the fashioning of national policy. At the end of 1860, when South Carolina became the first of many states to secede from the Union, the nation was torn by starkly contrasting visions of what path our country's national policy should follow.

The Parting is a story that brings American history to life and, in the process, makes you think, smile, and sometimes weep. While the subtitle alludes to this being a story about West Point on the eve of the Civil War, it turns out to be much more. The deft interplay between the three days before the First Battle of Bull Run and the events of the preceding year at West Point is surrounded by a broader treatment of American history and enriched by the infusion of seemingly unrelated facts and events. From the outset, the story is charged with tension between the hope for peace and the reality of war. Fast-moving, vivid, and gripping, *The Parting* is, at its heart, a story of a "band of brothers." Formed at West Point among the Class of 1861, it fell to these brothers to decide on which side of Bull Run to make their stand. This powerful and touching saga is written in a way that draws in readers who have never seen—or, indeed, known of—West Point, in no less a compelling way than it does graduates of the Military Academy.

The author's factual account of West Point at the beginning of the war is compelling. His attention to detail, vivid dialogue that captures the temper of the times, as well as his crisp portrayal of key personalities—including the legendary tavern keeper, Benny Havens— will capture both the imagination and the sentiment of every reader.

The author's adherence to documented relationships between actual cadets—some quite famous and some not so, but all significant to the plot—heightens the flow and flavor of the tale.

I applaud Rich Adams for taking on this ambitious project. His careful study and prodigious research have produced a fascinating and artfully crafted novel. In the process, it honors West Point and those who served as their consciences led them, during an enormously wrenching period of our nation's history.

> Peter M. Dawkins—First Captain of the West Point Corps of Cadets; President of the Class of 1959; football captain and Heisman Trophy winner; Rhodes Scholar; Airborne Infantry field commander; decorated combat veteran; White House Fellow; Brigadier General, U.S. Army (Ret.); and Distinguished Graduate of West Point.

MAIN STORY CHARACTERS

West Point Class of 1861 (later, the Class of May 1861):
John Pelham, Alabama
Henry du Pont, Delaware
Nathaniel (Nate) Chambliss, Tennessee
Edmund (Ned) Kirby, New York
Thomas Rosser, Texas
Emory Upton, New York
Charles (Chas) Patterson, Arkansas
Henry Walter (Walter) Kingsbury, Connecticut
Adelbert Ames, Maine
Charles Hazlett, Ohio

West Point Class of 1862 (later, the Class of June 1861):
George Custer, Ohio
Patrick O'Rorke, New York
Charles Ball, Alabama

West Point Class of 1863 (later, the Class of 1862):
Henry Farley, South Carolina

West Point Class of 1865 (later, the Class of 1864):
Daniel McElheny, Ohio

West Point Military Leadership:
Superintendents:
    Colonel Richard Delafield, Class of 1818
    Colonel Pierre Beauregard, Class of 1838
    Colonel Alexander Bowman, Class of 1825

Commandants of Cadets:
  Lieutenant Colonel William Hardee, Georgia, Class of 1838
  Lieutenant Colonel John Reynolds, Pennsylvania, Class of 1841
Other Military Staff:
  Lieutenant Fitzhugh Lee, Class of 1856, Tactical Officer, D Company
  Antoni Lorentz, Sword Master

West Point Academic Staff:
  Dennis Mahan, Class of 1824, Dean of the Academic Board,
    Professor of Engineering and Military Science
  William Bartlett, Class of 1826, Professor of Natural and Experimental
    Philosophy (Physics)
  Albert Church, Class of 1828, Professor of Mathematics
  Robert Weir, Professor of Drawing
  Henry Kendrick, Class of 1835, Professor of Chemistry, Mineralogy,
    and Geology
  Hyacinth Agnel, Professor of French
  John French, Reverend and Professor of English and Ethics
  Lieutenant Howard Oliver, Class of 1854, Assistant Professor of
    Mathematics
  Captain John Kelton, Class of 1851, Librarian

Clermont College:
  Clara Bolton, Philadelphia, Pennsylvania
  Ellie Lawson, Long Island, New York
  Carol Hill, Jackson, Mississippi
  Alice Paine, Boston, Massachusetts
  Jessica Danford, Clarksburg, Virginia
  Rebecca Astor, Concord, Rhode Island
  Miss Frampton, Assistant Dean and Chaperone
  Mrs. Wigglesworth, Chaperone

Other girls attending cadet hops:
  Eva Taylor
  Becky Thompson

Other Story Characters:

Jefferson Davis, Senator of Mississippi, later President of the Confederacy, Class of 1828

James Ewell Brown (Jeb) Stuart, Virginia, Commanding General, Cavalry of Northern Virginia, Class of 1854

Benny Havens (landing and tavern owner; wife Letitia)

Corporal Louis Bentz (longtime Corps bugler; dog, Hanzi)

James, head of service—Superintendent's Quarters

The Pelham family

Willie, Pelham family slave patriarch

Samuel, John Pelham's boyhood companion

Butch Jansonne, Pelham family overseer

Southern fire-eaters: Senator Louis Wigfall, Texas; Representative William Miles, South Carolina

Major Robert Anderson, Kentucky, Class of 1825, Member of the Davis Commission (Summer 1860) and Commander of Fort Sumter

Albert Edward, Prince of Wales, son of Queen Victoria and Prince Albert

PREFACE

Fewer than fifty miles north of New York City sits arguably the most beautiful college campus in America, the United States Military Academy, better known as West Point. Visitors who approach the gray castellated cadet barracks and academic buildings from the south see to their right eighteen black granite markers overlooking the majestic Hudson River and the distant Highland hills. The markers measure two feet by four feet and weigh five thousand pounds. Upon their polished faces is inscribed a history—unique, defining, and terrible. This is Reconciliation Plaza, the largest memorial complex at the nation's oldest military academy, a gift from the West Point Class of 1961 to commemorate its own and the members of the West Point Classes of May and June 1861. *The Parting* is a story based in fact, which enters the Victorian world of West Point during the period from August 1860 through the First Battle of Bull Run (Manassas) fought on July 21, 1861, and is told against the backdrop of slavery, states' rights, the Democratic and Republican Parties, the fire-eaters of the South, the abolitionists of the North, the election of Abraham Lincoln, the secession of the Southern states, the election of Jefferson Davis, the resignations of Southern cadets and officers from West Point, the posturings intended to avoid war, and the surrender of Fort Sumter that dashed all hopes for peace.

CHAPTER ONE

THURSDAY, JULY 18, 1861
WINCHESTER, VIRGINIA
THREE DAYS BEFORE THE FIRST BATTLE OF BULL RUN

In the haziness of dawn common to Shenandoah Valley summer mornings, Lieutenant John Pelham scanned the horizon from behind the battery of four old smoothbore six-pounder artillery pieces. All were aimed, as they had been for a month, to the northeast, at the eighteen thousand Union troops commanded by General Robert Patterson. As part of General Joseph Johnston's Army of the Shenandoah, which numbered twelve thousand, Pelham's mission was to deny Union movement toward Richmond, where the Confederacy had just moved its capital and where Provisional President Jefferson Davis was still scrambling to put his government in place. As acting commander of the Alburtis Battery, Pelham was providing direct support for Colonel Francis Bartow's brigade. His second in command, and the only other officer in the battery, was Jason Findley, a militia second lieutenant who a month earlier had been teaching math in a school in Lynchburg.

Pelham stood nearly six feet and eyed the gunner at the second of his four artillery pieces. "All right, Corporal Summers, the target is yours."

"You heard the lieutenant," the corporal growled at the five members of his gun crew. "You best perform or I'll be kicking your butts to midnight."

Pelham turned to the other gun crews. "You know what I expect. I want to know what this crew could have done better or faster."

1

The other crews understood well—that when it was their turn, they would receive no quarter.

For a month, Pelham had drilled his green troops with and without live ammunition. At the direction of those higher up, the live ammunition was reserved for real targets. Pelham understood the rationale, but he saw benefit only in tangible results, the hitting and missing of targets, and had a tendency to manufacture live targets where others saw none. Corporal Summers' crew fixed on such a target—a granite outcrop on a distant hillside.

Summers barked the commands to load and fire, and the gun muzzle flashed red. Every eye watching the enemy rock saw it explode in gray smoke, just as a hard-riding courier approached from nearby Winchester. The courier reined his horse and struggled to catch his breath.

"Easy, soldier," Pelham said in a calm voice.

"Lieutenant, sir. Your presence is desired at a meeting at General Johnston's headquarters."

Pelham smiled at the man's polite phrasing of a direct order.

"As soon as you can make it, sir!" The rider jerked the reins and galloped off.

Moments later, the thunder of many horses preceded the Confederate Black Horse Cavalry's return from the northeast. Its lead rider wore a cavalier hat flying a black ostrich plume. The man, Colonel James Ewell Brown Stuart, West Point Class of 1854 and known as Jeb, carried himself high in the saddle.

Pelham leaped up on a caisson wagon, waving his hat to draw Stuart's attention.

Stuart saw him and trotted up, touching his hat. "'Morning, John."

"'Morning, Colonel." Pelham saluted the man five years his senior. "General Johnston has called a meeting. Even I am to attend, so I'm sure he'll be expecting you."

"And I'll have news for him." The man with the red beard touched his hat a second time and dashed off.

Sensing deployment, Pelham ordered Findley to prepare the battery and limber the guns—attach them to chest-mounted carriages drawn by six-horse teams. Similarly, caisson wagons, overloaded with solid shot and canister rounds, would be readied.

Johnston's headquarters was the Winchester courthouse, and by the time Pelham entered the main courtroom, it was full of officers, all bearing high rank. After a few minutes, Johnston's aide-de-camp entered and announced the general's arrival. The assembled officers snapped to attention. Johnston, who bore a trim mustache, goatee, and thinning hair, returned the salutes and gestured for everyone to take a seat. He stood before the magistrate's bench, holding two telegrams.

"Colonel Stuart, what have you to report?"

"Favorable news, General. Union forces have pulled back to Harpers Ferry, and there is evidence that they intend no offense. Rumor is that Patterson has overestimated our strength and sees himself on the defense. Icing on the cake is that his army is dissolving. With each day, more of his ninety-day conscripts called up by Lincoln in April are deciding on home-cooked meals."

The room filled with laughter.

"God is indeed good." Johnston raised one of the dispatches above his head. "This is from President Davis. It was sent early this morning and asks that I consider moving the army with all speed to Manassas Junction to reinforce General Beauregard's twenty thousand troops, spread out as they are along Bull Run. As we all know, our good friend Irvin McDowell left Washington on the sixteenth with around thirty-five thousand Union troops. He arrived late yesterday in Centreville, about three miles east of Bull Run.

"This other dispatch is from General Beauregard. It says that one of McDowell's divisions is presently engaging him at Blackburn's Ford over Bull Run." Johnston scanned the faces in the room. "The telegram is an hour old, so I suspect there is more to the story. Anyway, I was wondering if we might want to help our Confederate brothers."

The room rocked with cheers.

Johnston turned to the blackboard behind him, which showed the relative locations of Washington DC and, in Virginia, Richmond, Manassas Junction, Winchester, Ashby Gap, and Piedmont Station. Between the locations were intervening distances: seventeen miles from Winchester southeast to Ashby Gap atop the Blue Ridge; ten miles from Ashby Gap south to Piedmont Station; and thirty-four miles from Piedmont Station east to Manassas Junction.

"We'll be pushing our green troops to the limit. Have them cook three day's rations. We leave at noon, and when we get to Piedmont Station, the infantry will load on trains for Manassas. Artillery and cavalry will travel by road."

Those in the room scribbled notes.

"General Jackson's First Brigade will take the lead, followed in order by the Second, Third, and Fourth Brigades. Tom, can you be ready by noon?"

The man with a full beard and piercing blue-gray eyes nodded.

Colonel Francis Bartow, General Barnard Bee, and General Kirby Smith, the other brigade commanders, likewise acknowledged the order of march.

"I am hopeful we can cross the Blue Ridge no later than midnight," Johnston continued. "For the defense of Winchester, we have two thousand local militia. We'll leave some artillery, and we'll leave the sick. Half of Stuart's cavalry will keep Patterson at bay for a day, and then join us as soon as they can."

Johnston cleared his throat. "Gentlemen, we have to do this quickly or it will be for naught. Worse, McDowell will have better than an even chance to run for Richmond."

The door to the courtroom suddenly flew open. A wide-eyed youth with a broad grin held a telegram high above his head. "Sirs, it is my honor as a Confederate to report that them bluecoats that tried to cross Bull Run at Blackburn's Ford, maybe three thousand of 'em, they never saw this side of Bull Run. We whipped them—yes we did! And it was General Longstreet and Colonel Early that did it!"

CHAPTER TWO

On Sunday, August 12, 1860, following Holy Communion, the organist played "Onward Christian Soldiers," and John Pelham sang with strength and emotion, catching many in the congregation by surprise. Flanked by his parents, Atkinson and Martha Pelham, and six siblings in a pew bearing a brass plate honoring his maternal grandparents, he was different from what any of them remembered.

The Presbyterian Church in Jacksonville, Alabama, was large by southern standards, seating two hundred whites in the main sanctuary and fifty blacks in the balcony. The sanctuary was a showcase, constructed of the finest materials, courtesy of a town and county where cotton was king and faith in Christ the foundation of life. The sanctuary and balcony were packed to overflowing for the mid-month Sunday service, which would be followed by a fellowship picnic. Outside the church, the day was already hot and humid. Two dozen black men and boys tended horses and carriages. Many of them sang their own version of the church hymn; others engaged in banter or waited in silence. Flies buzzed the grounds in anticipation of the feast.

In four years, Pelham had been home only once before. He too realized he bore little resemblance to the seventeen-year-old who had journeyed alone to West Point, New York, in 1856 to take the qualifying examinations for entrance into the United States Military Academy. In the time away from Benton County, recently renamed Calhoun County in honor of the former vice president and South Carolinian, his mind, body, and spirit had been much altered by the Academy's discipline and training, and by the rigor that had reduced the Class of 1861 from ninety-three to fifty. He was grateful for this unexpected second furlough. The coming year would be his fifth and last at the school, located some forty miles up the Hudson River from New York City and a thousand miles from Jacksonville.

Pelham struggled to focus on the service, to be honestly reverent. As he sang the last hymn, though, his mind drifted to the spirited debates he'd had with his father the past week over President Buchanan's successor.

He felt a small hand take his and gave it a squeeze. Its owner, Bettie, his only sister, now seventeen and more than a handsome woman, was home from her third year of college in Maysville, Kentucky. Two summers previous, when Pelham was on a longer furlough of two and a half months, he had traveled to Jacksonville by way of Maysville, so that the two of them could journey home together. This past week, they had spent nearly every afternoon as companions, riding or walking the plantation, reliving the past, and dreaming the future. She had proven quite a horsewoman and had been delightful company, though some of her northern sympathies frustrated him, despite her declarations that she was only teasing. He admonished her that she was too convincing a teaser and should be careful of her powers. In his eyes, she had grown up too quickly, and without his presence or permission. He would dearly miss her when he returned to West Point—the place she called Camelot.

Charles and William, Pelham's older brothers, stood on the other side of Bettie, and beyond them were the younger Pelhams—Peter, Samuel, and Thomas.

Suddenly the organist hit a wrong key and awoke the congregation, which responded with sideways glances and snickers.

When the music died, Reverend Peter Smith gave the organist a forgiving look, and in a booming voice, concluded the service. "Now may the Lord God of heaven bless you and keep you, make his face to shine upon you, and give you peace, now and forevermore. Amen."

The congregation waited patiently for their aged leader to shuffle down the aisle to the front vestibule, with the newly arrived and much younger Reverend Paul Knox following. Knox had been introduced to the congregation only that morning.

As the Pelham clan filed out, each took the relic's weathered hand and received a personal blessing or word of encouragement. When John Pelham approached the man, he took the arthritic hand.

The old eyes glistened. "What can I say, John, but that you give me great joy. What a blessing to your family and all of us to have you home these few days, but it's not fair you should leave so soon."

Pelham gently hugged the man, whose cleric robes smelled of naphtha. Reverend Smith had always been in the pulpit, and had tutored him for the academy entrance exams. The body that had been forever strong from raising barns for parishioners was a shell of its former self.

"You, sir, are ever on my mind, as is home. Anyway, just one more year and I'm done, and after giving the country its due, I'll return and you'll tire of me soon enough."

"Never, lad," the reverend vowed with a laugh that soured to a hacking cough. Recovering, he patted Pelham on the back. "Good luck, my son, and may God bless and protect you in all that lies ahead."

Pelham greeted the new minister, who was not much older than himself, and descended the church steps, conscious of his blue furlough uniform, highlighted with gold buttons down the front of the dress jacket. His brother Will had told him he looked like a peacock in heat. By a sense he did not fully understand, he was aware, as he had been in the sanctuary, of the glances nearly every young woman in the congregation gave him, and the furtive looks beneath fashionable hats and parasols were not unwelcome.

As the aroma of fried chicken teased his nose, he scanned the lawn from beneath the visor of his blue forage cap, but did not find who he was looking for. At the bottom of the stairs, a weathered man of some fifty years stepped in front of him. The man was Butch Jansonne, the family's new overseer.

"Master John, it was good to finally meet you, and I just wanted to wish you a safe trip back to your school."

The man extended his hand and Pelham shook it. "That's kind of you, Mr. Jansonne."

"I trust you found everything in good order, sir?"

"I'm sorry?"

"The plantation?"

"Why—I assume it's fine. I've no reason to think otherwise."

7

"Your blacks are a proud bunch, Master Pelham, and they work well, when encouraged, but then you know that, I'm sure. You have talked to some of them?" Jansonne turned his head, spat tobacco juice, and wiped his mouth on his sleeve.

"I had intended to, especially the man Samuel, but regretfully, no."

Jansonne seemed surprised, and offered a faint smile before taking his leave.

Pelham spied his father in conversation with a man at the corner of the churchyard, beneath a yawning oak tree. The discussion appeared serious, and he was drawn to it. The man was Judge Abraham J. Walker, a longtime family friend and a member of the Alabama Supreme Court. Pelham didn't recall seeing the judge in church.

"You two appear in need of an arbiter," he said, executing a slight bow.

The judge clasped Pelham's hand. "John, this has become a time of contingencies. And your father—the good doctor—and I appear to see a thing differently."

"Abraham, that would be an understatement," Atkinson Pelham said stiffly, but then his demeanor softened at the approach of his daughter.

"I'm so sorry to interrupt, Judge Walker." Bettie flashed a smile at her brother. "But, Pa, would you meet my classmate Lucy Bains from Birmingham? Can you believe she's here? You simply must."

The judge nodded his assent as the elder Pelham excused himself.

Pelham felt his father's touch as he passed by.

The judge, a full-bearded medium-height man of sixty, considered Pelham before speaking. "My, but you've become quite a man, John. Seems like yesterday, your christening." He paused. "In your short lifetime, the country's seen a lot of change. Much is afoot, John, and what I was saying to your father is that we Alabamians need to be prepared for an alternative future, should events unfold as they appear they might."

As was his habit when entering upon a subject, the judge pursed his lips, and Pelham prepared for words spent frugally.

"If the election goes badly and Alabama and other Southern states were to exercise their option, to strike out on their own, try something different, a different form of government, and between them a looser federation with less centralized power and greater respect of the individuality and needs of a state, would you favor Alabama joining such a federation?"

"You talked to Father about this, sir?"

"I suggested to your father that there will be mass secessions if Lincoln is elected, though quite frankly he thinks me wrong, and I suppose there is some chance he's right." The judge glanced across the lawn at the older Pelham, who was speaking to Bettie's friend. "Your father believes compromise is still the best wisdom, and that it will prevail as it has in the past. And beyond that, he is dead set against secession no matter what the circumstance. He even vowed to stump with Stephen Douglas to fight it."

"And you're wondering where I am on the subject, sir?"

"Knowing that would be useful, yes."

Pelham's father had lamented the divisiveness of the Democratic Party that had given the sectional Republican Party its opening, but vehemently claimed the Democrats would reunite before November and undo the botched conventions in Charleston and Baltimore. The split ticket of Stephen Douglas for the North and John Breckinridge for the South would be resolved.

"Then, sir," Pelham said, "I'm afraid it won't please you to know that, at least for the present, Pa and I are of the same mind." The words nearly stuck in Pelham's throat. "The issues are daily in the papers, as well as what you suggest. But, sir, I believe Pa could be right, that Alabama has very much to lose in what you propose. I can't see the real gain, not in basic rights and certainly not in economics." Pelham paused. "Sir, wouldn't you agree there is much risk in what you're suggesting?"

"There is risk in everything, John—everything worthwhile—but our rights as a sovereign state are in perilous jeopardy and have been for some time. As long as we've had a Democrat in the White House, we've had a measure of sympathy for our needs and our peculiar institution."

Pelham nodded. Slavery would always be the sticking point.

"As you say," the judge continued, "we've survived some divisive times through compromise. But the federal government has become a mean thing, continually growing and assuming for itself responsibilities

9

and rights that naturally, by the Constitution, fall to the states. Worse, its decisions invariably favor the North. If our William Yancey had his way, we would already be a sovereign state, flying our own flag."

Pelham was silent. His father had nothing good to say about Yancey, Alabama's chief fire-eater—the Northern descriptor for a secessionist. His father said that the only time Yancey wasn't preaching secession was when he slept. He made no attempt to hide his disdain for Yancey, and all those who he viewed as loose cannons.

"Do you know how onerously we are taxed by tariffs, John, and how unfairly our commerce is managed by the federals? Do you understand how our livelihood, our property institution, and our right to take property into the new territories are at stake?" The judge didn't wait for an answer. "I suppose you do not take the abolitionists seriously?"

Pelham couldn't help but admire the judge's quickness.

"No more than I should, sir. I believe we skew the group out of proportion, that what John Brown did at Harpers Ferry is distorted history. Personally, I believe abolitionists make more noise than allies and number but few."

"Perhaps, but Harpers Ferry has had the South looking over its shoulder."

Pelham couldn't refute the judge's point. Colonel Robert E. Lee's capture of John Brown in October 1859 had been a significant event. Brown had led a bloody, but botched, revolt of slaves in Virginia, hoping to catalyze the South into a slave rebellion. His grand vision had unraveled to a last-ditch stand inside the engine house of the Harpers Ferry Federal Armory in northern Virginia, where he, his sons, and a small number of committed slaves held several hostages. One hostage was the father of a fellow cadet at West Point, a grandnephew of George Washington. Pelham knew that Lee had sent under the white flag a recent graduate, Lieutenant Jeb Stuart, to negotiate with Brown. After Brown's refusal to surrender and the bloody aftermath, another West Point graduate and a hero of the Mexican War, Thomas Jackson, mobilized his cadets from the Virginia Military Institute to provide security for Brown's trial and hanging.

"How many in your class, John, from the Southern states—the slave states?"

"Perhaps one in three, sir. I do not believe more."

"One in three? A disturbing ratio, don't you think? I'm not saying that the Democrats can't win, but for the life of me, I don't see how. In any event, we can ill afford to lose more seats in the upcoming congressional elections, and they'll be strongly contested. If we lose them, without doubt the next president will be Republican, worse it will be Lincoln, and with Lincoln, Alabama or South Carolina will bolt and the dam burst."

The judge's bluntness struck Pelham. "Sir, have you ever been to West Point?"

"I have not had the pleasure."

"I assure you, it is the noblest of institutions, and bears none of the political rancor of which we speak."

"And that is to its credit, I'm sure. But the thing is—and let me be candid—if Alabama does secede, we're going to need every military advantage we can muster in the event Mr. Lincoln chooses to make an issue of it. More to the point, we'll need a strong officer corps. We'll need every West Pointer we can get."

Pelham said nothing.

The judge leaned closer. "I don't need to tell you how important this year is for you, for all of us. And I hear some very good things about your popularity as a cadet and your performance at the Academy. That among your pursuits you are excellent with the blade and the finest horseman at the Point. All this, of course, is very well, and cavalry is important, but what we'll really need are artillerists, expert artillerists. I encourage you to—"

The commotion of a carriage advancing up the church drive and shouts for Pelham interrupted the judge. He rested a hand on Pelham's shoulder. "Enough, John. You must be on your way, and I don't envy your journey. I simply ask that you think seriously upon what's happening and your role in it."

"Yes, sir, you may depend upon it. I seek only what is best for Alabama."

The judge nodded. "As do I."

As the judge turned to go, Pelham put a restraining hand on his arm. "Sir, may I write you as matters progress?"

The judge brightened. "Of course, John, and you may depend on my immediate reply. And if you will indulge me one last question, what is the one thing you want more than anything else at this point in your life?"

Pelham didn't hesitate. "To graduate from West Point, sir."

The judge smiled. "Of course. Foolish of me to ask."

Pelham made his way to the carriage and found a crowd wanting a speech. Seeing he had no choice, he mounted the church steps and delivered a convincing oratory, that home and all who made it so were sacred to him, and that what he was about to conclude at West Point was for them and for Alabama. This earned him a grand applause and the freedom to depart. He descended the steps feeling, oddly, both euphoric and uneasy. He shook countless hands and embraced friends, while across the church lawn, blacks busied themselves arranging tables and benches.

"Don't think I can't still whip you." Charles, the oldest of the Pelhams, waved his fists threateningly, and then hugged his brother.

"Not likely," William, the second eldest, said. "But I sure can." Pelham received another hug.

"I'm counting on you both to take care of Ma, Pa, and the family." He then sought out his younger brothers and finally Bettie, who was trying, unsuccessfully, to be brave.

"We'll have none of that, sis. You take care of yourself and mind the boys in Maysville. They can't be trusted."

His remark made her smile. "John Pelham, how is it you know that? And, anyway, I can take excellent care of myself, thank you. Besides, I'm waiting for you to find me a cadet."

"And I will, but in return, when you're back at school, take all that Yankee rhetoric with a grain of salt."

"I am not becoming a Yankee."

"I didn't say you were, but the Mason-Dixon Line is taking on more significance, and those from the North are of a different persuasion." He winked and kissed her forehead, at which she came undone.

"There, there, sweetheart." Martha Pelham consoled her daughter. Then she confronted her West Pointer. "John Pelham, promise me you will read your Bible every night and say your prayers."

"I do, and I will, Mother."

"Mother?" Her eyes glistened. "Lord, they've made you a man."

His embrace swallowed the small woman. "Ma—I love you so much, Ma."

"Willie has a jug of fresh water and ham and cheese sandwiches for your lunch." She wiped her eyes. "And this is for later." She handed him a muslin-wrapped package. "Some of young Ora's biscuits and Willie's beef jerky."

"It's time, John." Atkinson Pelham took his son by the arm and led him to the carriage. After a few steps, he whispered, "So soon. A three-week furlough with only a week at home and the rest traveling."

"I know, Pa. I almost wish I hadn't—"

"Nonsense! Nonsense. Having you for even a few days has meant everything to all of us, especially your mother. You will write?"

"Of course, Pa, as often as I can."

"There is so much going on, John, and our new man Jansonne gets the work done, but—" The older Pelham let it drop. "Judge Walker can be quite persuasive."

"No more than you, Pa, and as I promised, I'll give your opinion a chance. But tell me about Jansonne."

"He's a strict one to be sure, but claims it's needful, given the amount of cotton we have to bring in."

"He uses the whip?"

"I can't say that he overuses it, at least not yet."

"Aren't you concerned for runaways, Pa?"

"That is always a possibility, but one of the Watson slaves, Charlie was his name. You might remember he used to be old man Watson's driver. Anyway, he ran off and got himself killed in Illinois."

"Killed?"

"They said he resisted arrest, and news of that sort has a restraining effect."

"We've a good black family, Pa. We've never had a runaway, nor given cause for it." Pelham wanted to say more, but knew it wasn't his place. As for old man Watson, he remembered the man only too well.

"We just need to get through the next year," his father said, almost in prayer.

Pelham sensed change in his father. He looked uncharacteristically tired, and Pelham considered for the first time the stress of running a plantation, while at the same time being the county doctor.

"Pa?"

"Yes, son."

"I am going back to the Academy with every intention of finishing the year, getting my diploma, and being commissioned. You know what that means to me. But if it isn't possible, I won't be of age … I will need your permission to resign."

The elder Pelham smiled and patted him on the back. "No reason to visit that now."

They reached the carriage and its driver.

"Willie, you take good care of our boy."

The slim black man with a head of white wool smiled. "'Course I will, master."

Pelham climbed up beside the driver. "Okay, Willie, take me to West Point."

Willie laughed. "Well, Master John, I can take you as far as the stage." He made a clucking sound that propelled the one-horse carriage past the line of well-wishers and beyond the smell of fried chicken.

Pelham sat tall on the seat, looking back at the figures on the lawn until they disappeared from view. The carriage moved smartly down the lane and turned onto the main road. Willie whistled his way through a medley of gospel songs.

After a time of reflection, Pelham broke the silence. "Willie, how is it you never get older?"

"Lord, Master John, I suppose cuz I's always been old."

"But you'll outlast us all." He gave the black man a gentle nudge. Willie was the patriarch of the Pelham slaves, and as far back as Pelham could remember, the man had been old. For most of his life, he either had picked cotton or had supervised the picking, until his gift was discovered the summer an equine virus swept through the South, killing nearly two thousand horses. Willie's root-based cure saved the Pelham steeds. Within a week, Pelham's father had instructed Peter Martin, the previous overseer, that Willie was no longer to work in the field, but in the stables and doing directly for the family.

The carriage continued on, and Pelham finally challenged the obnoxious grin that had been on Willie's face the past half mile.

"What are you grinning about, Willie?"

The black man said nothing.

"Tell me, Willie, what is it?"

"Nothing, Master John. I just happy and proud—proud of you. You gonna make a fine officer, Master John."

"You think so?"

"I know it."

"Well, maybe I will, and for sure it's been a long time coming. And if it does happen, you, dear Willie, get all the credit."

Willie's face was radiant. "Ah, Master John, it wasn't none of me."

Pelham put a hand on the black man's arm. "Willie, next to God and family, you know I love you and Samuel best. And it was you, Willie, who taught me to ride, care for a horse, fish, and so much more."

"Oh, Master John."

"And the whole family feels the same, and shame on you if you don't know it better than your name. Pa has always said you're as good, as easy, and as consistent a soul as ever lived, and the glue that holds the place together."

The carriage made good time along the valley road that traversed the Alabama hill country, the air humid and flavored with cut hay and honeysuckle. Cottonwoods, magnolias, and sprawling oaks lined the road. Pelham feverishly stored images of home that would have to last a year: the rolling landscape, the woods, bottomlands, and dark-water creeks; the fields of cotton, wheat, and corn; the laborers in the fields; the houses, barns, and slave shanties; the daily wash hung out to dry; the fences of wood, stone, and wire; the horses, cattle, and hogs grazing dumbly; the cats and dogs lazing in the afternoon sun; and the chickens clucking about as if they owned the world.

A man on horseback approached from the opposite direction. Visibly impressed with Pelham's uniform, the man touched the brim of his hat. Pelham responded in kind.

After another mile of silence, Pelham cleared his throat. "And Samuel? How is he?"

"Oh, Samuel, that boy is fine, just fine, Master John."

"I had hoped to see him."

"In the field, Master John, got to bring in that cotton. You know that. Your daddy made Samuel the boss black man in the field."

Pelham was well aware of Samuel's promotion. The day before, his father had lauded Samuel's work. Still, it should have been easy for

Samuel to visit the big house either in the early morning or late evening, if only for a few minutes; and Pelham had very much wanted to see him, to know how he was doing, and to mend how they had left things when he had last been home on furlough. He thought of Samuel often and the history they had—and it was always Samuel, never Sam or Sammy. Memories of their time of innocence and fantasy came easy, when they had been inseparable from sunup to sundown, happy times until the day everything changed. The game had changed everything. He had never meant to hurt Samuel, and they had both survived. They had grown up. He thought of the year before he'd gone to West Point, when his father had entrusted him with a hundred acres of timber land, telling him to clear and farm the land with a work force of six of the blacks. His father had agreed with the men he'd selected, including Samuel. For ten months they had toiled as one. They felled trees, cut wood, grubbed the land, constructed living quarters, plowed fields, planted corn, and brought in a harvest, all before the fall frost. Through it all, Samuel had worked the hardest.

They crossed over the covered bridge at Four Mile Spring, the sun bursting through holes in the tin roof. Pelham reached for his valise and retrieved the ham and cheese sandwiches his mother had given him, handing one to Willie.

"Thank you, Master John."

"Tell me, Willie, how are things on the plantation? Tell me the truth."

"Oh, Master John—"

"Don't sweeten it."

"I suppose we do have some bumps with the new overseer, that's a fact. But I expect that's natural." The old man picked his words like watermelon seeds. "And I expect that's why you haven't seen Samuel. Master Butch rides Samuel pretty hard, he do." Willie forced a smile. "But everything gonna work its way around."

Pelham took a long pull on the jug of water and passed it to the black man.

They continued in silence until they crested a hill that brought Willie to life. "There 'tis, Master John. Blue Mountain." The old man pointed down at the small town.

They arrived at the stage office a few minutes before four o'clock, the fourteen-mile trip taking three hours. Pelham checked in for the morning stage and directed Willie to the Wilkes Boarding House, a block past the stage stop.

"You made good time, Willie, and after watering and feeding the horses, you should make it back well before dark."

"And that's good, cuz you know I don't take so good to the dark." The black man spoke with relief in his voice.

"Nothing is going to get you, Willie."

The man smiled and handed Pelham his duffel.

"Thank you, Willie. Thanks for everything." Pelham extended his hand.

Willie grasped Pelham's hand in both of his. "My pleasure, Master John, my pleasure. You take real good care of youself, you hear? All us want you back safe and whole."

"I will, Willie." Pelham gazed into the old man's eyes with the sudden urge to ask him if he had ever wanted to be free.

"Is there something else, Master John?"

Pelham smiled weakly. "No, Willie."

CHAPTER THREE

WEST POINT, NEW YORK

That same Sunday afternoon, the apprentice post courier, Alden Weir, the youngest of sixteen children born to Robert Weir, the Academy's drawing professor, ran as fast as his short, spindly legs would carry him, clutching a sealed envelope. In less than a minute, he covered the distance from post headquarters to the large well-appointed home of the superintendent of the United States Military Academy, currently occupied by its oldest superintendent, Colonel Richard Delafield. Delafield, in regal blue uniform and sporting bushy white chin-curtain whiskers, stood on the wide front veranda waiting to review the Corps of Cadets when they turned out for parade.

"Colonel, sir." The breathless boy handed the telegram to the superintendent. "For you, sir."

Delafield patted the boy on the head and rendered him a sharp salute. "Thank you very much, Alden."

"Thank you, sir!" The boy raced off in the direction he had come.

Delafield ran a finger around the inside of his collar, frustrated with uniform alterations that never kept pace with his weight.

"Colonel, sir, some ice water?" A distinguished-looking black man in a pressed white topcoat put a tray in front of the superintendent.

"Thank you, James." Delafield drew a pair of thick-lensed wire-rimmed spectacles from his coat pocket. The glasses rendered him fish-eyed, but were essential for reading. After digesting the telegram, another from General Winfield Scott, still general-in-chief of the army, he looked across the Plain.

"Bad news, sir?" After five years of daily contact, the head of the Delafield's service staff understood the superintendent better than anyone, and whether he wanted to be or not, James was privy to the man's inmost thoughts.

"Dammit, James. How are we to perform our mission when the secretary of treasury won't approve my budgets?"

"Yes, sir."

"Hopefully, Jeff Davis can do us some good."

James nodded at the reference to Jefferson Davis, the senior senator from Mississippi, who the day before had departed for Washington DC, after concluding his commission to evaluate the Academy. The commission had included three other members of Congress, along with Major Robert Anderson and two junior officers. The inspection and review of the Academy had lasted a month, and had included interviews with cadet officers in the First Class and selected members of the Second Class.

Delafield placed the telegram and his spectacles on the railing and peered across the Plain at the distant encampment. The field of white tents was barely visible through the encircling double row of elms that had been planted only a few years earlier. The city of tents was the annual summer encampment for the Corps of Cadets, this year numbering two hundred and seventy-eight. The cadets ranged in age from sixteen to twenty-six, and represented all thirty-three states. Across Jefferson Road from the superintendent's quarters, a steady stream of civilians, including wide-eyed ladies in Victorian dress, approached the array of benches in anticipation of the afternoon parade.

Delafield fixed his gaze on the flag that furled above the crown of trees at the north end of the Plain. When he first laid eyes on the flag as a new cadet in 1814, it bore fifteen stripes and fifteen stars, inconsistent with the eighteen states then in the Union. The flag had not been changed since 1795, and there was still disagreement on how to account for Tennessee, Ohio, and Louisiana. Not until 1818, under President Monroe, would the flag bear stripes for the original thirteen colonies and a star for each state. The standard that now waved boasted thirty-three stars, and Delafield wondered how many more would appear when the territories from Mexico were ready. The flag reminded him of

Davis's remark, that government intentions to keep slavery out of the new territories would fuel a fire no one needed.

Where had the time gone, Delafield mused, as he surveyed the backs of his hands, his skin wrinkled, liver-spotted. It seemed a lifetime ago when he'd graduated first in the Class of 1818. Twenty years of field assignments had followed, and then came his first appointment to West Point as superintendent. Those seven years had been a proud time, when the children were home, a time of fond memories. That idyllic assignment was followed by the Mexican War and more years of field service, until, in 1856, he was ordered back to West Point as superintendent for an unprecedented second term. At first, it had been a source of pride, but the shine had long worn off. He had held the Academy's top post for nearly a fifth of its lifetime, because, he had learned, if you design it, you build it. During his career he had architected, constructed, or otherwise had a hand in almost every significant structure at the Academy, including the academic building, the cadet barracks, the library and post headquarters building, the cadet chapel, the ordnance compound, the mess hall, the hospital, the riding hall, and the horse stables. But now, at age sixty-two, he was numb to the routine of Academy life and the responsibility of caring for, feeding, and evaluating the Corps of Cadets. And to this was added the headache of the little fiefdoms in the academic department and the upkeep of the Academy's physical plant.

He was mentally and physically tired. He was tired of the annual inspections by the secretary of war's five-member board of visitors. Those members, congressional delegates, senior military staff, and civilian academics, forayed way beyond their primary purpose of evaluating the cadets in their June examinations. Invariably, the board opened doors and pulled out drawers beyond their assigned scope, and challenged what they little understood. The latest board had arrived in late May, inspected the facilities, assessed the curriculum, monitored the faculty's final examinations, applauded the outgoing First Classmen, and monitored the examination of the civilian-attired, pimple-faced freshmen who would form the next class of plebes. And, as always, he greeted with politeness and feigned interest the board's opinions and recommendations.

After the board departed, Jefferson Davis and his commission arrived. If it had been headed by anyone other than his gaunt-faced friend, it could have destroyed his summer. But Davis made good on his word that the commission would impose no burden on summer training. Delafield knew that Davis loved West Point, and Davis had often been in a position to do it great service. After seven years of military service and escorting Chief Black Hawk to prison, the young Davis had left the military to prepare for a political career while raising cotton in Mississippi. From 1844 to 1846, he served Mississippi in the United States House of Representatives. At the outbreak of hostilities with Mexico, he resigned from Congress and raised a regiment known as the Mississippi Rifles, which gained considerable renown during the war. After the war, he returned to politics as U.S. senator for Mississippi, and served as secretary of war during the term of President Franklin Pierce. Delafield knew Davis was an ardent states' rights man, but not a secessionist. In fact, earlier in the year, Davis had submitted several resolutions in the Senate to salve the clamor of secessionist rhetoric. When last he and Delafield talked, Davis suggested that the Union might still be saved.

From the south, along Jefferson Road, Delafield noticed the approaching figure of Dennis Mahan, dean of the academic department and professor of military/civil engineering and military science. Mahan, a thin man, carried his signature worn leather briefcase and mounted the steps without invitation. His face bore a look of gravity, as it always did.

"Dennis." Delafield held out his hand.

The waiter poured the dean a glass of water.

"Colonel, sir." Mahan extracted a worn folder from his briefcase. "As requested, documents addressing the issue and illustrating my points."

Delafield nodded as he took the folder. Mahan had finished first in the Class of 1824—as had William Bartlett, professor of natural and experimental philosophy, Class of 1826; and Albert Church, professor of mathematics, Class of 1828. The three of them formed the core of the Academy's intellectual vigor and oversight.

"I'll give it priority, Dennis." Delafield lifted his eyeglass in the direction of the cadet encampment. "Care to stay for the review?"

"I'm quite sure I've seen enough parade reviews, sir. Classes begin in less than two weeks, so, if I could hear back from you—"

"I'll get back to you on the morrow. A question, Dennis. How long have you been dean of the academic board?"

Mahan paused to think. "I suppose thirty years, sir, possibly more."

"And every year at this time you bring me a folder."

"It's my responsibility, Colonel, to steward the curriculum."

"Um," Delafield mused. He raised his glass. "To the great defender of our hallowed institution."

After Mahan was gone, Delafield opened the folder, knowing that the contents addressed the matter of the Academy's ethics course. He extracted two documents. The first and thickest was the preliminary report from the Davis Commission, indicating that according to both cadet and officer feedback, the course was unnecessary. The character traits of honor and ethics taught in the course were sufficiently covered and stamped on every other aspect of Corps life, not to mention preached every Sunday. The commission favored, instead, another course in civil engineering or one in the new field of electrics. The second document was the academic board's defense of the course, authored by Mahan.

Delafield slipped the documents back in the folder. He understood his role and the need for peace. He would support Mahan.

He gazed back at the Plain, where two men in army blue approached from the encampment site. He recognized one as Lieutenant Colonel William Hardee, Class of 1838. Hardee was the Academy's commandant of cadets and second in rank only to himself. Hardee was in charge of the Academy's tactical department. Delafield couldn't make out the other man at first, but then recognized him as First Lieutenant Fitzhugh Lee, Class of 1856, and the newly assigned tactical officer of Cadet Company D. To Delafield, Hardee struck an imposing figure even at a distance. He was pleased to have the Southerner at his side. In the war with Mexico, serving under Zachary Taylor, Hardee had performed brilliantly, earning two brevets for gallantry. He was a fair but demanding steward of both the Corps of Cadets and the tactical department. His departure, scheduled for October, had been troublesome to Delafield. His replacement had just been named in the dispatch on the table.

Fitzhugh Lee was also an imposing figure, and the nephew of former superintendent Robert E. Lee, Class of 1829. The younger Lee had already been decorated for gallantry on the frontier, and, in the short month and a half that he had been on post, had become a favorite of the Corps.

The thought of Lee's uncle, who had run the Academy from 1852 to 1855, was a burr to Delafield, although he liked the man. But history would remember Bob Lee as the consummate leader, the soldier's favorite, and a hero of the Mexican War; while he would be remembered as a builder of buildings and a taciturn taskmaster. That cadets still talked of Lee in the most favorable terms was particularly irksome, as it was Lee who had advanced the idea to increase the Academy curriculum from four to five years, beginning in 1855. Since then, he was the one who had to live with it, and with the cadets who detested the extra year of schooling.

"James, would you pour two more glasses?"

"Of course, sir."

Hardee and Lee arrived, both sporting neatly trimmed beards and mustaches, and saluted at the foot of the veranda.

Delafield returned the salutes. "Evening, William, Lieutenant Lee. A hot day for our cadets."

"For all of us, sir." Hardee ascended the stairs, followed by Lee.

James handed out the ice waters.

"Been a continuous stream of hot days," Delafield said. "But not so bad, and another ten days and you'll be back with the family." He was referring to the large set of quarters adjacent to his own.

"Always good to be in a fine house, sir," Hardee said, "but I truly do enjoy being in the field with the cadets, and the tent living is as easy as it ever will be."

"So you think a Sunday review is necessary?"

"Trust me, sir, the plebes need more work."

Delafield handed Hardee the telegram.

Hardee's eyes narrowed as he read it. "Lieutenant Lee, would you excuse us for a moment?"

"Of course, sir." Lee saluted, descended the steps, and took a position on the lawn.

"Amazing stuff," Delafield said. "First the railroad and now the telegraph, and both so damn fast. They're changing how we live."

"Indeed, sir," Hardee muttered as he reread the telegram.

"So what do you think?"

"I'm more than disappointed. I thought, surely, Bob Anderson would be my replacement. Davis as much as assured me."

"My recommendation too. Major Anderson's already a legacy here, and the most popular artillery instructor we've ever had. On top of that, he's a gifted administrator and bona fide hero—brevetted three times."

"Does Anderson know?"

"I should think not. I think this is General Scott's courtesy to me. If I pushed the issue, I expect he would relent, but you read his reason?"

Hardee nodded.

"Apparently our Secretary of War John Floyd—that Virginian—is pulling strings."

"Which is inappropriate."

"Yes. And it is our right not to like it, but our lot to keep silent. What do you make of Scott's recommendation in lieu of Anderson?"

"John Reynolds and I have good history. He was Class of 1841, a plebe in my company when I was a First Classman, and even then mature for his years. We served under Zachary Taylor in Mexico. As I recall, he was twice brevetted for gallantry. Since then, he's been on the frontier. He'll do well here and leave a good mark, though his brand of discipline is likely different than mine."

"Not so different, I think." Delafield slipped the telegram back into the envelope.

"Will there be overlap?"

"I'll send my response first thing in the morning and press the point. I want a seamless transition. Of course, it is not too late for you to extend. I know that would satisfy both Scott and Floyd."

Hardee glanced at the encampment site. "Four years is more than enough, thank you. I need to get back to the troops and to the frontier. Besides, the family is looking forward to furlough in Georgia."

"Suit yourself, but don't be surprised if you come back as superintendent."

"You would wish that on me?"

Delafield's laughter was cut short by a cadence drumbeat from the military band on the Plain. As the lead company of the Corps of Cadets emerged from the encampment, Hardee and Lee followed Delafield across Jefferson Road to the reviewing stand.

CHAPTER FOUR

Monday morning, August 13, Pelham woke late and was the last to board the stage out of Blue Mountain. He stepped into the stage after instinctively scanning the wall postings for fugitive slave notices. He wore a pair of brown cotton pants and a bleached linen shirt, and was altogether indistinguishable from any other young man who might be traveling the country. He sat next to an older lady in black attire, who was as wide as she was short and accompanied by a slave girl who Pelham took to be in her early teens. Across from him were what he assumed to be two cotton men.

"Anybody mind?" he asked, reaching for a newspaper on the floor of the stage.

"Not at all, son. We've all read it—me twice." The man who spoke offered his hand. "Sidney Banks."

"Much obliged, Mr. Banks. My name's John Pelham."

"Mind me, there's not much in it." Banks gestured at the paper as the stage jerked forward. "How far you going?"

"New York, sir."

Banks raised an eyebrow. "Now that's a trip. What takes you so deep in Yankee land?"

"I school there."

"Do tell?" His eyes narrowed. "What do you think of them?"

"Yankees?"

Banks nodded.

"Not so different, really. Aside from the way they talk, they're pretty much like us, except they seem to take better to the cold and snow."

Banks involuntarily shuddered. "Don't like snow and don't like Yankees." With that, he tipped his hat over his eyes, and despite the jostling of the stage was soon adrift in sleep, lightly snoring.

The second man held a well-worn western novel up close to his eyes and was inclined to silence.

The lady introduced herself as Wilma Hawkins, and explained that she had just buried her husband, one Harry Hawkins, who had died of consumption, and that she was returning to her family in Indianapolis.

"I'm sorry for your loss, ma'am," Pelham said.

"We'd have been married forty-three years this October." She tilted her head toward the black girl. "This young thing is Rosie, she just turned fourteen. She takes some kind of good care of me."

Pelham leaned forward. "Hi, Rosie."

The girl kept her gaze on the floor of the stage, but returned his greeting with a nod.

"Tell the young man what's going to happen to you, Rosie."

The girl said nothing.

"She's some kinda shy, that one. When we get home, she's going to get her papers. She'll be free, yes she will. That's what's going to happen. My Harry wanted that. Isn't that so, Rosie?"

The girl looked up, her eyes exhibiting more fear than joy.

"Problem is she doesn't quite know what it means yet, to be free and all."

Pelham smiled. "I understand, and you are indeed a generous woman to do this for her."

The man reading the novel peered over his book at Pelham.

"She has no family, and is all I got except for my son. His name's Harry too, like his father." She lowered her eyes. "Harry's going west, but before he does, he'll sell our place and give me all but a little of the money and I'll live on that."

The stage driver announced the crossing of a shallow stream.

"Anyway," Mrs. Hawkins went on, "I think Rosie will take care of me 'til I'm gone. She said she would, and I'll pay her what I can."

"I'm sure she will, ma'am."

The widow smiled before being nearly pitched from her seat when the stage hit the stream.

Pelham was still holding the small package from his mother. "Ma'am, do you mind …?"

She patted his arm. "Lord no, son. Smells wonderful, and you got to keep your strength."

Pelham removed the muslin wrapping that contained strips of jerky from Willie's smokehouse and two of young Ora's buttermilk biscuits. He offered the widow lady a biscuit, but she graciously declined, which was well enough, because he was famished. He ate and washed the meal down with the bottle of beer he had purchased in the stage office.

Afterwards, he settled into the paper, soon in agreement with the man, Banks. The publisher was content to keep the same stale issues in the air, his journalism flat and biased.

"Young man." Mrs. Hawkins tapped Pelham's arm. "When we get to the rest stop, would you mind terribly getting us some water? I don't move so well, and don't want to leave the stage if I don't have to."

Pelham smiled. "Yes, ma'am, my pleasure."

"You are too kind. You come from fine family, I know it. I can tell these things."

"You are sweet to think so, ma'am."

"I'm quite sure of it."

After the rest stop, Pelham closed his eyes, hoping to nap, but instead juggled in his mind various thoughts, political and otherwise. He processed over and over the game being played by the new overseer, what his father and Willie had said, and the reality that not once had he seen Samuel. These were gristle in the chewing part of his mind.

Late in the afternoon, the stage driver hollered, "Talladega, one hour."

Pelham spent the night at the Talladega railhead, and the next morning caught the train to Selma, thinking it strange to travel southwest before heading east. In Selma, he caught the train to Montgomery, relieved to finally be heading in the right direction. Everywhere, he saw the same landscape of red earth, cotton fields, and pine trees. The widow lady and her young black were also on the train; and upon arriving in Montgomery, he aided them with their luggage and led them to the station hotel. The next day, he helped them onto the train for Atlanta. Outside of the Atlanta station, the three of them skirted a spirited rally of fire-eaters. That night, Pelham again slept fitfully, waking to another hot, sultry day and breakfasting on steak, eggs, and warm milk.

Returning to the Atlanta train station, he helped Mrs. Hawkins and her young attendant onto the train to Chattanooga, refusing the envelope offered by the widow, but accepting her best wishes. Before the train pulled away, Pelham caught the young black girl staring at him through the open window. He touched the bill of his cap, and he saw her smile for the first time.

CHAPTER FIVE

AUGUST 15, 1860
NASHVILLE, TENNESSEE

Nathaniel Rives Chambliss, known as Nate to his West Point classmates, stood conspicuous on the platform, and not just because of his height and uniform. It was his Romanesque face and piercing brown eyes. He strolled to the ticket counter and exchanged a nickel for a newspaper, tucked it under his arm, and rejoined two older brothers at the platform railing.

"You wait until now to tell us," Paul, the older of the two, said, more than miffed.

The other brother, Robert, lit a cigarette. "Yeah, Nathaniel, what's that all about?"

At the shriek of a train whistle, heads turned to see the iron snake appear a half mile down the track, nostril snorting black smoke.

"Because it's not important and more of a pain than it's worth." Chambliss attempted to conceal the pride he felt at being appointed first captain of the Corps of Cadets for the coming year.

"The hell you say!" Paul reached in his pocket. "You'll be a general one day and run the whole damn army." He pressed something into his brother's hand. "Mom and Dad would have been proud."

Chambliss opened his fist to see a gold coin. The size of a five-dollar gold piece, it bore the family crest on one side and the Union eagle on the other.

"John sent it," Robert said, referring to their eldest brother, now a colonel stationed in San Antonio.

Chambliss examined the coin. It had been John who got him his appointment to the Academy.

"Dad had it specially minted," Paul said.

Chambliss remembered little of a father and mother who had died while he was an infant. "But, why me?"

"Apparently you are the chosen one." Paul's sarcasm was unveiled.

"All aboard!" The conductor's voice rang through a bullhorn.

Chambliss slipped the coin into his pocket, hugged his brothers, and started for the train. Behind him, he heard, "Take it easy on the plebes." And over his shoulder, he responded, "And you two don't forget to write. Your letters mean a lot."

"To a tough guy like you?" Robert was smiling.

"Trust me—West Point can be a lonely place."

Chambliss disappeared inside the train and settled down for a trip that would take three days. As the locomotive pulled from the station, he unfolded the newspaper and read the cover article. He shook his head. John Breckinridge had defined his Democratic platform and there was no incentive whatsoever for any but a slaver to support him.

ELEUTHEREAN MILLS, DELAWARE

Henry Algernon du Pont, President of the Class of 1861 and son of the ardent Whig, Henry du Pont, himself a West Pointer and member of the Class of 1833, was the oldest of nine children. In the only home he had ever known, the massive family estate on the Brandywine River, du Pont determined that he would fully enjoy his meal, one of his last before returning to West Point. In three days, he would depart for New York City, and the following morning catch the steamer upriver to the Academy. He was nearly finished with a second helping of baked ham and sweet potatoes, careful to save room for the sugar-crusted apple pie that sat on the French buffet.

His question about the family munitions business, the largest in the country, still hung in the air. It had seemed odd to him that not a word about the business had been spoken since his arrival. His seven sisters and younger brother had tensed when he asked the question.

Furrows formed on the forehead of the elder du Pont. "Henry, it's not been a good year. And I was thinking it best not to burden you, but we've had three accidents, two minor and one major. Seven fatalities, seven good men. Anyway, what sparked the explosions I still don't know—not for sure. I've made changes and nothing more recent has happened. God willing, we're past all that."

Du Pont sensed uncertainty in his father's voice.

A kitchen helper began clearing the table, while another arrived with dessert plates. Du Pont's mother nodded to the youngest daughter. With eyes wide and a great sense of purpose, the six-year-old disappeared and returned carrying the apple pie like a crown to a coronation.

"Thank you, my dear," their mother said. "Henry gets the first piece." Turning to her son and passing the first piece of pie, she asked, "Do you think you'll still finish first in the class?"

"I suppose," he said matter-of-factly, as though nine years of Latin and one year of prior college made the outcome rather predictable. "I have a pretty good lead on Charlie Cross, and Charlie doesn't seem to want it that bad."

"Do you know yet where you will go for your first assignment?" his father asked.

"Based on what's happened to the Class of '60, I'll probably end up on the frontier, one of the territories, but where and doing what depends on my branch. I'm thinking Corps of Engineers, but ... Any more milk, Mother?"

"And when you've finished your service?" his father pressed.

Du Pont put his fork down and smiled. "After my obligated four years, if the offer is still there, I would be honored to return home and work for you, Father."

The older du Pont was clearly pleased. "With me, Henry, not for me. And tell me. After all we've talked about, concerning the election, who is your man?"

"I daresay anyone but Lincoln," the young Henry asserted without hesitation. "Lincoln and all the Black Republicans, I'm quite convinced, are but rascals bent on stirring a too-full pot of nothing good."

"I thought you might consider John Bell of the new Constitutional Union party. He's as good a man as ever there was." The senior du Pont, who had witnessed his beloved Whig party fall from grace, desired anyone but another Democrat. "For the nation's sake, I think we need change. Certainly, Buchanan has been a disappointment."

The young West Pointer, for the sake of peace, conceded that he would not decide hastily, though it struck him odd that his father, brilliant in every way and a prominent behind-the-scenes political player, was so thoroughly anti-Democrat, when Delaware was a slave state. That the family chose not to have slaves did not seem reason enough to repudiate the state's chief party.

Du Pont held out his plate. "Mother, might I have another slice of pie?"

BROWNVILLE, NEW YORK

"Eliza Kirby, that was without doubt the very best meal I ever et!" Garrison Blake made the pronouncement with jocular flair, waving a white linen napkin in surrender and patting his stomach. "And one I wager Edmund is not quickly to forget, given what I understand of Academy food. Am I right, Edmund?"

The two young girls at the table waited for their brother's response.

"Sadly, sir, you are entirely accurate," admitted the young man with dark hair and coal black eyes. Edmund, known as Ned to his West Point classmates, liked this widower who spent so much time with his mother, and who had known his father well. He knew his mother would never remarry, that his father could never be replaced. But she needed company, and Garrison Blake provided both excellent company and considerable humor.

"Shall we retire for a brandy and smoke, Edmund? I know that your mother keeps ample and quality supplies of both."

"Certainly, sir." Kirby rose to his feet and kissed his mother lightly on the cheek. Realizing what he had done, he gave her a proper hug.

"So like your father," the stately gray-haired woman whispered in his ear. She turned to Blake. "Don't let Edmund take too much of the brandy."

Kirby gave his mother a look and followed Blake into the study, where the older man selected two brandy snifters and poured from a decanter a liquid that appeared gold in the light of the gas table lamp. Blake removed a box of cigars from the desk drawer, offered one to Kirby, and picked one for himself. Both clipped their cigars and fired them with long matches. Given the constraints and abstemious nature of the Academy, Kirby smoked little and consumed alcoholic beverages infrequently. On this final night before returning to West Point, he would indulge himself.

As they sat savoring the brandy and puffing cigars, Blake shared an anecdote, which did nothing for Kirby, but made the big man nearly choke with laughter. At the end of the telling, Kirby saw that Blake's glass was empty and offered a refill. Blake nodded appreciatively, gesturing with a plump finger for a slightly larger portion, then raised his glass in a toast.

"You know, Edmund, your mother is very proud of you and brags upon you constantly. Says you are following wonderfully in your father's footsteps, and your grandfather's too. Am I correct?"

"Yes, sir, but that's a mother's job." Kirby's father and grandfather had been career militarists, and both had attained the rank of general. In 1821, his grandfather, Major General Jacob Jennings Brown, for whom Brownville was named, was the first general to be appointed "Commanding General" of the Army.

"My, I couldn't handle that kind of pressure," the portly man confessed.

"It's not so bad." Kirby, who had been the Corps' sergeant major the year before and the highest ranking man in his class, would be one of only four cadet captains in the coming year, commanding one of the four cadet companies, despite being the second youngest in the class.

"Edmund, are you aware that I was part of the coalition that got Lincoln the Republican ticket in New York?"

Kirby could not have been more surprised.

"And that without New York, Seward would likely have gotten the nod. But with New York, Lincoln gets the nomination on the third ballot."

Kirby would never have suspected Blake of such handiwork.

"Well, my take on the November election is that our man, Lincoln, not so much popular as convenient, will win. Not the people's vote, but the electoral vote."

He stood up and walked to the window and peered into the darkness. "Do you know what that means?"

"Sir?"

"That means that those who didn't vote for him will have to accept his victory."

The comment struck Kirby as odd.

"Yet that's not going to happen, is it? No. Some of the Southern states have as much as promised that if Lincoln wins, they'll leave the Union. Of course, you know all that. When South Carolina and Georgia walked out of the first Democratic convention, it split the Democrats, a brilliant stroke for our Republicans, as much as handing us the presidency. Indeed, if not for the split, I doubt the Democrats could have lost this one."

Kirby was of the same opinion.

Blake returned to his seat, his demeanor suddenly glum. "But that we win the election is not necessarily all good. This secession business is messy and cannot be sanctioned, Edmund." Blake's round face was suddenly a pinkish red. "We cannot allow it. We are sitting on a powder keg with firebrands everywhere."

This was a side of Blake that Kirby had not seen.

"After Brown's raid and the horrors in Kansas," Blake went on, "the entire country is just plain angry. Issues are quite literally black and white—no middle ground. Newspapers are disgustingly biased, defending the holiness of one camp and denouncing the hellishness of the other. The Kansas battleground for slave/non-slave election is an unmerited fiasco. Neither side concedes gains to the other. Both sides are guilty of murderous killings. There can be no winner."

Blake took a long pull on his brandy.

"I don't know what the answer is, and don't know that anyone does, save the Maker." Blake's face receded on itself as he pressed the snifter against his chin. "Still, the one saving grace is that the South has been preaching and threatening secession for forty years, and has yet to make good on it. God willing, it is still rhetoric. God willing, once the election is over, cooler heads will prevail."

Blake pointed a pudgy finger at Kirby. "Mark my words, the Academy is a crucible where what is to come will be played out in miniature. If the spectrum of cadets can keep their heads after the election, then perhaps the nation can weather the storm."

Blake drained his brandy. "Edmund, you are a gifted leader and a man of unswerving faith. I cannot urge you strongly enough to do whatever you can to calm the waters, because if they can't be calmed at the Academy ..." Blake rose heavily to his feet. "I wish your father were here."

He placed the empty glass on the desk and left the room. Kirby downed the rest of his brandy, welcoming the burn.

CHAPTER SIX

August 15, the train from Atlanta was oversold, and in the thick humidity of summer, the smell of humanity was almost too much for Pelham. Aisles were blocked with suitcases and dogs. Travel trunks, boxes, crates of chickens, and myriad other things were tied to the top of every passenger car. His salvation was a window seat with a window that worked. The chain of iron forged through the cool of morning into the heat of day, traversing valleys and trestle bridges, steaming across bottomlands, and climbing hills at speeds as slow as a walk. Fields of cotton eventually gave way to wheat, tobacco, and corn, and the landscapes of pine forests metamorphosed into oaks and maples and the gently rolling hills of Virginia.

After three days of inactivity, the grime of coal smoke, and straining to see through a sooted window, Pelham was done with trains. He longed for a horse, even one of the uninspired nags from the West Point stable. At every stop he got off, exercised his legs, breathed fresh air, bought a piece of fruit, and found a discarded newspaper to give his mind investment. He wrote letters to his mother and his sister, and a candid letter to his father about the new overseer. When not reading, writing, or napping, he studied fellow passengers and imagined their comings and goings.

When the train finished the four-hundred-mile trip to Richmond, Pelham checked into the Virginian Hotel across from the station. A fortyish man with one well-muscled arm took Pelham's money for room and board and a hot bath. The man caught Pelham staring at his pinned-up shirtsleeve, and without elaboration said, "Buena Vista."

Pelham found the hotel newly renovated, featuring hot and cold water and flush toilets at the end of each floor. In his room, he stripped, grabbed a towel, and headed down the hall. He gave the attendant the bath chit, and an hour later, shaved and much revived, he descended the staircase for supper, picking up a newspaper on the way.

The hotel's dining room was elegantly appointed, with cushioned booths along three walls and red velvet privacy curtains between the booths. Wait stations occupied the interior of the room, stacked with glassware, china, silver, and white linens. The headwaiter greeted Pelham with a deferential smile and sat him next to a corner booth, taking his order for a beer.

Pelham sipped his beer as he read a front-page article in the paper. It was a tongue-in-cheek proposition that the needs of both Democrats and Republicans could be amicably met by granting the South its right to property, including slaves, in the new territories. "Slave masters," the writer asserted, "should not be restricted from taking their slaves wherever they wanted. Do not hinder the Southern man from moving to the New Mexico territory or to the Colorado Territory and taking his slaves. It is his right. He, as much as the man from the North, fought for that right. However, once there, what will his slaves do? The land's geography and climate are not conducive to cotton, tobacco, rice, or sugarcane. Unless they can be made to harvest sage and cacti, they will serve little purpose other than to be fed, clothed, and housed." The obtuse argument amused Pelham.

A moment later the headwaiter sat two men in the corner booth, honoring them with a bow. "Senator, Congressman, it is very good to see you again. Something to drink?"

"Ale, please," said William Porcher Miles, U.S. congressman from South Carolina, as he retrieved papers from a black leather folder.

"I would have thought whiskey," chided Louis Trezevant Wigfall, U.S. senator from Texas.

Both men sported full beards, tailored dark suits, white linen shirts, and dark cravats. The congressman slid a single sheet of paper across the table. "Louis, lobbying will consume us if we're not enterprising. I see a series of dinners paid for by the party with increasingly expanded guest lists, beginning, of course, with those of the Cotton Belt."

"Dinner parties." The senator playfully patted his stomach and took up the list of names.

"And," Miles continued, "state conventions must be planned and all done orderly, with proper form and appearance—every element of propriety."

A black waiter returned with a frothy pitcher of ale, two mugs, and two bowls of peanuts; one roasted, the other boiled.

"And, of course," Miles said, "there are other delicate matters that will require attention."

"Indeed." The senator was eyeing the list.

"To test the loyalty—or lack of it—of those you see, we'll need a man who can ingratiate himself and discern the truth behind another man's rhetoric."

The senator looked up. "You mean a man who can outdrink another man."

"In a word."

The senator downed his ale as though it were water. "I see mostly Washington-based military men and men of commerce."

"Precisely. Avoiding conflict requires their support, or at least their neutrality."

"I will, of course, serve in any way I can."

"And we thank you for it, Louis. We must—" The congressman lowered his voice to a whisper. "We must convince the majority of Washington of the rightness of secession, that a state indeed has absolute sovereignty and an inherent right to leave the Union if its interests are not otherwise benefited. Nothing more than our forefathers intended, and what occasioned our break with Britain. That so many states now form the Union is almost explanation enough as to why interests and needs once similar and mutually beneficial, are now neither similar nor compatible. Rather, we find ourselves in a most unhealthy malaise, which festers the whole."

"A toast to righteousness." The senator downed the last of the pitcher. "Now, perhaps a whiskey?"

The congressman nodded, and straightway the senator placed the order.

On the other side of the velvet curtain, Pelham was captivated by what he was hearing and only pretended to read the paper.

A waiter delivered a bottle of whiskey and two shot glasses to the senator and congressman, and then took their dinner orders, as well as Pelham's. All three selected the daily special of T-bone steak, fried potatoes, green beans, and apple pie.

While the congressman nursed his whiskey, the senator poured himself a second double shot. "Still, on the main, we'll achieve the high ground soon enough, and then the bulwark will not be tested." The senator's voice was decibels louder than before. "I'll stake my fortune on it."

"Louis, please lower your voice."

Pelham caught a distinct edge in the congressman's tone.

"Relax, William, we are among friends. These are our people."

"Don't be naive. Those of a different persuasion are everywhere."

"Here, I've corked the bottle. Happy?" The senator caught the arm of a passing waiter, handing him the bottle. "Young man, bring us a bottle of French red. Bordeaux, if you have it." Wigfall smiled at the congressman. "My friend, you see a Pinkerton behind every newspaper."

A dusty bottle of fifteen-year-old Pomerol soon appeared, and the head waiter poured a taste for the senator as the food arrived.

Pelham understood well that he was sitting next to two fire-eaters, no less vehement than Alabama's William Yancey, and he had heard a word from the senator he had not heard before, *Confederacy*. He decided on another beer and inched closer to the privacy curtain.

The meal passed with little conversation, and when it was over, the senator ordered brandies and cigars. When they arrived, he announced in a voice for all in the restaurant to hear, "My friends, I should like to propose a toast!"

Pelham heard the sound of a fist on the table in the next booth and the jingling of silver and crystal.

"For God's sake, Louis, you are inebriated."

"Surely you jest, and if I am, it's from freedom's fruit, not drink."

The senator appeared from behind the velvet curtain, facing the waiters' stand. He was remarkably erect and composed, and walked easily to the center of the room, whereupon he turned a pretty pirouette, holding his glass high, his face beaming.

"I propose a toast to the Land of Dixie!"

From Pelham's vantage point, the toast seemed to be universally embraced.

"My friends, and I know you are," the senator went on in the practiced tone of political oration. "Would there be anyone here who intends to vote for the man Lincoln come November?" His voice held not a hint of alcohol.

After an awkward silence, a man sitting with four others stood up and thrust his fist in the air. "I would sooner kiss the devil!"

Others at the man's table echoed him, and then the entire restaurant erupted in hoots and hollers, castigating Lincoln, all Black Republicans, and lauding one great Southern state after another.

"I am indeed among friends," the senator said, "and I thank you that we are all of one accord!" He downed the last of his brandy and returned to his seat. "I rest my case."

Miles was indignant. "By all that is sacred, Louis, rest more than your case."

Early the next morning, August 16, a dense fog enshrouded Richmond. Pelham, somewhat slow-headed and cottoned-mouthed from the night before, changed into his furlough uniform and boarded the train bound for the nation's capital. The train slipped quietly out of the station as if respectful of the hour, and soon Pelham was asleep, his head pillowed on a flannel shirt he had rolled up against the window.

Unknown to him, the two politicians who had been in the next booth at the hotel had boarded the same train, and they had taken seats in the first class car forward of the dining car.

"How do you propose we proceed?" Senator Wigfall whispered as he wiped perspiration from his brow.

"Buchanan is key," Congressman Miles said. "A staunch Democrat, but a malleable duck. The bachelor enjoys good parties, and we'll see that he gets them. He'll see himself as the great compromiser and push for reconciliation, and so much the better for us. The rub will be his position on federal installations in the South. I and a few others will keep him occupied and convinced that what he wishes can be; and that what the South requires, the acquisition of all forts and arsenals within its borders, can also be."

The senator rubbed his temples, and then unfolded the sheet of names he had pocketed the night before. "On the military side, I suppose I should speak first with Floyd. The secretary of war is solid South and can give me his take on the who and the how."

An attendant pushed a cart down the aisle, and the senator wrestled a pitcher of steaming black coffee from the man. For the next half hour, the senator and congressman pored over the names and constructed a strategy. When the senator could no longer keep his eyes open, the congressman let him drift off to the shuffle of the train.

The smell of bacon roused Pelham from his slumber. The fog was gone, but dense low clouds masked the sun. He made his way to the dining car, and a waiter escorted him inside, where the senator and congressman were already seated.

Congressman Miles took notice of Pelham's uniform. "Citadel?"

"No sir, West Point."

"Impressive. What year?"

"Class of '61, sir. This is my final year."

"You look relieved. Where is home?"

"Alexandria, Alabama, sir. Near Jacksonville. I'm returning from furlough."

"Northeast Alabama?"

"Yes, sir, we have a plantation there."

"Great state, Alabama, and you have a fine man in William Yancey." Miles extended his hand. "I'm Congressman William Miles of South Carolina, and this is Senator Louis Wigfall of Texas, though formerly of South Carolina. Would you care to join us, cadet …?"

"Pelham, sir. John Pelham. I wouldn't want to intrude, sir."

"Nonsense, we insist."

"I'd be honored, sir."

The senator's face was pallid, but with effort he managed to extend a hand.

Pelham shook it and drew up a chair.

The congressman signaled the waiter. "Anything you want, son. It's on us, and you certainly deserve it."

Pelham made no pretense of refusing, and ordered coffee and enough food for two. They engaged in small talk until breakfast was served.

The senator talked into his coffee. "Mr. Pelham, my friend won't tell you, but before entering Congress, he was the most popular mayor Charleston ever had."

The congressman waved off the remark. "This is an unexpected pleasure, John, to meet one of our young lions. You West Pointers are a special breed."

Pelham cut a piece of smoked Virginia ham. "Thank you, sir. I know that I am very fortunate."

"Though I suppose now, with what's going on, it is a difficult time. You must find it a challenge to stay focused," the congressman said, almost as a question. "Would you mind sharing your take on the political climate at the Academy?"

Pelham had expected the question. "Most of us embrace an attitude of laissez-faire and respect one another, whatever our opinions."

The congressman nodded. "The proper response between gentlemen, though I suspect you cannot ignore what is afoot."

"No, sir, and I believe we are as aware of the issues as we can be. I think my classmate Henry du Pont put it best, saying none of us is another's puppet, but rather free thinkers who reflect the views of an entire nation. And as large a country as we are, we hold many views. To my mind, we have agreed to disagree." A smile crossed Pelham's face. "In any event, we are kept rather busy from reveille to taps the year long, which alone keeps the place quite civil."

"Your classmate is of the Delaware du Ponts?" the senator asked.

Pelham was surprised by the question. "Yes, sir."

The senator glanced at the congressman. "I know the man's father and his munitions company. He has been before my committee. Quite large government contracts, they have."

Pelham reached for another piece of toast.

"Then your classmate, du Pont, must be a Republican."

"Henry? I should think not."

"Really? His father is, or was, a staunch Whig, and … I would have thought otherwise."

"Sir, I'm quite sure he and his father differ on politics."

"You know him that well?"

"We are best friends."

"What are your own feelings about the election?"

"I am bred Democrat, but not optimistic about the election."

"Because the Black Republicans will win?" The senator buttered a piece of toast. "But is that so bad?"

"Sir?"

"A Republican victory might be celebrated by more than Republicans."

At this, the congressman gave the senator a stern look.

Ignoring him, the senator continued. "And the Academy as a whole, what would their position be on the election?"

"We are vastly Democrats, sir." Pelham finished peeling a boiled egg and applied to it generous pinches of salt and pepper. "But with two candidates vying for the post, I am sure you can speak better to that, sir."

The congressman nodded. "So there are no extremists at the Point?"

Pelham thought of Emory Upton. "There is one, but I believe him harmless enough."

The senator was suddenly animated, the vast quantities of coffee having finally done their deed. "What do you think of the Northern preoccupation with our peculiar institution, John?"

"I suppose I don't think of it, sir. It is what it is—in the woof and weave of our fabric. But I'm quite certain most Northerners don't have a bone to pick with us. After all, they benefit from it as much as we do."

"Your family has slaves?"

"Yes, sir."

"Many?"

"Fifty, sir—maybe more."

The congressman cleared his throat. "Senator Wigfall and I are headed back to Washington to do what we and other faithfuls can do to right the wrongs that are severing us from the North; ties that you must know are thread thin. Slavery, of course, is a part of it, but not all of it." The congressman looked at Pelham. "Would you care for anything else?"

Pelham, his mouth full, returned a sheepish grin and shook his head.

"Some of us are unequivocally convinced that the South and the North are oil and water—that we can no longer be agreeably mixed, that we have inexorably distanced ourselves from one another, and that compromise only further breeds anger and distrust and resolves nothing. Take the Fugitive Slave Act, a federal act to placate the South. It was passed on the moral ground of safeguarding our property, pure and simple, but if anything, it has emboldened a sympathizing North to paint us as inhumane and unchristian. And all the while, very few fugitive slaves have been returned to their owners. I'm not saying we are without sin—we have our faults. But the wrongs committed by the North, and which increasingly oppress us, will be sealed in cement if Abraham Lincoln is elected."

The senator leaned across the table. "John, Congressman Miles is prone to sugar coating. What he is saying is that we must not let Lincoln's shiny boot soil Southern pride. Do you understand my meaning?"

Pelham nodded.

"It takes little imagination," the senator continued, "to see why the blood of our people boils at his effrontery, his intent to steal what we possess and deny us the full blessings of the new territories."

The senator rubbed his temples again. "You've studied the Mexican War?"

"A little, sir."

"My cousin, name of Willard Wigfall, he had a wife and two young boys. He answered the patriot's call and fought in the war as a lieutenant. He was gut shot serving under Taylor at Monterrey. Took two days to die, and for what, John? He and thousands of Texas sons sacrificed, and to what benefit?"

Pelham remained silent.

"In the federal government, non-slave states control the House and have forever—and now with California a free state, they control the Senate. We are defenseless against the will of the North."

A part of Pelham wanted to support the senator's argument, but instead he sipped his coffee.

"John, can you imagine what it is like for us to sit in chambers and witness what takes place, the dismantling of the South?"

Pelham wiped his mouth and put down his napkin.

"It has come to this," the senator continued. "The South is no longer an equal to the North. We are a minority within the Union, a voice ignored and powerless to safeguard itself. Such a voice is no voice.

Mark my words, if Lincoln is inaugurated and the South remains in the Union, it will be reduced to servitude."

Pelham shifted uncomfortably in his chair.

The congressman apparently sensed Pelham's unease. "Louis, we've beat the drum enough. John, life at the Academy must be quite an experience. Perhaps you would share some of what you've been through?"

Pelham jumped upon the invitation. He recounted anecdotes from his plebe year and the rigors and stress of academic life, and soon had the senator and congressman laughing out loud. The meal ended on a positive note, with the congressman paying for breakfast and handing a cigar to Pelham.

"Again, John, we want to thank you. You've made our trip most pleasant."

"Sirs, I am very much in your debt, and I feel like I've been in the presence of—"

The senator cut him off. "I'm not sure I want to know what you've been in the presence of."

The three of them enjoyed a good laugh.

"Seriously, sir," Pelham said, "you and Congressman Miles have my utmost respect. I fear yours is a truly thankless job, but, in any event, my hope and prayer is that somehow good will come from what lies ahead."

The senator smiled broadly and extended his hand. "Count yourself lucky that you are a soldier and soon to be an officer."

"I do, sir."

The congressman offered his hand as well. "Best of luck in your final year, John. I hope we have the pleasure of meeting again."

"I would like that very much, sir."

Returning to his seat, Pelham found the train's smoke plume on the other side of the car, and quickly raised the window. The meal and coffee had made him light-headed, and he breathed deeply the country air. Settling back in his seat, he found himself considering William Yancey in a different light. If he was anything like the senator and the congressman, that could not be a very bad thing. Even the fire-eaters of South Carolina and Virginia might not be as irrational as his father had made them out to be.

Ten miles after Manassas Junction, the train sat on the track for several hours while a bridge underwent emergency repairs.

When the train finally stopped in Washington DC, the two politicians encountered Pelham on the platform and suggested a hotel for the night, before bidding him a gracious farewell. Finding the hotel, Pelham again slept fitfully before falling into a deep slumber. He awoke too late to catch the morning train. As a result, he spent the day seeing the sights of Washington DC, including the one-hundred-and-fifty-foot stump of the unfinished Washington Monument, and the mural painted by West Point's drawing professor, Robert Weir, in the rotunda of the unfinished capitol building. While touring the capitol building, he remembered John Meigs, a Fourth Classman and friend in his cadet company, and the highest-ranking man in his class. The man's father was Colonel Montgomery Meigs, Class of 1836, and he was supervising construction of the capitol extension and new dome. He found the colonel in his office, and the two of them shared a cup of coffee.

After a sound night's sleep and an early knock on the door by a member of the hotel staff, he boarded the train for Baltimore and Philadelphia. On the morning of the nineteenth, he boarded a final train, which snaked east and eventually crossed the sea grass of the Jersey flats, beyond which he disembarked from Newark onto a ferry to New York City.

CHAPTER SEVEN

Puffs of white in a lazy blue sky looked down on the Hudson River, whose origin was three hundred miles to the north in Essex County, New York. The dark wide ribbon divided the rolling landscape of greens and browns. The cliff faces of the river's west bank gleamed bright in the sun, and the valley that bore the river's name stretched northward to the Catskill Mountains and beyond. Maritime vessels and barges of every kind crowded the river, traveling north and south, tipping their hats with horns, whistles, and bells, while ferries labored against strong currents from one side of the river to the other.

Pelham checked his pocket watch. It was nine o'clock and the *Lovely Lady*, a newly commissioned paddlewheel steamer, was en route from the city harbor to destinations as far north as Newburgh, ten miles beyond West Point. The steamer had already made one stop, and the mid-August sun had climbed high enough for temperatures to be warmer than anyone desired, sending passengers to the top deck in search of breezes. Patrons talked loudly over the sound of steam boilers and the churn of the boat's massive paddlewheel. In the midst of the crowd, near the middle of the boat, John Pelham, Henry du Pont, and Nate Chambliss stood together in their furlough uniforms.

"All that is hard to believe," du Pont said, after hearing Pelham's account of his encounter with the senator and congressman. "And I'm not sure you were supposed to hear those things."

"Why not?" Chambliss said, his eyes shut and face to the sun. "What is he or any of us going to do with it?"

The previous night in the city had been a highlight for the three of them, with Chambliss particularly glad to have time with du Pont, who would be on his battalion staff as Corps quartermaster. The evening passed quickly, the friends sharing furlough stories and taking in a burlesque show after supper. That morning, anticipating Academy mess hall food, they drank coffee and ate steak, eggs, and biscuits until they could eat no more.

Chambliss gazed about the deck. "So, Henry, shall either of us find love in the waning days of summer encampment?"

"Not enough time, I fear." Du Pont sneezed, as he often did from perennial hay fever. "Female companionship, other than sisters, I've greatly missed as a result of furlough. Not much to pick from on the Brandywine."

Chambliss eyed Pelham. "But old John doesn't care. He's got that brunette from Cornwall."

"You are mistaken." Pelham produced a sad face. "I must report that I am no longer in Joanna Furman's plans."

"And pray tell, why?"

"Expectations."

"Regarding?"

"Marriage."

"She would have been quite the catch," Chambliss said, "and we all must be caught eventually."

"Perhaps," Pelham conceded. "But she pressed me and I could not mislead her. To my mind, a man must know himself, test himself, before settling down. And I am not there, yet."

Du Pont gestured equivocally.

Chambliss's attention was drawn to a group of girls at the bow of the boat.

"Mind me," Pelham added with a smile. "I'll continue to be sociable, for I am a gentleman, or soon will be by act of Congress, and a gentleman must attend to the ladies."

"Which is no problem for you." Du Pont's voice held a hint of irritation. "Those on the Hop Committee enjoy a distinct and unfair advantage."

"Now, Henry, don't tell me the uniform isn't enough." Pelham removed his furlough hat and breathed in the river air. "What a glorious day, my friends. Can it be that we are finally near the end of our suffering, that we will actually graduate and leave our rockbound highland prison?"

"Do you hear that, Nate?" du Pont said. "I claim honor violation, for if any of us loves the place, it's John."

Chambliss was still focused on the bow of the boat.

"All the same," Pelham said. "We are now First Classmen, and our suffering will be minimal."

The comment got Chambliss's attention. "And why would you think so? We're a far cry from graduated and face one hell of a year."

"Not with you at the helm." Pelham's tone was intentionally patronizing.

"You think I'll show concession?"

"To your friends."

"Not a chance—least of all to you."

Du Pont smiled. "Nate is right, my friend. Justice must be blind."

"So that's the way it's going to be? Going to be a horse's-ass? And that's the thanks I get for letting you to be my friend?"

Chambliss punched Pelham in the shoulder.

"I suppose I am to salute you," Pelham said, staring at the shore.

"That would be nice."

A young black man in a white jacket approached with a tray of ice waters. Du Pont handed out the ice waters and raised his glass. "A toast to the Class of 1861."

The three clinked glasses.

"A class whose fate is at the polls," du Pont added.

"Ah, ah. We agreed, no politics." Chambliss reminded du Pont of the moratorium they had pledged the night before. "Not until we're back at the Academy." It had been the only topic the night before, and although they were all Democrats, they were so for different reasons, which had precipitated much debate.

A small boy suddenly skidded into du Pont. "Excuse me, sir."

The boy turned to Pelham and held up a folded piece of paper, and in a squeaky voice announced, "Sir, I was told to give this to you."

Pelham took the piece of paper.

"Sir, it is from one of the ladies." The boy pointed to the bow of the boat.

Pelham, Chambliss, and du Pont eyed the bow of the boat as Pelham extracted a nickel from his pocket.

"Thank you very much, sir." The jubilant boy turned on his heels and disappeared into the crowd.

Pelham unfolded the note and read it.

"Out with it," du Pont demanded.

Pelham smiled and cleared his throat. "'Dear, sirs. We are traveling to the United States Military Academy to stay at the West Point Hotel and wondered if you were cadets.'"

"Nate, there is a God," du Pont exclaimed. "But why does John get the note?"

Pelham spied a girl dressed in light blue at the bow of the boat waving a gloved hand above her head. He instinctively touched the bill of his hat. "Friends, perhaps I may do us some good."

Chambliss patted Pelham on the back. "You, John, are a shallow fellow, unworthy of the fairer sex—but nevertheless our only hope."

"Merely your servant."

"On your way." Du Pont shoved Pelham.

"Okay, okay." Pelham straightened his forage cap and slipped through the crowd to the bow of the boat. A group of six young women stood there, in full neck-to-deck Victorian attire, each deftly shielding her face from the sun with a decorated parasol. Unthinkingly, he ranked them, finding none deficient on the exterior. As best he could tell they aged from late teens to early twenties.

"Ladies, allow me to introduce myself. John Pelham is my name, and I wish to respond in the affirmative to this note, written in such a beautiful hand. We are indeed cadets at West Point. We're all returning from furlough and are very happy to know that you ladies will be joining us."

The girl in light blue, in Pelham's estimation the prettiest, stepped forward. Her face was radiant and tanned, framed by flowing ash blond curls, and inset with large emerald eyes. She extended her hand. "Sir, the note you have is from my hand, and my name is Clara Bolton. My friends and I are from Clermont College on Long Island, and we are very pleased to make your acquaintance. Was it Cadet Pelham?"

"Yes, ma'am."

The woman's confident manner impressed Pelham. He took her hand and made a sweeping bow that tickled the others.

"Don't mind them, they're not used to a real gentleman," Clara said apologetically. "Let me introduce you to my roommate, Ellie Lawson." An attractive brunette stepped forward and extended her hand. "Ellie is our only native Long Islander."

Four more girls were introduced: Rebecca Astor, a petite, demure girl from Concord, Rhode Island, with an oval face, button nose, and long blond hair; Carol Hill, a vivacious redhead from Jackson, Mississippi, whose eyes nearly scorched Pelham; Alice Paine, an attractive and poised woman from Boston with black hair and high cheekbones; and Jessica Danford, a tall, curvaceous brunette from Clarksburg, Virginia.

Pelham greeted each girl in the manner he had greeted Clara, and with each greeting came fresh giggles.

After the introductions, Clara said, "We'll be at the hotel for almost a week, and we are so very excited." The joy and energy in her words was spontaneous. "None of us has ever been to West Point, but we hear the best things about the Academy, how nice the cadets are, and of course, the dance parties."

"We call them hops, ma'am."

"That's right, the hops. And isn't there one tonight?"

Pelham hadn't given it any thought, but it was Monday, and Monday was a hop night. "Why, yes. And if you are with us for a week, two more after that."

"Isn't that marvelous," Clara declared, leaning against the wall in the hallway. "Do you like to dance, Cadet Pelham?"

Pelham smiled, "Yes, ma'am, very much."

"Then, if you don't think me too bold, may I place you on my card for the first dance?"

Pelham wanted to pinch himself. "It would be my pleasure, ma'am."

Rebecca Astor stepped forward. "And the second dance—may I have it?"

The mother lode, Pelham thought, and before long he was conscripted by all of the Clermont girls.

"Where are you from, Cadet Pelham?" Clara asked.

"Alabama, ma'am. Why?"

"That's quite an accent you have."

"I could say the same for you."

"I, sir, am from Philadelphia, and we don't have accents there." Clara crossed her arms while the other girls laughed.

Carol Hill took Pelham's arm. "Sir, I don't think you have an accent."

"That's because you're from Georgia," Clara said effusively.

"Mississippi, dear."

"There's a difference?"

"Right—well." Pelham, quite pleased with himself, glanced toward the stern of the boat. "Perhaps I should introduce my friends?"

"Oh, yes, yes, you must!" Ellie Lawson's tone and eyes were insistent, but hardly had she spoken when her expression, and that of the other girls, blanched, and from behind Pelham came a loud, "Ahem."

He turned to face two gray-haired matrons, tented in dark dresses with thin white collars. One was tall, the other short, and both remarkably well fed. They stood cross-armed, staring at Pelham through wire-rimmed glasses.

Clara stepped between Pelham and the two women. "Miss Frampton, Mrs. Wigglesworth, I should like to present Mr. John Pelham. He is a cadet at West Point." She turned to Pelham. "Miss Frampton and Mrs. Wigglesworth are our chaperons, and Miss Frampton is our assistant dean."

Miss Frampton, the taller woman, cocked her head with an air of authority.

Pelham caught Clara biting her lip as he clicked his heels and bowed slightly. His greeting elicited only a perfunctory nod, and no word or change in expression.

Pelham weighed his options and chose retreat. "By your leave, ladies, and if I have intruded, I humbly beg pardon. I wish you a most pleasant voyage."

As he walked away, he heard the shrill voice of the assistant dean. "Fifteen minutes, just fifteen minutes, girls, and look at you, already flirting with total strangers. Be ashamed—be ashamed! Mrs. Wigglesworth, we're going to have our hands full. We'll have to watch them like hawks, and what are you smiling about, Miss Bolton?"

Upon his return, Pelham was greeted with downcast faces, Chambliss and du Pont having witnessed the whole.

Chambliss shook his head. "Beware the elders."

"They are harmless enough," Pelham said, his deadpan face erupting in a broad grin.

"We're in?" Du Pont was almost afraid to ask.

"We're in, Henry. Three of us and six of them."

"I like the odds."

"But let us be clear on one thing. The letter writer, Clara Bolton—the girl in blue—she is mine."

"Fair and done," du Pont agreed.

"Of course—first fruits." Chambliss slapped Pelham on the back. "So, my dear benefactor, which one for me?"

Pelham rubbed his chin. "Horse's-ass?"

Chambliss returned a look of innocence. "Who, me?"

"That's better. Then, it can only be the girl from Virginia, Jessica Danford. She's as trim a peach as you could desire, and nearest your height and homeland."

"And me, John?" du Pont asked expectantly.

"For you, Henry, I should think Ellie Lawson, Clara's roommate, and a very lovely lass from Long Island."

Pelham spent the balance of the trip deep in thought. He stood alone at the railing, his eyes tracing the craggy cliffs, shadowed inlets, and distant heights beyond the western shoreline. His imagination was alive with history. He understood history, that it was his greatest teacher, that he was living it. He saw in it the continuity and circling themes of life, and in the Hudson Valley the crucible of American independence.

He had often considered how overwhelming it must have been to the would-be nation in 1777, when the English general, Sir Henry Clinton, and his fleet of well-armed ships sailed from New York City up the Hudson, making short work of the colonial river defenses opposite West Point. He had planned to sail up the Hudson to link with General John Burgoyne, whose mission was to forge south from Lake Champlain. Had this occurred, the aspiring nation would have been cleaved in two, defeated piecemeal, and once again brought to heel. But Burgoyne had failed in the north, defeated at Saratoga, and had surrendered to General Horatio Gates, emboldening the young republic and forcing Clinton to abandon his Hudson prizes and return to New York City to winter in.

The steamer approached Verplanck's Point, and Pelham sought the buttress and ruins of Stony Point, where, in 1779, General Anthony Wayne had led troops up the steep embankment to recapture what the British had held for two long years. Pelham imagined himself in the pre-dawn attack, scaling the steeps and surprising the British, asleep in their quarters. In minutes, the half-naked mercenaries capitulated and the battle was over. The threat to West Point, scant miles to the north, was eliminated.

For Pelham, the War of Independence was his war. He had adopted it, reading about it much more than was required by the Academy. He claimed as his own the few victories and many defeats, the extraordinary hardships, and the insurmountable odds of beating the greatest army and navy on earth. His study of the colonial campaigns had placed him in Washington's mind. He embraced for himself the frustrations of the slow but inexorable transformation of ill-equipped and poorly trained militia into an army that would persist until France committed herself and British homelanders wearied of their investment.

In four years at West Point, Pelham had come to know what Washington fully understood—that the jut of land and the right-angle turn in the river that gave the place its name was the most defensible ground along the river's entire length. Washington had been brilliant in his choice of the Polish engineer Thaddeus Kosciusko to construct its defenses and father the new country's Corps of Engineers. In the late winter of 1778, Kosciusko had constructed water-level firing batteries and covering redoubts, and, when the ice was gone, a massive boom and chain to stretch across the river. The chain's links weighed a hundred pounds and were forged of two-inch square iron bar. He had engineered the parapetted fort on the Point's broad plain, which would initially bear the name Fort Arnold, for the once heralded Benedict Arnold. Farther west on higher ground, a second fort would be constructed, named for Colonel Rufus Putnam.

Pelham understood well that fortress West Point was impregnable to sea and land attack, but not to treason. When the namesake of the fortress, General Arnold, took command of it in 1780, his pride was much wounded from lack of recognition and what he perceived to be inferior assignments. To Arnold's credit, his decisive attack of British defenses at Saratoga, during which he was severely wounded, had been key to the colonial victory and the defeat of Burgoyne. In his eyes, he had been inadequately recognized for his efforts. Abetting his wounded pride was the death of his first wife and subsequent marriage to a prominent Tory's daughter. To salve his wounds and line his pockets, he bargained through Major John André of the British Army to betray Fortress West Point to the British for a sum of twenty thousand pounds and a general's commission in the British army. General Clinton had but to sail his ships up the Hudson to make good on Arnold's invitation. But God had intervened, of that Pelham was sure. Hours before the deed was to be executed, Major André, by all accounts a noble man, was apprehended by colonial militia, who found in his possession the condemning papers. He was not in uniform and summarily paid the penalty of a spy, while the forewarned traitor fled West Point to a British ship less than an hour before the arrival of General Washington, en route to make a routine inspection and unaware of Arnold's treasonous act.

What impressed Pelham more than all else in his study of the war was how circumstance raised up individuals to accomplish unique and extraordinary feats—people like Washington, John Adams, Alexander Hamilton, the Marquis de Lafayette, Thomas Jefferson, Nathanael Greene, Henry Knox, Israel and Rufus Putnam, Christopher Tappan, New York's George Clinton, Betsy Ross, and the Stillwell sisters. By the end of his Third Class year, his initial enchantment with the nation's founders was much tempered. The demigods had taken on flesh and descended from pedestals to instruct him on their weaknesses as well as their strengths, convincing him that the country's survival beyond gestation needed to be attributed largely to the merciful hand of providence.

Still, the war had been won, and he was immensely proud of a grandfather who had fought alongside Washington, and for himself to be a son of the first and only democratic nation in the world—a nation that in its infancy would sit at a global table of monarchies and embarrass itself in commerce and international relations; a nation that would fight another war with Britain before finally flexing the muscle that would make it a world power.

Of all the demigods, Pelham esteemed Washington most, and embraced his concern for the fledging nation's failure to provide for the common defense. After the Revolutionary War, the nation had disbanded its army, sending home all but a few soldiers. Of the less than one hundred professional soldiers that comprised the army, fifty-five were stationed at West Point. Washington argued vehemently for a standing army of significantly greater number, and for a national military academy to train its officer corps—and that the academy should be located at West Point, a recommendation that was shared by John Adams, Alexander Hamilton, and precious few others.

Not until 1802 would President Thomas Jefferson, an earlier opponent of what he perceived to be an elitist military school, establish the United States Military Academy at West Point.

Pelham breathed deep the air off the Hudson, his heart beating faster as the steamer passed Bear Mountain and Anthony's Nose. His mind drifted back four years to his first trip to West Point on the sloop *Oranje*. His mother, paranoid over the explosion and burning of the *Henry Clay*, made him swear not to book a steamer, saying he was too young to die.

Pelham realized that the most significant chapter in his life was coming to an end, the cadetship that would claim a quarter of his life. The thought evaporated with the sight of Buttermilk Falls, the small cloister of civilization south of the Academy. On the crest of the bluff was the five-story Cozzen's Hotel, and from it his gaze slid down the steep granite face to the shoreline. He found the small dock, and next to the dock the two-story structure of Benny Havens' Landing.

Chapter Eight

Beyond the crest of the bluff, Pelham could make out the nearest structures that made up the military school. Having just deposited passengers at the landing for the Cozzen's Hotel, the steamer blew its whistle twice, signaling approach to the Academy's South Dock. As the vessel drew near, Pelham saw figures on the road that descended two hundred feet from the bluff to the water's edge.

Two boats were moored at the dock, and two more anchored nearby. The narrow shore was stacked high with shipping crates, bales, barrels, stacks of wagon wheels, and various iron stock and mechanical implements. The dock swarmed with the activity of a dozen shirtless longshoremen. On the lower deck of the *Lovely Lady*, the crew made ready and tossed heavy ropes to hands on shore. The boat secure, the crew prepared to drop the gangway, and Pelham, Chambliss, and du Pont were first to disembark. It was Pelham who spied the welcoming committee.

"Well toast my buns, boys, look who's here to greet us."

On the dock in dress gray uniform stood Ned Kirby and Charles Patterson.

"You're the last of the class to return," Kirby shouted.

Patterson, a medium-height man from Arkansas with handsome features, piercing green eyes, and wearing the three gold stripes of a lieutenant on his uniform, handed Pelham a cigar.

Pelham sniffed the cigar and bit off the tip.

Patterson lit the cigar and, through teeth clenching a well-worn pipe, observed, "Our final year in the womb."

Pelham exhaled slowly. "Let's you and I enjoy it, Chas."

"No doubt we will, my friend."

Pelham threw an arm around Ned Kirby. "Did you get some smokes from your mother?"

"Half a box," Kirby said with a wink.

Pelham scanned the upper deck of the steamer for the Clermont girls, and as he did, two more cadets sneaked up behind him.

"Good thing you laggards showed up," a swarthy man announced in a gruff tone. "Hadn't been for Walter, I'd have reported you absent without leave."

Pelham spun around to see Tom Rosser, the tallest man in the class and his roommate for the past three years. "Your best and only friend? Surely not, you ugly dog. Let me look at you." Pelham was genuinely happy to see Rosser, who championed no stripes on his uniform. "You've kept the house pretty?"

"You'll find accommodations unchanged." The swarthy, dark-haired, and dark-eyed Texan took Pelham's valise.

"Walter," Chambliss exclaimed to the man with Rosser. The man was Walter Kingsbury, a lieutenant and the Corps adjutant.

"Expected you yesterday, Nate." The tall Connecticut man grinned through a face full of freckles.

"The trains run when they run. I trust the Corps is whole?"

"But without its leader." Kingsbury took Chambliss's bag. "Jefferson Davis and the commission are gone, and I think we got the message across on the mess hall. Not that it will do any good. I talked at length with Major Anderson. He's impressive—make a great commandant, even superintendent."

Chambliss was only half listening. He too was scanning the upper deck of the steamer.

"But the plebes are starting to come around. A few incidents in the last two parades and some hazing issues. The usual."

"Political issues?" Chambliss asked.

"Camps are forming, but no outright confrontations."

Chambliss nodded. "When's my first formation?"

"Evening parade."

Pelham got in Kingsbury's face. "Okay, mister mouthpiece, let's hear it."

Kingsbury gave him a look. "Here?"

"And now," Pelham insisted.

Kingsbury took a deep breath and, as if calling the Corps of Cadets to attention, boomed across the Hudson, "Battalion attention!"

Every head on the dock and steamer turned. After a moment's hesitation, Pelham gave Kingsbury an equivocal gesture. "Not bad."

"Then we're off?"

"A moment, Walter." Pelham again trained his eyes on the top deck. The two chaperones were there, as were all of the Clermont girls except Clara Bolton. Carol Hill saw him and waved a handkerchief, until collared by Frampton.

"Someone you know?" Patterson asked.

"Girls we met on the boat."

"No, I mean her." Patterson pointed to an open doorway on the lower deck, where Clara Bolton held up a piece of paper with the words "See You Tonight." Pelham grinned and touched the bill of his hat. The next instant, a nervous deckhand rushed Clara inside.

A horn sounded, and the steamer pushed away for its next stop, the Academy's North Dock, where the West Point Hotel omnibus would pick up the Clermont contingent.

"I'm liking this," Patterson said, stroking his chin.

"You like anything in a skirt," Pelham said.

"No, I mean it. She's really cute."

"Don't even think about it."

"Come on, John, 'Fair is foul, and foul is fair.'"

"What does that mean? Besides, she's a woman of breeding—not your type."

Patterson pulled Pelham's forage cap down over his eyes. "You consummate bastard."

Pelham adjusted his cap. "Premature, dear Shakespeare, for she has friends."

"Really? Then, begging your pardon. I mean, you consummate bastard, *sir.*"

"That's better."

The seven friends strode briskly up the inclined cinder road, passing the Academy's mammoth riding hall, where all but Pelham and Rosser harbored painful memories. They proceeded past the stables, approaching the level of the Plain and the east side of the two-story building that housed the Academy library and post headquarters. Before cresting the Plain, each of them extinguished his prohibited tobacco product.

The familiar sounds of summer training greeted Pelham: stern voices directing marching units, fifes and drums, the thunder of horses, the percussion of muskets, and the thunderous retorts of shore guns aimed at Crow Nest far to the north.

"Lieutenant Lee wants to see you," Kirby informed Pelham. "Any idea what it's about?" As commander of D Company, Kirby wanted to know everything that was going on, especially when the company tactical officer wanted to see one of his men.

"Possibly, Ned, but let me not say yet."

They stood at the southeast corner of the Plain. The flat expanse of land was a half-mile square, and in many ways defined the Academy. To the east and north, the Plain fell precipitously to the river's edge, while L-shaped Jefferson Road bordered the south and west.

"Moratorium over," du Pont declared, handing Pelham a newspaper and pointing to the headline on the front page: "Republicans Virtually Assured Presidency."

Pelham made short work of the article. "It's *Harper's Weekly*, Henry. What do you expect?"

Kingsbury put a hand on du Pont's shoulder. "Upton's been asking about you."

"Upton?"

"He wanted to know when you'd be back."

"Why?"

Kingsbury shrugged and jogged off in the direction of Kirby, Patterson, and Rosser, who were already heading back to the cadet encampment. Pelham, Chambliss, and du Pont made their way to post headquarters to sign in from furlough.

After signing in, Pelham indicated he was going to linger in the library. After Chambliss and du Pont were gone, he took the stairs to the second floor and the hexagonal battlement tower at the northwest corner of the building. Floor to ceiling leaded-glass windows and a landscape mural across the ceiling gave the room an old-world look. This was one of the two havens he had at the Academy.

Several of the windows were cranked open for ventilation, and he stood at one, looking north over the Plain. The smell of horse and sulfur were sweet to his nose, bringing to mind the time he, Tom Rosser, and Chas Patterson arrived on June 2, 1856, among the ninety-three bright-eyed seekers of glory who would take two weeks of qualifying examinations for entry with the Class of 1861. He could still see the faces, some long gone—faces that held the hopes and fears he had harbored. They had all had such grand dreams, and in the evenings they talked of glory, fighting Indians, and being generals. It was then that he and Rosser became fast friends. Having both been raised in the Cotton Belt, they tried to out boast each other on how much cotton they grew and how far they hauled it, Rosser claiming victory with a forty-mile trip to the gin. Day after day, gray-haired professors taught and asked questions and posed problems, mathematical and otherwise, to prepare them for the examinations administered before the stoic board of visitors. He remembered the evening before the names of those who would enter the Class of 1861 were to be announced. Convinced at first he had tested well, by midnight he was convinced otherwise, forfeiting an entire night's sleep. The next morning, he listened as the names were read. They included Nate Chambliss, Walter Kingsbury, Ned Kirby, Chas Patterson, Henry du Pont, Tom Rosser, Emory Upton—and his own.

He felt afresh the pain of not hearing the names of already good friends. He could still see their downcast, tear-stained faces; see them quietly packing bags and boarding the steamer home. He remembered how, soon enough, he had wished he'd been one of them. He was not prepared for plebe year, for the lowly estate through which he had to pass, through which every graduate had to pass. It was the toughest and longest year of his life, seeming to have no end. But end it did, and when it was over, an exhilaration that eclipsed any he had ever felt, or could imagine he might ever feel, suffused him. The relentless hazing by upperclassmen, the unending stream of plebe duties, the grueling academic schedule that claimed another twenty souls by the January academic board vendetta, and the absence of personal time— they all bore the sweet, sweet fruit of June. The feared and godlike upperclassmen extended hands in sincere friendship, professors nodded heads in approval. The intense pride at having survived plebe year was his. But most remarkable was that through the year, he had witnessed the transformation and amalgamation of his class. The man of silver suffered and succeeded no more nor no less than the man of pewter, their fates ordained by a system that granted neither distinction nor concession. The wide spectrum of personalities, beliefs, strengths, and weaknesses had become the Class of 1861, a class of uncommon mettle, whose motto would be "Faithful to Death." And now, more than ever, he realized the strength of that bond.

Pelham studied the scene in front of him. The western third of the Plain was alive with marching drill. Eight-man squads of plebes responded to commands from upperclassmen, their movements giving the appearance of indecision, first turning right, then left, then reversing direction, and then executing a series of complex movements that mysteriously produced a straight line, which then marched off in a new direction. In the center of the Plain, upperclassmen on horseback advanced in groups of five and ten, first in a trot and then in a cloud-raising gallop, sabers drawn, ready to clip heads off target dummies. In the eastern foreground, the polished brass barrels of the West Point battery gleamed in the sun, as sections of cadets conducted mock firing drills. Beyond the artillery pieces, cadets armed with muskets shot at targets raised at the crest of the bluff. At the north end of the flat Plain stood its only blemish, the fifteen-foot deep depression known as Executioner's Hollow.

Beyond the marksmanship range stood the cadet summer encampment site, and northwest of the encampment on the edge of the bluff, the West Point Hotel. North and east of the encampment site were the eroded breastworks of what had been Fort Arnold and was now known as Fort Clinton.

Pelham turned his gaze to the northwest, to the successive layers of steep verdant hills, over which he and his classmates had hiked for days on end with weapons and full packs during plebe summer. On a promontory, he could make out the stone wall around Fort Putnam. He took in the countryside and sweep of the Hudson River, affirming again that between them, the Academy could not rest on more beautiful ground.

As he left the building, Pelham spotted the familiar figure of a man in army blue approaching from the direction of the encampment. He was a smallish man with a bugle, and trailing at his heels was a dog.

Pelham grinned, "Old Bentz, my dearest nemesis!" He clasped the hand of Corporal Louis Bentz, whose leathered face also bore a grin.

"Mr. Pelham, I have not seen you about."

"I am just now back from furlough, and I see you and Hanzi are no worse for wear."

The bugler's dog nudged Pelham's leg and raised a paw. Pelham bent over and shook it, and then rubbed the dog's head.

"So this is it, Mr. Pelham, your final year."

"It is, and at long last."

"For my money, the years pass too quickly."

"Rubbish. You and Hanzi are eternal."

"But summer encampments are growing old, sir. I spend all my time going back and forth, back and forth."

"You are amazing, Bentz. How many years now?"

The Corps bugler rubbed his chin. "I don't know. Here at West Point, maybe twenty-five, maybe more. I lose track."

"Twenty-five years of destroying our sleep." Pelham put a hand on the man's shoulder.

"It's a job."

"And of course you realize what you've done to yourself. You cannot retire. We'll not stand for it."

"Then I'll die blowing reveille."

"That might be acceptable."

The two shared a laugh, and Bentz continued on his way.

Pelham whistled a cadence song as he approached the sentry post at the southwest corner of the encampment, and responded to the guard's challenge with the password provided at post headquarters. He found the encampment a bustle of activity, and turning down D Company's main street, he saw Rosser chewing out a plebe.

CHAPTER NINE

With a clear and majestic view of the Hudson River, the three-story West Point Hotel dominated the north end of the Plain from a nest of elm and oak trees and a flowered landscape. Northwest of the hotel loomed the imposing Butter Mountain. The people in the area had wanted it renamed Storm King Mountain, since the behemoth curried bad weather and blotted out the sun in the late afternoon, dropping temperatures ten degrees. The hotel was its own world, the only public lodging and dining facility on academy grounds, its only competition being the larger and quieter Cozzen's Hotel in Buttermilk Falls, a mile and a half to the south.

The hotel walls were masonry stone and brick, covered with a cream-colored stucco; its interior featured rich woods, polished brass, and crystal chandeliers. Its broad veranda, skirting all but the east side of the hotel, provided panoramic views of cadets training on the Plain and packets and white sails tacking back and forth across the Hudson. On the fresh cropped lawn and in the intoxicating light and warmth of summer afternoons, not a few guests pretended at Rip Van Winkle.

The imposing rock formation of Constitution Island, the northern anchoring point for the Great Chain during the Revolution War, commanded the opposite shore. On the island's sparsely treed surface lived the Warner family, whose daughter Anna had recently penned the hymn *Jesus Loves Me.* She and her sister, Susan, still crossed the river to the North Dock every Sunday to teach Sunday School to cadets and the post children.

Twenty miles upriver, framed by the highland hills, was the town of Newburgh; and thirty miles beyond it, the Catskill Mountains showed themselves only on the clearest of days.

The hotel, boasting eighty guest rooms, was a living thing, steadily expanding since its initial construction in 1829. For over three decades, it had played host to countless travelers, to the board of visitors, to purveyors of every kind of Academy business, and to dignitaries not otherwise accommodated in the superintendent's quarters.

But to the young men in gray, the hotel served a much more vital function. It was the abode of hundreds of young women who made the pilgrimage between early June and late August to give meaning to life. For a quarter of a century, West Point had been without peer as the venue for established and aspiring young ladies to meet the country's most eligible bachelors. To attend a cadet hop was a thing dreamed of and schemed over by mothers in the business of placing daughters. Every Monday, Wednesday, and Friday night, the hotel's first floor was transformed into a place of color, sound, and enchantment, where hearts were stirred, romance blossomed, and pledges were made and sometimes kept.

"And your room keys, ma'am." The desk clerk pushed four sets of keys across the counter to the Clermont assistant dean. Miss Frampton made a clucking sound as she snatched up the keys and waddled to the parlor.

"All right, ladies, I have your room keys. Mrs. Wigglesworth and I will be in room 207. Please remember that, room 207. Rebecca and Alice?"

Rebecca Astor stepped forward.

"Room 305."

Taking the key, Rebecca and Alice Paine ascended the hotel staircase.

"Clara and Ellen?"

"If you please, ma'am," Carol Hill attempted a straight face. "I believe they are on the back veranda taking fresh air."

"Taking fresh air?" Frampton's eyes narrowed. "Mrs. Wigglesworth."

Mrs. Wigglesworth, with upturned nose, took the key from the assistant dean and shuffled down the hall and out the back door, where she found Clara and Ellie sitting on a porch swing facing the river.

"Clara," she declared, "I'll thank you and Ellen not to leave the group without letting us know your intentions. You are our responsibility, and that is our rule. Here is your room key. A bellboy will bring up your luggage." She glanced at her watch. "You have precious little time to settle yourselves and rest before we meet in the parlor at five-fifteen. Is that clear?"

"Yes, ma'am, perfectly. And thank you, Mrs. Wigglesworth."

The pudgy chaperone eyed Clara suspiciously.

Alone again, the two girls giggled. "Ellie, is this not the most exquisite place on earth? I mean just look." Clara swept her hand across the turn in the river.

"It's quite wonderful—more than I could have dreamed of." Ellie closed her eyes and drew a deep breath. "I can't wait for tonight, to dance with Cadet Pelham and his handsome friends. Do you suppose I'll meet someone special?"

"Ellie, sweet dear, there are a lot of very fine fish in this delightful pond."

"And I'll dance with all of them, but be satisfied with one."

"Ellie, you're the catch, not them." Clara jumped to her feet. "Come, let's see our room!"

Clara inserted the key and opened the door to room 315. It was small, but contained a fine double bed with a quilted comforter and overstuffed pillows, a large armoire, a vanity with mirror and cushioned stool, and a washstand with a porcelain basin and a pitcher already filled with lemon water. A bowl of fruit and a vase of fresh flowers sat on a small dresser. The room's one window was large and open to a cooling breeze that passed through the room and out the transom over the door.

Clara stood at the window. "My God, Ellie, look! We have positively the best view in the entire hotel. See the river? Can you believe the mountains, and just look at the boats. I can't count the number of sails."

Ellie stood beside Clara, and together they breathed the scented air and ogled the landscape.

"See the children?" Clara pointed to a natural amphitheater fifty yards west of the hotel. A woman was lecturing a group of young girls and boys seated on a long bench.

"Class in the open air, how wonderful is that?" With an impish look, Ellie directed Clara's attention toward the bluff. "You know what's down there, don't you?"

"You mean the dock where we landed?"

"No, silly, next to the dock. Actually, you can't see it, but—" She dug in her reticule and produced a small pamphlet bearing the Academy crest. Thumbing through it, she found what she was looking for. "Read this."

Clara read. "Chain Battery Walk?"

"But everyone calls it Flirtation Walk!"

Clara's eyes widened. "Do you suppose we'll get to see it?"

"Well, you can't go by yourself. You have to be escorted by a cadet."

Clara and Ellie exchanged knowing looks and burst out laughing.

"Just magical," Clara exclaimed, plopping down on the vanity chair and tossing her bonnet on the bed. She untied her shoes and rubbed her feet. "You know, Charles Dickens was right about this place. I read that he and his wife lodged in this very hotel for two nights in 1842, just before they returned to England—maybe in this very room, Ellie!"

Ellie squealed.

"It's in his book, *American Notes*. I do love his books."

"Everyone does." Ellie proceeded to cut an apple into quarters. "But from what I remember, his book didn't do very well, at least here in the States."

"Well, he wasn't much impressed with us, was he? His expectations too high, I think. He likely thought the world's only democracy would be somehow perfect. Still, I believe he was only being candid about what he saw, about our working conditions—and slavery."

Ellie nodded and shared a slice of apple with Clara. "He was very much anti-slavery, but then he was English and the English abolished the horrid business long ago."

"Actually I don't think it was until 1834 that they did for the whole empire. I hope our expectations are not too high."

They both laughed again.

"Did Dickens talk to the cadets?" Ellie asked.

"I don't know, though I don't think so. At least, I don't think it's mentioned in his book."

"I should think the cadets would have enjoyed him immensely."

A knock on the door sent Clara scrambling for her shoes.

Ellie opened the door to a towheaded boy in his early teens, swimming in an oversized hotel staff uniform. The boy announced himself as Joseph and deposited four suitcases and as many hat boxes at the foot of the bed. Then he nervously delivered a rehearsed speech on what they should know about the hotel, from the dining hours, to the location of bath and privy facilities at the ends of the hall, to how it was best to bathe or shower early in the day when there was still hot water.

"You are a dear, Joe, but I have a question." Clara gave the boy an innocent look. "Are cadets permitted to call on female guests at the hotel?"

"Oh no, ma'am, I don't think so. Not unless they get permission from way high up."

"Really?" Clara let her disappointment show.

"But they can always call on the veranda, or on the grounds," the boy quickly added.

Clara brightened and winked at Ellie. "Thank you, Joe." She searched her purse and found a nickel.

"Thank you, ma'am, but that is not necessary."

"But deserved. And, Joe, do you work here every day?"

"Nearly, ma'am. During the summers and the long Christmas holiday, when I'm not in school, I work weekdays and Saturday mornings."

"That's reassuring, Joe. There's no telling when we might need some help."

"Yes, ma'am. I'm your man. I'm always at the bell stand."

After Joseph was gone, Clara turned to Ellie and squeezed her hand. "Ellie, you are my best friend, and this is going to be the best week of our lives."

In room 207, Miss Frampton sat in front of the vanity mirror. She felt haggard, and the mirror showed it. This was the third time she had escorted Clermont girls to West Point, and the memories of prior trips were having their effect.

"We'll not want to let them out of our sight, these girls, not for an instant. You'd think they never saw a man the way they gawked at those cadets on the boat. Imagine when they see the entire Corps!"

Mrs. Wigglesworth hung another dress in the armoire. "The transformation is indeed puzzling, for they certainly don't act that way around Long Island boys."

"We'll work in shifts and separately if needed, and give them very short leash. I want them to enjoy themselves, but I don't want them in trouble. Until convinced otherwise, and I have yet to be, I don't trust these young men. They may be cadets and model citizens, but they are men all the same."

"Indeed, ma'am." Mrs. Wigglesworth sighed. "I can't say this hasn't already been more than I bargained for." Wigglesworth had raised two girls and a boy, and her youngest girl had graduated from Clermont four years earlier. She had been in the last group escorted to West Point by Frampton, which was the reason Wigglesworth had volunteered to chaperon. Also, she had never seen the Academy.

"Still," Wigglesworth added, "it's only for a week, and when it's over we'll have them back in school and under books and homework. By the way, putting the girls on the third floor was a brilliant idea. We can guard the stairwells if need be."

"Count them, dear," said Frampton. "There are three stairwells. Anyway, at night the cadets are pretty much in their cage. They can get a great many demerits if they are caught not being where they should be." Frampton stood at the window, observing the intricate movements of a group of mounted cadets training on the Plain. "Still, the male libido is a fearful thing, capable of more than we want to know."

CHAPTER TEN

In less than an hour, Pelham was again immersed in the regime of summer encampment. The camp, conveniently located a hundred yards southeast of the hotel, had not changed its configuration in twenty years, except for the welcomed growth of shade trees around its perimeter. For nine months of the year, it was inhabited only by wooden post and cross-bar skeletons, to which tents were secured for the three months of summer. In June, after final examinations, the upper classes abandoned the barracks with bedding, uniforms, arms, and accoutrements, and raised the white tents of their summer home. The new plebe class, initially housed in the barracks, would not join them until after entry examinations.

The encampment measured five hundred and fifty feet east to west, two hundred and fifty feet north to south, and was unevenly divided into four sectors.

The western sector was a narrow parcel of land dedicated solely to the camp guard. The area contained five guard tents, an area for inspection of the guard, and an area for the stacking of muskets when not in use.

East of the guard sector, the second sector consisted of the parade ground. It was in this sector that the Corps daily assembled for meal formations, inspections, and abbreviated parades. Between the guard and parade field sectors was a well manicured, tree-lined walk, with benches for visitors to view the encampment parade field and a tent in which visitors could call upon cadets during inclement weather. From the north end of the walk, a path extended to the hotel.

East of the parade ground was the third and largest sector, the cadet bivouac area, consisting of eight parallel rows of white tents, in which two to four cadets were quartered. Two rows of tents faced inward to

71

form each of the four company streets—A Company to the north, B Company, C Company, and D Company to the south. At the east end of each company street were tents for cadet officers.

East of the cadet bivouac area, the fourth sector included the field command tents for the company tactical officers, including Lieutenant Lee, and the large field headquarters tent of the commandant of cadets, Lieutenant Colonel Hardee. The balance of the fourth sector contained Henry du Pont's Corps quartermaster tent at the east end of A Company, Walter Kingsbury's Corps adjutant tent at the east end of D Company, and several smaller tents for drum boy orderlies, boot blacks, and varnishers.

A visitor inspecting the bivouac area would have thought every tent the same, its arrangement precisely duplicated, from the stacks of neatly folded bedding; to the configuration of washbowls, shaving gear, and assorted other items; to the ordering within footlockers of books, socks, handkerchiefs, underwear, and white gloves. Uniforms hung from a bar strung between the front and rear tent poles. The uniforms consisted of full dress gray jackets, gray trousers, white trousers, utility drill jackets, reinforced utility trousers for riding, and light linen uniforms for summer training.

The purpose of summer encampment was threefold: to immerse cadets in every form of military training; to indoctrinate and assimilate the new class of plebes, instilling in them the discipline that would define them as West Point graduates; and to provide leadership opportunities for upperclassmen, as they assumed positions of command and staff within the Corps and fulfilled various cadet training assignments.

Throughout the summer, cadet guards were posted twenty-four hours a day at eight sentry huts positioned around the perimeter of the encampment. Cadet guards were to patrol the border of the encampment between two sentry posts, and to challenge all persons entering or departing the encampment. The guard detail for each day consisted of twenty-four cadets mustered from all classes. Only the sharpest and most disciplined plebes were allowed to participate in guard duty. Each man on the guard detail served four two-hour guard tours, and spent the balance of his time reading, sleeping, or preparing for the next guard mount inspection.

Guard mount inspection was conducted by the officer of the guard, a First Classman, and as soon as he returned, Pelham learned that he was to be officer of the guard the following Monday. The irony of the assignment, given Pelham's past performance, was lost on no one, especially Rosser. Guard mount inspections were universal grief for all those subject to inspection, as they were the breeding ground for demerits, or "skins," for infractions ranging from poorly shined brass, to lint in musket barrels, to inadequately polished shoes.

Once guard mount inspection was finished, a Second Classman, the sergeant of the guard, would march the new guard detail around the encampment. At each sentry post, the guard on duty would be formally relieved and fall in at the rear of the guard detail. At the same time, his place would be taken by a member of the new guard.

Pelham slipped into a pair of bright white cotton dress trousers, while a plebe in the company street announced mail call. Moments later there was a knock on the tent pole. At the entrance to the tent, a plebe stood straight as a rod with several letters in his left hand and one in his right hand.

"Sir, mail for Mr. Pelham."

Pelham had just lathered his face to shave, and mumbled for Rosser to take the letter. As the plebe turned to leave, Rosser ordered him to halt.

The plebe stopped and executed an about-face. "Sir?"

"Where's my mail?"

The plebe's face paled. Plebes were strictly taught to give only one of four answers: yes, sir; no, sir; no excuse, sir; or sir, I do not understand. To do otherwise was to invite grief. This plebe chose the last option.

"What do you mean, you don't understand?" Rosser growled as Pelham smiled in the mirror.

Without giving the plebe a chance to respond, Rosser bellowed, "Pea brain, next time you bring Mr. Pelham the letter, there better be one for me, understand?"

"Sir—yes, sir."

"What's your name, plebe?"

"McElheny, sir."

"Where are you from?"

"Ohio, sir."

"I'll be watching you, McElheny."

"Yes, sir."

The plebe raised his right foot to execute an about-face, when Rosser said, "Wait, I want you to do me a favor. You'd like that, wouldn't you, McElheny?"

The plebe slowly lowered his right foot. "Yes, sir."

"Tell Fannie I want my spyglass back."

The plebe blinked hard and repeated his earlier response.

In the mirror, Pelham could see beads of sweat forming on McElheny's face.

"You don't know Fannie?"

"No, sir?"

"Do you know who Mr. Custer is?"

"Yes, sir."

"Mr. Custer is Fannie."

"Yes, sir."

"Do you know why he is Fannie?"

"No, sir."

"Because I gave him that name when he showed up at West Point with long curly locks."

"Yes, sir."

"Do you think it a good name?"

"Yes, sir." McElheny blinked, and a drop of sweat landed on his shoe.

"So you'll do that for me, ask Fannie to return my spyglass?"

"Yes, sir."

"Exactly what will you say to him?"

"Sir, I will say, 'Mr. Fannie, sir, Mr. Rosser would like his spyglass back, sir.'"

"Excellent. Now get out of here!"

McElheny saluted and left to report to the next tent, his expression indicating he expected no better.

Pelham inspected his face in the mirror. "You going to the hop tonight?"

"I don't know. They are starting to blur. I may be all danced out. I might catch up on my reading."

A voice with a New England accent rang out from the company street. "John Pelham of Alabama!"

Pelham grinned. "Adelbert Ames of Maine!"

The handsome, round-faced commander of B Company appeared at the entrance to the tent in full dress uniform, with four large gold chevrons on the sleeves of his dress coat.

"So how was home?" Ames asked.

"Hotter than Hades, but otherwise better than it should have been. You?"

"Fine, but I've been back a week, and, hell, it's no cooler here." The fine-featured Ames narrowed his dark eyes. "Isn't there something you want to tell me?"

Pelham wiped the last of the shaving cream from his face. "Tell you?"

"Come on, John, you owe me. Nate says you've got a covey of quail, and I want in."

Pelham threw his towel at Ames. "Then I suggest, my lobster-loving friend, you not be tardy. Be at the hotel at ten to eight."

Ames threw the towel back. "Done."

After Ames was gone, Rosser slipped Pelham's sword from its scabbard, stepped into the company street, and began to perform officer sword drill. "I still can't believe you're a lieutenant. I'll never see one of these."

"Given our habits, my tenure is likely to be short. But until something happens, I'll enjoy not having a musket on my shoulder." Pelham was more than a little proud of the three gold chevrons on the sleeves of his dress coat. Ladies attending the hops seemed impressed by the distinction. While on furlough, he had never mentioned the promotion, for he was more than convinced that it was a mistake that would be rectified upon his return.

The Corps' eighteen officers were composed of four captains and fourteen lieutenants, and were drawn from the First Class, which for the Class of 1861 numbered fifty. A cadet captain commanded each company. Chambliss, in addition to being the Corps first captain, commanded A Company. Within each company, three lieutenants led each of three platoons. The Corps' battalion staff had two lieutenants: du Pont, the Corps quartermaster; and Kingsbury, the Corps adjutant.

Rosser raised the hilt of the sword to his chin, the blade pointing upward, and then brought his hand sharply down to his side, so that the blade pointed at the ground at a forty-five degree angle. Rosser returned the sword to its scabbard. "I've no problem with a musket, given the less disciplined life we lead."

"And that we do, don't we, Tom?" Pelham laughed at the obvious. Within the class, he had the most demerits, and Rosser only three less. Demerits above the monthly allowance of ten resulted in punishment tours for all but the First Class, which was one hour of marching in full dress uniform with shouldered musket for each excessive demerit. Now that they were First Classmen, except for the most grievous crimes, excessive demerits would be satisfied by confinement to quarters, one hour of confinement for each demerit.

Pelham and Rosser understood the demerit system better than anyone in the Corps, with the possible exception of Custer, who had the most demerits in the Second Class. Each year, the three of them flirted with the semi-annual limit of one hundred demerits, which, if exceeded, brought mandatory expulsion. But each tested the limit with the knowledge that if they did graduate, their peers would accord them a level of respect not much lower than that given the first captain. That they spent more money resoling shoes worn out by marching was a small price for glory.

Pelham checked himself in the mirror. His shoes were blackened and polished, his white trousers form-fitted his waist, and his black-trimmed and white-collared gray dress coat with three vertical rows of brass buttons was freshly brushed. He donned his blue forage cap, with its brightly shined gold wreath and the gold letters USMA across the front, and announced that he was off to see Lieutenant Lee.

Pelham waited outside Lieutenant Lee's tent until another cadet emerged, a Fourth Classman, bearing a defeated look. Pelham entered the tent and approached Lee's desk.

"Sir, Cadet Pelham reporting as ordered."

Lieutenant Lee returned the salute and motioned for Pelham to take a seat. "Welcome back, Mr. Pelham."

"Thank you, sir."

Pelham felt at ease with Lee. He admired him, and thought him the kind of leader he wanted to be. Lee was slim and of average height, but by his bearing gave the appearance of being taller. He was a positive person, competent to the extreme, and shrouded with an air of mystery. Pelham found Lee clear in his expectations as tactical officer; and if you met those expectations, he was content to let you live in peace. With Lee, a cadet stood on his merits, and knew where he stood. That Lee was a recent graduate with already so much frontier experience only enhanced his appeal. A near fatal confrontation he'd had with Comanches fueled speculation among the Corps as to the details. The rumor was that Lee had fought hand to hand with two Comanche warriors. He'd only wanted to disarm them, but had been forced to kill them. Whatever the truth, Lee was not inclined to visit the subject.

"Your furlough?" he asked Pelham.

"Too short, sir."

"I expect so. Traveling to and from Alabama could not have left you much time. I trust you considered what we talked about?"

"I have sir, and I would be honored to teach what little I know."

"Don't be modest. You're the finest horseman in your class and the Academy, and there are some Second Classmen in dire need of instruction. Such tutoring—if I may call it that—seems to stick better when it comes from within the Corps and not from a commissioned officer or enlisted man. I was a cadet instructor my First Class summer."

Pelham was well aware of Lee's prowess on a horse. "Yes, sir. I'm looking forward to it."

"I've asked Mr. Rosser to assist you."

Pelham could not hide his surprise. "Yes, sir. No one more qualified."

"He'll give you the details. And from the Second Class, I've picked Mr. Custer, as he'll likely take the lead next year—assuming he's still with us."

Pelham managed to keep a straight face. "Yes, sir. He rides very well."

"Then we're agreed." Lee got to his feet. "I know you need to ready yourself for parade."

When he returned to the tent, Pelham found Rosser shining brass—his breastplate, waist plate, the Corps insignia for his dress hat, and a handful of dress coat buttons laid out on a white handkerchief on his footlocker.

"Why didn't you tell me?" Pelham demanded.

Rosser looked up. "We should be royally entertained."

"And the schedule?"

"Tomorrow, again on Wednesday, a day of rest, and then on Friday. We'll have two sections of eight to ten, an hour each, one at eight and one at ten. The section rosters are in your locker."

Pelham pointed to Rosser's breastplate. "It's not my place—"

"Damn right, it's not." Rosser picked up the breastplate and applied more polish.

In the company street a plebe minute caller shouted, "Sir, there are five minutes until parade formation. Uniform is full dress gray over white."

Pelham checked himself in the mirror. "Tell me it's an encampment parade."

"That would be a negative. Hardee wants full blown parades in front of God and country to settle the plebes."

Pelham perused the hop card Charlie Hazlett had dropped off, and considered what Hazlett had said. It would make the evening more complicated.

The plebe minute caller announced, "Sir, there are four minutes until parade formation."

Pelham fitted a starched white cross belt over his dress coat and positioned the polished breastplate with a white-gloved hand. He fastened the leather sword belt around his waist and wrapped his waist with the red satin sash of an officer.

The minute caller barked his final announcement. "Sir, there are two minutes until parade formation."

Pelham fitted the seven-inch tall black dress hat on his head, from which extended a long, thick black feather plume. Across the front of the hat was a large gold spread-wing eagle positioned atop the castle of the Corps of Engineers. He turned in the small mirror and, satisfied with his visage, announced, "After you, my friend."

Rosser stepped into the company street, his dress hat with black pompon in one hand and his musket in the other.

CHAPTER ELEVEN

At five-thirty, the Clermont girls sat around a large circular table in the hotel parlor. Clara rolled her eyes at Ellie as Miss Frampton droned on, already five minutes into another lecture on the lechers that might inhabit the Corps. Mrs. Wigglesworth was not in attendance, as she was napping before her evening assignment. When Frampton finally rested her tongue, she produced a rubbery smile. "Right then, where is that nice young man?"

Joseph appeared out of thin air.

"We will follow this boy to the parade viewing area, and after the parade return directly to the hotel. Is that clear?" Frampton was looking directly at Clara.

Joseph led the Clermont contingent down the hotel lane, past the display of Revolutionary War and Mexican War cannons on Trophy Point, and then around the northwest corner of the Plain to the public seating area. A large crowd had already formed, including patrons of Cozzen's Hotel, and those arriving by road or packet from Cold Springs, Garrison, Cornwall, and resorts upriver. Some were still making their way up from North Dock.

Owing to Joseph's fast gait, the girls quickly distanced themselves from Frampton. En route they gracefully deflected the sun's warm rays with parasols, and talked only of the evening hop and cadets. They soon arrived at one of several long benches on the edge of the Plain. The bench was tagged with a reserved sign, which Joseph removed.

"Best seats in the house, ma'ams." Joseph beamed, pleased with himself. "Now, if there is nothing else I can do for you, I got to get back to my duties."

"We'll be fine, Joe." Clara smiled and squeezed his hand. "You've been too kind, and thanks for everything. I'll see you tomorrow?"

Joseph blushed red. "Yes, ma'am. Thank you, ma'am."

Miss Frampton finally arrived, somewhat winded, and took a position behind the bench.

Ellie searched the Plain. "So where are they? I don't see any cadets."

Just then drums from the regally uniformed West Point band began to beat cadence. In a matter of seconds there was movement from the south side of the cadet encampment.

"Here they come, girls!" Carol Hill declared in a husky voice.

"Miss Hill!" Frampton's voice was shrill.

Martial music suddenly replaced the drum beat and pealed across the Plain.

Rebecca Astor and Alice Paine stared with mouths open and eyes wide, and Jessica Danford peered through the group's only eyeglass. "Oh, my gosh! They're beautiful!"

"Let me see." Alice Paine reached for the eyeglass.

Ellie clutched Clara's hand. "I've got goose bumps."

"Me too," Clara admitted.

The Corps of Cadets marched forward led by its battalion staff, with Nate Chambliss in front. Centered two paces behind him were Walter Kingsbury and Henry du Pont.

Chambliss halted the battalion staff directly in front of the reviewing party and fifty feet from the reviewing stand. Colonel Delafield, Lieutenant Colonel Hardee, and two visiting French diplomats stood on the elevated reviewing stand. The five-man color guard formed on the company line fifty feet behind the battalion staff. Then, beginning with A Company, company guides posted forward to assigned positions on the company line, and the four companies formed on the company guides.

The martial music abruptly stopped. The sun's rays reflected brightly off the dress hats and bayonets of the assembled Corps. To Clara, the cadets appeared as Greek warriors clutching spears.

After a profound silence, Chambliss executed an about-face and bellowed, "Bring your companies to order arms and parade rest!"

The Clermont girls exchanged expectant looks.

"Order!" company commanders barked in unison. "Arms!" On that command, every rifle-bearing cadet executed the five-step drill that brought the butt of his weapon to a spot on the ground next to his right foot.

"Parade, rest!"

Every man's left foot shifted eighteen inches to the left, and every man's left hand was brought crisply to the small of his back.

Ellie pinched Clara. "Do you see him?"

"Who?"

"Clara!"

"I can't make out anyone. They're too far away, and they all look alike."

"They all look handsome," Ellie said dreamily. "What's going to happen now?"

"Will you shush? I don't know any more than you do."

Beneath a pastoral sky, Delafield and Hardee critically eyed the Corps' performance. The march-on had been acceptable, though Hardee observed that the spacing between Companies B and C was greater than he would have liked.

Chambliss executed another about-face and rendered to the reviewing party a salute with his sword. "Sir, the Corps is formed!"

Delafield returned the salute.

Chambliss turned back to the Corps. "Bring your companies to attention and present arms."

The Corps, as one, executed both commands, and Chambliss again faced the superintendent. Then he, du Pont, and Kingsbury presented arms in a flash of steel blades.

Carol Hill made a swooning sound, eliciting giggles from the other girls.

"I am not amused, Miss Hill," Frampton said, in a pitch that could break glass.

Delafield returned the salute and gave the command, "Pass in review."

Chambliss faced the Corps and repeated the command. "Pass in review!"

Company commanders brought their companies to "order arms" and then "right shoulder arms." On Chambliss's cue, the band struck "The French National Defilé," a Corps favorite and a delight to the crowd. Chambliss wheeled the battalion staff and proceeded to a point directly in front of A Company's first platoon. On his command, the platoon stepped off on its left foot in perfect cadence with the battalion staff. The first platoon was followed by the second and third platoons. B Company, with Adelbert Ames at the head, followed A Company, and then came the color guard, C Company, and D Company with Ned Kirby at the lead. As each platoon made the final turn to pass in review, it executed a maneuver that formed two long ranks of twelve cadets, with the challenge, little appreciated by the assembled throng, of maintaining perfect alignment while passing the reviewing party.

At a marker near the reviewing stand, unit commanders gave the order "eyes, right," and heads snapped forty-five degrees toward the reviewing party. On the same command, each officer raised his sword and brought it down sharply at a forty-five-degree angle.

Clara's heart seemed to jump in her chest as the band played and the grim-faced cadets approached and marched before her. Around her, the crowd roared for each platoon. With the passing of each unit, her heart seemed to beat faster, and she wondered if she would survive long enough to see Pelham. As companies and platoons marched past the reviewing stand, they continued straight ahead for fifty yards, and then made a left turn toward the encampment.

The color guard passed the reviewing stand, carrying the Stars and Stripes, the army flag, and the colors of the United States Corps of Cadets. On either side of the shoulder-to-shoulder flag bearers, marched a cadet bearing a musket with fixed bayonet. As the national flag passed before the crowd, those in uniform stood at attention and saluted; those not in uniform placed their hands over their hearts.

"There he is!" Ellie screamed after C Company had passed in review, her voice all but drowned out by the crowd noise.

Clara had already spied Pelham in front of D Company's second platoon, and was shuddering with excitement. She waved impetuously, unable to take her eyes off Pelham.

Ellie suddenly stood up and cheered loudly.

"Miss Lawson, be a lady and sit down!" demanded Frampton.

At Frampton's voice, Clara checked herself. Frampton was right. Be a lady, she told herself. It was just a parade. She hardly knew this man, John Pelham. It was the martial music—yes, and the crowd, the men in uniform, and their terrible weapons. She wiped perspiration from her brow and took a deep breath. But try as she might, she couldn't look away from Pelham.

Pelham commanded, "Eyes, right!" in a voice that shocked her. She swallowed hard, and when his sword slashed through the air, every eye in the platoon looked straight at her. She froze, unable to breathe until the platoon had passed and Pelham had ordered, "Ready, front!"

And then he was gone, followed by the last platoon of D Company, and just that quickly, the martial music stopped again and the parade was over.

"Come, girls, back to the hotel," Frampton said with a perfunctory air. All but Clara and Ellie stood up and dutifully filed off behind the mother hen, their tongues a whir.

Clara and Ellie sat alone on the bench as drummers continued to beat cadence until the last of the Corps disappeared into the distant encampment.

Ellie put a hand on Clara's arm. "Are you all right?"

Clara hid her face beneath her parasol, and wiped her eyes with a handkerchief. "Ellie Lawson, you will never speak a word of this to anyone."

Chapter Twelve

Half an hour after the Corps returned from parade, Bentz sounded the call for supper formation. Pelham and the rest of the Corps formed on the parade field, not at all optimistic about the meal that awaited them. The chatter of the four companies came to an end with Kingsbury's command to come to attention.

When roll call reports were rendered to Kingsbury, he turned to Chambliss. "Sir, all present or accounted for."

At Chambliss's command, fife and drum began to play, and the battalion staff led the Corps the half mile to the mess hall. They marched across Jefferson Road onto South Gate Road, between the Cadet Chapel and the academic building, and on to the mess hall, located south of the academic building.

The mess hall, constructed in 1852, was a large structure made of locally quarried gray granite, with imposing towers and medieval battlements. The main dining room easily contained the entire Corps, and a wing at the south end of the mess hall served as the dining facility for the Academy's academic and tactical departments.

As each platoon approached the steps leading up to the imposing entrance, commanders gave the order "at ease, march," at which all semblance of order was abandoned.

After releasing his platoon, Pelham joined the Babel scene in the dining hall. The hall measured one hundred and fifty feet long by fifty feet wide, with a ceiling height of twenty-five feet. Large windows ringed the hall, spaced every fifteen feet, and were open for ventilation. Within the hall were three long rows of five tables, and at the north end was a single table for Chambliss, du Pont, Kingsbury, and members of the lower classes from A Company. Each table sat eighteen cadets.

Breakfast was served at seven, the midday meal at one, and supper at seven.

Crossing the mess hall to D Company's area, Pelham brushed up against Emory Upton, standing at the head of an A Company table. "Behaving yourself, Emory?"

The abolitionist almost smiled. "Only challenging what must be challenged, my friend."

"I'll take that as a yes." Pelham moved on across the dining room, until a hand restrained him.

It was Walter Kingsbury. "You never mentioned the girls."

"You never asked."

"I had to?"

"Sorry, Walter. Supply and demand. But as it happens, Tom isn't going to the hop, so if you're interested …"

"You know I am, and if I may be so bold—neither too thick, nor too thin."

"Hotel steps, ten till eight." Pelham slipped Kingsbury a note. "If you wouldn't mind."

"My pleasure."

Pelham weaved between the tables to the D Company dining area, and assumed a position next to Rosser at the head of one of the tables.

"Battalion, attention!" Kingsbury boomed from the north end of the hall, drawing immediate silence from the Corps. "Father God, we thank you for our country, the Academy, and this food, and ask that you to bless us in your service. Amen. Take seats!"

More than two hundred wooden stools scrapped the gray slate floor, and plebes, already seasoned in their duties, dispensed to upperclassmen beverage preferences of water, milk, tea, or coffee. At the same time, sixteen waiters emerged from the kitchen with huge trays bearing platters of meat, boiled potatoes, and string beans.

"McElheny, bread, please," Pelham said, realizing that he hadn't eaten since breakfast. McElheny, his eyes straight ahead and chin drawn back into his neck, passed the bread platter up the table.

Pelham tore a piece from the loaf and took a bite.

The imposing dining hall was a curious paradox of white linen tablecloths and napkins, sterling silver and bone china, and food that was neither inviting nor sufficient. But whatever else was passed as food, the bread, always fresh for supper, never disappointed.

Standing guard around the hall were solemn portraits of men in uniform and men in suits, soldiers and academicians past and present. And above the short hallway leading to the south wing was a portrait of Colonel Sylvanus Thayer painted by Professor Weir. Thayer, a former superintendent, was acknowledged as the father of the Military Academy for his sweeping contributions.

As would be the case for breakfast, only a few faculty and staff were present for the supper meal. However, for the midday meal, all faculty and staff would be in their seats, as this was the established time for dissemination of information and discussion of matters academic and otherwise.

At opposite ends of the table located at the west end of the wing were places for Colonel Delafield and Professor Mahan. These and the remaining seat assignments at the table were as fixed as reveille and retreat. William Bartlett, professor of natural and experimental philosophy, had a place to the right of Mahan; and Albert Church, professor of mathematics, to the left of Mahan. Next to Professor Bartlett sat Professor Weir and next to Professor Church, Henry Kendrick, professor of chemistry and geology. Next to Professors Weir and Kendrick, and consequently next to Delafield, were places for Hyacinth Agnel, professor of French, and John French, professor of English and ethics, who, as an ordained minister, also served as the post chaplain. Of the faculty, Kendrick, a major brevetted twice for heroism in the war with Mexico, held the highest regular army rank.

At a second table sat active duty army officers assigned to the Academy to teach. At the head of this table was Lieutenant Oliver Howard, assistant professor of mathematics.

At a third table, Lieutenant Colonel Hardee sat with Lieutenant Lee, the three other cadet company tactical officers, the post adjutant, the post quartermaster, the post engineer, and the master of the sword, Antoni Lorentz.

After another bite of bread, Pelham pointed to the platter in front of Rosser. "What's the mystery meat?"

Rosser sniffed the platter. "Mutton."

Pelham thought it remarkable and altogether deceptive, the similarity between boiled mutton and boiled beef.

At the end of the mess hall, du Pont eyed Kingsbury, who was actually eating the mutton.

"Walter, how in all that's holy do you eat that stuff?"

"It's not so bad, Henry, and it's excellent protein." Kingsbury sliced off another piece, oblivious to the fat and gristle that dominated the cut.

"Protein? You see it as protein, when it tastes like—"

"Right, a strong taste. But that's the nature of it, a distinct flavor."

Du Pont shook his head. "And smell."

"Henry, you've got to rest your senses and eat what's before you. You need your strength."

Du Pont thought of the steak, pork, chicken, vegetables, fruits, cakes, and pies he had eaten on furlough, and groaned.

A tall wiry man walked up behind him. "Welcome back, Henry." The man's voice was low and whispered.

"Emory." Du Pont didn't bother to turn around.

"I didn't think you would stoop so low, Henry."

Du Pont turned to face Emory Upton. "What is that supposed to mean?"

Upton gave Chambliss and Kingsbury a pasty smile. "I think you know exactly what it means. You surprised me. I would have expected loyalty from the class president."

"Drop the riddles, Emory." Du Pont didn't bother to whisper.

Upton raised his hands in a defensive gesture and departed. Kingsbury, his cheeks full of more mutton, gave du Pont a look. "What's with Upton?"

Du Pont shrugged.

"You okay, Henry?" Kingsbury pressed.

"Yes, why?"

"Look at your fork."

Du Pont saw the gristled mutton on his fork and gagged audibly.

Ten minutes into the meal, waiters appeared from the kitchen with bowls of bread pudding, a dessert staple of leftover bread that had been cubed, sugared, and wetted with cream. Pelham noticed amber specks in the pudding and suspected cinnamon, which would preclude the need for Sammy, the dark molasses in silver pitchers on every table, universally applied to anything that needed sweetening or disguise.

Having made the evening matchups, Pelham's mind was at peace. He had Nate Chambliss for Jessica Danford, Henry du Pont for Ellie Lawson, Chas Patterson for Alice Paine, Adelbert Ames for Rebecca Astor, and Walter Kingsbury for Carol Hill. Of course, the matchups would only be initial introductions, a chance for a foothold.

A single chair scrapped the mess hall floor. Kingsbury rose and stood at the small lectern beside the battalion staff table. "Attention to orders!" he bellowed as he sorted through a handful of notes.

"There will be a meeting of the Ring Committee at the battalion staff table immediately after supper. The Year Book Committee will meet Thursday evening after supper in the academic lecture hall. And Lieutenant Howard's bible study will meet at Trophy Point Friday morning immediately after breakfast."

When Kingsbury paused, Pelham thought his friend had forgotten, but Kingsbury was only clearing his throat. "And the meeting of the Dialectic Society originally scheduled for tonight has been postponed until tomorrow evening after supper in the First Class Club."

Pelham, president of the Dialectic Society, breathed a sigh of relief.

When Kingsbury boomed, "Corps dismissed!" the hall exploded in a rustle of stools, as members of the Corps returned to the encampment.

Outside the mess hall, a tall Second Classman came up alongside Pelham and Rosser. "My lieges!"

"Fannie." Pelham slapped George Custer on the back. "Are you ready to train up your classmates?"

"More than ready—and ready to get out of Dutch with the tactical department."

"Funny, Tom and I were thinking the same thing. Going to the hop?"

"Nope. I'm not taking any chances between now and tomorrow."

Rosser tousled Custer's hair. "Now don't overthink this, Fannie. Eyes not on you might be on us. And where's my spyglass?"

Behind them, du Pont, chairman of the Ring Committee, raced out of the mess hall, intending to be the first to meet Pelham at the hotel.

CHAPTER THIRTEEN

Half an hour before the hop, Clara sat rigid in front of the vanity in a pair of white pantaloons and a white cotton half-slip. The face in the mirror was screwed up in pain.

"Tighter," she insisted, exhaling more air. "It has to be tighter, Ellie."

Neither girl was by any measure overweight, and their feminine lines accented all the right places. But in Victorian tradition, even the slimmest of figures had to be further compressed.

Ellie pressed her foot against Clara's back and with one final tug, cinched the last of the corset.

"The inquisition is not over!" Clara gasped.

Side by side, they stared in the mirror at cleavage and hips that would excite a dead man.

"Now the bird cage." Clara's face was filled with expectation as she and Ellie reached for their hoopskirts, substructures that would make their gowns look like dinner bells. Layers of petticoats followed, and finally a dress that all but covered their cleavage.

The two brushed their hair and applied final makeup.

"I almost feel sorry for them, don't you?" Ellie rubbed her cheek with a final touch of rouge, pursed her lips, and cast a practiced glance over her shoulder at the mirror. Then she leaned forward and ever so slightly squeezed her arms against her breasts. Pleased with the results, she said, "Yes, I do pity them."

Clara laughed and again took over the vanity.

A minute later there was a knock at the door.

"Come in," Clara declared without hesitation.

In the vanity mirror she saw in the doorway a girl her own age, her face bearing a panicked expression She was not a Clermont girl, but Clara remembered seeing her in the lobby. Even then, she had been striking, and was even more so now, being fully dressed for the evening.

"Forgive me, you must. I'm so sorry to intrude, but my hair brush exploded. Well, not quite. I dropped it and the glass handle shattered, and my roommate only uses combs, can you believe it?"

Clara smiled, intrigued by the southern accent and amazed at the speed of the girl's tongue.

"But where are my manners. My name is Eva Taylor, and I was hoping, no praying, you might lend me a brush—I mean, when you're finished."

"Of course, dear. I'm Clara Bolton, and this is my dear friend, Ellie Lawson. Please, come in." Clara stood up and handed Eva her hairbrush. "The vanity's yours. Where are you from?"

"You are a dear, and Kentucky is my home." Eva applied long strokes to shimmering black hair.

"You came all the way from Kentucky?"

"My sister, Becky—she married a cadet, David Jones—he's in the army now—a captain, I believe. Anyway, she said I needed to come to West Point and meet some cadets, and so here I am. Finally. I've been promising for the longest time. I was visiting family in New York City until yesterday."

"Have you come to find a husband?" Ellie asked innocently.

"Ellie!" Clara chided.

"Well, truthfully, I've got all the offers I need back home, but ..." Eva looked thoughtful. "Becky seems so happy with her David, and she gets to move around, see the country and all. I would love that. So, I thought ..." She turned around and smiled coyly. "What's the harm in a little window shopping?"

The three girls laughed.

"You two have been so kind." Eva returned the hairbrush. "Thank you very much. It was Clara Bolton and Ellie Lawson?"

Clara nodded, smiling, and Ellie extended her hand.

"Aren't you the dearest thing!" Eva walked back to the door. "See you girls on the dance floor."

CHAPTER FOURTEEN

Fifteen minutes before the hop, Pelham was alone at the base of the hotel staircase. A breeze off the Hudson tickled his ear, and the braided scent of roses, lilacs, and honeysuckle amused his nose. The evening was more pleasant than he had expected, the air less humid, and the temperature no more than seventy degrees. He knew that in two hours it would drop another ten degrees. Under the light of a gas lamp, he glanced at the hop card and reviewed the program. Engraved on the cover of the tasseled dance card was a scene of the Plain, with the encampment in the foreground and the hotel and river beyond. Inside were printed the evening's twenty-six dances, which included eleven waltzes, four gallops, three lancers, three deux temps, one trois temps, one polka, two redowas, and one polka redowa. All of the selections pleased him. Adjacent to each dance entry was a space for the card bearer to enter the name of a partner. Pelham smiled, knowing the intrigue and romance that would play out over the next few hours.

Ned Kirby approached with Becky Thompson on his arm. "'Evening, John."

"'Evening, Becky, Ned." Pelham bowed slightly.

"Congratulations on the teaching assignment. I thought Lee wanted a bite of you."

"He might yet."

"I understand some Clermont girls are here," Becky said with an expectant look. "Mother went to Clermont. She says it's a wonderful school."

Pelham nodded. In his opinion, Becky Thompson was the prettiest of the Thompson girls, with a fine figure, blond hair, and perfect teeth, but at eighteen, she was too young for him.

As Kirby led Becky up the stairs, she batted blue eyes over her shoulder and whispered, "I'll save you a dance, John."

Pelham smiled and tapped the railing with his fingernails. Three weeks absence had left him with little more than a week of his final encampment. For him, summer encampment was the best part of the year. He often thought of the first encampment, after surviving entrance exams and entering the Corps as a plebe. He hadn't known how to dance or that there were so many kinds of dances. Few in the class had, and none had understood the protocols of the ballroom or gentlemanship, the social graces of being an officer. He still carried the image of Mr. Flambeaux, the plebe dancing instructor, ranting like a drill sergeant, but managing over the slow cooking fire of plebe year to transform boys with only left feet into men of poise and grace. By the end of the year, he had been schooled in every dance that might surface at a hop, and during the year had partnered with Rosser, du Pont, and Kirby, learning quickly to avoid Rosser's feet. The next encampment, Flambeaux's good work was affirmed when he danced with a live female, and at the end of the dance found her all smiles and without injury.

"You look lost," a man with a southern drawl suggested.

"Hey, Charlie." Pelham shook Charlie Ball's hand. Ball was a fellow Alabamian, a Second Classman and close friend, although unlike Pelham, he played the Academy game well and was the odds-on favorite to be first captain the next year.

"John, I still can't believe you went all the way home and back in three weeks."

Pelham smiled. "I don't recommend it."

"Wish me luck." Ball touched the bill of his cap. "There's a northern belle waiting for me."

Du Pont was the first to arrive, though less than a minute ahead of Nate Chambliss, Chas Patterson, Adelbert Ames, and Walter Kingsbury. Like Pelham, they each sported a gray dress coat, white trousers, blue forage cap, the red satin waist sash of a cadet officer, and white gloves.

The appearance of another man drained the color from Pelham's face.

"Hi, roommate, guys." Rosser glanced up at the sky. "Another glorious night."

"Tom—" Pelham was speechless.

"Don't worry, I'll fend for myself."

From the hotel veranda, a girl's voice called down, "Mr. Pelham."

Pelham looked up to see Clara Bolton surrounded by her friends. "Why, Miss Bolton, ladies, what lovely sights you are."

Clara flicked open her fan. "And aren't you the handsomest of men."

Pelham led his troop up the stairs, while Rosser remained on the lawn.

"Shall we meet one another?" Pelham suggested.

"Please." Clara stepped back and organized her friends in a semi-circle.

Quickly and masterfully, Pelham made the introductions. As he did, Clara slipped back inside the hotel, past two figures hiding in the shadows, and emerged with Eva Taylor in hand.

"That tall handsome man on the lawn," Clara said. "Is he one of your friends, Mr. Pelham?"

Pelham didn't hide his surprise. "Why, uh, yes."

Rosser, who stood straight as a pole, executed an overdone bow.

"Do you think he would like to meet my friend, Eva Taylor?"

"Indeed! The man is Tom Rosser, my roommate, and a consummate gentleman from the State of Texas."

Patterson couldn't suppress a snicker.

Rosser mounted the veranda in two steps.

The matches made, Pelham took Clara's gloved hand, saying in a voice only she could hear, "It appeared you enjoyed today's parade."

Clara blushed. "You saw me?"

"I'm a soldier. I'm supposed to see everything."

In the shadows of the entrance, Miss Frampton whispered something to Mrs. Wigglesworth.

Pelham suggested that the matches mingle, and while Alice Clausen was getting the correct spelling of the first captain's name and Rosser was introducing himself to Carol Hill, Walter Kingsbury approached Eva Taylor.

"Miss Taylor, forgive my boldness, but may I request the favor of a dance?"

Eva smiled easily, checked her card, and offered Kingsbury the seventh dance.

"You honor me, ma'am, and ..." Kingsbury hesitated, glancing at Rosser. "If I might be even more bold, have you given away your last dance?"

Eva studied the Corps adjutant with interest and decided in his favor.

"Your servant." Kingsbury touched his cap and retreated.

Clara pulled Pelham aside. "Cadet Pelham, you have acquitted yourself most admirably."

"Not me, but we, for without your Miss Taylor—" He gave Clara a look. "I daresay, had I shown up with another friend, you would have manufactured another match."

Clara laughed. "I can't thank you enough for what you have done. You have made us all feel so much at home. I am going to take so many very special memories from this week. I just know it."

"I hope you feel the same at the end of your stay, but now I must confess something."

His pronouncement caught her off guard.

"Alas," he continued, "I was informed by Charlie Hazlett that I'm floor manager for the second half of the hop. I suppose the penalty of being gone for three weeks."

"What does that mean?"

"Once I'm on duty, I'm prohibited from dancing or otherwise enjoying myself. Rather, I must mingle, make sure everyone is having a good time, settle partner disputes, check the punch bowl, that sort of thing."

"So, we shall have just one dance?"

"Have you committed for the thirteenth?"

She opened her card, holding it so he couldn't peek, and made an entry. "Now I have."

"Excellent." He lowered his voice, confounding the two women in the shadows. "May I suggest that later in the evening, if you find yourself in need of fresh air, that you'll want an escort on the veranda? That happens to fall within my assigned duties."

"Fresh air?" Clara tried not to laugh. "Well, I am usually a woman of great stamina, but tonight I very well might need some fresh air."

"Yes, ma'am."

"Cadet Pelham, will you get a great many demerits if you call me Clara?"

"No, ma'am—I mean, Clara."

"That's much better, and will I get a great many demerits if I call you John?"

Pelham smiled.

"John, I am so looking forward to this whole week."

The paired young women and West Point cadets continued to converse, and soon the girls, not wanting to show favoritism, had entered the names of all seven cadets on their hop cards.

Charlie Hazlett, the night's head hop manager and a good friend of Pelham's, stuck his head out of the door. "We're about to begin, mates."

Pelham offered Clara his arm.

The main dining room had been cleared, so that it had every appearance of a ballroom. Hazlett, short but handsome, with dark hair and deep blue eyes, rang the dance bell that signaled the start of the evening, and then raised a hand to the expectant crowd.

"Welcome one and all to tonight's hop. Let's hear it for the band, for if they are encouraged, they will indeed play better."

Laughter filled the room as the ladies clapped gloved hands, producing little effect. In contrast, the cadets stomped their feet on the wood floor, whistled, and made catcalls, drawing smiles from the fourteen uniformed members of the dance band.

"Thank you, ladies and gentlemen. Our first dance is a waltz by Johann Strauss. Enjoy your evening!"

Hardly had Hazlett finished, when Pelham slipped Clara past Patterson and Alice Paine onto the dance floor. Seconds later, the floor was packed as the bandleader's baton twitched to life.

Clara expressed unveiled surprise. "You, John Pelham, are an excellent dancer."

"You make me so, my lady, though I should confess that instruction in dancing is a requisite here."

"A requisite?"

"The belief is that officers must be gentlemen, and gentlemen must be able to lead on the dance floor as well as on the battlefield." Pelham scanned the room, his gaze resting on the refreshment table. "I see your Miss Frampton is well positioned."

Clara glanced at the table with the punch bowl. "Always."

"She looks like a fun person."

"Just tending her flock," Clara replied in amusement. "And there." She nodded in the direction of the dining room entrance. "Mrs. Wigglesworth. We're trapped."

Pelham noticed du Pont gracefully leading Ellen Lawson around the dance floor, the two talking and smiling. Soon the mother instinct in him confirmed all matches were off to a good start.

In the meter and pulse of the waltz, the ladies in their elegant long dresses seemed without feet, floating across the floor at the slightest pressure from white gloved hands at their waists, all the while maintaining proper distance from their partners.

Too soon the first dance was over, followed by applause and more foot stomping.

Eva Taylor, with Rosser towering beside her, touched Clara's arm. "And don't you two make a fine couple."

Clara glanced at Pelham, who appeared not to have heard.

As Pelham escorted Clara off the floor, he gently squeezed her hand. "Thank you, my lady. I would not have thought that Quakers cottoned to dancing."

"Cottoned?"

Pelham smiled. "Never mind."

"You flatter me, John, but get me for a lancers and you might change your mind."

"Doubtful, my lady."

"Miss Bolton?" Chas Patterson's Arkansas accent was unmistakable.

"Mr. Patterson." Clara extended her hand.

"Ma'am, please call me Chas." Patterson led Clara onto the dance floor.

Pelham was already across the room offering his arm to Carol Hill. "Miss Hill, my southern neighbor and kindred spirit."

"Indeed, Cadet Pelham, in the thick of these vulgar Yankees, we must stick together. And do call me, Carol."

The two squeezed onto the already packed dance floor, as men lined up one side and ladies the other for a lancers quadrille.

The magic of the evening continued to build, with music, movement, and gaiety claiming hostage all in attendance. Hearts on both sides of the battlefield planned strategies, and as the evening wore on, gallons of iced punch were downed from ridiculously small glass cups.

By the time Pelham approached Clara for the thirteenth dance, her face, like that of every girl in the room, had been re-powdered and her hands clad in fresh gloves.

"You are flushed, my lady." He offered Clara his arm.

"And you are shiny." She drew a scented handkerchief from her sleeve and wiped his brow, letting her fingers linger on his cheek. "Thank goodness for another waltz," she said. "And do be gentle, for I think I shall really need that fresh air."

They were again swallowed up on the dance floor.

"Enjoying yourself?" Pelham asked.

"Oh, John, how could I not! And to think, you do this three times a week, three months a year. Do you know how lucky you are?"

"Lest you forget, my lady, there are twelve months in a year, and for nine months the hotel is empty of any reason to come to it. We are veritable monks. I have but Rosser to look at—can you imagine?" He twirled her, and as he did he confirmed that the two chaperones were still at their posts. "Will you be able to elude your guards?"

"Leave that to me, and don't think ill of them, for they only want to keep us lambs safe from wolves. Be there wolves here, John?" She batted her eyes.

"Nary a one," he said with a straight face.

"Yes, I believe you could be a bad boy, given half a chance." She squeezed his hand. "Give me fifteen minutes. I'll meet you at the reception desk."

Pelham stood alone with his back against the lobby counter, snapping to attention each time someone exited the ballroom. Ned Kirby and a giddy Becky Thompson suddenly emerged.

"Waiting for someone?" Kirby gave Pelham a knowing look.

"Just resting," Pelham said, and then he raised a finger. "Ned, a moment, please—"

The two huddled for half a minute, and then Pelham winked at Becky. "You had a good time tonight, young lady. I was watching you, and you are putting the visiting competition to shame. Old Ned here better keep an eye on you."

"You hear that, Ned?" She kissed Pelham on the cheek.

Kirby whisked the youngest Thompson through the front door.

"So quickly into another girl's arms?" Clara declared, leaning against the wall in the hallway.

"You can't trust men," Pelham confessed. "I see you got by the trolls."

"Diversionary tactics, isn't that what you would call it? Ellie drew their attention. So, just where is this fresh air?"

Pelham led Clara onto the veranda, where they encountered Lieutenant Lee and another officer enjoying cigars.

Lee touched his hat. "Mr. Pelham, ma'am."

Pelham saluted Lee and the other officer. "Lieutenant Lee, sir, may I introduce to you Miss Clara Bolton."

Clara extended her hand.

"Lieutenant Lee is my company tactical officer."

Lee clicked his heels. "A very good evening to you, Miss Bolton. Mr. Pelham, please pass on my compliments to the orchestra. They are more than usually superb tonight." Lee turned to Clara. "Ma'am, you are in the company of a real gentleman."

"Thank you, sir. I can see that."

"Miss Bolton has requested some fresh air, sir." Pelham's tone was officious.

"Yes, a number of the ladies seem to be in need of it tonight. Must be stuffy in there. I believe you'll find the air freshest on the river side of the hotel, Mr. Pelham."

"Yes, sir, I'll trust your judgment."

Though not alone on the back veranda, Pelham and Clara enjoyed a measure of privacy in the darkness. Flickering lights on the two sides of the river and the glow from the town of Newburgh beneath a starry sky gave the Hudson an air of enchantment. A breeze off the river sent a sudden chill down Clara's back. Sensing it, Pelham put an arm around her shoulders.

"A button for your thoughts," he said.

"I thought it was a penny."

He took her hand and pressed something in it. "It's one of my brass uniform buttons with the Academy crest. A keepsake for your visit."

"John, you shouldn't have. I will treasure it always, and thank you." She slipped it into her silk purse. "Shall I tell you what is on my mind?"

"Only if you are having a good time."

"That, you must know." Her smile was wasted in the darkness. "Tell me about your home, John."

"Now that could take a while."

"I want to know."

"Well, for me, home is everything. We have a cotton plantation in northeast Alabama—about seventy miles northeast of Birmingham."

"And your family?"

"Pa runs the plantation and also serves as the county doctor."

"He does both?"

"And has for years."

"How does he find the time?"

"I don't know. And I can't count how often I've driven the buggy so he could mend a bone or deliver a baby in the middle of the night, only to see him up bright and early the next morning, managing the plantation."

"You love him, don't you?"

"I do. He's the hardest working man I've ever known, and a just man, though he could apply the belt with the best." This time it was Pelham who wasted a smile in the darkness.

"You were naughty?"

"I was a Pelham. I had to keep up with Charlie and William."

"Your brothers?"

"And mentors."

Clara inquired about the rest of Pelham's family, particularly interested in his mother. That discussion led to his grandmother, and he talked at length about both women, until he realized the time. "I'm sorry. I ramble, and I can't imagine how many boys inside have been looking for Clara Bolton."

"You have a dear family. A large family is so wonderful, and to live in the same place all your life is very special."

"So it's only you?"

"I have a brother, Harry, but he's eight years older and more like an uncle. He practices law in Newark. Father is a doctor, like yours, but teaches now at the University of Pennsylvania. Mother is gone. She died when I was fourteen, after we moved to Penn—" Clara's voice quavered.

"I'm sorry." Pelham drew her close.

"Some form of consumption. But now she is in heaven with the angels, and all is perfect for her."

"I understand Penn is a beautiful campus. Do you get much snow?"

"A little," she said. "Your friend, Henry du Pont ... he is a nice man and a fine dancer in his own right."

"Henry, oh yes, he's the best."

"We had time to talk." She paused. "And I inquired about you."

"Me?"

"I asked him if you had someone special in your life—a particular lady friend."

Pelham was grateful for the darkness. "And what did Henry say?"

"That you had a good many friends and that some were indeed ladies, but that there was no one in particular now."

Pelham relaxed.

"He said that this very day, when we all came up the river, you vowed not to get serious with a woman for many years. I think he said, until you knew yourself, or something like that."

Pelham fumbled. "Did he now?"

"I just wanted you to know"—Clara's voice was surprisingly cheerful—"that I feel the same way. Honestly. I too must avoid a serious relationship. I have my goals and can't afford to complicate my life. I can't be distracted from my studies."

Pelham wasn't certain whether he was relieved or wounded.

Clara drew herself up to him. "John, that is not to say I don't like you, for I very much do, and I think you like me." She hesitated. "I want to be with you as much as I can this whole glorious week."

"All right," Pelham said, unsure where Clara was going.

"So I propose we become the dearest of friends," she said with childlike enthusiasm. "Unlike you, I have not one friend who is also a boy, and it would give me great joy if you would be my one true friend, who is a boy."

"A boy?"

"A man." She giggled. "Will you, John?"

The more he digested the thought, the more agreeable it tasted. "Clara Bolton, I would consider it an honor be your friend, who is also a boy."

Clara kissed him lightly on the cheek, an affection he did not expect, and squeezed his hand. "You have made me very happy, John. We shall have the grandest time." She kissed his other cheek. "Now, I think I've had enough fresh air."

For Pelham, the rest of the evening passed slowly as he played the floor host. When not otherwise engaged, he found himself searching the dance floor for Clara, always finding her smiling and with someone new. Twice she had caught him looking and twice she had flashed him a generous smile.

At the end of the hop following the final dance, he came up to her. "You, my lady, have broken more hearts than the Academy allows and still have two hops to go. The Corps will be decimated by the time you leave."

"You silly. I've had an incredible time, John. You better not have duty Wednesday night."

He smiled. "I don't, and ..." He leaned forward. "If you would like, there is the possibility that I can call on you tomorrow afternoon."

Her eyes grew wide with anticipation. "Could you, John?"

"Would you like to see the campus?"

"I would love to!"

"I'll know in the morning and get word to you."

"There's a young bellboy, Joseph. He is a dear. Ask for him. I'm in room 315." She placed a hand on his arm. "John, please make this happen."

Ellie Lawson came up to them, her face flush. "Hello, John. I so enjoyed dancing with you, and thanks for introducing me to Henry.

He is tremendous fun." She turned to Clara. "Come on, girl, we've got to go, or Miss Frampton will lock us in our rooms tomorrow."

All of the Clermont girls quickly disappeared from the ballroom, and Pelham made his way to the punch bowl. Du Pont joined him a moment later. "I saw you talking with Ellie. Did she say anything about me?"

Pelham studied the man who had complicated his life. "As a matter of fact, she did."

"So tell me."

"She said that you were … fun."

"Fun?"

Pelham nodded.

"What the hell does that mean?"

Pelham shrugged, and du Pont left shaking his head. Pelham poured himself another warm punch—the ice was long melted—and spied Rosser and Patterson across the room. He waved them over.

"Chas, my man, how are you and Miss Alice Paine doing?"

"Shall I compare her to a summer's day?"

"She would be more lovely and more temperate?"

"Exactly."

"And, Tom, how about you and Miss Taylor?"

Rosser shrugged.

"What, you don't like her?"

"Miss Taylor …" Rosser's face bore a look of disbelief. "I think she sees something in Kingsbury."

"Say it isn't true, roommate. It cannot be that a southern belle prefers a Connecticut Yankee?"

"Incredible, isn't it? However, Cathy Hill—"

"Carol Hill."

"Right. She couldn't take her eyes off me."

"And she speaks our language."

"Precisely."

Pelham motioned for the three of them to huddle. "Enough of the fairer sex, my friends. We've respects to pay."

"Respects?" Patterson asked.

From the look on his face, Rosser knew exactly what Pelham meant. "No, John."

"How can you say that, Tom?" Pelham's hands were on his hips. "Isn't it time we visited our friend?"

The light went on for Patterson. "Benny?"

Pelham nodded.

Rosser rolled his eyes. "Not from encampment—there are too many guards! Wait until we get back to the barracks."

"We don't pay respects when it's convenient, but when we've reason."

"And just what is the reason?"

Pelham smiled. "Making it this far."

"What about last time?"

"That was a fluke."

"We were nearly caught!"

"But weren't, were we? And Chas is in, right?"

"Definitely," Patterson said without hesitation.

"And so is Ned."

"Kirby's in?" Rosser expressed surprise.

"He gave me the nod earlier. But, Tom, we'll understand if you're not up to it."

The gauntlet stung Rosser. "When?"

"Tomorrow night, after taps inspection."

Chapter Fifteen

Choosing not to attend the hop, Emory Upton, who for all his eccentric behavior was acknowledged by his classmates, even du Pont, as the class genius, labored under candlelight in the encampment, penning a response to Sarah, his favorite sister and most faithful correspondent. As always, her letter, which had arrived that afternoon, had boosted his spirit and commitment, but for the first time, she had urged caution. She counseled specifically against exhibiting too ardent a stand for precipitously unslaving the country. She was as ardent an abolitionist as he, but reasoned that while Lincoln might be elected easily enough, the new Republican administration would need time, even years, to see its desired end realized. Its very electability depended upon millions of voters who, while staunchly anti-Democrat, for sundry reasons had no interest whatsoever in unseating slavery. She reminded him that for the vast majority of the needed votes, the central issue was not slavery, but the federal government, tariffs, the sovereignty of states, and the grievances of Southern states regarding the new territories.

"Unconverted intentions are worthless," he wrote and underlined. "Unless Lincoln changes his position, the black man will never be free," he added. However, he did acknowledge that the man must first be elected before he could cross the Rubicon. He thanked her for the family news, which had filled three pages of her letter, and included something she could share with each member of the family, which included parents and eight other siblings.

He sealed the letter in an envelope and called out into the night air, "Mr. Saunders."

Seconds later an A Company plebe appeared.

"You will ensure this gets into tomorrow's mail." Upton's tone was firm but polite, and when the plebe was gone, his thoughts turned to Henry du Pont. There was no reason to let the matter fester.

Hearing the bell announcing the end of the hop, he regretted missing it. He had planned to attend, until receipt of Sarah's letter. Stowing his writing materials, he stepped out into the star-studded night and stretched his limbs. The sky shimmered above the blackness of the surrounding hills. He breathed deep the cool night air and lifted his hands to heaven. *Father God,* he prayed, *your will be done in my life and in the life of our nation. Grant me and those around me wisdom and mercy, forgive my imperfections, help me to forgive others and to guard my tongue. Father, especially help me to forgive those who dismiss the truth, and above all, Father, keep me resolute.*

Unconsciously, he rubbed the four-inch scar on his cheek inflicted by the South Carolinian, Wade Hampton Gibbes, a year ago. It would be a lifelong reminder of his temper and that he needed to think before acting. What had happened to Alexander Hamilton could easily have happened to him. He still believed that Gibbes had sullied his name and honor with rumors of sleeping with a black woman while at Oberlin College. He had been so enraged, he had challenged the First Classman to a duel, which had taken place that very evening in the cadet barracks. Not only did he find Gibbes the better swordsman, he was told that Gibbes was likely not the one who had spread the rumor. That Gibbes had shown mercy, Upton credited not to the First Classman, but to God's providential grace. He had shared the episode with his Oberlin mentor, the evangelist Charles Finney, expecting sympathy and support for his actions. But to the contrary, Finney had expressed disappointment, declaring that violence reconciled nothing.

CHAPTER SIXTEEN

Tuesday morning, August 21, Pelham awoke to the retort of a single cannon and old Bentz bugling first call and reveille. The disturbance was made complete by two overly eager drum orderlies. At the same time, two hundred yards to the northwest, the nation's flag was raised. The rest of the day would be similarly ordered, when Bentz sounded assembly, mess call, drill call, tattoo, call to quarters, and taps. At six o'clock, five o'clock in the late fall and winter, Bentz would sound retreat and the flag would be lowered.

After the Corps returned from breakfast, Pelham paid Lieutenant Lee a visit. He left the tactical officer's tent in fine spirits, heading directly for the hotel. In the lobby, he found the boy Clara had described.

"Joseph?"

"Yes, sir."

"Would you be so kind as to give this note to Miss Clara Bolton? I believe she is in room 315." He handed the boy the note and a nickel.

"Oh, yes sir, you can depend on it, and thank you, sir."

Shortly after ten o'clock, Pelham was on the Plain, perched on his sorrel mount and awaiting the second section of Second Classmen, who were on probationary status for deficiency in horsemanship. The first section had come and gone, clearly proving why they needed additional instruction. Satisfactory completion of the remedial instruction would require completion of a three-jump obstacle course and delivery of a deathblow to a target dummy at the end of the run, all within the space of one minute and exhibiting competent control of a horse.

From the direction of the stables, Rosser and Custer approached with eight Second Classmen attired in riding apparel and armed with dragoon sabers.

The section formed around Pelham.

"Before you lies the obstacle course," Pelham said, wasting no time. He nodded in the direction of the linear course, three hundred yards long and consisting of a jump of three feet, a second jump of four feet, a third jump of three feet, and then a flat of seventy-five yards leading to a straw-filled dummy.

"Be confident," Pelham encouraged the cadets. "The course is no different from what you faced in the spring. Some of you ran it well enough, but too slowly, while others ran it swiftly enough, but not well, which is to say, not in control."

Some in the group focused on Pelham, while others stared anxiously at the course. All understood that if they failed to pass the remedial training, they would be dismissed from the Academy.

"So why don't we warm up a bit, get the legs loose, get used to whatever gallant steed the army has issued you today? Mr. Rosser, please lead the way."

Rosser rendered a very casual salute and hollered over his shoulder, "All right. Follow my gait and don't run up my ass."

Rosser led the section in a sequence of trots, canters, and gallops around the Plain, returning the section to Pelham.

Pelham forced a smile. "Yes, we are a bit rusty, aren't we? Some of you are out of balance, too far forward or back. Some of you are fighting the natural rhythm of your horse. Either will cost you speed and points on poise. And, yes, the army wants you to look good in the saddle."

Several in the class snickered.

"Okay, once again, this time with Mr. Custer in the lead."

When the section returned, Pelham admitted to some improvement and, with that, led the section at a trot to the obstacle course.

"Before we start, let's break it down so we take chance out of the equation. A horse is neither dumb nor stupid, not even these glue nags. A horse is intuitive, it can read its rider—sense whether he lacks confidence. If the horse senses fear, you'll quite literally be along for the ride, like a flea on a dog. The key, then, is to manage your fears and project confidence." Pelham spoke with easy authority. "The other key is balance. You have to move and flex responsively with the horse and remain centered when you jump." He turned to his assistants. "Mr. Rosser and Mr. Custer will demonstrate."

Rosser, and then Custer, separated by less than ten yards, accelerated to a gallop. They executed the jumps and stuck the red heart of the target dummy with ease and grace, as the class looked on in awe.

Upon their return, Pelham announced, "Forty-five seconds. Not bad." Turning to the Second Classmen, he smiled. "I know what you're thinking. You weren't reared to ride, you haven't enjoyed your time in the riding hall, and you've spent more time under the horse than on it."

There were more snickers.

"We've all been there, and it's the same with every class. But that will change, and of course, it has to. You are in the army, and your career depends on your ability to ride. You must ride well, and over rough terrain, through timber fall, across battlefields, and it certainly wouldn't do for your troops to see you timid on a horse. And riding this course is simple. Finish in a minute or less, tag the dummy, and stay balanced. That's all we want. Do it and you're free to leave. Any questions?"

"Sir, you make it sound easy," Andrew Collins of B Company spoke for the otherwise catatonic section.

"It is, Mr. Collins," Pelham said. "Mr. Rosser, call out each runner. I'll be positioned at the four-foot jump, and Mr. Custer will keep time at the finish line."

Once in position, Pelham signaled Rosser.

"Mr. Collins," Rosser announced from his clipboard.

Custer's arm dropped, and Collins and his horse lurched forward. His run began well, and he cleared each of the three jumps with good form and speed. However, he fumbled for his saber, barely nicking the dummy's shoulder.

The next rider was Ron Williams from D Company. After executing the first jump, Williams made the mistake of pulling back on the reins on his approach to the four-foot jump. His horse reared, depositing him in a heap.

Pelham looked down at the man. "You okay, Ron?"

Williams jumped to his feet and brushed the dust from his riding pants, his face red with embarrassment. "Sure, John—I mean, sir."

Pelham wasn't used to being called sir. "You've got to trust your horse, Ron. He's made that jump a thousand times, so let him take the lead. You're fortunate the ground is still soft. It will be brick hard this afternoon."

"Yes, sir."

Custer trotted up with William's horse.

"Thanks, Fannie." Williams returned to the section.

Of the remaining six riders, all but one failed the course because of time, poise, or inadequate contact with the dummy.

Pelham assembled the class, making a show of Jason Lott of B Company, the one cadet who had passed. "See, it can be done! Let's hear it for Mr. Lott, who is now free to go about his business."

Approbation, muted with envy, attended Lott's rapid departure for the stables.

Pelham canvassed the seven remaining members of the section, their faces long and defeated, and offered a conciliatory smile. "You've two more sessions to pass the obstacle course. Pass the course and you join Mr. Lott."

Pelham saw fear in their faces. "Who was the finest horseman ever to ride at West Point?"

Without hesitation, and with an obvious smirk, Andrew Collins declared, "Why, John Pelham, sir."

The rest of the section and Rosser guffawed, and Custer quipped, "Collins, your nose has a definite color to it."

"Grant, sir," Ron Williams volunteered.

"Very good, Mr. Williams. Ulysses S. Grant, Class of 1843. He jumped a horse a height of six feet inside the riding hall and could ride anything with four legs. And why could he do it, Mr. Williams? Because he grew up in the saddle, that's why. But we don't expect you to imitate Grant or us. You just need to pass the obstacle course—the same one we've all had to pass, and you have the ability. I've seen it." Pelham paused. "Okay, we're done for today. But I'll wager that before the end of the third day, all of you will have passed the course, and Mr. Rosser knows I can't afford to lose a wager."

From behind the section, Custer cleared his throat. "If it's okay, John, I'd like to take you up on that wager." He produced a Liberty Head five-dollar gold piece for all to see.

Back in the encampment, Emory Upton marched the short distance to the quartermaster tent and found du Pont sitting at his desk.

Without preamble, he demanded, "I want to know why, Henry."

Du Pont put down his pen. "What has crawled up your ass, Emory?"

"As if you didn't know." Upton's face was red. "Last week, I'm officer of the guard and report to the commandant's tent for my guard detail briefing."

Du Pont sat back in his chair.

"He's not there and neither is his orderly. There are papers on the floor, so I pick them up."

"Your point?"

"One of them is a record of communication—signed by you."

Du Pont stiffened in his chair. "You read a confidential memo?"

"Dammit, Henry, you harpooned me!"

"I didn't harpoon you, Emory."

"You deny the report?"

"Lieutenant Colonel Hardee asked me a direct question. I had no choice."

"You said I was extreme, Henry. That's not true."

"Not true? Hardee asks me who has radical views in the Corps, and you're telling me you're not in the mix, the only self-avowed abolitionist in the Corps? If you were of the closet variety, I could let it slide, but Emory, you're not, and you know it."

"I have a right to my opinion, same as you."

"Emory, you almost lost an eye to Wade Gibbes."

"It was a point of honor."

"What do you want from me, Emory, an apology?"

"I am not an extremist, Henry."

"Okay, maybe I could have picked a better word. Anyway, if you read my memo, which was a clear violation of confidentiality and a five demerit offense, you would have seen that you weren't the only one mentioned."

Upton shook his head, obviously unappeased.

"Are we done here?" Du point said dismissively.

After washing up for the midday meal, Pelham and Rosser fell in for the march to the mess hall. On the mess hall steps, Walter Kingsbury pulled Pelham aside. "I'm in love, John."

"Again?"

"No, I mean it. Do you think Tom holds a grudge?"

"He's shattered. Tell me more."

"It's crazy. I can't get the girl out of my mind. Eva Taylor is in every thought I think, every breath I breathe."

"Have you written that down?"

"It's embarrassing."

"It's demeaning."

"I'm serious."

"The adjutant is smitten."

"She's of the Zachary Taylor clan. The president was her uncle. She remembers visiting the White House."

"I'm impressed."

"Her father is assistant commissary general for the army, and the best part is that her sister is married to a West Pointer. So she knows what's coming."

"My friend, I smell a fully cooked goose."

"And a distraught bird, I am. She leaves Saturday—and Sunday I die." Kingsbury wrung his hands.

Pelham put a hand on his shoulder. "Then I suggest you make the most of life before Sunday."

CHAPTER SEVENTEEN

At two forty-five, Pelham approached the hotel expecting to find Clara waiting on the veranda, but instead saw only two bearded gentlemen taking coffee and enjoying a pipe.

"Cadet Pelham." The voice behind him attempted sternness.

Pelham spun around to see Clara in a floral gown, peeking from behind a large elm tree, her face radiant.

"Aren't you the sneak?" He offered his arm.

She sprang forward and took it. "So what are we to do, John?"

"What I promised."

"Oh, I can't wait." She opened her parasol and gave him a perplexed look. "How is it you can be with me, when I see so many of your colleagues still training?"

Pelham smiled. "Colleagues. I've never thought of them that way. But in answer to your question, it's my compensation for being a cadet instructor. I am teaching horsemanship this week, and in return I get Tuesday and Thursday afternoons off from two-thirty to five."

"You clever man!" Clara squeezed his arm.

They walked a short distance to a curious circling of large iron links supported on short posts. "A necklace for a giant?" she said with amusement.

"Part of the great chain that stretched from West Point to Constitution Island. During the Revolutionary War, it was intended to keep British ships from sailing north of West Point."

Clara ran her hand over one of the large links. "Did it work?"

"The British never tried it."

"And what about those?" She pointed to the cannons she had seen on the way to the parade.

"Spoils from the Revolutionary War, the War of 1812, and the Mexican War." Pelham motioned toward the bluff. "Before we get started, I want to show you one of my favorite spots."

He led her to a cast iron bench that overlooked the Hudson. A cluster of large elm trees shaded it. From the bench, one could see the entire valley and the river alive with sloops, schooners, ketches, and dinghies.

The sound of horses announced the hotel omnibus coming up from the North Dock.

Clara sat on the bench. "Look at all the birds. If only I had some bread." She patted the bench. "Come sit with me."

Pelham looked about for a blue uniform, and seeing none, obliged her.

"Beautiful," Clara said, looking north up the Hudson.

Pelham nodded and the two sat quietly, enjoying the moment. Squirrels soon appeared in number, scampering from tree to tree. Various birds joined them, stabbing the ground for worms.

"Is it true that cadets are not to hold hands with a lady friend except at a hop?" Clara made her hand available, and Pelham took it and squeezed it.

"We have a good many rules, my lady."

She pointed to a small gothic house nearby. It was steeply gabled and boasted extensive filigree trim. "That is the cutest little gingerbread house I've ever seen."

"That is the Simpson House, our confectionary—where we leave our teeth." Pelham smiled. "Let's go. There is much to see."

He led Clara past Executioner's Hollow, the localized depression in the Plain, remarking that he was not personally aware that anyone had actually been executed there. They crossed Jefferson Road and walked slowly past the quarters of the commandant, the superintendent, and Professor Mahan. Pelham gave detailed histories and anecdotes for each.

"The gardens behind the houses are very impressive," Clara said. "And the flower beds are beautiful."

"The flowers are for show. The gardens are functional, providing vegetables of every kind and fodder for livestock."

"I did notice a lot of chickens and a cow."

"And sometimes a chicken wanders off never to be seen again." Pelham gave her a look of innocence.

"You are bad boys," she declared, wagging a finger. "But I must say, you are a most accomplished guide who keeps me wanting more."

"Trust me, four years in this place and you could do the same." He directed her attention to the house adjacent to Mahan's quarters. "That is the Thompson house, a Corps favorite. You remember Becky, the girl with Ned Kirby?"

"The one who kissed you?" Clara gave him a critical look.

"Becky is the granddaughter of Mr. and Mrs. Alexander Thompson. Her family has been on post since 1806, and in that particular house since 1838. Her grandfather was the Academy's military storekeeper. He passed away prematurely in 1809, but his widow and three daughters were allowed to stay on post. In the early days the Academy had no organized dining facility, and the cadets boarded with local families, the Thompsons being one of them. Now that we have a mess hall, only those with a good grade point are invited to take meals at the Thompsons. The widow Thompson, while advanced in years, still does a great meal. Kirby got to know Becky when he was invited to dine. Henry du Pont takes meals there every chance he gets."

"I can see that she and the family are quite special to you." Clara closed her parasol when they reached the shadow of a behemoth four-story Tudor-Gothic structure. "What, pray tell, is this?"

"That, my lady, is the cadet barracks, my prison for nine months of the year." He described in detail the configuration and organization of the barracks as they continued east on Jefferson Road.

"And this?" she asked, pointing to a long, massive three-story building next to the barracks.

"That is the academic building, where I suffer most." He made a pitiful face. "I take most of my classes there, and soon, after but another week and a half and when you're back at Clermont, I will return to its bowels and grow pale and pink once again."

"Yours is a difficult curriculum?"

"So we are told. We lose between thirty to forty cadets each year, mostly plebes, and not many of us are at a loss for brains."

"And you—you are a good student?"

"Well, I have yet to be invited to the Thompsons," Pelham said. "I'm in the middle third of the class. Actually, the bottom of the middle third. But I retain what I learn, and learn what I think is important. The rest—I just get by."

"And your favorite subjects?"

He smiled again. "Same as any college man. Cavalry, artillery, infantry, fencing, ordnance, doctoring horses."

"Don't be silly. Isn't West Point an engineering school?"

"The best in the country," he said with obvious pride. "And I find the engineering subjects very interesting. There will be a lot of them this year, and I can see their application once my four years of service are up."

"You'll not make the army a career?"

"I'm not planning on it. But it's a free education. In fact, I'm paid to be here, though not much. No, as a Southern boy, my dream is to run a plantation—my own. After defending the frontier and safeguarding the sagebrush, I'll make room for somebody else in this army."

"So that you can be a farmer?"

"You cut me, my lady. I'll be more than a farmer."

"I'm sure you will," she said without conviction.

As they crossed South Gate Road, Pelham pointed down the street to the mess hall, beyond the academic building.

"Why is it called a mess hall?"

Pelham considered for a moment. Realizing he didn't know, he shrugged his shoulders.

"The food is good?"

"It … can be."

She spied a three-story granite structure in the distance, and asked what it was.

"The cadet hospital."

"Impressive, but it seems overly large."

"The post surgeon and his assistant surgeon quarter in the building with their families, and the hospital attendants quarter in the basement."

"Have you spent much time in the hospital?"

"Very little—until this past year. I got kicked royally by a horse in the stables." He raised a pant leg and showed Clara a not-so-faint purple and yellow bruise on his shin. "I was in bed for four days."

"You poor baby. May I?" She stooped down and inspected his leg. "You're lucky the tibia wasn't fractured, or worse."

"You know about tibias?"

She smiled as she rose to her feet, gazing with interest at the building on the other side of the road. It was unlike any other on the campus, possessing arched stained glass windows and a balustrade roofline, incongruent with any of the other Academy architecture. "Your church?"

"The Cadet Chapel. It's Greek revival or something, and every Sunday we are in it, whether we believe or not."

"Excuse me?"

"Relax, my lady. I mean that after Sunday morning inspection, church attendance is mandatory for every cadet. Al Mordecai, as devout a Jew as there is, frequently sits next to me. The Catholics are marched to services in Buttermilk Falls, south of post."

"You believe, don't you, John?"

"What do you think?"

"I hope with all my heart you do."

"And you would be right."

She smiled. "Can we go inside?"

"If that is your wish." He glanced about, and then led her up the stone steps, past the portico of four Doric columns and through the massive entryway. As he removed his forage cap, Clara crossed herself.

"You are a Catholic Quaker?"

She ignored him and proceeded down the center aisle.

Pelham followed, indifferent to the fact that he had broken every rule in the Academy book by taking an unchaperoned woman inside an Academy building.

"This is a beautiful sanctuary, John." Her eyes devoured the church interior: the worn gray slate floor, the massive dark mahogany pews, the eighteen-foot Corinthian wood columns, the downward facing cannons embedded in the white plaster walls, the ornate wood and marble altar, and the large mural high on the somewhat concave wall behind the altar.

She stared a long moment at the mural. "That is an outstanding piece of artwork."

"It's called *Peace and War*, painted by our Professor Weir. He heads the drawing department. The mural is eleven feet by twenty-two feet, and you can see that it's painted on a curved surface, giving it a three-dimensional look."

"It really is quite excellent."

"Professor Weir is internationally recognized, and has a painting in the U.S. capitol."

Clara proceeded down the aisle to inspect the mural in more detail. The painting consisted of an altar framed against a starry sky. On the left side of the altar, Peace, in the form of a woman clad in white, held an olive branch; in her other hand she held a Bible. War, on the other side, was a Roman soldier with his a hand on the hilt of a sword. The two faced away from each other. On the face of the altar were the words, RIGHTEOUSNESS EXALTETH A NATION, BUT SIN IS A REPROACH TO ANY PEOPLE, PROV. XIV.

"What symbolism and depth for a school that instructs men on soldiering. It truly is a masterpiece."

"You have studied art?" Pelham asked.

"We study everything—a little. They want us well rounded." She gave him a prissy face, and then continued to look about the chapel. Embedded in the floor and on the walls were a number of black shields and bronze placards.

Pelham answered her question before she could ask. "We memorialize everything."

Clara smiled, and then gestured to the balcony above the entrance to the sanctuary. "Can we go up?"

"Anywhere you like." Pelham led her up the curved wooden staircase. In the balcony, more pews and more plaques greeted them.

"Surely this man isn't still alive?" She pointed to a plaque that was like the others, but bore only the inscriptions *Major General* and *Born 1740*. There was no name and no date of death.

"That was," Pelham said, "or I suppose is, for Benedict Arnold."

"The traitor?"

"The same—the thought being that traitors are nameless and live forever in dishonor."

117

Clara surprised Pelham by slipping into a pew and drawing him in beside her. She folded her hands, closed her eyes, and bowed her head in prayer. Pelham watched her for a moment, and then closed his own eyes. As they sat in silence, his senses were fully keyed. He smelled her light perfume and felt her softness. He cracked an eye and took in the smoothness of her skin, the tiny brown mole on the nape of her neck, and the fineness of her blond hair.

"What are we praying for?" he asked.

She finished her prayer with an audible "Amen." "For you, my friend. My dearest new friend."

"For me?"

She kissed him lightly on the cheek. "I prayed that God would grant you a noble life, for you are indeed a good and noble man. You are my knight, and I have never known a knight before."

She hesitated, studying his face. "Am I distracting you?"

"Distracting me?"

"By kissing you on the cheek. I don't mean to—"

"No, no. Not at all." Pelham fumbled for a fabrication. "There is no reason that friends can't express affection for each other. A kiss on the cheek … I'm sure friends do that."

"Of course they do." She beamed and kissed him on the other cheek.

Pelham cleared his throat. "We better be off. I want you to see the Academy's showcase before we head back."

"Lead on, dear knight!"

East of the chapel lay the Tudor-Gothic building that housed the library and post headquarters. The monolith was constructed of steel gray granite, and trimmed with reddish-brown sandstone.

Clara studied the building's exterior and its three towers, and then pointed to the middle tower that boasted a rounded cupola.

"That is our planetarium," Pelham explained.

"Can we go inside?"

"Let me check."

In a minute he was back with the report that they could, and once inside, he described the building's floor plan. The east side of the building housed one of the finest libraries in the country; and the west side, the post headquarters and offices for the superintendent and his staff. When he mentioned that the second floor was home to the Department of Natural and Experimental Philosophy lecture hall with all of its displays, she asked to see it.

They ascended the stairs, and once in the lecture hall strolled between the various physics displays and new inventions. Pelham attempted to describe them to her satisfaction, but soon realized he was no match for her questions.

"You've a most curious mind for a woman."

She gave him a look. "Does that door lead to the planetarium?"

"It does. Would you like to see some stars?"

"Can we?"

Once inside and seated, and after allowing their eyes to adjust to the darkness, the heavens exploded above and around them, and again Pelham was aware of Clara's femininity. Her gentle breathing and her hand resting harmlessly on his thigh made him thankful for the darkness and her inquisitive mind. He answered her questions with all he knew about the major constellations and their importance to navigation, and how cadets spent a great deal of time using instruments to glean from the stars where they were and where they wanted to go.

When they returned to the ground floor, Clara asked if she could see the library. Once inside, she exclaimed, "My gosh! So many books and stacked so high."

Fifteen feet above them and circling a portion of the interior wall, was a narrow wrought iron walk by which books on the highest shelves could be accessed. Portraits, large and small, covered much of the room's dark wood paneling.

"Good afternoon, Mr. Pelham."

Pelham spun around, surprised and disconcerted to see the post librarian, Captain John Kelton.

"Captain Kelton, sir, I didn't realize you were here."

"I was in the stock room. We received a shipment of new books." The librarian's face was unreadable behind a bushy mustache. Pelham knew full well that if the man reported him with an unchaperoned woman, he would spend the rest of his life in confinement.

Pelham chose directness, and with a casual air introduced Clara. Turning to her, he said, "Captain Kelton guards these books as if they were his children."

"Especially watchful of you, young man." Kelton produced a ready smile. "Mr. Pelham is a voracious reader."

"I am pleased and not at all surprised to hear it, sir." Clara said, proceeding to inquire as to how many books were in the library, what kinds of books they were, and about the portraits on the wall, especially the portrait above the man's desk.

"That, ma'am, is Sylvanus Thayer," Kelton said with pride.

"An impressive man."

"Indeed, Colonel Thayer was, and is, quite an impressive man, though gone before my time as a cadet. But I think Mr. Pelham will agree that much of what you see of the campus and how the cadets are trained are his doing and his dream. He was superintendent from 1817 to 1833, and had considerable influence on our current superintendent, Colonel Delafield. Thayer might still be here if he hadn't got crosswise with President Andrew Jackson. During Jackson's presidency, cadets dismissed from the Academy because of gross misconduct were easily reinstated if politically connected, and Jackson was one for granting such favors. This infuriated Thayer, and flew in the face of what he considered essential order and discipline. Right or wrong, he resigned as superintendent and has never been back to West Point. He is currently serving with the Corps of Engineers, though I'm not sure where."

"Sir." Pelham made a show of checking his watch. "I want to thank you for your time, but we better be heading back."

"Of course. I'm pleased you dropped by, Mr. Pelham, and I'm very happy to have met this young lady."

"Thank you so much, Captain Kelton." Clara extended her hand.

Outside, Pelham resisted the impulse to tell Clara what he had just risked, and since marksmanship was over for the day, he took her on the most direct route to the hotel, along the bluff road.

"So, my most interesting lady friend, what is it that you study at Clermont?"

"I'm finishing what is called a preparatory medicine program."

"Excellent. You are to be a nurse?"

"Well, that's the intent of the course—but actually, no." She paused to measure his response. "I am going to be a doctor."

Pelham was certain he had not heard correctly. "A what?"

She nodded. "A doctor."

"A ... female doctor?"

"I am a woman, yes. Is that a problem for you?"

"Well ... I mean—no, of course not, but I've never met or even heard of a female doctor."

"Precisely, and I know of only one myself—Elizabeth Blackwell—but someone needs to be the next, and why not me?"

"A doctor." Pelham voiced the word as though trying it on for size.

She stopped abruptly and crossed her arms.

He raised his hands in defense. "This takes some getting used to, but to your credit, you are clearly intelligent and curious to a fault. From the patient side, I believe you could be at ease with anyone, and you certainly have what I know of a doctor's demeanor, but ..."

"But what?"

"You are—don't take this wrong—a rather nice-looking woman, and I am not sure how that would—"

"I can make myself homely, if I have to." She screwed her face up in a way that made him laugh out loud.

"Well, it seems you have much in your favor," he said in a more serious tone. "Especially with your father being a doctor."

"After Clermont, I will have three, maybe four years of medical training."

"Have you been accepted for schooling?"

She hesitated. "No. Not yet."

Pelham sensed frustration. "I'm sure it will happen."

"My grades are nearly perfect. I will graduate Clermont first in my class." The irritation was evident in her voice. "I don't mind the sight of blood, I know the human body, male and female, and I can down a shot of whiskey as well as you can."

Pelham rubbed his chin. "Yes, imminently qualified. And for what it's worth, I would very much like for you to be my doctor."

She smiled. "Don't patronize me, young man."

"Here we are," he announced as they reached the foot of the hotel stairs.

"John, I have truly enjoyed this afternoon and being with you. I feel so at ease with you." She paused. "I was wondering ... Ellie mentioned something about a lovely walk along the river."

Pelham smiled. "Flirtation Walk?"

She waited for him to say more, but he didn't. "Is it pretty this time of year?"

He smiled again. "How about you see for yourself, say Thursday afternoon?"

"Oh, can we, John? I could make us a glorious picnic. What is your favorite dish?"

"I'm not picky, but if you're asking, I love fried chicken, and we never get it in the mess hall."

"You poor baby. Fried chicken it is, and I'll surprise you with a dessert."

He squeezed her hand. "Until tomorrow's hop."

"Actually, I'm going to watch you parade this evening. I'm not going to miss a single one. Thank you again, John, for being such a wonderful friend. And don't eat too much before the picnic."

"That won't be a problem."

Clara glanced around and gave him a parting peck on the cheek.

CHAPTER EIGHTEEN

Following her afternoon with Pelham, Clara briefed Ellie and the other girls on her tour. They were more envious than pleased for her, and she didn't blame them. An hour later, at the abbreviated parade on the encampment grounds, she waved without restraint as Pelham led his platoon past the reviewing party, and she was convinced he had winked at her. Accordingly, she was in a particularly jubilant mood when she and Ellie returned to the hotel. But at the top of the staircase, they were greeted by Miss Frampton.

"Ellen, do you mind if I have a word with Clara?"

Ellie looked at Clara. "No, ma'am, of course not."

Frampton motioned for Clara to follow and waddled to the corner of the veranda. "You are having a pleasant time here at the Academy, Clara?"

"Yes, ma'am," Clara said cautiously.

"Would you mind filling me in on your afternoon?"

"I'm sorry?"

"Your rendezvous with Cadet Pelham."

"Are you referring to my campus tour?"

"Why did you not inform me? You know the rule. You are my responsibility."

"And you are quite right, Miss Frampton. I was remiss and I am sorry. It was a spur of the moment thing. I just didn't think to tell you."

"You didn't think to tell me," Frampton repeated. "I think you see too much of that Pelham boy."

"Meaning no disrespect, ma'am, but he is hardly a boy."

"I am sure you are quite right," Frampton said, raising an eyebrow. "Clara, I am not singling you out, but your father, when he first brought you to Clermont after your mother passed, God rests her soul, made some things quite clear to me. He wished to be fully satisfied that you would be trained in all that was necessary to the proper upbringing of a lady. I pledged to him I would do just that, and have personally attempted my best to do so."

"I'm sorry, ma'am. I don't understand what you mean."

The assistant dean drew back, not a little surprised at Clara's tone. "Miss Bolton, Clermont is a finishing school, a true seminary for girls. While we are happy to provide you with a profession appropriate to a lady, our primary goal is to make you a woman of refinement."

"Am I failing in that area?"

Frampton was momentarily nonplussed. "Your father was insistent that you receive the finest instruction in every aspect of becoming a woman, and that you be able to fit seamlessly into any level of society."

"'Fit seamlessly.' That sounds like Father. Has he complained to you?"

"Of course not." Frampton hesitated. "At least not about that."

"What then?"

"Well … last week, I received a pointed letter from him seeking an explanation."

"About what?"

"I had written him about your aspirations."

"My aspirations?"

"Of your … wanting to be a doctor, Clara."

"Did I ever say I wanted to be a doctor?"

"Well, maybe not in so many words, but you did ask to take the anatomy course at Columbia, which is an all male school."

"And what did Father say?"

"In a word, he did not want me or Clermont making a man out of his daughter."

Clara flushed red. "Miss Frampton, do you doubt my female nature?"

"Of course not, dear, but how can I ignore the perceptions and desires of a parent?"

"You mean a parent who pays the bills."

"A parent who is deeply concerned about his daughter. You know that, Clara. In any event, in my response to him, I made it clear that I would not counsel you to pursue any profession that rightly falls in the male domain."

"Miss Frampton, may I ask you a question?"

"Of course you may."

"Have you ever seen a man naked?"

CHAPTER NINETEEN

Before supper, Pelham had an unexpected visit from Emory Upton; and after supper made his way to the tunnel-like sally port that extended through the cadet barracks. He entered the door next to the sally port and climbed the stairs to the First Class Club, a high-ceilinged room with a long conference table, a few smaller tables for card and board games, a billiard table, and several lounge chairs. The north and south walls were set with large leaded-glass windows, and the interior walls bore paintings, etchings, and shelves for books, newspapers, and magazines. The facility also served as the meeting place for the Dialectic Society, now entering its thirty-sixth year. Pelham took a seat at the head of the conference table and waited for the rest of the society's eighteen members to arrive. Included in that number were Henry du Pont, Adelbert Ames, Chas Patterson, and Emory Upton.

After a few minutes, the society's sergeant-at-arms, Patrick O'Rorke, signaled to Pelham that all were present, and announced, "This meeting of the Dialectic Society is hereby called to order."

O'Rorke, the oldest member of the Second Class, was tall, slim, and freckled, and a brilliant and eloquent man. He was the first Irish cadet to make a real mark at the Academy, ranking just below Charlie Ball in class standing and serving as first sergeant for D Company.

At Pelham's direction, O'Rorke read the minutes of the previous meeting, which had been held in May.

"The minutes have been read." Pelham looked around the table. "Are there any corrections?"

No one offered any corrections.

"Then they'll be filed as read."

"Now." Pelham rose to his feet and placed the tips of his fingers on the table. "A point of privilege, if I may, since you have seen fit to place me in this chair."

His remark brought laughter, since he had been elected president during the May meeting, when he was in the hospital mending from his leg injury. The vote was deemed reasonable, since he had been vice president the year before.

"I have given considerable thought as to what we might do to make a real difference this coming year, a year in which politically so much is at stake for the country and all of us. I've asked myself, should we ignore the issues? Should we play it safe and like last year and years past, settle for simply poking fun at ourselves? Or should we face the enemy toe to toe and give voice to what is on everyone's mind and debate it accordingly?"

"And pray tell, what is on my mind?" Patterson asked, pinching an empty pipe between his teeth.

"Whether or not a state has the right to secede from the Union."

The expletive from Patterson seemed to speak for the room.

"Thank you, Chas." Pelham was unfazed. "But when I reflect upon what the Dialectic Society should be about, I see an opportunity and a responsibility to place squarely before the Corps, and anyone else who attends our debate, the arguments for and against this incredibly central issue."

Silence followed. Emory Upton, sitting at the opposite end of the table, showed no emotion.

Adelbert Ames broke the ice. "You don't believe in foreplay, do you, John?"

Pelham raised his hands in a gesture of surrender. "I have only made a suggestion. I am not even allowed a vote, unless it's to break a tie. I'll go with whatever you decide, and we can certainly pick another topic. My only fear is that we become irrelevant at a time when the Corps needs relevance."

Du Pont, initially off balance with Pelham's candidness, spoke next. "The superintendent will never sanction it, John. He would see us as teasing a hornet's nest—and he would be right."

"Perhaps, but we won't know unless we ask him, will we? I don't mind defending the topic if we are in agreement."

The room was again quiet.

"I understand the hesitancy," Pelham said. "And so I propose we adjourn early this evening and task ourselves to come up with a debate topic in the form of a one-sentence proposition for our next meeting in September. Mine is just one idea. We'll vote on the topics and decide on our debaters, and schedule the debate sometime in mid-October. Whatever the topic, I'll take it to Delafield to get his stamp on it. If he denies it, I'll offer our second choice."

Du Pont so moved, and the motion was seconded by Patterson, and followed by a mumbling of "ayes."

Pelham glanced at the clock on the wall, which showed only twenty minutes had elapsed since the meeting began. "I would entertain a motion to adjourn."

Ames made the motion, which was seconded by du Pont and approved by all.

"Then," Pelham said, "I declare the shortest Dialectic Society meeting in Academy history adjourned."

CHAPTER TWENTY

After camp lights were extinguished at ten o'clock, the cadet officer of the guard made his inspection, starting with A Company and ending with D Company. He walked methodically down each company street, confirming with a lantern that each bed was occupied.

Fifteen minutes after bed check, Pelham whispered, "Let's be at it." Rosser followed him under the canvass, past Lieutenant Lee's tent, the commandant's tent, and the tents of drum orderlies and boot blacks. They found Kirby and Patterson already waiting on the eastern perimeter of the encampment.

They waited for the guard's predictable movement from north to south. When the guard was beyond earshot, Pelham gave the signal, and they snaked Indian style through the darkness to the monument for Thaddeus Kosciusko and the safe haven of the river bluff.

Pelham turned around, grinning. "Be we thirsty, lads?"

"Parched," Kirby said.

Patterson made a choking sound.

Rosser said nothing.

"Then we're committed."

Pelham proceeded under a full moon and decidedly cooler air. With the practiced silence of a tactical patrol, they hugged the tree line that bordered the bluff. Barely a hundred yards into the journey, Rosser grabbed Pelham about the waist, and Pelham immediately understood. He was inches from the edge of a fifty-foot cliff, and he chastised himself for being distracted.

They skirted the ring of gas lampposts around the library and post headquarters, and at the rear of the building descended through moon shadows to South Dock Road.

Try as he might, Pelham couldn't purge Clara Bolton from his mind. She had taken up residence, confusing all that was otherwise in good order. Worse, she had changed the playing field—introduced an unfamiliar game—and he didn't understand the rules.

At the switchback in South Dock Road, Pelham took the footpath that ascended the bluff. Before reaching the crest, he detoured onto a little used trail that bypassed the South Gate guardhouse. Beyond the guardhouse, the four scrambled up the embankment to the cinder road leading to Buttermilk Falls.

Patterson slapped Rosser on the back. "You can relax now."

"Me? It's you three risking stripes."

"Isn't life one big risk?" Patterson opined grandly.

Kirby, with the most at risk, was whistling a bright tune, and quickly enough Rosser's mood improved, with the pronouncement, "I think I'll start with ale."

"Aye, while the flip is made," Patterson said, in full agreement.

Pelham, lost in his own thoughts—and every thought was of Clara—said not a word as they strode briskly down the dark road. He struggled with how to proceed. Her nature was disarmingly transparent and kind, and she was seasoned with endearing sincerity and wit. No pretense or façade in her. About these things, his heart and mind wrestled. His heart challenged—*is that what you really want, the platonic? It is untried country and likely to wear thin. Not so,* argued his mind. *The platonic affords intimacy a person would never know otherwise, real friendship born of respect and noble intention.*

But are you not a man, countered his heart, *and is she not a girl easily more attractive and intriguing than any you have ever known? Befriending her with a friend's motive is a slippery slope, and serves what end?*

Pelham shook the contradictory thoughts from his head. Clara had made her desire clear enough. At the approach of a rider, he whispered to the others, "To the woods."

After the rider passed, they continued on, as did the debate within Pelham. *What of the kisses, the way she touches you?* his heart questioned. *You think her so naive as not to understand your nature, your chemistry? Don't confuse naïveté with genuine affection,* parried his mind.

Pelham found himself smiling in the dark. Whatever the temptations, he would bear them.

Ten minutes later, they reached the sleepy village of Buttermilk Falls, and sneaked past the nearly dark Cozzen's Hotel, its young ladies and their mothers readying for another day and another hop. A quarter of a mile beyond it lay the stone steps that led down to the river and the lights far below. The nearness of their destination spurred a trot and a swift descent down the stone steps. At the base of the steps stood the wood structure, cheerily silhouetted against the river. The candle burning in the second story window was evidence that their friend was home and it was safe to enter. Against the landing's small dock, a single sloop rolled in the light chop, its jaundiced eye, an oil lamp behind the mast, blinking eerily.

CHAPTER TWENTY-ONE

The tavern was alive with light and laughter, and the unmistakable sound of Benny Havens.

"I'd say he's got a fair business," Pelham said, mounting the porch steps with Rosser, Kirby, and Patterson on his heels. He swung open the heavy door and announced, "Benny, we're back!"

From within the small tavern, three tables of patrons eyed the intruders.

At the far right of the tavern, behind the bar, a man with silver gray hair threw up his hands. "Well bless my soul, if the prodigals ain't returned!"

Pelham and the others waited for the old man to round the bar and greet them with a hug.

"Masters John, Tom, Ned, and Chas. And here I was thinking you'd given up on your old friend." Havens crossed his arms. "And would you be having a thirst?"

"A mighty thirst, Benny." Pelham tossed his forage cap on the hearth.

"We're here to celebrate," Rosser proclaimed. "Start us with ale, but make us our flip." The Texan produced a fistful of coins. "And this is for arrears."

"Master Tom, you're an honorable man." Havens pocketed the money. "Rest yourselves and trust me to keep vigil out back."

Pelham and Rosser sat opposite Kirby and Patterson at a table that was flanked by barreled provisions and a stone fireplace.

Benny soon returned with four frothy pints of ale. "This is indeed a grand surprise and blessing to my old age."

"Your health, Benny." Pelham raised his mug.

"Your health, Benny," echoed the others.

"Moreover, to the man who's seen us at our worst and still loves us," Rosser added with a wink.

"Pshaw, let me get the flip going." The Irishman returned to the bar to assemble the ingredients for the beverage for which he was renowned.

Pelham looked around the tavern as Patterson filled Rosser and Kirby in on the challenge Pelham had given the Dialectic Society.

There was a rustle of chairs, and four men who appeared to be the crew for the sloop settled their bill.

Pelham sipped his ale as his gaze fixed on the old tavern keeper. If ever there was a constant in the world, it was the man behind the bar. Benny Havens was known by all in gray, but only as a true friend to those willing to risk dismissal for a different brand of education. Pelham knew Benny's story. The man had been born in 1787 in New Windsor, some thirteen miles north of West Point. In 1802, at the age of fifteen, the year the Academy was founded, he was hired by the sutler who ran West Point's general store. While working for the sutler, Benny was expelled from Academy grounds for selling a bottle of rum to a cadet wanting to better enjoy Christmas. The man went straight to his cups and made a spectacle of himself, and at the encouragement of authorities revealed his source.

Havens glanced up from behind the bar and caught Pelham's stare. He nodded and smiled as Pelham raised his mug in salute.

In the War of 1812, Havens had served as a first lieutenant in a company of volunteers drawn partially from Buttermilk Falls, which at the time boasted barely one hundred souls. His company had been stationed on Long Island and saw no action. But a woman named Letitia Stuyvesant captured his heart, and later became his wife. In due course, she gave birth to a son and two very pretty daughters. The daughters both married, one an officer. After the war, Havens became a woodcutter and a carpenter, primarily cutting and making hoop poles for barrels. In such capacity, he was allowed back on Academy grounds. He built a small, attractive cottage close to the cadet hospital, and after a time, reverted to his natural calling. For several happy years, he and Letitia befriended cadets and supplied them with food and drink, though in the earlier years it was more Letitia's buckwheat cakes, roast turkeys, and the like that made them a living, rather than Benny's bartending. Soon enough, however, his recipe for hot flip gave him the edge over competing establishments.

The master barman pulled a large brown earthenware pitcher from beneath the counter, a tray of eggs from the cold box, two bottles of ale, a jug of rum, a tin of sugar, and an assortment of spices essential to the making of his flip, a concoction far and away the favorite of patrons—cadets especially. He deftly cracked eggs over the pitcher and added ingredients measured by sight and feel.

Next came a generous quantity of ale and an ample measure of rum, the whole beat into a frothy mixture. He then extracted a white-hot "flip dog" from the stove, and in dramatic fashion plunged the iron into the pitcher. The resulting hiss filled the tavern, drawing the attention of all present. The aroma of caramel soon filled the room.

Pelham reflected further upon the thorn in the Academy's paw. In 1825, the nearly sainted Sylvanus Thayer, bent on temperance for the Corps and well aware of the propensity of cadets to visit the Havens' cottage, achieved his aim by convincing Congress to purchase for ten thousand dollars the land upon which the Havens' house stood. As Havens owned the house but not the land, he was paid for the house and directed to vacate. While an effective measure in the near term, the move interrupted the Havens' business only a short time. The entrepreneur moved his growing family to temporary accommodations in neighboring Buttermilk Falls. In a matter of months, his trade was in full vigor and beyond Academy reach. But it was not until 1843, when Havens purchased property for the landing, that the tavern was built in which Pelham and his friends found themselves.

While Patterson speculated with Kirby and Rosser on the next commandant, Pelham inspected the tavern, tracing with his finger the initials he had carved years earlier in the tabletop. It had been three months since he and Rosser had escaped through the tavern's back door, when the duty officer followed up on a report of cadets leaving post.

Had anything been added, had anything been changed?

Pelham surveyed the tavern as if he might be required to sketch it for Professor Weir, who had never been much impressed with his sketches. Weir had taught him to see a thing first in its whole, before seeing it in its parts. The tavern was a single room, twenty by forty feet, its length parallel to the shoreline, its wonderfully worn pine plank floor stained by whatever spilled or missed the spittoon. The ceiling was rough mahogany with massive dark ceiling beams, from which stubby whale oil lanterns hung on iron hooks, providing soft, soothing light. Its entrance was bordered on one side by a window, which in the daytime opened to glorious views of the river and the hills beyond. The plastered walls bore a dull yellow-ochre finish, nearly black around the stone fireplace. The thick rough-cut square columns bore hooks for every miscellany.

Pelham registered the line, color, and sense of everything: the tarnished brass lionhead doorknob, the narrow stairs rising to the second floor where Havens and his wife lived, the mahogany bar with stools crafted by Havens himself, the liquors and wines behind the bar, the cork dart board, the cracker barrel in the center of the room, and the collection of unmatched tables, chairs, and benches that made the place a tavern. The walls were alive with paintings, etchings, and sketches, and swords, sabers, and musketry that gave the place the feel of an armory.

"How went your trip, Master Pelham?" Havens shouted from behind the bar.

"A blur, Benny. Too much and too fast."

"I expect so, so little time."

Rosser pointed an accusing cigar at Pelham. "So why did we wait so long to visit our friend?"

The last of the other patrons settled their accounts, receiving a hearty farewell from Havens.

"Benny," Pelham declared, "you are undoubtedly the most congenial soul in the valley and likely upon earth."

"Don't know about that, Master Pelham." Havens's eyes twinkled. "But I do believe a stranger is but a friend I haven't met." The tavern keeper assumed a more serious tone. "These are interesting times, lads."

"'Twill all resolve itself," Patterson said with assurance.

"You think?" Havens forced a smile. He removed the flip dog and spooned a taste. Removed too soon, the beverage was flat; left too long, it had a burnt taste. He smacked his lips and smiled, and rang the bell above the bar, which he rang only for hot flip.

Patterson drained his ale and found his pipe. "Glorious is the here and now, but, oh, how we'll pay for it with sleep."

"Not if we mind and limit ourselves." Pelham lit the cigar Kirby had given him. "But we had to come. Think of what little time remains. When we graduate, Benny and all of this will be a memory. But we're agreed, one flip and we're gone."

Havens dispensed the four steaming tankards of hot flip. "This will cure your demons, and, certain, you'll not find a serving like mine nowhere's else."

Patterson sniffed the beverage and loosed a guttural purr.

"Pure heaven," Kirby announced, his upper lip covered with flip.

The four toasted Havens again and then each other, then the class, and finally their last year at the Academy.

Patterson stood up. "And it's only right we toast our benefactor, John Pelham, and his Clermont girls."

"Hear, hear." Rosser tousled Pelham's hair.

"And I'll let you know that Miss Alice Paine and I are getting along famously," Patterson added confidently.

"A poor judge of men, is she, Chas?" Kirby winked at the others.

Patterson ignored him. "It pains me to say it, John, but I am indeed obliged to you."

"Then pay me back in academics, for it's there I'll need it."

"Not as much as Tom." Patterson poked Rosser in the ribs. "And just how are things with Miss Taylor?"

"We have a name change," Pelham interjected on Rosser's behalf. "Seems Tom prefers the southern lass, Carol Hill."

"What about poor Walter?" Patterson asked.

"I suppose he'll have to make do with Miss Taylor." Pelham's face was deadpan.

Patterson seemed satisfied. "And you and Clara?"

"Clara and I are where we need to be, thank you."

"As it should be, for she's the queen of six royal bees."

Letitia Havens descended the staircase. "Hello, boys. What's our topic?"

Benny rounded the bar. "Mum, I believe it would be manly passions."

Pelham nearly choked on his flip.

"Though, dear wife, I can't quite recall exactly what it is they are talking about."

Now it was Rosser's turn to choke.

Letitia winked at the young men. "Seems he figured it out a few times."

When the laughter died, Havens asked if he could join them.

Pelham drew up another chair. "So what's new with you, Benny?"

Before he could respond, Patterson had a hand in the air. "Is it true, Benny, what John says, about the Marquis de Lafayette coming to visit you?"

Pelham shrugged his shoulders. "What can I say Benny? The man is a Thomas."

"Master Chas," Havens remonstrated, "there are likely some things I've said you might want to test, but as far as that fine Frenchman goes—you know he was adopted by George Washington—he most certainly did pay me a visit. It was …" He searched his memory. "In 1824, I think, when he was making his grand tour of the country that he served so well in our struggle for independence so many years ago." Havens smiled curiously. "You're not pulling my leg, Chas? You really don't believe me?"

Patterson assured him he was serious.

"So you want to see the nail holes, do you? Give me a minute."

Havens got up and rooted behind the bar, surfacing with a well-polished cherry wood chest. He unlocked it with the small key that always hung about his neck, and after some searching retrieved a small polished wooden box. Returning to the table, he placed the box in front of Patterson.

"Go ahead, open it."

Patterson lifted the lid and found inside two buttons. "May I?"

"By all means."

Patterson removed one of the buttons and examined it. "Real gold?"

"It is."

"Fine workmanship."

"I should think so, and that fine French general was the guest of Superintendent Thayer. And I'm sure it was none to Thayer's satisfaction that the general was determined to pay me a visit. Why, I don't know, or how he even knew I breathed the air, but he arrives with others in his company, and I didn't know whether to bow or curtsey. He marches right up to me and asks if I am the one who makes hot flop. I don't correct him, but say I am, and I make him and his friends a very fine batch indeed. From then on we got on famously, becoming the best of friends, with me, of course, doing most of the talking."

"Of course." Pelham grinned.

"The marquis," Havens continued, "enjoyed a good story, no less than you, and laughed better than most men, and we had a gay old time. When he finally left, it was after midnight. Before he goes, he gives me them two buttons with his face engraved on them. Made in Connecticut, he said. Then he thanks me and says if ever I get to France, he'll show me Paris personally."

The others looked at Patterson.

"Okay, okay, I believe you, Benny." Patterson put the button back in the box. "You're incredible! So what did the Marquis look like?"

"What did he look like?" Havens paused to think, and suddenly guffawed as only he could. "What did he look like? Lord, he looked old. That's what he looked like, by then nearly seventy." Havens thumbed his chest. "Damn if the disease ain't catchy."

When they stopped laughing, Pelham exhaled a cloud of gray smoke. "Benny, how is it that you, who hardly ever travel farther than the city, regale and endear a Frenchman and international hero in one evening?"

"Don't know about endear'n, Though there's something about a tavern keeper that puts people to ease. But let me say, if we're talking heroes, I'd offer up the likes of you. I've seen it before. You'll leave this place, and come a Mexican War or whatever, you'll prove me right or die trying."

Letitia came up alongside her husband and placed a hand on his shoulder.

"I'm proud I get to know some of you," Havens continued, his words sincere. "Though not as many as I'd like, and glad enough when some of you come back to visit your old friend, like Jeff Davis and Edgar Poe before he passed away, too soon before his time."

Pelham nodded, thinking that Davis had probably visited Havens during his commission trip. He could picture the tall wiry senator and the tavern keeper talking through the night, reminiscing about the old days, about the time thirty-five years earlier when Davis was caught in the tavern by a tactical officer and subsequently court-martialed, only to be reinstated by President Jackson. They would have also joked about a later incident, when Davis eluded a raid, but in his escape had stepped off a cliff, nearly killing himself.

"I'll be back, Benny," Pelham promised. "Davis and Poe won't have a step on me."

The others pledged the same, Rosser adding, "That Poe gives me the creeps."

"He shouldn't, Tom. Poe was as brilliant a mind as ever graced West Point, and possessed a very fine sense of humor, God rest his soul. He was beloved by his classmates."

Pelham and the others knew the story, that when Poe arrived at West Point to join the Class of 1834, he had already published his earliest works. He was attending West Point to appease his stepfather, who thinking himself rid of the young man, proceeded to disown him. Learning that, Poe decided he wasn't where he needed to be, and did all he could to get himself dismissed, including missing formations, skipping classes, and spending many hours with the tavern keeper. As a consequence, he and Havens became fast friends. Sylvanus Thayer tried to persuade Poe to stay, but he departed the Academy in February of 1831, eight months after his arrival.

After Poe's departure, Havens would talk about the man's admiration for the Corps and his bond with his classmates, pointing to Poe's next published collection of works, entitled *Poems*, with the sentiment on the title page, *To the U.S. Corps of Cadets this volume is respectfully dedicated.*

Pelham knew that Havens had copies of all of Poe's works, and was quick to recite his poems, his favorite being "The Raven."

"No, you would have liked him, Master Tom, believe me. He could actually be quite like you at times and delighted the Corps with his satire—always aimed at the leadership."

Rosser laughed. "Then assuredly I would have liked him very much."

"And imagine what fun we had," Havens continued. "Each time, him coming in with something new to rattle my nerves."

"Can you imagine living inside that head?" Kirby said.

"I'd never get to sleep," Patterson said.

Pelham put a hand on the tavern keeper's arm. "Yours is a long list of friends, Benny."

"Aye, there have been many. I think of Grant, Jackson, Sherman, Longstreet, Burnside, Meade, Heath, Sheridan, Pickett, Thomas, and Strong—all of them, my boys. And others, of course."

"I've heard of Grant and Jackson from the Mexican War," Rosser said. "But the others ..."

"Were like you," Havens said. "All of them did what you're doing now, took risks, and for what? Its own reward."

"For flip," Rosser insisted, raising his tankard. "'Tis the elixir that courses down my throat that draws me."

"So smooth and soothing, so friendly, fruity, faultless, flawless, this flip of ours." The words dripped off Patterson's tongue.

"But, alas, mine's gone," Rosser said in a mournful tone. "What say another round, my friends?"

"I thought we were going easy tonight," Pelham ribbed his roommate.

"Blast that idea," returned Rosser.

As Havens prepared a second batch, he shouted from the bar, "You think you know a thing or two, don't you, boys? But I bet there is something you don't know. There is one at the Academy who has headed an academic department for more years than I can count, who used to come and visit me. Can you name him?"

The interest of the four was piqued, and they pooled their guesses, with Pelham finally announcing, "Can be none other than Professor Kendrick." Kendrick, who made his own peach brandy, would on occasion invite cadets to sample his wares. Patterson could personally testify to the quality of Kendrick's brandy and good humor.

"Don't believe I ever had the pleasure of Kendrick's company," Havens said. "So perhaps, a clue. Who is the man most responsible for the departure of cadets from the Academy?"

The clue gave away the answer, but none of the four believed it.

"Professor Church?" Rosser shook his head. He had almost been dismissed by that very same professor.

"Aye, Albert Church, professor of mathematics, Class of 1828. Same as Jeff Davis, though Church was at the top and Davis near the bottom. But I assure you," Havens said in defense of Church. "His predecessors were just as villainous as he, and I'm sure his successors will be no less. There's just something about math that undoes people. Church was a good lad, and he and I hit it off well. I expect because mathematics was a passion for me. Indeed, I used to tutor some of you in the old days."

Pelham knew this. "But Church is so ... normal."

"Normal now and no longer an imbiber, I understand. But I remember a different Church, and one night in particular. He and three others came to visit, and they were into a fine time when an informant warned them that they had been discovered absent from the barracks and officers were on their way. Letitia and I hid them as best we could. Church, being a small fellow, we hid in the flour barrel." Havens pointed to the barrel in the corner. "But to no avail, as all four were discovered, and one as white as a ghost."

Pelham's stomach hurt when he finally stopped laughing.

"All but Church were court-martialed and dismissed. The clever Church raised a point with the court officer that I was never clear on, but it prevailed and his fate was settled favorably by President Van Buren."

"You find us amusing, don't you, Benny?" Pelham wagged an accusing finger.

"I find you a blessing. I find that you undergo great change during your time here. And after you're gone, your lives are exciting, and Letitia and I live through you as we hear how you spend your lives." Havens turned thoughtful. "And soon the four of you will be gone. Anyway, if I didn't have the likes of you as part of my life, dropping in at all times of night, I would have retired from this business long ago."

"Now that's a naked lie, Mr. Havens," Letitia declared, now washing dishes.

Havens produced a weak scowl. "What do you know, woman?"

Pelham seized the moment. He got to his feet and began to sing, joined by Rosser, Kirby, and Patterson. They sang the first verse of the song penned decades earlier in honor of the tavern keeper, a song sung to the tune of "Wearing O' the Green."

Come fill your glasses, fellows, and stand up in a row
To singing sentimentally we are going for to go
In the Army there's sobriety, promotion's very slow
So we'll sing our reminiscences of Benny Havens, Oh!

Oh! Benny Havens, Oh!—Oh! Benny Havens, Oh!
We'll sing our reminiscences of Benny Havens, Oh!

Letitia crossed the room with a brown bound book. "You honor us, boys. Horace Porter of last year's class presented Benny with his book, entitled *West Point Life*. In it are most of the verses that have been written for my Benny."

Pelham hugged the aged woman. Porter was a good friend, and last year he had been the Corps adjutant and president of the Dialectic Society.

As the young men sang two more of the more than sixty versus penned for Havens, verses collectively known as "Benny Havens, Oh," the old man's eyes required drying.

CHAPTER TWENTY-TWO

Wednesday morning at precisely five o'clock, Bentz played the first note of reveille, his bugle again punctuated by two energetic drum orderlies. Immediately, the dead arose amid yawns and oaths, the lighting of lamps, and rustled movements across wooden tent floors. In each company street, a plebe announced the minutes remaining until reveille formation, and by the time the two-minute call was made, the last of a stream of dark figures scurried onto the four company streets for the first formation of the day.

The three platoons of D Company stood at attention in front of First Sergeant Paddy O'Rorke.

"Report," O'Rorke directed in a tone respectful of the hour.

"First Platoon, all present and accounted for," a man in front of the lead platoon reported.

O'Rorke returned the man's salute.

"Second Platoon, all present and accounted for."

O'Rorke returned a second salute.

"Third Platoon, all present, except for Cadets Pelham and Rosser."

Laughter followed by cheers erupted from the three platoons of D Company. O'Rorke executed an about-face and rendered the report to an expressionless Ned Kirby, who in turn rendered the report to the battalion adjutant, Walter Kingsbury.

Minutes later, Kirby flung the tent flap aside and kicked Pelham's footlocker. Pelham shot up on his pallet. "What the—"

Rosser peeked out from under his comforter.

"Fine example, boys. You haven't left the tent and already have a skin."

"Morning, Ned," Rosser said with a sheepish look, stretching his arms. "And I thought you worse off than me."

Pelham was more circumspect. "Hell, why should this year be any different?"

After Kirby left, Rosser invested himself mentally and announced, "At this rate we can still graduate."

While the cadets breakfasted in the mess hall, Colonel Delafield sat at a small table that James had set on the veranda of the superintendent's quarters. He was finishing the last of his morning meal and reading the newspaper, savoring the serenity of solitude. His wife Harriet, along with Professor Weir's wife, had ferried the Hudson to catch the train to New York City for three days of necessary and not so necessary shopping. They would not return until the following day. His disposition was further improved by the thought that this would be his last summer encampment. General Scott had as much as promised him that come January, he could either retire or mark time in a Washington job until the chief of engineers post opened. Either way, in his mind he would be gone from the campus that had become claustrophobic. His only wish was that his wife shared his viewpoint, but she didn't. She rather enjoyed the idyllic life and her position as queen of court. Beyond this, clouding his more or less sunny countenance, was the continued hesitancy on the part of Scott to actually name his replacement.

"More coffee, sir?" James asked. Without waiting for a response, he tipped the silver coffee pot and filled the superintendent's cup.

Delafield put down the newspaper and studied the black man.

James felt the attention. "Sir, is there something?"

"James, in the nearly five years we've been together, you've told me nothing of yourself."

"Sir?"

"I see more of you than my wife, and yet know nothing of you."

"It is … not my place, sir."

The superintendent waved off his excuse. "Nonsense. Have a seat, James."

The house servant placed the coffee pot on the table and sat stiffly, his back straight as a board.

"So, tell me of yourself, James."

"Sir, there is not much about me. I was a slave, and now I am a free man, and I have worked for the government as a house servant here at the Academy for the past eight years."

"Don't tell me there is not a story there," Delafield insisted.

The black man appeared agitated. "Fifteen years ago, sir, I was given my papers after my master died, he being true to his promise to free me."

"A good man, him. And where was that?"

"Brusly, Louisiana, sir. I was born into sugarcane, third generation, and had worked my way from the field to the house."

"That must have been a red letter day for you, James, getting your freedom."

The waiter's face suggested otherwise, as he glanced over his shoulder across the Plain. "Sir, I was very close to a young woman. She had been purchased by my master only months before he died. Her name was Juniper. She was the kindest, sweetest soul I had ever met, and to me the most beautiful woman I ever seen."

Delafield sensed he was unearthing something.

"This woman, sir, was to be the master's new cook, and she and me came to know and understand each other in special ways, both of us working in the house and all. I intended to ask her to be my wife, as much as I could have a wife, and I believe she would have said yes. I even asked permission of the master, and it pleased him to know it."

"Where is your Juniper now?"

"Sir, only God knows. Master died sudden like from his heart." The black man hesitated. "His son came down from Opelousas to settle the estate. It all happened so fast, sir. The day after he come down, I get my papers and am beyond myself with joy. I go looking for Juniper to tell her—but she is gone."

"Gone?"

"That morning, sir. Sent away to a plantation near New Orleans to settle a debt." James had to regain his composure. "I'm sorry, sir, but I never even had a chance to …"

"Please, James, go on."

"The master's son, he was a good man, but he knew nothing of me and Juniper. When I told him, he said he would do whatever he could to get her back and that I could pay him as I was able. He wrote the new owner to say he'd pay in cash what the man wanted to settle the debt and to send Juniper back. He told me not to worry, that he would send Juniper to join me in New York City." The servant's eyes filled with tears.

"New York City?"

"It was all arranged by my master before he died. Before noon, I am on a steamer out of Baton Rouge with a small purse of coins and a letter I am to give a family in New York City."

"And you've not seen your Juniper since?"

"Weeks later, a letter come from the master's son. He is so sorry, but the new owner of Juniper has already sold her to a man in Mobile who had lost his wife and needed a mammy for his children. I got two more letters from him, but he never did hear from the man in Mobile. The last letter said he could do no more—and that was the end of it, sir."

When the servant fell silent, Delafield searched for something to say, but could think of nothing.

"I held to hope, sir, for the longest time, I did."

"And that's why you've never married?"

"Hope is a powerful thing, sir—till it's dead. And when it's dead, it leaves such a hole. Anyway, it just don't seem right, me to marry and all."

Delafield stood up and put a hand on the black man's shoulder. "I am indeed sorry, James. I was wrong to put you through this. I truly wish there was something I could do."

"I can't see how, sir. It's been so many years." The servant's lip suddenly quivered. "Sir, I can't even remember what Juniper looks like any more."

The black man got to his feet and began clearing the table. "Will there be anything else, sir?"

"No, James. Thank you, and, again, I'm very sorry."

"Yes, sir. Thank you, sir."

The servant raised the tray to his shoulder and disappeared inside the house, at the same time as an army private appeared at the foot of the stairs with a telegram.

Delafield returned the man's salute and took the telegram. After reading it, he called into the house, "James, good news from Jeff Davis. The Senator says the mess hall fare will improve posthaste, and our boys

146

and the rest of us will get a decent meal. On top of that, we can expect more and better horses within two weeks."

"Yes, sir, that is indeed good news," James replied from inside the house.

Delafield had hoped for more, but Davis had warned him that federal dollars were scarce, and congressional interest in the Academy was, at best, tepid. He reread the last of the telegram, where Davis congratulated him on the state of the Corps and the Academy facilities.

Later that morning, after every man in the first section of remedial instruction had passed the obstacle course, the chagrin on Custer's face turned to delight when roll was called in the second section, and Mr. Collins reported that Mr. Williams was in the hospital with a stomach virus.

"I had nothing to do with it," Custer told Pelham with a toothy grin.

One by one, each man in the second section eventually passed the obstacle course. As they did, they eagerly awaited dismissal. However, before granting anyone leave, Pelham admonished the section to visit Williams in the hospital and encourage him for Friday. Otherwise they might never see him again.

For the First Classmen, a refresher surveying class followed the midday meal, and those in D Company sat Indian style in a semicircle at the northwest corner of the Plain. The instructor was a stocky sergeant sporting a fiery red handlebar moustache.

"Gentlemen, the Theodolite instrument is man's greatest invention, affording him the ability to map any topographic feature. With it we can know the world as it really is." The sergeant removed the cover from the instrument and continued in his thick Scottish brogue, "Mr. Patterson, would you be so kind as to set and level the instrument."

Patterson did as instructed, setting up the tripod, affixing the Theodolite, and leveling the instrument with its precision thumbscrews.

The sergeant examined the setup, checked the level, and nodded his approval. He perfunctorily described the component parts of the instruments and how the instrument was to be used. This was all a rehash for them, especially for Pelham, who struggled to pay attention. His gaze kept wandering in the direction of the hotel, where even at a distance, he could see activity of interest on the front lawn.

"So then, Mr. Pelham," the instructor said, picking up on Pelham's wandering. "Let's see if you remember how to use the Theodolite. Would you please demonstrate for the class by selecting a target and giving us an azimuth?"

Pelham got to his feet, approached the instrument, and intentionally looked through the wrong end of the scope, drawing laughter from his classmates.

"We are not amused, Mr. Pelham, and have a schedule to keep." The instructor's voice was terse.

Pelham swung the eyepiece toward the hotel and sighted through the aperture at a group of girls huddled by the hotel omnibus. Rosser picked up on it and poked Kirby.

In the magnification of the eyepiece, Pelham saw Clara with her friends. She was talking and gesturing, and suddenly all of the girls were laughing.

"Sergeant," Pelham called out in a loud voice, "azimuth, eighty-one degrees, thirty-six minutes, fifteen seconds."

"Your target, Mr. Pelham?" The sergeant asked after writing down the reading.

"The center of the oak tree, Sergeant."

The non-commissioned officer sighted through the instrument and found that the crosshairs were indeed centered on a tree. He read the angle and compared the measurement with Pelham's reading. He fingered his mustache and grunted. "That will be all, Mr. Pelham. Mr. Kirby, would you care to give us the vertical angle to the top of the flag pole?"

CHAPTER TWENTY-THREE

Later that day, before the parade review and after shining the brass hilt of his sword, Pelham selected a well-used rag to polish his shoes. He was interrupted by a knock on the tent pole and the figure of Emory Upton.

"Emory." Pelham spit on the black polish he had applied to the toe of his shoe. "Have a seat." Pelham pulled the remnant of the old handkerchief tight around his forefinger and rubbed polish into the shoe leather in a light, but rapid circular motion.

"I thought the meeting went well." Upton's statement was more of a question.

"Were you at the same meeting?" Pelham asked, cracking a smile. "I sensed a rather cool reception, but regardless, as we agreed, the subject could not have been proffered by you with any hope of acceptance. And I remain in your camp that we should give it voice, both sides of it."

"Who do you see as debaters?"

"That all depends on how it comes down and, of course, on whether the topic passes muster with the superintendent. Delafield is a very cautious man."

"John, I want to debate against secession."

Pelham put down his rag. "And I'd like to be King of France. Be realistic. Your chances are not good."

Upton said nothing, which surprised Pelham.

"Face it, Emory. The society, like the Corps, is heavily Democrat. If the topic is accepted, the group, not I, will select its debaters. And you must know that some view you as an—extremist."

Upton remained deadpanned.

"The important thing, Emory, is that we get the forum you want."

Upton greeted the comment with a single nod, and rose to his feet.

"Are you coming to the hop?"

Upton's face brightened, and Pelham thought he saw the hint of a smile.

"I am."

"Then I'll introduce you to my friend, Clara Bolton."

Upton's smile was now unmistakable. "I have heard about the young lady."

Much to the joy of the Corps and the regret of visitors, including Clara and her friends, the evening parade was canceled due to a short drizzle that stopped just before supper. After the evening meal, Pelham and Rosser made ready for the hop and walked the short distance to the hotel. On the way, they talked strategy for the Friday session with Williams. He was the one most in need of the second session, and, having missed it, would have his mettle sorely tested.

"Hi, Tex," Carol Hill called down from the veranda.

Rosser bounded up the stairs and presented his arm, and the two disappeared inside.

A second figure appeared on the veranda. "And how was your day, dear knight?"

"My lady, my day was excellent, most excellent. And yours?"

"They canceled the parade." Clara feigned a pout and took his arm.

For Pelham, the second hop passed all too quickly. He partnered with Clara for six dances, all of them waltzes, which afforded them conversation and a measure of intimacy. The rest of Clara's hop card bore names like Chambliss, Patterson, du Pont, and, courtesy of Pelham, Emory Upton.

As the end of the evening approached, Pelham approached Clara. "Can we skip the last dance?"

"I'll meet you in the lobby."

Moments later they were on the rear veranda, again facing the river.

"So many stars," Clara said. "So beautiful—so very like a dream. One I wish might never end."

"I'm pleased you are having a good time, and I noticed you haven't lost your effect on the Corps. You even got Emory Upton to smile."

"You know, he's actually a good dancer," she said, adding with a hint of melancholy, "John, I am so happy, but so sad too. Half the week is gone and we have only one more hop."

Pelham squeezed her shoulders. "I know. The stuff of time is fleeting. But we have our picnic."

"And such a picnic it will be," she promised, finding her gaiety again. "Promise me you'll have a sailor's appetite?"

"I always do."

Neither said anything, but rather gazed out across the Hudson at the distant lights until the final strains of music played out.

Clara turned in Pelham's arms. "John?"

"My lady."

"Cadet Upton … Tell me he is your friend."

"Emory?" The question surprised him. "Yes, he is. Why?"

"He was so easy to talk to. I told him about us."

"About our being friends?"

"Best friends. Do you mind?"

Pelham was glad for the darkness. "Why should I mind?"

"I find him most interesting, but also—"

Pelham couldn't imagine what she might say next.

She laughed. "He talks so very fast."

"Um."

"He reminds me of Father. Yes, he is very much like Father."

"My lady, 'tis time I was off." Pelham placed a finger on her nose. "Would you bestow your friendship seal upon your humble servant?"

"Of course, you silly."

Instead of her customary peck, she drew him close and pressed her mouth full against each cheek.

"Until tomorrow, dear knight."

CHAPTER TWENTY-FOUR

Thursday afternoon at two o'clock, Clara, carrying a picnic basket with a red gingham coverlet, glanced nervously over her shoulder as she glided down the back stairs of the hotel. Walking quickly past a stand of well-leafed maples, she found Pelham waiting with a neatly folded blanket tucked under one arm. They exchanged expectant looks, and she kissed him lightly on the cheek, finding the sun warm on his face.

Without a word he led her down a gravel path, over the crest of the bluff, and beyond sight of the hotel. After a few minutes, he asked if he could peek in the basket.

"You'll have to wait, young man, and you already know there's fried chicken. The rest is a surprise, but I'll let you smell." She raised the basket to his nose.

Pelham sniffed and tried to peek, and for the offense had his hand slapped.

"Temptress! What is that on your neck?"

"What?"

"Little red dots?"

"I didn't get them all?" Clara matter-of-factly wetted the finger of her glove and rubbed her neck. "Gone?"

Pelham smiled. "Gone."

"It was Ellie's idea." Clara giggled. "The sneak made me up a sickly face and then had Carol Hill run get Miss Frampton."

Pelham shook his head.

"When she came, I carried on awful, and she made a big fuss. Said I should rest—that she would procure a tonic."

Pelham helped Clara down some stone steps.

"She came back with castor oil—imagine! Thank God for Ellie. She said I was asleep and shouldn't be wakened, and that she would administer the medicine when I awoke. And so, here I am."

"Your roommate's beauty is exceeded only by her cunning. She and Henry are still a number?"

Clara smiled. "Henry has promise."

Pelham led her down the steepest part of a hillside path, through the trees and around exposed granite faces, until they reached North Dock Road at a point near the river. As they walked down the road, Clara saw letters and numbers cut into the massive granite stone of the hillside.

Anticipating her question, Pelham explained. "These are names and dates of battles, some Revolutionary War and some Mexican War."

Thinking her distracted, he attempted another peek in the basket and suffered the same fate.

"Don't they teach you patience here?" Clara shifted the basket to her other arm.

"Oh, but you are a hard lady." Pelham directed her attention to the river's edge, where men unloaded coal from a barge, and other men loaded the coal onto haul wagons.

Soon they arrived at a wooden sign in a clearing to the east of the dock. Clara read the fine lettering: Entry Prohibited to all but Cadets and their Accompanied Guests. She smiled and squeezed Pelham's arm. "So this is Flirtation Walk. I am actually here."

"You may be anticipating more than there is." Pelham led her into the wood on the narrow path of crushed stone.

After they had gone but a short distance, she said, almost in a whisper, "Such a secluded place. I am glad to have my knight for protection."

"Your servant."

"Aren't you glad we don't have to play games, John? That we can simply be together, have fun the way real friends do?"

"Best friends," he said, his smile somewhat affected.

"The very best."

She gripped his arm tighter as they walked the twisting path, a cooling breeze rising off the river. When they came to an opening in the trees, she exclaimed, "So many boats!"

The Hudson was alive with vessels of every variety, including a large whaler.

"Do you sail, John?"

"I can row a bit, but otherwise there is not a nautical bone in my body."

She stooped down over a small bush to inspect its tiny white flowers. "I've never seen these."

"Shadblow," Pelham said. "They normally don't last this long."

"Aren't they the most delicate creatures? They look like edelweiss."

Pelham picked a cluster of the tiny flowers and with a grand gesture, presented them to Clara.

"For me?"

"Beautiful flowers for my lady, whose heart exceeds their beauty."

"Thank you, though I suspect you've used that line before." She placed the flowers in a silk handkerchief and tucked them in her basket.

They continued along the winding path, Pelham answering a continuous stream of questions, until Clara suddenly froze mid-step. "Oh! What was that?"

"What was what?"

"You didn't hear it? There in the bushes." She was already behind him, pointing over his shoulder.

"Relax, my lady, it's just a family outing." Pelham directed her attention to an opening in the trees, where a doe and two fawns grazed on grass.

"They don't seem much interested in us."

"Trust me, this is home to the king's deer, and we've many birds, squirrels, coons, and possum. And don't faint if we flush some quail."

"Snakes?"

Pelham saw the concern in her face. "Strictly prohibited."

She smiled.

The two of them ambled on, at times close to the river's edge, where they could hear the waves lapping against the shore; at times distant, with only the sound of their footsteps and the twitter of birds.

"I feel like we are in some sort of enchanted forest," she said, her voice full of wonder. "You come here a lot, don't you, John? I mean— with girls."

Pelham didn't respond.

"Don't say you don't, John Pelham, I bet you have a different girl every week."

"Not every week, but neither am I a monk."

"You are a bad boy." She playfully punched his arm.

As they rounded a bend and the path ascended, Pelham stopped and raised a finger to his lips.

"What?" she whispered.

"Professional courtesy. Let's give them a minute."

Ahead of them, a couple embraced beneath a granite overhang.

"Why—that's Alice Paine and your Mr. Patterson," Clara declared, almost indignant. "I'll stake my life on it."

"I do believe you're right."

"That little sneak. How did she get out?"

Pelham smiled. "I love it, that thing you do with your nose."

"What?"

"Look, they're gone."

"Do you think they will kiss again? I mean, down the path, where there is no rock?" Clara gave him a look of innocence.

"I suppose, if the situation demands." Pelham bore an equally straight face.

In a moment they too were beneath the overhang. Pelham intended to pass it by, but Clara restrained him.

"So, this is your Kissing Rock?"

"It is," Pelham said evenly.

"I understand there is a legend about this rock."

"Yes, but I don't know that it's true," he said dismissively.

"Tell me."

"Well, it is said that if a cadet and his date do not kiss beneath this rock, the Academy and indeed the entire country will fall into ruin."

"Dear me. How terrible!" Clara affected great emotion.

"But to this day, thanks be to God, none have failed to do their duty, and the country and the Academy are secure."

"What then are we to do?"

"We? I must leave that up to you, my lady."

"Well, I can't have the demise of civilization on my conscience. I suppose we must do our duty." Clara put down her basket and positioned herself beneath the rock. Closing her eyes, she tilted her head back and presented her lips. With firmness of purpose, she said, "Do it."

Pelham had to repress a laugh. He leaned forward and kissed her lightly on the lips.

Her eyes opened. "There, it is done," she said. "We have done our duty and preserved the nation and your school." In an instant, she was several steps up the path, asking, "Where should we picnic?"

Within Pelham, the game was on, the skirmish lines of heart and mind clearly drawn. "Not far from here," he said.

Onward they walked, up and down and around the steeps of the shoreline, past the point where the great iron chain had been attached, until Pelham stopped at what was Gee's Point, the easternmost tip of West Point. An unattended lighthouse and a glorious view of the Hudson and the town of Garrison on the other side awaited them thirty feet below.

"This will be a little tricky," he said, taking the picnic basket from Clara. He descended the sloped rock face backward, holding Clara's hand and allowing her to brace against him. When they arrived at the water's edge, he spread his wool blanket on the ground and assisted Clara off her feet.

"Oh, John, this is absolutely the loveliest spot that could possibly be. And look, those people are waving at us!"

Fifty yards offshore, a sloop heeled into the wind. Clara waved at the crew.

Pelham reclined on his back.

"So," Clara said, "not counting me, how many girls have you brought to this rather magical spot?" She removed her bonnet and undid her bun, allowing her hair to fall down about her neck.

"I'm not good at math," he said with eyes closed.

She giggled and leaned over him, shaking her hair so that it teased his face. "You are my best friend, aren't you?"

"More so with each minute."

"Look at me," she demanded, holding a rock above his head with an all-too-serious look upon her face.

Pelham raised his hand in defense. "My lady, have I offended?"

"Silly, this is no ordinary rock. This too is a kissing rock. I pronounce it so." She leaned over and kissed him on one cheek and then the other,

her breath tickling his nose. "Yes, we are the very best of friends, and what we did at Kissing Rock was our duty."

"It was. We had no choice."

She reclined on the blanket beside him. "The sun feels so good, doesn't it?" She folded her arms beneath her head and closed her eyes.

A boat sounded its horn, and Pelham announced, "That would be the Garrison ferry."

"To destroy our peace," she said, her eyes still closed.

Pelham turned his head and gazed upon Clara, upon the rising and falling of her bodice.

"That does it, my lady. You are the greatest tease I have ever known. I believe you enjoy my torture, and, frankly, I will stand for it no longer."

She opened her eyes. "I take it you're famished."

He grinned and tweaked her nose. "Exactly."

Clara reached for the picnic basket and found what she was looking for. "Close your eyes and open wide."

Pelham obliged, and something with a creamy texture was inserted into his mouth. "By all that is holy, this is like a dessert. What is it?"

"It's cheese. French brie. It would go well with wine, don't you think?"

"You tease me further, my lady," Pelham said, his eyes still closed.

"*Voila!*" Clara produced a bottle of red wine.

Eyes wide, Pelham couldn't believe it.

"I had it opened." She handed him the corked bottle and two small glasses. "Care to do the honors?"

He poured a little into the two glasses and made a toast. "To my truly extraordinary friend, who is also a girl."

Clara clinked his glass. "This is such a special experience for me, John." She clinked his glass again. "To our amazing friendship."

She watched him drain his glass. "I know that this is entirely forbidden to you and your friends, so I thought—"

"You thought rightly, my angel of mercy." He poured himself another glass. "Benny Havens would love you."

"Benny who?"

"It doesn't matter. Have you more of that cheese?" She gave him the rest of the small wedge. "Where did you come by this?"

"Your hotel chef. He and I have become fast friends. He gets it from the man who teaches you French."

"Professor Agnel?" Pelham was impressed.

"Close your eyes again."

She placed a plump drumstick against his lips, and he nearly swallowed it whole.

Clara arranged two ceramic plates on the blanket, along with knives and forks, the tin of fried chicken, a bowl of potato salad, and half a pecan pie.

For the next few minutes, Pelham was poor company, rather unceremoniously downing everything Clara placed in front of him.

When he had finished the main course, he asked her if she was going to finish her potato salad.

"Such an appetite. How is it you are not the fattest of men?" She pushed her plate in his direction. "Save room for pie."

The pie was no challenge, and when there was nothing remaining but the gingham coverlet, Pelham offered Clara the last of the wine, which she graciously declined. "My lady, I am replete and toast you for a most incredible meal. But more importantly, for a most unusual week."

"Hmm. And how am I to take that?"

"In the very best of ways." He winked, enjoying the effect of the wine.

Clara smiled, but then her smile faded. "John, in two days I'll be on the steamer back to Clermont, and you'll forget me. You will, won't you?"

"You underestimate yourself."

She smiled again. "I pray you are right."

The two reclined, neither saying anything for a long minute. Then Clara rolled onto her side and placed a hand on Pelham's chest, fingering one of his uniform buttons. "We've had so little time."

"How much is not important, but the use of it."

"We have had a glorious time, haven't we, John? Tell me more of yourself, more of what it was like to grow up in Alabama."

He laughed. "At this time of year, hot." He rolled over, his face inches from Clara's. "And speaking of hot, do you mind if I unbutton my coat? I seem to have grown."

"Of course not."

As he did, she pressed him. "Tell me more about your family. I still can't get my mind around such a large family."

He smiled and tweaked her nose again, and then described in more or less humorous fashion each member of the family, trying not to repeat what he had already told her.

When he finished, Clara observed, "Your family comes to life in the way you describe them. I should very much like to meet the sister who has six brothers and her sanity. And your grandmother, she was like a second mother to you."

"She was wonderful." He rolled over on his back. "It's hard to believe she's been gone nine years."

"Southern life is so much about family, isn't it? You pull together for everything, and, I think, differently than we do in the North. Your father is amazing. How he can run a plantation and heal the sick, fix bones, and deliver babies is beyond me!"

"True enough, but I think for us, it is the land that is key. There is very little that we can't provide for ourselves from it, and the money we need to take care of the rest comes from the cotton and the other crops we grow." He pulled at the sleeve of her dress. "You, my lady, may be wearing my cotton."

"Do you like the way I wear it?"

"Very much." He found himself staring at her in a way he had not intended. "Anyway, it might surprise you to know that my father's medical practice doesn't bring much income. Most patients pay us in eggs, milk, chickens, a side of beef, a hog, preserves, or a promise to do this or that. It is the cotton that brings us cash."

"I'm embarrassed, but does cotton grow on trees?"

He smiled and said it didn't, and described briefly the nature of the cotton plant, how it was planted, tended, and harvested, and how much labor was needed. He described the problems of bole weevils and killing frosts and the details of the ginning process. "From the gin, it is shipped north to textile mills."

"All of it?"

"I suppose not all of it, but there are precious few mills in the South. Of course, some of the cotton is shipped in bulk direct to Europe."

"By labor, you mean Negro workers?"

He sensed her hesitancy. "Yes."

"Have you many—"

"We have about fifty blacks."

"They are ... slaves?"

"They make up our black family, yes."

"John, I don't mean to pry, and if you don't want me to, I won't ask, but I've never met or even seen a slave. The Negroes I know are like you and me—intelligent. They speak well and have manners."

Pelham thought of Samuel. "That is natural, but I understand that blacks in the North make up less than one percent of the population. In the South, it's more like thirty-five percent."

"Your slaves, John, are treated well?"

"What do you think?"

She smiled. "I knew they would be."

"To understand the South, its culture, and life on a plantation, you need to understand how important the Negro is in our society. I can't picture the South without blacks. The black man, woman, and child are extensions of every plantation family. But understand that everybody on the plantation, white or black, works for the common good. It's not a case of whites sitting back and letting blacks do the work."

She nodded. "I guess all I know is what I read."

"And you've read *Uncle Tom's Cabin*, right?" He took her silence as confirmation. "That book is an affront, Clara, and pure fiction. It paints a very narrow and jaded view." He forced a laugh. "And why wouldn't it? The author is an avowed abolitionist. Its premise is clear, and the book has done more to harm relations between the South and the North than anything William Lloyd Garrison has printed."

"But, John, you can't say some of the blacks aren't mistreated."

"If you are suggesting there are bad people in the South, I grant you that, just like there are in the North. Think of those who run textile mills, who have treated many thousands of children worse than slaves."

Clara dropped her eyes.

Pelham squeezed her hand. "Can we declare a truce?"

She smiled. "John, you are a wonderfully honorable man, more noble and kind than I could ever hope for in a friend."

"My lady, in truth, you hardly know me."

"I do know you," she said firmly. "You're a man of faith and high virtue. It's just that slavery is so—" She stopped herself. "I'm sorry."

"Cruel? That's what you were going to say, isn't it? If you could only see your face." He cupped her chin gently in his hand. "If I wasn't so full, I could eat you up." He sat up and gazed across the Hudson. "This river has seen more slave trading than you or I could ever imagine. Every colony had slaves, though your Pennsylvania gave it up at the outset."

She began to massage his back. "Truce."

But Pelham continued. "Times have changed, and things are different. The industrial revolution has transformed the North, eliminated the need for slaves. But what did the North do with their slaves? Free them? Trust me, precious few were freed. Most were sold at a nice profit. I've no problem with the right of Northern states to abolish slavery. They are sovereign states, and can do as they please. One day Southern states may do so, but it will be a time coming. For now, we are nothing without our blacks."

"I understand, John, I really do. It's just that morally—"

"Morally?" Pelham could not resist interrupting her. "There are nearly four million blacks in the South. They represent our single greatest asset. What comes of us if they are suddenly freed to satisfy someone's sense of morality?"

"The government could pay you for them, like England did."

"We are not England, my lady. Our government doesn't have the money to buy decent horses for the Academy."

Clara picked up the gingham coverlet and waved it. "I surrender."

Pelham couldn't help but smile. "My lady, there are a lot of inequities in this world. But slavery has been around for all of history. And I can tell you that in the South, most Negroes are treated fairly. We know they have souls, and that they are children of God. Owners provide them shelter, clothing, food, medical treatment, all the necessities of life. Some are even paid a stipend to spend upon themselves. Believe me, there are very few Simon Legrees."

"How long do your Negroes work each day?" Clara asked.

"It's not just the blacks, my lady. We all work from before sunup to sundown, Sundays off, except for minor chores. Again, it takes everyone on the plantation working together to keep it going. Most days we all go to bed exhausted."

"Then slaves aren't whipped for the littlest thing?"

"There are exceptions, I'm sure, but whites don't have a corner on laziness. If a black puts in an honest day's work, he should never feel the whip."

"So much for our truce," Clara said apologetically.

"It's all right. Yours are good questions."

"Then please allow me one more. Do you lock them up at night?"

Pelham couldn't resist laughing. "You intend to know it all, don't you? Of course not. A slave who runs away is caught easily enough. But, my lady, please understand that a slave's life isn't what you imagine. They have their own quarters, we respect their privacy, and they have their joys. Come Christmas, most have the entire week off. They celebrate every night and dance till they drop, and Lord, can they dance, and sing too. They enjoy a Christmas feast, no less than our own, and can get passes if they've earned them. If a man has a pass and wants to visit a friend on a neighboring plantation, he can do so."

"You love life in Alabama, don't you?"

"You would too, if you were to visit. A visit would make all the difference. Then you would understand." He watched the ferry pull away from Garrison across the river. "The hill country of Alabama is truly beautiful to behold, and the weather ... Well, it's delightful most of time, except when it's not."

She laughed.

"Yes, Alabama is very special, and it is almost impossible to meet a stranger there. Life is honest. Work is hard, but rewarded, and we know who gives us our daily bread."

Clara responded with an amen, and asked, "Are slaves able to have families?"

"Perhaps not under the law, but they have unions that are respected, have children, and for the most part stay together as families. It seldom benefits an owner to split a family—for obvious reasons. If a family is split, it's normally because an owner has no other choice."

"That would be so sad. Tell me they go to church, that the Negroes are Christian."

"In truth, more so than a lot of white folk. They sing the sweetest gospel songs going to field, working their rows, and coming home at night, beautiful songs, mostly about the Promised Land."

"Your friend, Emory Upton—he only wants the best for them."

Pelham wondered if Upton had gotten to Clara. "Emory has some strong views."

"I am glad you are friends, that you respect each other."

"I'm not so sure how much he respects me, but when he goes on about freeing the slaves, I say nothing more than what I've said to you. How does such a thing happen without destroying the South? And he has yet to give me a rational answer."

"Four million slaves," Clara said it to herself, as though finally grasping the enormity of the problem.

"One day it may be so—slavery abolished everywhere in the country, in the world. In my heart I believe it should be, but how we get there, I cannot begin to know. What I do know is that slavery in the South is not a question of equity. It just is, and always has been."

Clara was ready to leave the subject. "Who was your very best friend growing up?"

"Either Charlie or William, one of my older brothers."

"Brothers don't count."

"Then, I suppose … Samuel."

"What a wonderful Bible name. Tell me about Samuel."

"Samuel is a slave."

Clara didn't hide her astonishment.

"Samuel and I were the same age and inseparable from when I can first remember until we were almost eleven."

"And he was your best friend?"

"That surprises you?"

"Well …"

Pelham told Clara how Samuel and his mother had come to the Pelham plantation when Samuel was five, how Samuel's mother had died within the year, and how Pelham's grandmother had taken Samuel under her wing.

"Ma still talks about Olivette, Samuel's mother, being the most beautiful high yella woman she had ever seen, but so frail. After she died, Samuel lived until just a few years ago with Bones, the skinniest of our blacks. Bones and his woman had no children. Each day, except Sunday, Samuel would report to Grandmother and would be in her charge until the blacks came in from the fields. Pa resisted what he saw as a breech in the social system, but Grandmother prevailed. As a result, Samuel and I were daily companions—thick as thieves." Pelham smiled. "And we had the run of the plantation."

"Those were good times?"

"The best. Anyway, Grandmother became quite attached to Samuel. She intended from the start that he would one day take over Willie's role."

"Willie?"

Pelham told Clara about the black patriarch.

"So, what about Samuel now?"

"He's the field foreman, responsible for all the field workers."

"I think I would like to meet your Samuel."

"You'd be very impressed with him."

"And you two ruled the plantation?"

"My father says we were a handful, from spooking the stock to harassing the field hands. He would tell us to go fishing to keep us out of mischief, and it seemed we fished every day until we were maybe seven, when it was determined I should start school."

"What was school like?"

"I was taught at home. My grandmother was my teacher."

"Your grandmother?"

"She had done a passable job with Charlie and William, and my mother was still raising Bettie and my younger brothers. So I started my lessons to read and write and do numbers. In the beginning, Samuel would wait in the parlor for me to finish. When I was done, we would play or go fishing."

A blast from a steamer startled the two of them, and soon the steamer's huge bow appeared in the turn of the river.

"Anyway, before long, Samuel is repeating to Grandmother things he's heard from the other room and doing so with a white accent—I mean, without any slave dialect."

"Amazing."

"She thought so, and it was then she decided on what I think she knew wasn't right."

"I'm sorry?"

"She decided that Samuel should sit in on my lessons, if we both swore to keep it secret, which we did."

"And that was a mistake?"

"I didn't think so at the time, and I was glad to have someone else for her to pick on. Anyway, Grandmother never failed to tell Samuel how lucky he was, that while he was learning things that I needed to know to make my way in the white world, he would have no worries when he was grown. All he had to do was whatever the family needed done, and if he did, he would be cared for for the rest of his life, and his life would be pleasant enough."

Pelham looked out across the water.

"She taught the two of us for three and a half years, and Samuel proved to be one smart boy. She told him that he was the smartest black boy she had ever known. After our lessons, when we went out to play, Samuel would want to work out problems instead of play."

"That is wonderful!" Clara didn't hide her joy.

"We'd write in the dirt or sometimes on my slate with chalk, but it was safest to write in the dirt, so we could erase the evidence with our feet. One of us would write a word or sentence, and the other would read it and check it for spelling. Samuel was a better speller than I was. We did math problems the same, and I had the edge on him there."

"You weren't afraid of getting caught?"

Pelham smiled. "We weren't afraid of anything."

Clara leaned over and kissed him lightly on the lips. "You were a little stinker, weren't you?"

"I felt Pa's belt often enough," he admitted. "But one day it all changed." There was finality in his words.

"I don't understand."

"The day we played the game."

"The game?" Clara waited for an explanation, but it didn't come. Instead, Pelham started buttoning his coat.

Clara gathered up things in the picnic basket. "I wish I had known your grandmother."

"We really must be good friends. I've never told anyone what I've told you."

"You are so sweet to say so." She kissed him on the cheek.

"My lady, I wish we might never have to leave this place, but if we don't get a move on, I won't get you back in time."

Half an hour later, after a quick peek at Kosciusko's Garden, overgrown and in disrepair, they arrived at the hotel.

At the base of the stairs, Pelham squeezed Clara's hand and gave her a grand bow. "My lady, you have made both me and my stomach exceedingly happy."

CHAPTER TWENTY-FIVE

Clara watched Pelham from inside the doorway as he returned to the encampment. When she turned around, she almost knocked the spectacles from Frampton's nose. The two stared at each other until the stoic assistant dean said, "Clara, would you join me for tea in the parlor?"

"Tea?"

"Or coffee, your preference."

Clara followed Frampton into the parlor, where the two sat at a corner table. Frampton ordered, and the waiter returned with a pot of steaming water and an assortment of teas and small biscuits.

"Earl Grey or Darjeeling?" Frampton asked.

"Earl Grey, please." Clara was more confused than apprehensive.

"You appear to have survived your illness." Frampton's tone was bland. "Sugar?"

"I—"

Frampton waved her off. "You asked me if I had ever seen a man naked."

The assistant dean's words stung Clara. "Miss Frampton, please, I spoke out of turn. You must forgive me."

"When I was your age, perhaps a year younger, I was taken to Europe by my parents. I was an only child. We spent almost three months, from late spring through most of the summer, visiting close acquaintances of my father, who then was a renowned art critic. He and Mother are now deceased."

"I'm sorry, ma'am."

"It was a glorious time in my life. We visited the most incredible sights, and met the most wonderful people in England, France, and Italy. As you might imagine, I saw some of the most exquisite pieces of

167

artwork that Europe had to offer. In Italy, we stayed with the owners of a magnificent chateau near Florence, complete with a small vineyard. My room was in a large turretlike corner on the third floor, and I thought myself a true princess." She paused. "Anyway, the vineyard was cared for by a young man from the village … Oh, I see you are empty. I'm such a poor hostess."

Frampton refilled Clara's cup.

"He would remove his shirt as the day got hotter, and his bronze skin would glisten in the sun as he clipped the plants, and tilled and weeded."

Clara sensed she was hearing something that Miss Frampton had never shared with anyone.

"I watched him, or you might say I spied on him, for nearly a week from my bedroom window. He was more than handsome—and a well-muscled man." She cleared her throat. "He knew I was there, I felt certain, and I thought he was ignoring me, but one day he surprised me. As I looked down upon him, he suddenly turned and looked at me. I felt his eyes. We stared at each other for a long time. Then he cocked his head and gave me the most charming smile, and I smiled back."

Clara couldn't hide the delight she felt in what she was hearing.

"Then, he went back to his vines."

"No! He didn't!" Clara didn't hide her disappointment.

"But the next day, I left the house on the pretense that I needed some help moving a piece of furniture, and would he be so kind. Well, he was … more than kind."

Clara found herself giggling. "He spoke English?"

"Not a word, nor I Italian."

Clara felt her pulse quicken.

"But we had that common language." Frampton glanced out the hotel window.

"Miss Frampton, you little vixen."

"It may be hard for you to believe, Clara, but in those days I was what you would call a looker, and considerably more petite than you see me now. Before the trip, in Baltimore, a prospective lawyer seriously courted me. And there were others who called upon me, though if I were you, I would want proof of my former self."

With that she produced from her purse a photograph wrapped in silk. She handed it to Clara.

"My father had a man by the name of Louis Daguerre take this with his equipment while we were in Paris. His daguerreotype process is now, of course, quite common."

Clara studied the face and the figure of the girl in the image and shook her head. "Miss Frampton, you were indeed a beautiful girl. And, of course—"

"No need for that. Anyway, we were in Italy for almost a month, and the young man, his name was Dino, learned some of my English, and I learned some of his Italian. I don't think a day went by that we didn't see each other . . . all of each other."

Clara gasped and laughed, not believing what she was hearing.

"Some days, I would come to him in the vineyard. Other days I would wave for him to join me in the house, and to my knowledge my parents never suspected a thing. But then ..." Her voice quaked. "It was finally time for us to leave. It was the hardest day of my life. That morning, we pledged our love to each other."

The sparkle that had shone in Frampton's eyes was suddenly gone, and she blew her nose.

"I can't express to you my sense of loss. My parents thought me gravely ill, for I kept nothing down on the trip home. Anyway, I wrote him every week for two months and waited for his first letter."

She stopped and smiled, and seemed to be collecting herself.

"Please, tell me," Clara said.

"It never came." Frampton's voice was not much more than a whisper, and the smile was gone. "I, of course, clung to the hope that it would. I imagined that he'd been hurt, that he'd joined the army, been in a battle, maybe wounded or worse. I even imagined that my parents were intercepting and destroying his letters, which of course they weren't. It never occurred to me until my heart was utterly undone that it was simply over, that we had experienced something temporal, a summer fling."

Frampton managed another smile as she composed herself, and reached for Clara's hand. "All this is to say that I have no desire to kill your joy, Clara. I just don't want to see you hurt."

Her final words caught Clara no less by surprise than had her story. "But, Miss Frampton, you don't understand. You needn't be concerned for me. You see …" she found herself stuttering. "Y-you … are mistaken. We—Cadet Pelham and I are not … that way. We are just friends."

"Of course you are, my dear."

CHAPTER TWENTY-SIX

That night, Pelham struggled to sleep, unwilling to admit that Clara Bolton had undone him. He fought the passions that would kill the platonic, at the same time realizing the emptiness of how things would play out on their current course. Clara Bolton would soon be gone; her smile, her touch, her light, her joy, all that she freely gave him would be gone. And, as she had said, time would pass and memory would fade. Yet he knew one thing with clarity. She had penetrated his shield, she had walked freely in his inmost world—she had unearthed Samuel. When sleep finally came, it brought with it a long dormant memory.

He and Samuel lay side by side beneath a lone oak tree, in the corner of a field not being worked by the blacks. The tree was perfect for shade. The morning lesson with his grandmother had gone easy, and they had just finished lunch. It was the heat of the day, and they were shirtless and barefoot.

He stared vacantly at the gray spidery branches of the oak tree. "I'm bored."

"So, whatcha want to do?" Samuel, content, was half asleep.

"Don't matter, just something different."

"How you mean different?" Samuel opened one eye and squinted at the rays of sun that diffused through the crown of the tree. "S'pose we could swim. I'm boilt alive."

"No, I mean something we ain't never done."

"John, we is ten, almost eleven years old. Ain't nothing we hain't done."

He thought a long moment, and then scrambled to his feet. "I got it, Samuel!"

Samuel didn't answer.

"Wake up, Samuel! I got it. I know what we can do!"

Samuel struggled to his elbows, his eyes bleary. "Huh?"

"You ever want to know what it's like to be somebody else?"

Samuel rubbed his eyes. "I already been a sheriff, a Injun, a knight, a musketeer, a preacher—"

"That's not what I mean. I mean for real."

"I don't get you."

"Let's you and me switch." He was beside himself with the idea.

"Switch what?"

"You be me."

"You?"

"Yeah, you be white and I be black."

"You want to be black?"

"It's just a game, Samuel. Then I can know what it's like bein' you, and you can know what it's like bein' me." His chest expanded with the energy of the thought.

"I don't get it. How do I play white?"

"You make me do stuff."

"What stuff?"

He was ahead of Samuel, and pointed to the nearby rows of nearly ripe cotton. "Pick cotton."

"You want to pick cotton?"

"I never tried."

"Believe me, you don't want to pick cotton."

"Samuel, it's just a game, but first we need …" He rubbed his chin. "Wait here." A minute later, he returned from nearby Cane Creek with a willow switch. "You got to have a whip."

Samuel looked at the willow branch as if it were a poisonous snake.

"Take it, Samuel."

Samuel backed away. "I—I don't want it."

"Just take it, Samuel. It's just a game. Then we can play whatever you want."

Samuel shook his head, but finally took the willow switch.

"I ain't gonna whip you, John."

"What, it was okay to give me a black eye last week?"

"That was fair and fair, an even fight and you know it."

"Relax, Samuel, this ain't no different. Nothing more than a game."

He led Samuel to the edge of the cotton field and began to pick cotton boles, stuffing them in his pockets. The sun beat down mercilessly, and after only a few minutes, sweat streamed from his chin. "You're right, Samuel, this is harder than it looks."

"Don't recall anybody saying it was easy."

He continued to pick until Samuel noticed a plant that still had some boles on it. "You got some left on that one."

He saw his mistake. "Damn, you're right, Samuel. Now you got to whip me."

"What for?"

"Because that's the way it works. I missed that cotton and you caught me."

"I ain't gonna whip you, John."

He had already prostrated himself on the ground, and mumbled into the dirt, "Samuel, it's just a game. Do it."

"I don't like this game." Samuel's voice trembled.

"Just do it, Samuel. Then we can play something else."

Samuel was silent, motionless.

"Do it, Samuel, this dirt is hot!"

He felt the willow switch barely graze his back. "What was that, Samuel? You got to really do it, or it don't count."

He was surprised when he felt a sharp sting, and had to bite his lip to keep quiet. "That's it, Samuel. Four more and we're done."

Samuel raised the switch, but before he could bring it down a second time, a man galloped up on horseback.

"Samuel, you stop that! Stop it, Samuel!" shouted the man.

Samuel dropped the switch and without even a glance at the rider, ran as fast as his spindly legs would carry him in the direction of the plantation house.

The man jerked his horse to a dead stop. "John, what in God's creation is this all about?"

He scrambled to his feet, his head down. "Nothin', Pa."

"You call this nothing!"

"It was just a game, Pa."

His father dismounted and shook him by the shoulders. "Did I not just see Samuel, a black boy, whipping you? A black boy whipping a white boy?"

"It was part of the game, Pa. He weren't gonna hurt me. He didn't want to do it nohow. It was me that told him he had to."

"You? Son, why would you do that?"

"I don't know, Pa." He looked up at his father. "You gonna give me the belt, Pa?"

Later, after he had felt the belt as he'd never felt it before, he lay on his bed in his room. Charlie and William had come to visit and wanted to know what he had done. He lied and said he had spooked cows through the best of the cotton. Come suppertime, when he was told he could come down to eat, he found his grandmother crying in the parlor.

She didn't look at him. "You get along to supper."

There was a pall over supper, and after they finished eating his father took him outside on the porch. "I want you to tell me one more time how this all came about."

He explained the game again, that it was his idea, and that Samuel wanted no part of it.

"Son, do you not know how thoughtless you were? Don't you understand the way it is?" His father grasped him by the shoulders. "You don't ever make light of the relationship between whites and blacks—not ever! You understand me?"

"Yes, sir." He quavered in his father's grip.

"Think what you've done to poor Samuel, how the boy must feel."

"Yes, Pa."

"You hitch up the buggy. I need to get to the Williams house for Miss Beatrice."

"Yes, Pa."

The next day, when he took his lessons with his grandmother, she looked pale and worn. He thought her sick, and he didn't see Samuel all morning.

That afternoon, Willie asked him to come outside on the back porch, and when he got there, Samuel was already sitting at the table.

The black man sat across from them.

"Master John, what do you see on this table?"

He looked at the table. "Nothing."

"Oh yes, there is. What is it, Samuel?"

"De salt and de pepper shaker," Samuel replied in the slave dialect he always used when he wasn't alone with his friend.

"Exactly so," Willie said. "Master John, is what is in the two shakers the same?"

"No, sir,"

"Samuel, I ask you the same."

"No'em. One gots salt, de other pepper."

"Exactly so. Master John, why do you suppose that both shakers are always on the table?"

"To season our food."

"Exactly so, again. To make the food taste just right. But they are different, salt and pepper, ain't they? Yet being different, they are good together, ain't they?"

Both he and Samuel nodded.

"Master John, are you mad because Samuel ain't white like you?"

He said nothing.

"And Samuel, are you mad because you're black and not white?"

Samuel said nothing.

"Don't appear to me to be so. You two are having the time of your life." Willie smiled. "And that's a good thing. And both of you know how life is, don't you?"

There was silence again.

"Ain't right for you and me to question how God set all this up. No sir. We are each born to be either salt or pepper, different but both pleasing in his sight."

Samuel stared at the porch deck.

"Look at me, Samuel. Ain't no easier being salt than pepper. You ever see the good doctor or any of the Pelham family lazing around this place?"

Samuel shook his head.

"The light in the big house is on long after you and me are asleep, ain't that so? The doctor and Master John's momma got powerful stress over how to make all this keep goin', keep us in food and clothes and everything else. And all them in the Pelham family got to go to school and learn them words and numbers that are such a mystery to me."

Samuel lowered his head.

Willie picked up the salt shaker in his right hand. "The Pelhams are the best salt there is, and I believe that to be a gospel fact." He picked up the pepper shaker in his left hand. "And this pepper shaker is all us in the colored family, with plenty enough to keep us busy and pleasing to our maker. Ain't he made us special to work the fields, to take that hot sun and work til dark, to put in and take out the crops year after year? Look at me, boy!"

Samuel raised his eyes.

"Ain't no shame being pepper, Samuel. You understand me?"

Samuel nodded weakly.

"Without both the salt and pepper, things around here would fall apart pretty quick. That's a fact."

Willie turned to Pelham. "As for you, Master John, ain't never going to be easy being salt, so much gonna be on your shoulders, but I expect you know that."

He nodded as if he did.

"Now all that being said, there is no reason the two of you can't forever be the best of friends as you work out your part in God's plan. You just got to respect his plan." Willie stood up and reached out to the two boys, taking them in his arms. "Now you go out and play, and don't pick any more of that cotton. It ain't ripe yet."

Chapter Twenty-Seven

Friday morning at breakfast, Nate Chambliss, Adelbert Ames, and Chas Patterson made a point of thanking Pelham for the matches he had made—they had all stuck. Chambliss had taken Jessica Danford on Flirtation Walk twice. Ames had taken Rebecca Astor once, but secured an invitation to visit her in the city if he could get leave.

"So how is it with you and Clara?" Patterson asked Pelham as they left the mess hall.

"Couldn't be better," Pelham lied.

"As it should be, for the man who would be king."

"Just let me graduate, Chas."

An hour later, Pelham, Kirby, Upton, and twelve cadets from junior classes sat on wooden benches in the natural amphitheater below the bluff. Lieutenant Oliver Howard, an 1854 graduate who had experienced a profound conversion while serving in Florida, one that had nearly led him into the ministry, stood before them and turned to a verse in his large black leather-bound Bible.

"So what then are we to think when the Apostle Paul says to the Church in Rome, 'For all have sinned and fall short of the Glory of God'?"

"That none, save Christ himself, can live a life without sin," Upton said with his head bowed.

"Do we believe it? In all of history, not one person?"

"I don't see how anyone honest with himself could think otherwise," Pelham offered.

"So you are with us, Mr. Pelham." Howard voiced surprise. "I thought you distracted."

"Sorry, sir." Pelham smiled sheepishly. "As for sin, God created us in his image and gave us free will, freedom of choice, and with this freedom, I for one tend to seek my own interests, which I suspect aren't always, or even ever, his."

Howard nodded. "And so we thank God for his grace, for his unmerited favor, and for the gift of his son, that through his blood we have forgiveness of sins and are co-heirs of the kingdom."

A breeze off the Hudson rustled the leaves of trees.

"And, of course, we can't seem to stop sinning, can we?" Howard continued. "We live in a world of sin, constantly tempted by Satan and subject daily to trials and temptations. So is this person, Satan, still alive today?"

"Alive and well, it would seem," Kirby said.

"An example?"

"The existence of slavery," Upton offered without hesitation.

"Slavery is the work of Satan?" Howard pressed. Though an abolitionist, he was silent on the subject with cadets.

"Absolutely. I believe Satan begets this worst of evils."

"Are we in agreement?" Howard anticipated a response from at least one of the cotton state cadets.

Charlie Ball was the one to reply. "We are not, sir, and to suggest it is so is unbiblical and condemning of the South, if not the whole country. Slavery existed before, during, and after the time of Christ, and to my knowledge Christ never said, 'Thou shalt not have slaves.' Slavery is a condition of society and foundational to the Union, certainly to the South." Ball eyed Upton, whose head was again bowed. "Whatever it is, it is man's doing, not Satan's, and were it not to exist, how many unsaved blacks would have been enslaved or butchered in Africa?"

"So the end justifies the means?" Howard let the question hang in the air.

Pelham took up the defense. "In the South, sir, slavery is a fact of life. There, they at least have Christ and their souls are saved for eternity."

Howard looked to Upton, who remained silent.

"Well then, let's widen the scope. What other tactics does the enemy use against the faithful and the undecided? What else confounds our faith and seeks to separate us from the love and peace of God?"

Henry Farley, a redheaded South Carolinian and a Third Classman in Pelham's company, raised his hand. "He pits us against one another, just as now demonstrated, and ... sir, it has troubled me greatly since last year when we studied world history, when we learned how Protestants and Catholics for centuries have killed each other in the name of Christ. How does God deal with that?"

"Now that is a question, isn't it? And I'm afraid I don't have the answer any more than you do. But it is, indeed, one of Satan's chief tactics, to take us from grace and truth into his realm of legalism, which ferments all manner of self-righteous pride as to what religion should look like, trivializing the all important 'who' and 'why' of faith."

Howard placed a finger on his Bible. "Is there any mention in this book of the people we call Protestants or Catholics? Is there any mention of Lutherans, Presbyterians, Baptists, or Methodists?"

They all shook their heads.

"It is man's doing, with encouragement from our one true enemy, and it divides us, divides his church."

Howard glanced at his watch.

"Our time is up. Let us pray to the God of the universe. Let us ask him for wisdom to discern that which is of his kingdom and that which is of the world. Let us pray for grace, that while we live in the world we would follow kingdom rules, and that we would allow the Holy Spirit to work through us and make us salt and light to the lost. Mr. Kirby, if you would start us, I will conclude. And as we depart, Mr. Pelham, please lead us in the singing of the first two verses of 'Amazing Grace.'"

In the stillness of the morning, after each person had offered prayer, the group departed and followed Pelham's lead, singing, "'Amazing Grace, how sweet the sound ...'" They continued singing the hymn as they made their way up to the Plain.

After the hymn, Emory Upton came alongside Pelham. "I don't know about your Charlie Ball."

"Charlie's fine, Emory. He just doesn't think like you."

"You are both Alabamians, John, but so different.

"How do you mean?"

"Your heart is not behind slavery. You told me so yourself."

"Emory, your hearing is selective. I agree that it is a most unfortunate institution, but that doesn't change its reality. I don't see it ending in our lifetime."

"John, save for pigment, Negroes are no different from you or me. Slavery is the sum of all evils, worse than stealing, the same as killing, rendering children of God hopeless and helpless."

Pelham knew better than to argue with Upton. "Emory, there are fruits of the spirit, aren't there?"

"Of course."

"Is one of them patience?"

Upton didn't respond.

"You've got to allow time for change. Your zeal is a two-edged sword. If you're not less judgmental, no one will listen to you or take you seriously. And what is this beef with du Pont?"

Upton was surprised by the question. "That's between Henry and me."

"Henry is a prince, Emory, the best of men. And he works like a dog for our class and the Corps. Attacking him does you no good."

Upton looked at Pelham, but said nothing. Instead, he quick-timed up the hill.

Kirby took his place. "It truly amazes me how you and Upton get along."

"The man means well."

Pelham and Kirby continued up the hill, unaware they were being watched from the third floor of the hotel.

At the window, Clara stood in her sleeping gown. Ellie was still in bed.

"For the last time, Clara, what's going on?"

Clara had heard the singing and had opened the window. She had watched Pelham, Upton, Kirby, and the others walking up the hill.

"John was leading the hymn. Wasn't it beautiful?"

"Did you see Henry?"

"I don't think so." Clara returned to bed and crawled in beside Ellie. "Ellie, we've just one more night, and then we're gone." Her tone was momentarily morose. "But hasn't it been grand and everything we could have hoped for?"

"Much more," Ellie said dreamily. "I may one day visit Delaware. Henry has invited me to his home. How about you? Does John know how you really feel?"

The setting on the Plain was unlike any Pelham had seen before. He had given Williams permission to run the course the second hour of the morning, and the entire Second Class had turned out for him, lining both sides of the obstacle course. Custer had escorted him from the stable.

"How do you feel, Ron?" Pelham asked upon his arrival.

"Scared."

"Nothing wrong with that. Take a warm-up lap and let me know how you feel. We're not going to do this unless you're ready."

"I want to get it over with, sir."

"No sirs today."

William forced a smile and kicked his horse into a trot, and then a gallop.

Rosser joined Custer and Pelham. "He should still be in the hospital. He's white as milk. I'd be surprised if he makes one decent run."

Custer surveyed the crowd. "And all this attention doesn't help."

Upon his return, Williams said he was ready, and Pelham dispatched Rosser to the midpoint of the course and Custer to the finish line.

"You're sure?"

Williams nodded, beads of sweat on his forehead.

"Look around, Ron. These guys are going to kick your ass if you let them down."

Pelham signaled Custer, who in turn raised his hand.

When Custer dropped his hand, Williams kicked up a cloud of dust and was quickly at a gallop. He easily cleared the first jump, his form good, and was soon upon the second jump. Pelham held his breath as Williams's horse pushed off his back legs into the air. The sound of the horse's hind legs hitting the crossbar echoed across the Plain, and with it came the collective groan of a hundred spectators. Williams returned to the starting point, his eyes locked on Pelham.

"I'm done, John. I just can't make the four-foot jump. I think I'm going to throw up."

They were joined by Rosser and Custer.

"Fannie, tell your classmates not to go anywhere. I'm taking Williams."

"Gotcha, boss." Custer rendered a casual salute.

Pelham led Williams into a stand of trees at the eastern perimeter of the encampment. Ten minutes later, they reemerged.

Upon their return, the number of spectators along the course had grown. Pelham directed Rosser and Custer back to their stations.

Custer again dropped his arm, and Williams began his second run, clearing the first jump in perfect alignment for the second. As the horse's front legs left the ground for the second jump, it was as if the whole of West Point had stopped breathing, every eye on the crossbar. When the front legs and then the back legs of the horse touched the ground and the bar was still in place, the Plain shook with cheers. Williams was again at a gallop, easily clearing the third jump and drawing his saber. He leaned forward over the horse's mane and delivered a deathblow to the hapless dummy; and then sprinted past Custer and the finish line.

Every eye was on Custer, whose hand shot up in the air, triggering jubilation across the Plain.

Pelham was quickly to Williams's side. "You did it, Ron!"

The Second Classman returned a disoriented look and slid off his horse to one knee.

"Drink this." Pelham gave his canteen to Williams.

Barely had Williams taken a few swallows, when he was swarmed by his classmates and hoisted on their shoulders.

"Well done, Ron! Damn fine work," Custer shouted. "Thanks to you, I am a poor man, but a small price to pay for a miracle."

Custer ceremoniously tossed a five-dollar gold piece in the air, which Pelham caught with an appreciative nod.

Rosser slapped Custer on the back, nearly unseating him.

Pelham drew his saber and held it high for attention. "To the Class of 1862, I salute you. You are indeed a proud bunch, with reason to be. Ron Williams is but an example! You are now all fair game for the fall jump masters. Good luck to you."

With that, he, Rosser, and Custer headed for the stables.

"So what happened with you and Williams?" Custer asked. "He was a different man that second run."

"Same man." Pelham cocked his head. "Different horse."

"You switched mounts?"

"I told Williams that Old Red had never touched a crossbar, and that's why I rode him. I told him to sit back and let Old Red do the work."

"Is it true?" Custer asked.

Pelham gave Custer a wink." Of course not."

Rosser couldn't contain himself. "So, Fannie, are you going to the hop, tonight?"

"Hell, why not? The way I'm hiding in my tent, the guys are starting to talk."

"Indeed, and we've all missed your dashing presence," said Pelham, tongue-in-cheek.

"I'll ask Carol Hill if she'll toss you a crumb," Rosser said. "Though, frankly, she has better taste."

"Done!" Custer announced, his spirits improved. "And you, John, may I expect a crumb from your table—a twirl with your Clara?"

"If she isn't already promised, for she doesn't lack suitors."

"So I've heard." Custer kicked his horse to a gallop.

CHAPTER TWENTY-EIGHT

Ten minutes before the final hop of the week, Clara waited for Pelham on the hotel veranda. She saw him coming from the encampment and met him at the foot of the stairs.

"Do you mind if we walk a while?" She took his arm.

"Of course not. How was your day?"

"Fine. I took Ellie down to the river, to Flirtation Walk. We broke your regulations." She gave him a defiant look. "Henry was going to take her, but your commandant gave him a job." She giggled. "I showed her Kissing Rock. She so did want to see it. Henry missed his chance."

"I'll have to tell him."

"Don't you dare!"

"Maybe he can make up for it."

"I think he should."

Pelham led her to the rear of the hotel, behind a flowered trellis that afforded a measure of privacy.

He sniffed the air. "Your perfume is different."

"It's Eva Taylor's. Do you like it?"

"Indeed." He squeezed her hand. "My lady, until now you have had free rein to kiss my cheek. I wondered if such license extended both ways."

Clara couldn't suppress a giggle. "It might."

He leaned forward and brushed her cheek with his lips, and she freely turned her other cheek.

"That was very nice," she said, a dreaminess in her eyes. "But I think I'm better at it." She stood on tiptoes and delicately kissed him on both cheeks, finishing with a feathery kiss to the lips.

"Yes," he agreed. "Infinitely better."

She removed her shawl, revealing bared shoulders and, for the first time, a hint of cleavage. "Do you like my dress?"

Pelham endeavored not to stare. "Indeed, though I fear you will attract much attention."

She took his arm. "I suppose we had better make an appearance."

When they reached the hotel steps, she turned. "John, I have had the most wonderful week, the best week of my life to be truthful, and I know tomorrow is coming. I will miss you, John. I will miss my dearest friend. But tonight, let us have the most incredible time of our lives."

"We shall," he promised.

She showed him her hop card. "I've saved all the waltzes for us."

"Have you a free dance for a friend, George Custer?"

"Of course." She penciled him in. "And, John, I had hoped we might have some time to ourselves at the end of the evening."

"Block out the last three dances."

"Done." She smiled and pointed an accusing finger. "You watch out for that Becky Thompson. She definitely has eyes for you."

After ringing the dance bell, Charlie Hazlett set the stage for the evening by announcing the obvious, that it was the last hop of the week and that everyone should make the most of it, since nearly all of the ladies would be leaving the next day. He winked at Pelham.

The first dance, as always, was a waltz, and Pelham and Clara glided across the floor as though lifelong partners. There wasn't a couple on the floor that didn't envy the grace of the cadet from Alabama and the woman from Philadelphia. After the dance, Pelham handed Clara off to Emory Upton.

Clara's third dance was with Nate Chambliss. Chas Patterson had the fourth, and her partner for the fifth dance was Ron Williams, who later met Pelham at the punch bowl.

Pelham gave Williams a playful thump on the shoulder. "You think because you can ride a horse, you can steal my girl?"

Williams smiled. "I want to thank you again, John."

"Nonsense. And by the way, you looked good on the dance floor."

"Miss Bolton is a very special woman."

The band was in rare form and high spirits, and it was not until they had taken a short break that Custer got his turn with Clara.

185

After the dance, Custer confronted Pelham. "Did you tell Clara Bolton I bite?"

Pelham smiled. "Fannie, she had to know."

Custer was unamused. "It is hard to be dashing when one is so thoroughly dashed."

When the music started for the next dance, Pelham was paired with Eva Taylor. He informed her that she had captured Walter's heart.

"And he mine, though sadly, I must break one in Kentucky."

Pelham smiled. "I feel sorry for the man."

"Excuse my boldness, John, but I think you are making a mistake with Clara."

"How so?"

"You should be more than friends." She gave him a discerning look. "At least, that's my opinion."

"You have talked to her?"

"Not in so many words."

"Clara and I are close," Pelham said, hoping to draw more out of her.

"That may be well and good, and if you are happy being ... friends, so be it. And if you are, I know the girl you must meet."

"You know me that well?"

"I have eyes," she said in a teasing tone.

"And are a matchmaker?"

Eva cocked her head, as though sizing him up. "You, John Pelham, are an uncommon spirit. You need a kindred spirit, one with comparable energy."

Pelham wanted to say that Clara Bolton fitted that mold, but settled for a nod.

"My friend is at least your equal," Eva said as the dance came to an end. "She and I roomed together two years at William and Mary." She smiled over Pelham's shoulder at Clara and Adelbert Ames, who joined them at the edge of the dance floor.

"Clara, Adelbert." Eva extended her gloved hand. Ames pressed it to his lips, and then left in search of Rebecca Astor.

"Clara, you are the queen of the ball," Eva said. "And I must have that dress. I was telling John about a friend of mine, that he would like her. I know he would, and she's more than pretty. Her name is Sallie Dandridge of the Virginia Dandridges."

Clara's face was devoid of emotion. "And how would you propose John meet this girl?"

"Just leave that to me, Clara. I know that Sallie and John would have chemistry. I am quite sure of it. They would be more than friends, or nothing at all."

"Eva, you are too kind." Clara's tone was gracious. "I'm sure John will want to take you up on the offer."

Pelham mumbled something inane.

Eva smiled. "I will first write Sallie and make sure she is not otherwise engaged."

Walter Kingsbury came up behind Eva and tapped her on the shoulder. "Shall we, my rose?"

As they turned to the dance floor, Eva added, "If Sallie's not engaged, I'll get you her address."

As the evening progressed, Hazlett, to heighten everyone's sense of urgency, announced the declining number of dances. When he announced but three left, Pelham caught Clara's eye, and the two met at the refreshment table. Pelham poured them each a cup of punch.

"I see the chaperones have switched posts." Frampton was at the door.

Clara said nothing.

"You are unusually quiet, my lady."

She took a sip and let the cup linger at her lips. "It is almost over, John, our time together."

Pelham was about to agree, when his jaw dropped. "I don't believe it."

"But it's true."

"No, I mean Miss Frampton. She's smiling."

Clara turned, and indeed, the assistant dean was smiling. Clara waved at Frampton, and Frampton waved back. "She's full of surprises," Clara said.

"Or has been nipping at something."

"Follow me," Clara said, and the two of them proceeded unmolested past Frampton, who nearly floored Pelham with a cordial nod.

187

Moments later, they were on the rear veranda, gazing at another starry night sky, the moon dancing off the Hudson.

Clara squeezed Pelham's hand. "A penny for your thoughts."

"It will cost you more than that."

She slipped something into his hand. "Don't look. Just put it in your pocket."

He did, and before he could say anything, Clara put a finger on his lips. "Don't say a word." After a few seconds, she took both of his hands. "John?"

"My lady?"

"I want you to kiss me."

"My pleasure." He leaned forward to kiss her cheek, but she pushed him back.

"No, John. I want you to kiss me as if ..."

"As if what?"

"As if we were ... more than friends. As if you found me attractive."

"Attractive?"

She tilted her head.

"Are you sure?"

"Kiss me."

Pelham took Clara in his arms and drew her to him, feeling her bosom compress against his chest, her breath tickle his nose, and tasting the sweetness of her mouth. He lifted her chin, and in the darkness explored the margins of her mouth.

Clara gave herself willingly. Her tongue greeted his, and together they played at hide and seek. With scarcely a pause for breath, they made up for time played at friendship.

Then, locked in Clara's arms, Pelham heard boots on the veranda.

"Attention, soldier!"

The voice was deep and commanding, and Pelham prayed for a prankster.

A man's face appeared in the moonlight.

"Sir!" Pelham stood apart from Clara and snapped to attention.

Lieutenant Colonel Hardee emerged fully from the shadow. "Is that you, Mr. Pelham?"

Pelham fumbled for a response.

"Mr. Pelham, are you in the habit of not saluting a superior officer?"

"No, sir." Pelham immediately rendered a sharp salute.

Hardee returned the salute. "Would you mind following me, Mr. Pelham?"

Clara caught Pelham's ashen face as he turned and followed the commandant.

Around the corner of the veranda, Clara heard muffled voices, footsteps, and then nothing. Seconds later, she heard footsteps again, and a man in uniform appeared and identified himself as the aide to the commandant.

"Ma'am, I am truly sorry, but Cadet Pelham will not be able to accompany you for the balance of the evening."

CHAPTER TWENTY-NINE

Saturday morning, Pelham awoke to the humiliation of the night before, his malaise heightened by the certainty of discipline and a thick fog that had ascended off the Hudson. Rosser did his best to steer free of his roommate's transgression, and said not a word to Pelham through reveille and the march over to the mess hall.

At breakfast, word of Pelham's fall from grace quickly spread through the Corps. In addition to Rosser's attempts at consolation, du Pont, Chambliss, Ames, Patterson, Upton, and Custer took turns trying to lift his spirits. Chambliss offered to intercede with the commandant, but Pelham declined, insisting that he not receive special treatment. The only other person in the Corps more distraught than himself was Walter Kingsbury, whose lamentations over Eva Taylor's departure later that morning rendered him incapable of being consoled or giving consolation.

After breakfast, Rosser returned to the encampment to find Kirby emerging from the tent occupied by him and Pelham.

"What's it to be, Ned?"

"The formal charge is gross public display of affection. Thankfully, Hardee chose not to report him for failure to render respect to a superior officer. He gets confinement to quarters until the end of encampment and reduction to the grade of cadet private."

"That's tough, but like you say, he could have been dismissed for disrespect. How did he take it?"

"Hard to say."

"When does it start?"

"Immediately."

Rosser raised the flap to the tent and found Pelham sitting on his footlocker. "Ned filled me in."

Pelham cradled something in his hand.

"What's that?"

He handed Rosser a locket attached to a delicate gold chain.

Rosser opened the locket. Inside was a photograph of Clara. "My friend, she truly is beautiful."

For the next fifteen minutes, he and Pelham scurried about the tent in silence, preparing for Saturday morning inspection, the most rigorous inspection of the week, which would be conducted by both Lieutenant Lee and Lieutenant Colonel Hardee.

Rosser suddenly tossed his hands in the air. "Damn, I can't believe I forgot. I've got to take care of something. Look after my side."

Before Pelham could object, Rosser was gone.

Rosser sprinted up the tree-lined path to the hotel, taking the hotel steps three at a time. He found a young bellboy in the lobby. "You have a guest here, Miss Clara Bolton—do you know her?"

Joseph snapped to attention. "Yes, sir."

"Would you tell her John Pelham is waiting for her in the parlor? It's urgent."

"Yes, sir, Mr. Pelham." Joseph bolted up the stairs.

Two minutes later, Clara appeared, her face radiant. "Hello, Tom." She glanced about. "Where's John?"

"He's not here, Clara. Let's go in the parlor."

"I don't understand." Clara wrung her hands, while Rosser led her to a settee.

"It's about John, Clara."

"He is all right, isn't he?"

"He's fine, but confined to quarters until the end of encampment."

"Oh, Tom, that's dreadful and all my fault." She shook her head despondently. "It's all my fault."

"Don't blame yourself, and trust me, he'll survive."

She gave him a pleading look. "He'll be able to see me off at the dock, won't he?"

"I'm sorry, Clara. That's not possible."

"Oh, Tom, what have I done?"

"I wish there was something I could say."

"I can't leave without seeing him. I must see him." Her tone was desperate.

"Clara, it's not possible. He can't leave the encampment. If he attempts anything else … well, you'd then be able to see him all you want."

"Oh, Tom, this is awful."

"I can take him a note. He would like that. But it must be short. I have to get back before inspection."

Clara's expression became stern. "I will see him, Tom, if only for a minute."

"Clara, you don't understand."

"No, Tom. You do not understand!" She stood up, her hands on her hips. "You must take me to him."

"Me?"

"You heard me, Tom." Her voice was sharp as glass.

"You can't be serious. The encampment is under guard. There is no way to get in or out unless you're a cadet or an officer."

"I will see him, Tom." Clara's tone was unyielding. "With or without your help. Just tell me which tent he's in."

"God in heaven, you can't be serious, Clara. You can't just waltz into the encampment."

She crossed her arms. "I will see him."

Rosser glanced out the parlor window. The encampment was still obscured by fog. "You're going to do this?"

"With or without your help."

"No matter what I say?"

"I can't leave without seeing him, Tom."

Rosser stifled an expletive. "Stand up. Now, turn sideways."

"What?"

"Let me see your profile."

Clara turned.

"You're five-five?"

"Five-four."

"This is insane. No, worse. Crazy, brainless, stupid—stupid—stupid." Rosser's mind raced. "When I was a plebe, a First Classman snuck a girl into the barracks. But that was during graduation week."

"Yes, Tom." Clara was unable to hide her excitement.

"And it was at night. This would be in daylight in front of God and country."

"I'm willing, Tom. Anything."

"But there is fog, and it might last."

"Yes, yes, anything!"

"If the fog persists, I'll be back in forty minutes, after inspection. We can only do this if there is fog. Can you be very uncomfortable for an hour?"

"How do you mean?"

"No time to explain. The bellboy, do you trust him?"

"With my life."

"I'll come to the back of the hotel. Have him meet me."

"I will." She hugged Rosser. "God bless you."

"Clara, this is insane. You need to know that. The chances are better I'll join John in confinement than you getting to see him. Do you understand?"

"I do," she said. "And thank you."

Pelham and Rosser survived inspection with only a demerit apiece, due in no small part to the confounding mist that still enveloped the encampment. Pelham wasn't surprised that nothing in Lieutenant Colonel Hardee's demeanor or actions reflected his indiscretion the night before. He had broken regulations and would serve his punishment, and that would be the end of it.

After inspection, Rosser abandoned Pelham in search of Doug Woodridge, the smallest man in the class. Minutes later he was en route to the hotel with a carpetbag. He found Joseph waiting at the back steps. Ten minutes later, Joseph appeared with Clara. She was dressed in a cadet uniform—white trousers tight across her hips, gray dress coat with gold buttons tight across her chest, and a forage cap that sat high upon her head.

She descended the stairs and crossed the lawn in a pair of black shoes, attempting to walk like a man.

Rosser couldn't help but smile. "Well, just look at you." He reached in his pocket and produced a nickel for the bellboy, but Joseph shook his head.

"No, thank you, sir. I do this freely and with the highest regard for Miss Bolton." He turned to Clara. "Good luck, ma'am."

The cadet impersonator kissed the boy on the forehead and ruffled his hair. "Thank you, Joe. If only you were a little older."

The boy beamed and was gone.

"Cadet Bolton, reporting for duty, sir." Clara attempted gruffness.

Rosser pressed the forage cap down on her head. "You know, this just might work. The fog is incredible, but we've no time to waste."

He led Clara to the northwest corner of the Fort Clinton parapet, and then south along its west side. Nearing the southwest corner of the fort, he warned her of the sentry they would encounter and pulled her behind an elm tree. From the corner parapet, they could almost make out the nearest of the A Company tents.

"When the guard passes, we move. Once in camp, look like you own the place. Understand?"

Clara nodded as she peered into the thick mist. She smiled despite the blisters forming on her feet.

"Are you wearing perfume?"

She dropped her eyes. "Sorry."

"We'll make our way between the tents and cross each company street until we get to D Company." He saw the fear in Clara's face. "Are you okay?"

She returned a weak smile.

"You're doing fine."

The sentry came and went, and Rosser made his move.

The two crossed the encampment perimeter to the first row of A Company's tents. They walked at an even pace, Rosser carrying on a meaningless conversation. He kept an eye on Clara, and was pleased with her relaxed manner and acquired swagger. Together, they sauntered through the heart of the encampment, the mist still holding.

Clara suddenly clutched Rosser's arm, shielding her eyes. "Tom, that man is relieving himself."

Rosser couldn't resist a chuckle.

In less than a minute they reached the first row of D Company tents.

"That's us." Rosser pointed straight ahead.

"He knows I'm coming?"

"No, he doesn't."

"You didn't tell him?"

"I didn't think we'd make it."

"Bless you, Tom." She surprised Rosser with a kiss.

A moment later, she slipped soundlessly under the rear flap of the tent, and found Pelham sitting on a locker. He was wearing white trousers and an undershirt, and was reading a book.

"Care for company?"

Pelham whirled at her voice.

She stood trembling, tears streaming down her face.

Pelham shook his head as Clara raised a pitiful salute, and then was upon her with kisses. "God, this cannot be happening," he said. "Don't let me wake up."

Rosser cleared his throat at the front of the tent. "Two minutes, you two. Then it's back to the hotel."

"You listen to me," Clara said. "I love you, John Pelham."

Pelham laughed, his eyes moist. He drew her close, squeezing the breath from her. He lifted her off the ground and swung her side to side, and in the process shook the forage cap from her head, revealing hair tightly braided and pinned.

"You did this for me?"

She flashed a sheepish grin. "John, I'm so sorry." She hugged him, the buttons on her coat digging into his chest. "I've ruined it for you, for us."

"You have no idea what you've done," he announced joyfully. "You've resurrected my life, given me a memory to feed on forever. You are incredible, my lady!"

"Hold it down in there," Rosser cautioned.

Pelham shook his head. "Clara, I can't believe you're here."

"I wouldn't be, if weren't for your amazingly dear friend."

Pelham kissed her a dozen times more, until she drew back. "John Pelham." Her tone was deadly serious. "You are not to listen to Eva

Taylor. I don't know who this Sallie Dandridge is, but I don't want you with her or anyone else."

"Is that so?" Pelham squeezed her even tighter.

"I don't want to be your friend—or even your best friend. I don't know what I was thinking." She took his face in her hands and smothered him with kisses. "John, I want to be your girlfriend, a real girlfriend, the way God intended me to be."

"Hey, Romeo." Rosser's voice was terse. "Wrap it up."

"Tom," Pelham replied joyfully. "There most certainly is a God, and you, blessed brother, are his divine instrument. A moment more."

He turned back to Clara. "Truly, this is answered prayer." He kissed the tip of her nose, then the full of her mouth, all the while his hand exploring her uniform.

"John, my heart beats only for you." She took his hand and pressed it to her breast.

"God, you are so very beautiful." He pulled her hard against himself.

She smiled an impish smile.

"Time's up, John." Rosser's tone was insistent.

"Dr. Bolton." Pelham kissed Clara's ear. "You have changed my life and stolen my heart."

The delight in Clara's face suddenly melted to apprehension. "John, what are we to do?"

"Whatever we must. Our timing is the worst, and it won't be easy. We'll have to discover each other from a distance. By letters, we'll know each other fully. I will live for yours and you for mine. I'll pray for you and you for me. Each night I'll dream of you and you of me, of this day, and of a day that will be."

"And when will that be? How long?"

Pelham hesitated. "I'm afraid it will be a long time from now."

"When?"

"Graduation."

"But that is next June!"

"I know."

"John, that's ten months."

"We have no choice. Will you come to graduation?"

"I will live for it."

Rosser kicked the tent post. "Dammit, John, the sun is burning through."

"I do love you, John Pelham from Alabama, and I'm not asking you to say you love me. Not until you are ready."

Pelham smiled. "You do know me, don't you?"

She fitted the forage cap on her head. "John, let me write the first letter. Will you do that? As soon as I get to Clermont, I shall write you my heart."

"If that is your wish."

CHAPTER THIRTY

Shortly after noon, the steamer for New York harbor pulled away from the North Dock. Pressed against the stern railing on the top deck were Clara Bolton, Ellie Lawson, Eva Taylor, Carol Hill, Jessica Danford, Alice Paine, and Rebecca Astor. They shouted and waved at Henry du Pont, Walter Kingsbury, Tom Rosser, Nate Chambliss, Chas Patterson, and Adelbert Ames, who stood on the dock until the steamer disappeared from view.

From the confines of his tent, Pelham heard the steamer's horn as it approached Gee's Point. He smiled as he snipped the threads that attached the three gold chevrons to his dress coat. If only for a few months, he had been a cadet officer. When he was done, he put the chevrons and the red satin sash, his dress sword and accoutrements in his valise, and carried it to the cadet clothing store. Afterwards, he reported to the armory to pick up a musket, bayonet, and cartridge box.

After the midday meal, Pelham heard the arrival of the northbound steamer that would deposit the final group of starry-eyed girls before the end of summer encampment.

Late that afternoon, Kirby stuck his head in the tent. "Lieutenant Lee wants to see you."

"What about?"

"He didn't say."

Pelham marked the page of the worn James Fennimore Cooper novel he was reading.

At the entrance to Lee's tent, Pelham saluted. "Sir, Cadet Pelham reporting as ordered."

Lee returned the salute. "Come in, Mr. Pelham. Confinement suiting you?"

Pelham sensed a smile behind the beard. "I'm into a good novel, sir, and intend to reread Nolan's book on cavalry next. He has much to say on the use of horse and field artillery."

"He does. Something the French have been experimenting with—horse artillery—but it takes a powerful lot of horses."

"Yes, sir."

"I've news that we are to receive twenty fresh mounts early this week, and they'll likely need breaking. I was hoping I might be able to enlist you, Rosser, and Custer again."

Pelham couldn't help smiling. "Anything to get out of confinement, sir. I'll let them know."

"By the way, despite your ... error in timing with the young lady, I want to commend you on your work with the Second Classmen. Not only did they all pass the course, but I understand they thoroughly enjoyed your instruction."

"Thank you, sir. I'll pass it on to Mister Rosser and Mister Custer."

"One last thing. Mathias Henry checked into the hospital this morning with a bug. He's in a bad way, and we're going to need a replacement gunner for the artillery competition. Had you not been an officer, you would have been my choice for the competition. The position is yours if you want it."

"Yes, sir. Again, anything to escape confinement."

"Good." Lee stood up. "I'll let you know when the horses come in."

When Pelham returned to the tent, he found Rosser cleaning his musket and filled him in.

"Hot damn," Rosser declared gleefully. "It's been ages since I broke a horse." He pointed to Pelham's musket. "You better get with it, John. Ned's got us on guard detail in the morning."

"That didn't take long." Pelham hung his coat and rooted around for his cleaning rod. "You and Carol Hill have it going pretty well."

"Aye, my luck may be changing, and we had a good send-off at the boat. A good thing Hardee wasn't around. But I'm to write first, and you know what that means. She's hoping for a letter this week. You'll help me?"

"Of course," Pelham said. "Just remember that less is more, until you know where she stands, and you won't know that until her first letter."

Rosser nodded. "I know, and I can't figure it out. Face to face, I'm great with the ladies, but put a pen in my hand and I panic."

Pelham smiled. "Your encampment flairs do seem to fizzle in the mail."

An hour later, when Rosser was off to the confectionary, du Pont knocked once on the tent pole and entered. He found Pelham reclining on his footlocker.

"You got dealt some bad cards, brother," du Pont said, and when he saw the locket, he asked, "What have you there?"

Pelham handed him the locket.

"She is indeed a plum. I spoke with her on the dock—she hugged us all. You've made her a very happy woman."

"She's made me a very happy man."

"It was a sweet time on the dock, not a few tears."

"And you and Ellie?"

"We'd be as tight as you and Clara, had we made it to Flirty. I intend to write her this evening." Du Pont produced an envelope. "Clara asked me to give you this."

Pelham waited for du Pont to leave before opening the envelope. Inside was a delicately formed bow of red and white ribbon, with a note in Clara's hand. *You gave me a button, I give you a bow, expect my letter soon. Love, your lady, Clara.*

At supper, except for Rosser and du Pont, there was universal surprise at Pelham's ebullient mood. Kingsbury, on the other hand, was so beside himself that Chambliss had to ask du Pont to make the announcements.

After leaving the mess hall, Pelham caught up with Patterson. "So how goes it with you and Alice Paine?"

"I fear the woman has misled me."

"Pray tell."

"Ellie Lawson told me that Alice has been courted by a lawyer on Long Island for more than two years. It's been an on and off thing, and apparently it is in the off stage for now. At any rate, Alice said she would write, so—we'll see."

Pelham slapped Patterson on the back. "A taste of your own dessert?"

The remaining week of summer encampment passed quickly, with alternating days of rain and shine, and throughout the week coveys of Third Classmen returned from their two-and-a-half-month furloughs, bringing the Corps to its full complement. Pelham had to start over with Rosser's first letter to Carol Hill, but Rosser still managed to post the letter in Monday's mail. Tuesday morning came with word from Lee that the shipment of horses was in, and Wednesday morning, Pelham, Rosser, and Custer reported to Lee at the stables.

"Notice anything unusual?" Lee asked, as they got their initial look at the new mounts.

"Hard to miss, sir." Pelham pointed to the nearly white steed in a corral of nineteen sorrels.

"He would make a fine target on the battlefield," Custer said.

"But here at West Point, just another mount," Lee said. "Who wants him?"

"I'll take him, sir," Pelham said.

The four of them inspected the twenty mounts, and spent the better part of Wednesday, Thursday, and Friday mornings breaking the horses to the point that they wouldn't break cadets. By the time the job was done, they had named all of the horses. Pelham had named the white horse Cotton.

Friday after the midday meal, the Corps, the Academy staff, and a great number of visitors assembled in the area south of the cadet encampment for the Corps field artillery competition. The competition was the culmination of summer training, and involved four of the Academy's six bronze field artillery pieces, the muzzles of the cannons sparkling gold on the Plain.

A crew of five serviced each gun: a horse-mounted gun captain, a gunner and cannoneer at the trails of the cannon, and two cannoneers at the muzzle. For the competition, the gun captain was more or less for show. The gunner and cannoneer at the trails would set the primer and firing lanyard, and maneuver the weapon into position. The men at the muzzle would load and ram the powder bag and ammunition. After the gunner fired the cannon, they would sponge the barrel, so that the whole process could begin again.

For the competition, each of the four cadet companies proffered its most proficient gunnery team. Pelham entered the competition, having worked with the D Company crew an hour Monday and Tuesday, and half an hour late Thursday.

"I'll wager a dollar on D Company," Rosser announced loudly to no one in particular.

Adelbert Ames responded to the announcement. "Against the field?"

"Why not?"

"Care to make it two?"

"Why not five?"

The two shook hands.

The Plain exploded with cheers as the teams formed around their field pieces, and continued until Lieutenant Colonel Hardee raised a hand for silence.

"Welcome to today's annual field artillery gunnery competition." Hardee went on to recognize special guests and explain the nature of the competition, that the winner was the gun that fired first at the assigned target. For the many visitors in attendance, he assured them that no projectiles would be used, and that the good people on the other side of the Hudson had nothing to worry about.

The four company commanders served as gun captains. Ames, now on horseback, positioned himself behind the B Company gun crew, and Kirby behind the D Company crew.

"Give 'em hell, Alabama," Custer yelled to Pelham.

Hardee announced, "On my signal," and raised his arm. At the drop of his hand, the four gunnery crews flew into action.

Pelham and the three other gunners shouted the commands, "Load," "Ram," and "Heave—Halt," commands that readied the guns and moved them forward the required ten yards. Then Pelham and the other gunners shouted adjusting commands to aim their pieces.

Satisfied, Pelham bellowed "Fire" and then "Swab."

The stillness of the valley reverberated with the retorts of the four cannons.

Rosser wasn't sure. Pelham's gun and a second gun had advanced to the firing line at the same time, and had fired at nearly the same instant, but he thought the other gun had the edge.

As the Corps and the crowd argued the winner, Hardee, Lee, and the other company tactical officers trooped the line and independently sighted down the muzzle of each cannon. The group then caucused beside the podium.

Ames dismounted next to Rosser. "I'll be taking your fiver, Tom. B Company was first, I'm sure of it."

Ignoring him, Rosser's eye was on Hardee, who approached the podium.

"Ladies and Gentlemen, and men of the Corps, this year's winner of the gunnery competition is the gunnery team from D Company."

Loud cheers and boos erupted from the Corps and the crowd.

"While second to fire," Hardee continued, "their gun was accurately aimed at the target, unlike the piece that discharged first. D Company and its cannoneers are to be congratulated."

Rosser presented Ames with a gratuitous smile and an open palm.

Leaving the mess hall that evening, Ames cornered Pelham. "How did you do it? You had your crew only days and the rest of us all summer. And you busted horses for three days. We beat you, but only by a split second."

"I posed a question to my crew." Pelham whispered what it was in Ames's ear.

"You asked if they wanted to die?"

"I said there are no second place ribbons on the battlefield, that the first target is the enemy's guns. The infantry can wait. I suggested that we imagine the other guns pointing at us, and respond accordingly."

Saturday night was the last night of encampment and the occasion for the summer's finale, Camp Illumination. Amid final preparations, Pelham remained in confinement in his tent. Four hundred candles in sanded bags were placed around the perimeter of the parade field; and beyond the lights, several hundred spectators waited for the spectacle. From his tent, Pelham could see the glow over the parade ground.

At eight o'clock, a single pistol shot signaled the beginning of festivities. Entering the parade ground through an opening in the perimeter of spectators and lights, were cadets dressed as everything ridiculous—from military caricatures to ghosts, girls, Indians, and animals. Trailing them, and similarly attired, were a dozen more cadets playing fiddles, banjos, and harmonicas, and beating makeshift drums.

Bawdy exchanges between paraders and those on the sidelines attended the procession. After the procession had circled the parade ground twice, and there had been time for stag dancing on the parade ground, another pistol shot declared the affair over. The candles were extinguished, the procession retired to company streets, and the spectators dispersed.

Throughout the whole, Pelham lay on his pallet, contemplating the year ahead and the prospect of Clara in his life. But as the final note of raucous music died, a verse from a Corps favorite, "Army Blue," struck him with sobering reality. He would never again greet "… the ladies who come up in June."

Chapter Thirty-One

Reveille the next morning came at the usual five o'clock, announced by the lone cannon, the inveterate Bentz, and the pitiless drummers. Pelham stumbled from his tent, lamenting an interrupted dream, blindly following Rosser to the first formation of the day. In the morning chill, he stood his place in ranks awaiting dismissal.

"Report," Paddy O'Rorke commanded in his usual morning voice. Receiving reports from the company's three platoons, he executed an about-face and rendered an "all present" to Ned Kirby.

Kirby returned the salute and announced in a loud voice, "All right, gentlemen, summer encampment is over. Let's hear it for Mr. Pelham, who is once again a free man!"

Instantly, the sacrosanct quietness of the hour was shattered by the hoots, hollers, and whistles of every man in D Company, the noise escalated by the rest of the Corps, the sound cascading across the Hudson.

Pelham blinked hard.

After breakfast, what took a day to erect was, in ritualistic fashion, brought down in three hours. By noon the only evidence of the encampment was the graveled grid of company streets and skeletal posts. The morning saw a steady stream of horse-drawn wagons loaded with footlockers, uniforms, bedding, washbowls, tents, and tent poles. Each cadet carried his own weapons.

The migration's end was the large cinder-covered expanse known as Central Area, measuring three hundred by five hundred feet, and defined by the cadet barracks to the north and west, the academic building to the east, and the commandant's office, boiler house, and shower facilities to the south.

Constructed principally of sandstone block, the massive four-story barracks consisted of eight divisions. The First Division was at the east end of the barracks, nearest the academic building, and each division extended the width of the building, with entrances to the front and back of the building. Each division had a central stairwell with four cadet rooms on each of four floors. The exception was the first floor, where one room served as the company orderly room.

From the Central Area side of the building, seven stone stairs that led to a broad covered stoop accessed the first floor. The basement of the barracks housed mechanical equipment and miscellaneous storage, and was interconnected between divisions by a narrow passageway.

Nate Chambliss, his battalion staff, and part of A Company quartered in the First Division; the balance of A Company quartered in the Second Division. B Company quartered in the Third and Fourth Divisions, C Company in the Fifth and Sixth Divisions, and D Company in the Seventh and Eighth Divisions at the west end of the barracks. With the exception of the more spacious quarters of the battalion staff, where on the second floor Nate Chambliss would enjoy a two-room suite reserved for the first captain, every cadet room was the same.

"I am ready for a real bed," Rosser declared as he and Pelham carried their weapons to the Eighth Division.

"Aye, but remember what comes with it," cautioned Pelham.

They climbed the three flights of iron stairs, with varnished wood handrails and handsome iron scrollwork, to reach the fourth floor of the Eighth Division. Turning left, they entered an empty room, the same room they had vacated two and half months earlier. Pelham and Rosser had chosen the room the previous year for the privacy it afforded.

The room measured twenty feet by twenty feet, and had a twelve-foot ceiling. The space was divided into a ten-foot by twenty-foot common area to the right, and the same size area for sleeping to the left. The sleeping area was partitioned into two separate alcoves. Against the outer wall of each alcove was a simple metal-spring bed with a mattress. In front of the partition wall was a wooden stand with towel racks, a washbasin, and two slop buckets.

Centered on the right wall of the common area was a large leaded-glass window. On either side of the window were shelves and pegboards for muskets, sabers, swords, and accoutrements. The floor was pine plank, stained a light gray, and the walls were plaster, painted an off-white. The high baseboard and the window trim, as well as the wooden shelves and pegs on which uniforms, hats, duffel bags, and miscellaneous were stored, were painted blue. Printed curtains, affording a measure of privacy and drawn back as required during the day, fronted the two alcoves.

Opposite the door was a small brick fireplace with a metal floor grate and firebox, and a metal hearth set flush with the floor and extending twelve inches from the fireplace. The fireplace was trimmed in wood and capped with a six-inch mantel, and both the wood and brick of the fireplace were painted black. To the right of the fireplace was a five-shelf bookcase. The bookcase was painted beige and fronted with blue curtains. On the shelves, Pelham and Rosser would precisely arrange their clothing, extra linens, and personal items. The top shelf was reserved for academic books arranged by height and specific order.

To the left of the door, along the interior wall, was a long wooden desk with two chairs. A gas light was mounted on the wall above it.

Pelham opened Clara's locket and hung it from the gas lamp.

"Sir," a plebe announced from the bottom of the division stairwell. "Class assignments have been posted in the sally port!"

"The other shoe drops," Pelham said, scrambling for pad and pencil.

"Most merciful God," Rosser mumbled as they descended the staircase. "Protect me from Professor Mahan."

Arriving at the first floor, Pelham inspected himself in the wall mirror, while Rosser checked the company bulletin board, which was bare except for the stick figure cartoon he had drawn before encampment, depicting an upperclassman towering over a plebe.

Behind the bulletin board was the company orderly room, the command and control center and mail drop for the company.

Pelham stuck his head inside the room. "Welcome back, Jim."

James Wright, a Third Classman serving as charge-of-quarters, looked up. "Hey, John."

"Any mail yet?"

"Nope, not yet."

When Pelham and Rosser arrived at the sally port, it was a sea of bodies, each man scribbling down class assignments posted on the framed bulletin boards that lined the walls. These same boards would post weekly class grades.

"Yo, Pelham," Chas Patterson shouted from the end of the sally port. "Check this out."

Pelham answered the call and found himself in front of the demerit list. His name was at the top, his total twice that of the next offender.

"Over here, John," Rosser shouted. "We're in the same civil engineering section."

Within five minutes, Pelham and Rosser had journaled their class assignments and in the process had crossed paths with du Pont, Upton, and Chambliss.

Back in their room, Pelham and Rosser unpacked their footlockers and prepared in advance for Sunday morning inspection. During the academic year, inspections were on Sunday rather than Saturday.

Rosser brooded over his class schedule. "I have a bad feeling about this year."

"You say that every year."

"But this year we have Mahan."

"Tom, he's just another professor."

"No, he's Mahan."

"I'm going to see if mail's in," Pelham said.

He descended the three flights of stairs and asked the charge-of-quarters if the mail had arrived.

"Just delivered, and I've given it to the plebe mail carrier. But I don't recall anything for you."

Pelham suddenly realized that it was Friday. There could be no letter. Had she written the day she left, Clara's letter could not have been posted before Monday. He bounded back up the stairs in high spirits.

"Alabama," Custer shouted from the room across the hall from his. He appeared in the doorway with musket and cleaning rod. "Can you spare some cleaning oil?"

"Sure, you know where it is."

Custer followed Pelham into his room, found the cleaning oil, and departed. Pelham sat at his desk and transcribed his notes into a coherent class schedule. When he finished, he weighed the semester workload and sensed he might actually have to apply himself.

CHAPTER THIRTY-TWO

Saturday, after the midday meal, McElheny knocked once upon the open door to Pelham and Rosser's room.

"Sir, mail for Mr. Pelham and Mr. Rosser."

"Well, well, well, beanhead." Rosser was on to his feet. "You've a letter for old Tom?"

McElheny did.

Rosser ripped it open and removed a single sheet of paper. After reading it, he shot McElheny a look. "You find this amusing, Mr. McElheny?"

McElheny stood stoic, his eyes fixed on the wall across the room. "No, sir."

Rosser handed the letter to Pelham, who read it out loud.

Dear Tom,

My feelings for you are beyond words. I cannot wait to see you again, to have you hold me the way you do, and until then I must nurse a broken heart. Take care, my gallant one, and know that I miss you more than life itself, and if you would, please be nice to the plebes, especially Mr. McElheny.

Love, Carol.

It was nearly a full minute before Pelham regained his composure. He gave McElheny a knowing wink and handed him an outgoing letter.

"I want you back in this room after taps," Rosser growled "You understand me, beanhead? After taps!"

McElheny acknowledged that he understood and crossed the hall to Custer's room.

The supper meal came and went, and Pelham ate little for reasons other than the food. Returning to his room, he picked up the letter McElheny had given him. It was from Clara, and he had yet to read it.

Rosser, in a stupor at the other end of the desk, cursed unintelligibly as he flipped the pages of one of a dozen books he had picked up from the bookstore. "How the hell am I supposed to know what's in all of these?" He closed the one book and opened another.

Pelham sniffed the three scented pages of vellum from Clara. At the upper left-hand corner of each sheet, she had artfully drawn and colored a small flower, a different flower on each page. The date on her letter was August 27, 1860, and the subscript to the date was "Clermont College, Long Island, New York." As he read, he could hear her voice.

My dearest knight,

You will not believe the trip home and how we six jabbered on and on, each convinced we had a better time than the rest. I, of course, know the truth, for you made it so! Ellie is nearly done with her letter to Henry, and the other girls are writing "thank-yous" to Chas, Nate, Tom, and Adelbert. They are all expecting replies! I quite marvel at the clever matches you made. Eva Taylor and I talked all the way back to New York City, and I think your Walter Kingsbury is a very lucky boy. You may find it curious, but I did not tell Eva about us, or about my visiting you in camp. Thus, don't be surprised if she follows up on her friend, Sallie Dandridge. If she does, I will trust your feelings toward me.

I feel I should warn you on behalf of Chas Patterson that Alice Paine has not been entirely open with him, which is as I suspected. On the boat, she admitted her fondness for him, but also the uncertainty of her allegiance. She has been dating a local boy for some time—a rather timid man by your standards—but the two have history. While she is for now taken by your man from Arkansas, as time passes, I fear she will lean toward the "bird in the hand."

Pelham read on as Clara shared her first semester courses, and her chagrin at not having been placed in the anatomy laboratory course she had requested. Her letter concluded with:

After receiving your return letter and knowing you have not changed in feeling toward me, I shall write Father to tell him of you, and to insist upon his blessing. I will also ask his support for the lab course and for channeling my applications to medical colleges. He is indeed "old school," but he is my father and loves me (so he says). With his influence, I can succeed, though I am not altogether optimistic and am prepared for rejection. Still, I shant give up until every way is exhausted.

Miss Frampton has been somewhat encouraging, though still wanting me to pursue nursing.

In closing, dearest John, I know God's providential hand is upon us for good. How else could one week mean so much and have so changed my life, and I pray yours. We can and will survive our separation, if we will it so, and you must know I do. Be careful, my love. There, I've said it with my pen. Know that my heart awaits your reply.

Your lady, Clara

P.S. I still grieve at the punishment you received on my account, and pray for your forgiveness.

Pelham read Clara's letter a second time, this time with her locket in his hand. He then withdrew from the desk drawer a sheet of embossed Academy vellum and dipped a quill pen in the inkwell. He wrote carefully, thoughtfully, not wanting to be anywhere other than where she needed him to be in this first letter. When he was finished, several wadded sheets on the floor testified to revisions. He blew on the last page, blotted the ink, and read what he had written.

September 1, 1860
West Point, New York

My Lady and Dearest Clara,

You need no forgiveness, I assure you, and indeed had events not transpired as they did, I cannot know how we would be in the wondrous place we are. What you have prayed for has indeed occurred regarding my feelings for you, and in no way have they been diminished since your departure. Which is to say, my lady, you may be assured of my deepest affection and faithfulness. I appreciate your indulgence as I grow accustomed to the word you so bravely use, and which gives me such joy. For now, it seems to stick not only in my throat but in my pen.

With regard to her medical pursuits, Pelham counseled against depending wholly upon her father, and suggested she attempt contact with the practicing female doctor she had mentioned. She might even consider a face-to-face visit.

He was surprised by the call for lights out, and folded the sheets of vellum and inserted them in an envelope. He then applied a hot wax seal. By the time Bentz sounded tattoo, both he and Rosser were in bed; and when the charge-of-quarters made his rounds, he was relieved to find Pelham and Rosser in their room.

Minutes later, there was a whisper at the door as McElheny reported to Rosser. Rosser slipped from his bed and proceeded to supervise McElheny's swim to Newburgh, the euphemism for lying on one's stomach and executing the crawl stroke until collapsing from fatigue.

Chapter Thirty-Three

PIEDMONT STATION, VIRGINIA
FRIDAY, JULY 19, 1861
TWO DAYS BEFORE THE FIRST BATTLE OF BULL RUN

Pelham was exhausted. The trip from Winchester, across the Shenandoah River, over the Blue Ridge, and south to Piedmont Station had taken thirty hours, and he had been in the saddle all but four of them. Behind General Jackson's brigade, Pelham's Alburtis battery had been tucked between two regiments of Colonel Bartow's brigade. The brigades of General Bee and General Smith followed Bartow. When the long column headed southeast from Winchester, Pelham had heard the retorts of small arms and Union artillery, as Colonel Stuart's cavalry put on a show for General Patterson's Union army. Providentially, Patterson's army would never become a factor in the ensuing battle.

The journey had begun on a sour note. General Johnston, for security reasons, had instructed commanders at all levels not to divulge their true destination until well clear of Winchester. As a result, Pelham's men expressed considerable displeasure at retreating in the face of Patterson's army. Not until Pelham finally informed them that they would be reinforcing General Beauregard at Manassas Junction to repulse a much larger Union army's push for Richmond, did their spirits improve.

For Pelham and the Alburtis battery, the first leg of the trip from Winchester had been the most grueling and costly, especially crossing the Shenandoah and climbing the Blue Ridge. Half a dozen wagon wheels had been changed out, and he had been forced to put down three horses that gave out from muscling wagons and guns up the deeply rutted road.

During the brief stop in Paris, after cresting the Blue Ridge, Pelham had been invited by Stuart to share a smoke. The two had talked of West Point and Benny Havens.

That morning, descending the eastern slope of the Blue Ridge and facing the sun, the heat, humidity, and parched earth greeted the long snake of humanity. While horse and wagon traveled easily enough, every soldier's nose and mouth was covered, and eyes squinted into the unending dust.

On the final leg to Piedmont Station, Stuart had ridden for a time alongside Pelham, emphasizing that they were in for quite a row, and the importance of the Alburtis battery setting the example. Pelham's response had been direct—his men were ready and would do their duty.

Now at six o'clock, the sun low on the horizon, Pelham sat slumped in the saddle, watching the rail hands at Piedmont Station detach the locomotive from the string of Manassas Gap boxcars. The train had just returned from Manassas Junction after off-loading General Jackson and half of his brigade. As the locomotive took a spur to the other end of rolling stock to recouple and face the other direction, fifteen hundred troops advanced on the empty boxcars. When the cars were full, others climbed on top. After the train pulled away, more than seven thousand Confederates at Piedmont Station still awaited transport to Manassas.

The train, lunging forward and straining for speed, would average only four miles an hour, making the trip to Manassas Junction an eight-hour ordeal. Pelham wondered at the wisdom of putting infantry on trains that had a tendency to accidents and delays. He shared a further apprehension with most Southern troops: that the railroads held Northern sympathies. But none of that was his concern. Along with the cavalry, the guns would travel by road to Manassas.

"Lieutenant, sir, the horses are watered and the men ready," reported Sergeant Miles, Pelham's senior gunner.

Pelham returned the man's salute. "Very well."

"Damn hot evening, sir." The sergeant passed a dirty salt-encrusted handkerchief across his brow.

"Be glad you're not in one of those boxcars."

"Cannons, Lieutenant?" the gunner said, referring to distant thunder.

"Possibly," Pelham said, sure that it was.

"We're going to a have us a real battle, aren't we?"

"We are, Sergeant."

When the limbered battery and caissons took to the Manassas road, they found its macadam surface worn away over long stretches, rattling the teeth of all not in a saddle. From time to time, Pelham trooped the length of the battery, making light and encouraging the men that soon they would be putting their talent to good purpose.

In the monotony of the journey, Pelham found himself reflecting on the reality of war, and wondered how his former roommate and other classmates were faring at Bull Run. He knew Rosser was with Ewell's brigade, commanding the First Company of Washington Artillery, a battery from New Orleans. He presumed that Charlie Ball and Henry Farley were commanding artillery pieces elsewhere along Bull Run.

CHAPTER THIRTY-FOUR

TEN MONTHS EARLIER
WEST POINT, NEW YORK
FIRST SEMESTER, 1860

Monday morning, September 3, Pelham awoke to the sounds of reveille and rain against the window, thankful for a warm bed and an uninterrupted night of sleep. Rosser announced himself with a moan from the next alcove. The two of them sat up in bed, their feet touching the floor at the same time. As room orderly for the week, Pelham got up and lit the gas lamp.

The two donned uniforms and rain capes and cap covers, and joined the rumble of feet down the stairs, across the stoops, and out onto the dark quadrangle of Central Area.

"Our last first day," Pelham whispered to Rosser, as water dripped off the bill of his forage cap.

Breakfast in the mess hall was quiet, the mood of the Corps sullen in anticipation of academics. Rosser buttered a biscuit, drenched it with Sammy, and ate quietly, absorbed in his thoughts.

Pelham sipped black coffee and considered his roommate, who was neither dumb nor slow. In fact, Rosser was a quick study of whatever was placed in front of him. Pelham couldn't understand why Rosser didn't bury forever the stigma of having arrived at West Point with only four years of formal education. Rosser had done the right thing, arriving six months earlier than anyone else and being tutored for the entrance examinations. The investment had paid off. He had passed and was a member of the class. Yet the self-esteem so evident in every other aspect of his life did not extend to academics. In his mind, every September would be his last, and every September he prepared for dismissal. Yet come every June, he was still around. At the end of the previous year, he had climbed from the bottom of the class to forty-second out of fifty.

Pelham, thirty-fourth in the class, waited for what he knew was coming.

"John, just shoot me." Rosser's elbows were on the table, his head in his hands.

"Cheer up. We have Mahan first class. You'll be at your sharpest."

When they returned to the barracks, the rain was heavier, and the slapping wind sent it pinging against the window. It occurred to Pelham that it had rained the first day of every academic year. It had ushered in plebe year's algebra, geometry, trigonometry, English, literature, fundamental tactics, and fencing. It had announced Fourth Class year and more math, differential and integral calculus, more English, more literature, first-year French, artillery and infantry tactics, use of small arms, and more fencing. Third Class year, it had served up physics, astronomy, the final year of French, the only year of Spanish, the first year of drawing, more artillery and cavalry tactics, equitation, and still more fencing. And last year, in a deluge that lasted a week, it announced chemistry, the final year of drawing, philosophy and ethics, advanced cavalry, artillery and infantry tactics, advanced equitation, frontier outpost service, and, as always, more fencing.

Pelham failed to notice that the rain was only a drizzle when he made his way to the academic building and Professor Mahan's classroom, which on Mondays, Wednesdays, and Fridays would be filled with the concepts and formulas of civil engineering; and on Tuesdays and Thursdays with instruction in military science and the art of warfare.

Bentz's bugle call announced five minutes to class, and Pelham took a seat in the back row, where Rosser soon joined him. The two of them watched the clock on the wall, and at precisely eight o'clock the tiny form of Professor Mahan, his chin decorated with a white goatee, marched through the door to the front of the class.

Mahan opened his briefcase. "Attendance report."

Chas Patterson, the section leader, reported that all were present.

"Welcome, gentlemen, to civil engineering. I know you are excited to be here, to have made it this far." Mahan's attempt at humor was lost on Rosser. "This course will be the crowning achievement of your academic education, and I wish all of you the wisdom and commitment necessary to arrive safely at its end." The dean's eyes narrowed. "For I assure you, luck will have nothing to do with it."

Rosser nudged Pelham. "I'm dead."

Mahan picked up a reference book. "Open your text, *Moseley's Mechanics of Engineering*, to the table of contents."

Pelham's attempts to console Rosser on the way to the ordnance laboratory below the north end of the Plain fell on deaf ears.

"Gentlemen, may I join you?" Captain James Benton, the ordnance instructor, made the request.

"Certainly, sir," Pelham said.

"The sun's out," Benton observed. "An omen?"

Rosser seemed to respond to this, and as Benton briefly described what they could expect in his class, Rosser's spirits improved. Ordnance, he could get his arms around. He confided to Benton that he was eager to learn what was needed to produce the various kinds of munitions for soldiering, and to improve his skill with the array of coastal guns that comprised the Academy's shore battery.

The midday meal was followed by mineralogy and geology, taught by Professor Henry Kendrick, popularly known as "Old Hank." Kendrick had an engaging way of bringing the inanimate to life.

In the hallway after class, Pelham encountered the drawing professor, Robert Weir, and greeted him.

"Good day to you, Mr. Pelham." Weir put a hand on Pelham's shoulder. "Your final year, and I believe you will survive despite my efforts."

Pelham laughed. "I continue to sketch, sir. What you teach is important, and I will endeavor to improve."

"To your credit, Mr. Pelham, your drawings were always accurate. It was your technique that I took issue with. Seems I want all of you to be fine artists. But we all have our style, and you have yours."

From Kendrick's classroom, Pelham walked the length of the second floor hall to the tactics classroom, for the first in a sequence of classes on advanced cavalry tactics, taught by Lieutenant Lee.

The next day Pelham and Rosser again sat on the back row in Professor Mahan's class. For his military science class, the otherwise dour Mahan displayed an entirely different persona, his eyes fairly twinkling.

"Gentlemen, what is the Academy if not a crucible for shaping military leaders? You have come a long way through a maze of training that has brought you to this day. Beginning today, you will venture outside your own time in history. We will look back at the great captains of the past, learn from them, and examine their victories and defeats. You will be challenged to enter the minds of these great men and to suffer with them through their campaigns, to judge them on how well they assessed the situation, the enemy, and the terrain, so that you might carry their strengths with you when you leave this cloistered place."

Pelham looked forward to the class. Indeed, every First Classman anticipated the class, even Rosser. Mahan promised that the class, which he preferred to call Military Art, would connect the seemingly disjointed military experiences of the past four years into a seamless whole.

"You have a legacy to follow, don't you? Graduates of West Point distinguished themselves most handsomely in the war with Mexico— whether it was justified or not, that being a different thing. What was it that Winfield Scott said, which Robert E. Lee required every plebe to memorize, and which is still required today?"

Pelham was surprised to see Rosser's hand in the air.

"In the back, there." Mahan called out to Rosser.

"Sir, that would be General Scott's Fixed Opinion, in which he said, 'I give it as my fixed opinion, that but for our graduated cadets, the war between the United States and Mexico might, and probably would have lasted some four or five years, with, in its first half, more defeats than victories falling to our share; whereas, in less than two campaigns, we conquered a great country and a peace, without the loss of a single battle or skirmish.'"

Rosser's recitation was flawless, and drew disingenuous approbation from his classmates.

"You, sir," Professor Mahan said, "are either very sharp or were a plebe the upperclassmen picked on quite regularly."

The room filled with laughter.

The next class was the popular practical military engineering class taught by First Lieutenant James Duane, in which earthworks, pontoon bridging, and military defenses would be studied. This was followed by the midday meal, which in turn was followed by a curiously combined class entitled "Law and Literature," and taught by Professor and Reverend John French. Pelham struggled to stay awake as French introduced notes on the rules and articles of war and the text by DeHart on courts-martial.

The day concluded with what Pelham considered a crucially important study, a tactics class taught by Lieutenant Colonel Hardee himself, in which he introduced the combined use of arms—infantry, cavalry, and artillery—in what he called "modern warfare." Pelham, like the rest of the Corps, would miss Hardee, and knew nothing about his replacement, Lieutenant Colonel John Reynolds, who was to succeed him in a week.

Saturday morning from eight until ten o'clock was more practical military engineering with Captain Duane, followed by fencing, a class that involved the entire First Class for two hours in the expansive basement of the academic building. Pelham and the rest of the class arrived with their fencing foils and cavalry straight sabers, and were greeted by Mr. Antoni Lorentz, the Academy's long time master of the sword. The slim man, gaunt-faced and fully sixty years old, wore fencing pads, and he directed the cadets to carts that held fencing pads and masks.

Properly protected, the cadets configured themselves in long rows, with ample room between each of them. They faced Lorentz, who slapped his foil against an open hand and commanded, "Starting position!"

Each cadet assumed the *en garde* pose, and for ten minutes responded to well-known drill commands, their individual performances criticized and corrected by Lorentz.

"That will have to do for now," Lorentz said with more than a hint of disappointment in his voice. "To your seats, please."

The class took to a set of bleachers along the back wall.

Lorentz eyed the class with his hands behind his back. "Your final year, yes?" His Italian accent was thick. "And have we not spent many enjoyable hours together these past four years?"

Pelham would have described them otherwise.

"This year, we should be better with the blade, do you not agree?"
No one cared to speculate.

"Mr. Pelham, you are the best swordsman in your class. Will you please join me?"

Lorentz's question was not a request, and this was not the first time Pelham had been the object lesson. Seated on the top row, he dropped down the back side of the bleachers.

"Let us see what we remember."

Lorentz began slowly, parrying Pelham's thrusts and allowing Pelham to easily parry his.

After a minute, in a voice all could hear, Lorentz asked, "Have you ever stuck or cut a man with a blade, Mr. Pelham?"

Pelham awkwardly parried a move he had not seen before. "No, sir."

"It is different than anything you might expect." Lorentz glanced at the class as he said this, and in that instant Pelham lunged for the instructor's heart. Without even looking, Lorentz flicked Pelham's blade aside with his own, and used Pelham's momentum to jab the tip of his blade into the padding over Pelham's heart.

A collective gasp filled the room.

The point of the blade, though blunt, sharply stung Pelham's chest.

Lorentz recovered his foil and nodded to Pelham. "One more time, please."

As before, the match had the appearance of parity, until Lorentz again turned his attention from Pelham to the class. "Gentlemen, can a headless enemy continue to fight?"

Before anyone could answer, Lorentz executed a combination of moves that culminated in a horizontal slash that spanked the padding around Pelham's neck.

The class was no less stunned than before.

"Thank you, Mr. Pelham. You may take your seat."

Pelham removed his mask, and Chambliss and Kirby made room for him on the front row.

"Private Norris," Lorentz called out, "if you please!" A blue-uniformed soldier pushed a tall canvass-covered cart through a set of double doors. He rolled the cart across the fencing room to a point in front of the bleachers.

"What's that smell?" Rosser murmured to Patterson.

"Gentlemen," Lorentz began. "To date you have thrust your blunted blades into the air, tickled each other's padding, and stuck your sabers into sawdust dummies. I suggest that in war there are no dummies. Your adversary, your enemy, young or old, will be no different from you. He will be keenly aware of your intent, since it will be his own. With every fiber of his being he will endeavor to run you through with his own brand of steel. With these long knives"—Lorentz brandished his saber lovingly—"you will fight as men have fought since the dawn of time. You will stab and slash human flesh and bone until it is no longer a threat to you, or else be so stabbed and slashed that you are no longer a threat."

Lorentz nodded to the soldier, who removed the canvas cover.

"Holy sh—" Rosser's voice was more audible than he intended.

Hanging from atop a seven-foot tall tripod, hooks embedded in the flesh of its shoulders, was the carcass of an enormous hog, the height of a man, its pink eyes staring blankly at a world it no longer graced.

Lorentz allowed the image to set in.

"Have you ever wondered what it would feel like to really use your saber? To pierce flesh?" A faint smile crossed his face. "Well, this is your chance to find out. A volunteer, please."

No one volunteered.

"Come now, this is your chance," teased Lorentz.

Pelham stood up and, without a word, retrieved his dragoon saber. He looked at Lorentz, who gestured to the carcass. Pelham approached the carcass, set his feet, and ran his saber through the hog's chest, the blade crunching through bone, the tip appearing out the backside of the animal.

Lorentz smiled. "Pretending it was me, Mr. Pelham?"

CHAPTER THIRTY-FIVE

On September 10, following the Monday afternoon parade in honor of the departure of Lieutenant Colonel Hardee and the arrival of Lieutenant Colonel John Reynolds, and after another disappointing supper, Pelham headed for the First Class Club. The passage of an entire week of academics had removed the uncertainty of what the first semester courses would impose. It was no more than he had expected, and would not overburden the time he wanted to reserve for himself. That he was stripped of his rank had the benefit that he was no longer responsible for the discipline and academic performance of a platoon of twenty-four men.

Earlier in the day, he had rejoiced with Rosser over a letter from Carol Hill. While the girl had not expressed quite the sentiment that McElheny had, Rosser had reason to feel whole and confident in his game. The others too had received letters: du Pont from Ellie Lawson, Chambliss from Jessica Danford, Ames from Rebecca Astor, and Patterson from Alice Paine. Knowing what he did, Pelham asked Patterson about Alice Paine, and Patterson spoke candidly, saying that she still seemed to be in his camp, which suited him, since he had nothing better to pursue. A letter from Eva Taylor to Walter Kingsbury had mended the broken man to such a degree, Pelham and others found it hard to pass more than a few minutes with him.

When he bounded up the steps to the First Class Club, Pelham was buoyed by the expectation of another letter from Clara. In the First Class Club, there was lively discussion in response to the announcement at supper that both Maine's and Rhode Island's congressional elections had gone Republican. The first person he encountered was Emory Upton.

"No gloating?" he asked Upton.

"Not necessary."

Chambliss, Patterson, and du Pont stood looking at a map of North America.

"There are a total of three hundred and three electoral votes at stake in the election," Chambliss said. "Maine and Rhode Island together account for only ten votes. It's Pennsylvania with twenty-seven votes and Indiana with thirteen that we'll need, and they vote in two weeks."

Patterson shook his head. "Even so, Pennsylvania and Indiana won't help if we can't settle on a compromise candidate."

"True enough," du Pont said, shrugging, "but which one do you pick—John Breckinridge, Stephen Douglas, or John Bell?"

"Douglas must step down," Patterson insisted. "He's the bane of the South, and if he does, Bell might. And he should, because he doesn't have a chance. That would leave Breckinridge, who, as Buchanan's vice president, at least has name recognition. He could do well."

"I don't see it happening," Adelbert Ames said, drawn to the discussion. "Even if Douglas steps down, Missouri won't go with Breckinridge on account of his slavery stance. Same for Delaware."

Du Pont was unsure about Delaware, but chose to remain silent.

Ames turned to Upton. "You must be feeling rather cocky about this."

Upton surprised Pelham again with the evenness of his response. "The people will vote what they know, or think they know. And the sad thing is that they'll vote emotions fired by party-line half-truths, without really understanding the issues."

"I have to echo Emory," du Pont said. "A lot of gnashing of teeth, but little constructive dialogue. In the South, fire-eaters have the platform they want. In the North, abolitionists headline the papers."

Pelham chose to remain silent on the subject and returned to the barracks, finding Rosser penning a letter.

"Carol?"

"Nope—Sam Houston."

"The Texas governor?"

"Houston got me my appointment. I might as well get his take on what to do if Texas secedes."

Chapter Thirty-Six

By the third week of September, the Corps was fully immersed in academics, and the election had moved to the back of the stove. Every day they were graded in every subject, a legacy of Sylvanus Thayer. Grades were on a three-point scale, with 3.0 a perfect grade and 2.0 a minimum passing grade. Every Friday afternoon Pelham, Rosser, and the rest of the Corps made the pilgrimage to the sally port to see the postings of the latest grades.

Rosser, who had started out better than he had expected in Mahan's civil engineering class and had earned a 2.2 grade point after two weeks, was devastated by the grades of the past week. He'd been reduced to a deficient 1.9 grade point. His cheerful disposition and sense of humor were the casualties of the lost three-tenths. Compounding his anxiety, a second letter from Carol Hill, fully ten pages long, suggested a real relationship, a thing he had hoped for and often discussed with Pelham. But that she was proving such a prolific writer presented a problem. It forced him to make a decision that surprised even Pelham. He presented Pelham with a one-page return letter. In it, he stated simply that he thought it best, in light of his academic difficulties, not to pursue an ongoing correspondence until he could get a handle on his grades. It was of little consolation to Rosser that Pelham found not one thing to edit in the letter.

Wednesday, September 19, Rosser and Pelham fell into formation for the midday meal, waiting on Paddy O'Rorke's attendance reports.

"Hey, Tom, did you hear the one about the mess hall cook?" Custer whispered in ranks, wanting to raise Rosser's spirits.

"No," Rosser replied dully.

"Seems a cadet told the cook that his soup was terrible. So the cook says, 'Look, soldier, I cooked for Winfield Scott throughout the

Mexican War and was wounded three times.' The cadet comes back and says, 'Hell, I'm surprised he didn't kill you.'"

The man in front of Custer nearly doubled over with laughter, and Rosser growled, "Is that you, McElheny?"

The man stopped laughing. "Yes, sir."

"About-face, McElheny."

McElheny turned about.

"You think Mr. Custer's joke was funny?"

"Yes, sir."

"Are plebes permitted to laugh in ranks?"

"No, sir."

"Come to my room after taps."

"Yes, sir."

That night after taps, McElheny reported as ordered to Rosser, and Rosser closed the door behind him. The gas lamp dimly lighted the room, and the window drapes were pinned to hide the light.

Rosser rubbed his chin. "Mr. McElheny, are we in agreement that you have a laughing problem?"

"Yes, sir."

"Then you'll be pleased to know there is a cure."

McElheny said nothing.

Rosser positioned his chair in the middle of the room.

"Stand upon the chair, McElheny."

McElheny complied.

"Are you comfortable?"

"Yes, sir." McElheny's face was emotionless.

Rosser handed McElheny a duffel bag. "Put the bag over your head."

"Sir?"

"The duffel bag—put it over your head."

McElheny complied.

"Still comfortable?"

"Yes, sir."

"Dark in there?"

"Yes, sir."

"I want you to repeat after me, ha-ha, ho-ho, hee-hee; ha-ha, ho-ho, hee-hee. And I don't want you to stop until I tell you to stop. Is that understood?"

"Yes, sir."

In a surprisingly strong baritone voice and easy meter, McElheny repeated the words over and over. Ha-ha, ho-ho, hee-hee. Ha-ha, ho-ho, hee-hee. Pelham observed the proceedings passively from his chair.

After a few minutes, Rosser said, "All right, McElheny. Now I want you to begin double-timing in place on the chair."

McElheny complied with difficulty, carefully lifting and dropping his feet on the chair and barking, ha-ha, ho-ho, hee-hee.

"McElheny, I'm going to assume that you enjoy a good cigar." Rosser had already lit one and was puffing it to a good burn.

Smoke soon filled the bag that covered McElheny's head, while McElheny continued to double-time and repeat, ha-ha, ho-ho, hee-hee.

McElheny's delivery gradually began to weaken.

"I can't hear you, Mr. McElheny," Rosser growled.

McElheny began to cough and teeter on the chair, but righted himself.

Suddenly, the duffel bag listed to an unrecoverable angle, and Pelham was on his feet in time to help Rosser catch the plebe.

Rosser removed the duffel bag and sat McElheny on the chair.

"You okay, McElheny?"

McElheny coughed and gasped for air, but nodded.

"How do you feel?"

At first McElheny couldn't answer, but after regaining his composure, he asked, "Should I put the bag back on, sir?"

Pelham had to bite his lip.

"Well, it depends." Rosser circled the plebe. "Do you still feel like laughing?"

McElheny, his face wet with perspiration and his eyes blood shot, responded, "No, sir."

"Then hallelujah and praise God, McElheny. You're cured!"

Chapter Thirty-Seven

The next day, Pelham finally received the letter he had been expecting from his father in response to the one he had sent a month earlier. His father apologized for his tardiness, explaining that he had wanted to observe the overseer, Butch Jansonne, to see if he was, in fact, stepping out of line. He suspected Jansonne got wind of his intentions, for the man was nearly angelic for almost three weeks. But returning home from a house call, the senior Pelham had caught the overseer in the act of culling out the man, Amos, from the picking line and whipping him beyond any sense of necessity. Pelham's temper flared as he read on. "I called Jansonne to account and gave him strict notice that if I ever caught him abusing one of the blacks, I would fire him on the spot."

The warning bothered Pelham, for the overseer had but to carefully pick his times for brutality. The man held absolute power over the slaves, and unless he was actually caught in a condemning act by a responsible white, the overseer's word in a court of law would take precedence over the testimony of any slave.

Late that night, Pelham prayed for the slave family, for Willie and Samuel specifically. He prayed that Jansonne would be found out and discharged before anyone was seriously injured—or worse. After these petitions, he thanked God for the one piece of very good news in his father's letter. Samuel and fifteen-year-old Ora were to be a couple.

After class that day, Pelham noticed Rosser lifting the ash grate from the fireplace. He removed a tin cigar box and took off the lid, and then extracted something from his pocket and put it in the box.

"What is that all about?" Pelham finally asked.

Rosser crossed the room and let Pelham look in the box.

"A rat?"

"Not a rat. A mouse. There's a difference." Rosser retrieved the tiny creature and stroked the animal's fur as it sniffed his thumb. "This morning when I swept the room, he was in the corner looking up at me. Didn't run—just stared me down."

Rosser crumbled a sliver of stale bread in his fingers, producing a small pile of crumbs in the tin box. He returned the creature to the box, which he had fitted with tiny air holes.

He and Pelham watched as the creature sniffed the bread, ate one crumb, then another, and then the entire pile.

"He's got a good appetite," Rosser said with pride.

"Has he a name?"

Rosser returned a thoughtful look. "Mouse?"

"Just Mouse?"

Rosser reconsidered. "No. Mr. Mouse. Yes, that's his name, Mr. Mouse. And see, John, he looks like you and me."

"Like us?"

"Yes. All gray." Rosser returned the box to the fireplace.

The following Monday after supper, Pelham listened passively to members of the Dialectic Society debate the debate. A small faction wanted to steer clear of politics, but the majority was in favor of some sort of relevant issue. What it might be ranged from debating the right of women to vote, to party platforms, to adopting what Pelham had suggested in the previous meeting. It was Adelbert Ames who made the argument that debating party platforms was futile as there were four parties, the Northern Democrats, Southern Democrats, Republicans, and Constitutional Union. With Pelham's topic, he reasoned, there was clear relevance and two sides to the argument. A state either had a right to secede or it didn't. Ames eventually prevailed on the group with a motion for Pelham's topic, and it carried by the needed majority. Whether women should be given the right to vote was adopted as a fallback topic.

Choosing the debate topic proved easier than choosing the debaters. At one point there were six names under consideration, including Pelham's, which he immediately withdrew since he intended to be the moderator. The chief obstacle to agreement was the complaint that the prospective debaters held views that were too similar. The resulting debate would be skewed to one side; specifically, the side of a state having the right to secede.

Henry du Pont finally offered an opinion. "I think our best choice for debating that a state does not have the right to secede is Emory Upton."

The mere mention of Upton's name seemed to drop the temperature in the room, but Ames immediately supported du Pont. "Henry's right. Emory is nearest to a true Republican and an independent thinker."

If Ames expected an "amen," he didn't receive it. Still, no one argued the point.

"Providing," Ames continued, "that the man doesn't go to meddling, which I sense he won't. Am I right, Emory?"

Upton nodded agreement.

"And," Ames said, "if I may be so bold as to offer up his opponent, who better to espouse the opposing position than our own Henry du Pont?"

Du Pont could not have been more surprised. "Me?" His name had not even come up in discussion. "Yes, I am a Democrat, but I am not a secessionist."

"I didn't say you were," Ames said. "But you are Upton's equal in advocacy, in considering an issue, and in defending a position." Ames addressed the broader group. "If we were to offer up a fire-eater, and I mean them no offense, John would not stand a snowball's chance getting the superintendent to go along with us."

Pelham gave Ames a nod of thanks and turned to Upton. "Are you agreeable, Emory?"

Upton said that he was.

"Henry?"

Du Pont was clearly ill at ease, but acquiesced.

"Don't panic, Henry, there is still the vote." Pelham recapped the situation. "We now have du Pont and Upton in the mix with the others. Are there any other names we should consider?"

There were rumblings, but no additional names were mentioned.

"We'll do a secret ballot, each man writing down his choice of debater for and against secession."

O'Rorke distributed small slips of paper to each member of the society, gave the members time to make their choices, and then collected the slips. He excused himself to a corner of the room and tallied the votes. He returned to the group, his face unreadable, and announced, "To debate that a state has the right to secede from the Union, we have by large majority decided for Henry du Pont."

Of little consolation to du Pont, he was roundly applauded.

"To debate that a state does not have the right to secede from the Union," O'Rorke went on, "by a margin of one vote, we have decided upon Emory Upton."

A leaden silence filled the room, until Pelham, joined by Ames, applauded the selection.

"Now that wasn't so hard, was it?" Pelham said. "And now that we have our debaters, it is up to me to earn my keep. I will sugar this as best I can and present it to the superintendent tomorrow, assuming I can get in to see him, and then report back to you. If he doesn't agree with our first choice, I'll offer up universal suffrage and we'll pick new debaters."

The group was in unanimous agreement.

"Whatever Delafield's decision," Pelham added, "we'll want to get the word out and give our debaters at least two weeks to prepare." He poked at a calendar on the wall. "Shall we strike for October 27, a Saturday, and the academic building lecture hall as the venue for debate?"

The date and place were agreeable to all.

CHAPTER THIRTY-EIGHT

On Friday morning, after Professor Mahan's class on Alexander the Great, Pelham visited post headquarters and made an appointment to meet with the superintendent following Lieutenant Colonel Reynolds's afternoon tactics class.

Shortly after five o'clock, he returned to the superintendent's office.

"I'll let the colonel know you are here, Mr. Pelham," the superintendent's aide said.

A minute later Pelham stood inside the superintendent's office. "Sir, Cadet Pelham reporting."

Colonel Delafield, in apparent good humor, returned Pelham's salute and motioned for him to take a chair in front of his desk. "What brings you to my office, Mr. Pelham?"

Pelham began the pitch he had rehearsed a dozen times. "Sir, as president of the Dialectic Society, I wanted to share with you the main program we have decided upon for the fall semester."

Delafield nodded.

"Sir, we want to host a debate timely to the upcoming presidential election."

"A political debate?" The superintendent's tone was not encouraging.

"Exactly, sir."

"Mr. Pelham, you should know my policy that, for good reason, I think it best to avoid public discussion of political issues within the Corps."

"Yes, sir, I am aware of your position on political matters. May I ask why, sir?"

Delafield eyed Pelham. He could have easily dismissed him without a word, but didn't. "Mr. Pelham, you are conscious of the delicate nature of the national scene, and I trust you appreciate the need to safeguard an environment in which we can accomplish our mission to educate. I cannot sanction anything that would fuel more rancor or aggression than is already evident in the Corps."

"Understood, sir, and I agree that quite vocal camps have formed, as I suspect they have in the academic and tactical departments."

Delafield seemed surprised by Pelham's observation, but nodded in agreement. "But doesn't that go to my point?"

"Sir, if I may, I think it profits little for us to ignore what is happening around us. We of the Corps are mature men in a course of instruction and a profession of arms that demands that we use the gift between our ears."

"You are being trained to follow orders and lead." Delafield's tone was terse.

"Yes, sir, but how are we to lead without independent thought? Our intention with the debate is only to inform those in attendance about an important issue, so that all might better see the opposing viewpoints and sift fact from fiction."

"What is it you want to debate?" Delafield asked bluntly.

Pelham responded as bluntly. "Sir, whether a state has the right to secede from the Union."

Delafield was certain he hadn't heard correctly. "Come, again."

Pelham repeated himself.

"Mr. Pelham, are you purposely trying my patience? Do you actually think I would sanction talk of secession, even in the guise of a dialectic debate?"

"Sir, the point of the debate would not be to argue whether states should secede, but whether there is a legitimate basis in law for doing so. We believe, sir, that there is a difference."

Delafield pressed the tips of his fingers together. "I see no difference, young man."

"The problem, sir, is that sectionalist talk is already rampant behind closed doors and in cliques that undermine our unity. The debate, at the very least, will place the arguments on the table."

"To what benefit?" Delafield asked, his tone sincere.

"Sir, to the end, we have what the founders fought for, free speech and expression of opinion. The debate might even quench some of the anarchical fires that already blaze."

Delafield drew a deep breath and rapped his desk with a pen. "You know full well, it's about slavery. There'd be no talk of secession if slavery were allowed in the territories."

"I don't doubt that, sir," Pelham conceded. "Yet I don't see how it is healthy to ignore an argument that goes to the broader question of states' rights."

"Ah!" Delafield wagged his finger. "That's the debate, isn't it, states' rights?"

Pelham repressed an urge to smile. "Sir, why not give opportunity for reasoned debate so that both camps, Unionists and states' rights advocates, can hear what the other has to say? I don't see how an even-handed debate, and I assure you it will be so, will do harm. Rather, I think it might take much of the sting out of the air."

Delafield pulled at his whiskers.

"Sir," Pelham said, "if you agree, the debate will be held in the academic building lecture hall on Saturday, October 27. It would be open to the Corps and anyone else who might want to attend."

"I suspect it would be well attended," Delafield conceded. "And your debaters?"

"Henry du Pont, for a state's right to secede."

Pelham perceived a slight nod of approval.

"And for the opposing argument—Emory Upton." Pelham chastised himself for hesitating.

The superintendent's eyes narrowed. "The dueling abolitionist?"

"He's an excellent debater, sir," Pelham said in defense of Upton. "I admit the man has personal views beyond the issue, but he has assured me that he will not stray beyond the bounds of the debate. He understands that to do so would cost him the debate and an otherwise improved standing within the Corps."

Delafield continued to pull at his whiskers. "What assurance do I have the debate won't become something ugly?"

Pelham straightened himself. "I will moderate it, sir."

That evening at supper Pelham informed members of the Dialectic Society that the debate was on and that he would call a meeting to consider how best to publicize the event. With one exception, the news was well received. Henry du Pont, more convinced than ever that he was miscast, pled for a replacement. It was to no avail, as Pelham's ear was deaf to altering anything that had formed the basis upon which he had attained Delafield's approval.

Returning to the barracks, Pelham found Rosser humming "Three Blind Mice" as he removed the grate from the fireplace and retrieved his pet. It had been nearly two weeks since the arrival of Mr. Mouse, and the creature had become a celebrity, receiving numerous visitors bearing morsels of cheese or crumbs of bread. Rosser had placed McElheny in charge of D Company's plebes to ensure that the tin box was kept clean and Mr. Mouse's water was changed on a regular basis.

"Mr. Mouse." Rosser's voice was shrill and squeaky. "I've an edible for you." He removed the lid and dropped a tiny piece of cheddar inside the box, inquiring how Mr. Mouse's day was.

Pelham found Rosser's mouse communications irritating, but had resolved to remain silent.

"C'mon little fella, it's your favorite." Rosser prodded the creature with his finger. "Up and at'em, little buddy, time to wake up."

Pelham flipped another page in Kendrick's geology text.

"John!" Rosser placed the tin box in front of Pelham and prodded the nonresponsive creature. "I think Mr. Mouse is—"

Pelham finished his sentence.

"But I don't understand." Rosser continued to nudge the creature.

In truth, Pelham could see that the mouse, while tiny by most standards, was enormous for its size, and for several days had moved about on its stomach. That it had eaten itself to death was not what Rosser needed to hear, so in sympathy Pelham offered, "Critters like these have very short life spans, Tom. He likely died of old age."

"You think?" Rosser seemed much relieved.

A knock at the door was followed by the appearance of McElheny. "Sir, a letter for Mr. Pelham."

"A bit late for mail, isn't it, Mr. McElheny?"

"Sir, Mr. Wiggins got yours by mistake, and he asked that I run it up."

"Then, I thank you." When Pelham saw that it was a letter from Clara, he added, "I thank you very much."

Before McElheny could retreat, Rosser blocked the door. "Mr. McElheny."

"Yes, sir." McElheny stood erect, no doubt numbing himself to whatever might follow.

"You remember Mr. Mouse, don't you?" Rosser showed McElheny the tin box.

"Yes, sir."

"Mr. Mouse is no longer with us."

"Yes, sir." McElheny eyed the deceased. "I'm sorry, sir. My condolences."

"Yes, thank you, McElheny. That means a lot to me."

McElheny waited in silence. "Sir … is there anything else?"

His voice seemed to steady Rosser. "Yes. Yes, there is."

McElheny waited, but Rosser didn't say what it was. "Mr. Rosser, sir?"

Rosser put the lid on the tin box. "Sorry, McElheny. I was just … Do you mind if I impose upon you?"

"Sir?"

"Would you make the final arrangements for Mr. Mouse?"

McElheny said nothing.

"And, if you would, maybe some appropriate remarks on his behalf—about the deceased?"

Pelham could hardly contain himself.

McElheny betrayed no emotion. "Certainly, sir. I'll see to it straightaway and let you know the particulars as soon as they are settled."

CHAPTER THIRTY-NINE

Friday, October 5, a dark cloud descended over a majority of the Corps. The results were in for Pennsylvania and Indiana. Both had gone Republican, and a cursory examination of the Electoral College showed that Lincoln had more than enough votes to secure the presidency. Nothing could change the outcome, not even the adoption of a compromise candidate by the Democrats. Knowing this, Pelham was even more convinced of the need for the debate. That evening he called a meeting of the society, at which it was agreed that an announcement of the debate would be prepared and posted on each company bulletin board, as well as distributed to the tactical and academic departments.

That evening, before he cracked a book, Pelham opened Clara's fifth letter in as many weeks, to find her flowered illustrations larger and more colorful. She had been admitted to the human anatomy course at Columbia University, despite the fact that she had missed the first four classes. Additionally, she had written to Dr. Elizabeth Blackwell and had received a warm reply from the country's first female doctor. Dr. Blackwell was encouraging in her letter, and informed Clara that she was not the only one attempting the hard climb. The doctor added that she would both welcome a visit and do whatever she could to help Clara secure acceptance to a reputable college. On her father's front, Clara had written him about her intention to become a doctor and to curry his support, but she had not yet broached the subject of the man from Alabama. She suggested that her father might choke on more than one pill at a time. Pelham smiled. To have done otherwise would have been foolish.

Her next paragraph, a short one, was for the benefit of Chas Patterson, whose Alice Paine was wavering. The previous Saturday and

237

Sunday, she had been observed in the company of her erstwhile lawyer friend.

The last of Clara's letter was a confession that, if she could vote, she would vote for Lincoln. Her defense was the desire for change that she believed Lincoln represented. While not detailing the change she expected, she said that Lincoln was an independent mind, not tainted by the games of Washington (at least not yet), and might bring a needed freshness and energy to the country.

Despite a paper due the next day in Professor French's law class, Pelham spent the best part of the evening replying to Clara's letter, urging her to visit Dr. Blackwell as soon as she could, supporting her decision to remain mum about their relationship until her father had digested his first pill, promising to soften the blow for Patterson, and honoring her right to vote as she saw fit—were she able to vote. He also wrote that she could rest easy, that Eva Taylor had communicated through Kingsbury the news that another man was courting Sallie Dandridge.

CHAPTER FORTY

News of the funeral for Mr. Mouse spread throughout the Corps, and on Sunday, October 7, after the midday meal, nearly all of D Company, a number of other upperclassmen, and all of McElheny's classmates showed up at the riding hall in full dress gray to pay their final respects. The arrangements were orchestrated by McElheny, and the scene in the riding hall was one of somber reverence. In the middle of the enormous hall, fifty chairs were arranged in five rows. In front of the chairs was a lectern, and to the right of the lectern, a flat waist-high dolly curtained with black crepe.

McElheny stood where he could greet those who arrived and direct them to their seats. His demeanor of deference and piety was contagious, and adopted by all in attendance. Upper classmen were ushered to seats, and those of the plebe class stood in a horseshoe around the upper classes.

By the time Rosser and Pelham arrived, all but the two chairs reserved for them had been taken.

"A sad day, Mr. McElheny," Pelham observed, as McElheny ushered them to the front row.

"Sir, perhaps you and Mr. Rosser would care to put on one of these." McElheny offered them each a black armband.

"Of course." Pelham's tone was reverent.

All seated, the silence and mood of the proceeding would have honored the passing of a head of state.

McElheny, with hands folded in front of his chest, approached the lectern, looked upon his audience, and cleared his throat.

Pelham fought for composure.

"My friends, it occurs to me that before we begin the service, I should ask Mr. Mouse's guardian, Mr. Thomas Rosser, if he would like to have a viewing of the open casket following the service."

Rosser, who himself was struggling for composure, whispered to Pelham, "What casket?"

"Mr. Rosser, sir?" McElheny pressed.

Rosser looked up. "Well, sure. I think we'd all like to see Mr. Mouse one last time."

"Very good, sir." McElheny nodded solemnly.

On cue, a door at the side of the riding hall opened, and through it walked eight of McElheny's D Company classmates, four on either side of a full-size casket, each plebe wearing a black armband. The funeral procession moved slowly and in lockstep across the hall. With synchronized movements the pallbearers placed the closed casket on the dolly, and then assumed a position of parade rest behind the casket.

"And, Mr. Rosser," McElheny went on, "I understand that you have requested Mr. Mouse be cremated after this service, and his ashes scattered over the Hudson."

Rosser didn't remember saying so, but responded, "Yes. He would have liked that."

McElheny nodded perfunctorily, again cleared his throat, and faced the assembled. "We are here to say farewell to one who in the short time he was with us, spread great joy, lightened the burden of our days, and never once had a regard for himself. Selfless, is a word that personifies the departed …"

McElheny continued for twenty minutes, his eulogy straining the insides of every man present. Yet, remarkably, the decorum of the proceeding remained respectful.

"And so," McElheny finished, "we take heart, knowing that in heaven, we reunite with the Lord and our loved ones, and hope that God in his infinite mercy has a place for the tiniest of his creatures, even our beloved Mr. Mouse. Amen."

Pelham glanced at Rosser, whose eyes were glistening.

Responding to a nod from McElheny, two of the pallbearers removed the lid to the casket.

"My friends," McElheny said, "if we could proceed from right to left. Mr. Rosser, Mr. Pelham, if you would care to be first …"

As Pelham put a hand on Rosser's shoulder, the muscles of his diaphragm ached. "Come, Tom. It's time."

Pelham was the first to view the casket, and he had to bite his lip. In the center of the padded, silk-lined casket was the tiny gray form of Mr. Mouse, his body somehow straightened, his forelegs crossed. His lower half was discreetly covered with a small swatch of black felt. Pelham consoled an emotional Rosser and stepped to the side, where the two of them received words of sympathy from those who followed.

In minutes, the viewing was over and the riding hall empty except for Rosser, Pelham, and McElheny. The pall bearers and the rest of McElheny's classmates had closed and removed the casket, the chairs, the lectern, and the dolly, and had readied the hall for its intended use.

"Mr. McElheny!" Rosser's voice boomed in characteristic fury. "Front—and—center!"

In a flash, McElheny, stripped of persona, stood at attention in front of Rosser.

"Mr. McElheny!" Rosser's voice rumbled off the walls of the great hall.

"Yes, sir."

"What is your name, beanhead?" Rosser's voice rose to a higher, even more intimidating pitch.

"McElheny, sir."

"Your full name, beanhead!"

"Sir, John Daniel McElheny, sir."

Rosser leaned forward, his nose nearly touching McElheny's. "What do your friends call you, beanhead?"

"Sir, Dan, sir."

"Then that will be your name!" Rosser's menacing glare unscrewed into a huge grin, his right hand extended.

Speechless, but unhesitating, McElheny grabbed Rosser's hand. He understood full well what was happening. He was being "recognized," the cadet term for acceptance of a plebe by an upperclassman as an equal, which before graduation was a rare occurrence, and a practice strictly prohibited within the same company.

Rosser and Pelham enjoyed a long laugh, before Rosser put a hand on McElheny's shoulder. "An incredible piece of work, Dan. Absolutely incredible. From now on, you call me Tom."

"Thank you, sir. Thank you very much, sir."

"Tom."

"Yes, sir."

"The name is Tom!"

"Yes, Tom, thank you … Tom."

"Highly irregular, this is. You know that?"

"I do, sir, I mean, Tom, and I'll not abuse it. None will know from me that you are anything but the same bastard you've always been."

Rosser and Pelham laughed heartily.

"And with one of us, you get the both, Dan." Pelham extended his hand.

As they left the riding hall, Rosser was shaking his head. "Where the hell did you get the casket?"

CHAPTER FORTY-ONE

At breakfast the next morning, Adelbert Ames informed Pelham that he was visiting Rebecca Astor in the City the next weekend, and was there a message he might deliver to Clara. Concealing his envy, Pelham said there wasn't, but to have a wonderful time.

Before first hour class, Pelham was finishing his civil engineering homework, when Rosser flew into the room, livid, the fluency of his profanity flawless.

"We win the war, hell we win both of them, and still are made to suffer at their hands!" Rosser collapsed in his chair.

"Whose hands?"

"The bleeding British! That's who!"

"What do you mean?"

"They're coming! The bonny Prince of Wales is coming to West Point."

"Who told you that?"

"Kingsbury and du Pont. Reynolds briefed the battalion staff after breakfast. First ever heir to the British throne to visit North America."

Pelham loosed his own, albeit slightly less oiled, brand of profanity. "Dammit, somebody's always rocking the boat. And he wants to come here?"

"He and his entourage are set to leave Canada. They'll bunk at the White House next, then a big parade in New York City, and last of all us."

"Bless his limey little heart," Pelham said. "We'll be drilling until the day he arrives. When is the show?"

"In a week. They come on Monday and leave the next day."

An oddly satisfying thought occurred to Pelham. Adelbert Ames would not be seeing Rebecca Astor that weekend.

On his way back to the barracks after the midday meal, fellow Alabamian, Charlie Ball, stopped Pelham.

"John, I can't believe it." Ball was beside himself.

"I know," Pelham said. "We've enough on our plate without the royals."

"Not the royals," Ball exclaimed. "What were you thinking, putting Upton into the debate? The man's nuts!"

"Calm down. He's not nuts, he's an abolitionist. He'll behave himself, I promise."

"We're talking Upton!"

"Listen, Charlie, Lincoln has the votes, right? He's going to be the next president of the United States, right?"

Ball nodded.

"The debate will give an important issue, secession, a fair forum. Henry will fairly represent what the South wants, and the North deserves equal billing. The debate is meaningless without competent advocates."

"There was no one else you could think of?" Ball pressed.

"Charlie, you're my only negative response. Listen, any forum to argue states' rights is a forum for us."

"You obviously haven't heard from the South Carolinians. Henry Farley of your own company is incensed. It's not the debate—it's Upton!"

"Upton can do us no harm. Do me a favor and talk to the naysayers. Trust me, this is a good thing."

Tuesday afternoon, Lee summoned Pelham to his office in the commandant's building and wasted no words. "General Scott is coming for the royals. He wants a demonstration for them, a display of horsemanship for the visiting prince."

"Yes, sir."

"Our visitors will debark at South Dock and arrive on the Plain via omnibus. They'll troop the Corps on foot in front of the barracks, and then proceed to the superintendent's quarters for the parade review. After the review is where you come in."

"Me, sir?"

"Set up a series of jumps, different heights, different types, behind the parade area. Make it interesting."

"I'm volunteering, sir?"

Lee smiled. "Of course."

Pelham nodded. "The prince, sir. Do you know his age?"

"Twenty, I think, about your age."

Before supper, Patterson informed Pelham that he was no longer in the life of Alice Paine, that her lawyer beau had formally proposed and she had formally accepted. Pelham expressed insincere condolences.

After supper, Kingsbury caught up with Pelham on the way to the barracks. "I did it, John!"

"Did what?"

"I'm engaged! Eva and I are to marry."

"You're kidding! When did this happen? We talked last night and you said nothing—"

"All by telegram. I decided at breakfast and sent Eva a telegram asking for her hand. By noon, I had her telegram and her hand."

Pelham smiled.

"Then I sent her father a telegram asking his blessing, and just before supper I have that. Can you believe it—in a matter of ten hours, over and done?"

"And the big day?"

"Right after graduation."

CHAPTER FORTY-TWO

Sunday, October 14, the Corps, less Pelham, drilled for two hours on the Plain for the sixth day in a row, passing in review time and again. Their marching, alignment, and manual of arms were critiqued beyond reason by Reynolds and Hardee, the latter still lodging at the West Point Hotel awaiting passage to Savannah. The day before, General Winfield Scott, Old Fuss & Feathers himself, arrived to join in the critique. By virtue of his size, the general, who weighed more than three hundred pounds, proved quite a challenge for James and the other attendants of the superintendent's quarters, where the Delafields hosted the Scotts. Left to his own devices, Pelham experimented with various configurations for the obstacle course. When he finished each configuration, he tested it, but only when the Corps was not in a position to see him.

The next morning at breakfast, word quickly spread that the British contingent would arrive on the federal revenue cutter *Harriett Lane* at the South Dock shortly after noon. It was also reported that the previous day half a million people had lined Broadway in New York City for a glimpse of the heir apparent.

The British landed at one o'clock, greeted by Delafield and Reynolds and a squadron of blue uniformed cavalry. Since the royals declined the omnibus, preferring to walk, Delafield and Reynolds dismounted and led the royals on foot up the bluff road to the level of the Plain. There, a brilliant backdrop of fall color beneath a crisp blue sky greeted them, along with a national salute thundered by the West Point battery. The West Point band struck up "God Save the Queen," followed by "The Flower of Edinburgh." The principal spokesman for Crown Prince Albert Edward was the prince's consort, General Bruce, Duke of Newcastle, who walked on one side of Delafield, while the royal walked on the other.

By the time the prince and his contingent began to troop the Corps, the Corps had been standing formation on Jefferson Road for over an hour. During the inspection, a plebe passed out and had to be taken to the hospital. The prince, at the lead of the reviewing party, was of medium height and blond, with engaging blue eyes, and the young royal passed within feet of the first rank of cadets in each company. When he reached D Company and the west end of the Corps formation, Pelham whispered to Rosser, "He looks a lot like Adelbert, but with a mustache."

"He looks impressive," Rosser admitted. The young royal sported a regal uniform with gleaming medals and a cross sash that suggested a seasoned warrior.

When the contingent had passed by, Pelham took his leave and retreated through the sally port into Central Area, where a flustered enlisted man was struggling to control Cotton. Pelham approached the immaculately groomed horse, rubbed its nose, and stepped lightly into the saddle. "Easy, Cotton. We'll get our chance."

The royal contingent moved past the throng of spectators to the superintendent's quarters, where refreshments were taken and General Scott was introduced to the crown prince. Delafield then announced it was time for the review, and he, Scott, and Reynolds led the visiting British to the reviewing stand.

The silhouette of six diverse jumps and a well-dressed target dummy were visible beyond the portion of the field reserved for the parade review, and captured the attention of the six thousand visitors.

A single drum broke the relative silence, beating a cadence that set the Corps in motion. The commands of Chambliss were echoed by company commanders and platoon leaders. The crowd, four deep within the tree line along Jefferson Road, turned their heads in anticipation. As Chambliss and the battalion staff led A Company onto the Plain, the fife and drum section of the West Point band struck up the British march, "Garry Owen." The brisk lightness of the unfamiliar music delighted the Corps.

Later, at the supper meal, in reference to the Corps' performance on the Plain, General Bruce would tell Reynolds that his British Palace Guard could not have executed as well as the Corps of Cadets had that afternoon.

After the Corps passed in review and marched off the field, they joined the array of onlookers to watch Pelham perform. Colonel Delafield explained to his guests what was to happen next, and Reynolds raised his hat—the signal for Pelham. Until then, he had been positioned near the east corner of the barracks, inside the tree line bordering Jefferson Road.

"Time to dance, my friend," Pelham whispered into Cotton's ear, as he pressured Cotton's white flanks and galloped directly for the reviewing stand. He reared Cotton in front of the reviewing stand to the delight of all in attendance, and made eye contact with the prince. The two exchanged smiles. After a salute to the reviewing party, which included a bow by Cotton, Pelham kicked the horse to a gallop and sped to the north end of the obstacle course. He cleared the first jump with ease, as he did each succeeding and increasingly higher jump; and after clearing the final jump, he drew his saber and decapitated the target dummy. The crowd roared.

The tumult continued as Pelham then initiated the unexpected. Instead of returning to the Jefferson Road and thence to the stables, he proceeded at a full gallop for the reviewing stand. As he approached, the roar of the crowd evaporated, accentuating the sound of Cotton's pounding hoofs. Rosser would later tell Pelham that Scott, Delafield, and Reynolds could not have been more confused, and that the royal party had shuffled to the rear of the stand. From a full gallop and less than fifteen yards from the reviewing party, Pelham abruptly drew Cotton to a halt. Instantly, he dismounted and pulled the horse down by the bit onto his flank. Kneeling, with Cotton between him and the reviewing stand, he drew his pistol and brandished it high in the air.

The six thousand spectators remained stunned until the Corps of Cadets gave Pelham a rousing cheer. It was then that Reynolds explained to the great delight of the visitors that Pelham had just demonstrated the final tactic of a mounted trooper on the frontier defending himself against an Indian attack, a tactic taught in the second semester of the Second Class year.

Pelham sprang to his feet and holstered his pistol, and Cotton bounced easily to his feet. Surprising all on the Plain, the Crown Prince descended from the reviewing stand and greeted Pelham with an extended hand.

"Bravo, young man, bravo. Truly extraordinary!"

"Thank you, your highness," Pelham said, shaking the royal's hand.

The Prince rubbed Cotton's neck. "Yours is a most magnificent steed."

Pelham touched the bill of his cap in acknowledgment, his face dirty and streaked with sweat.

"And you, sir," the prince went on, "have great skill. Do all in the Corps possess such skill?"

"Your Highness, you could pick anyone from the First Class, and they could do the same."

As the crowd dispersed, the Corps was dismissed to the barracks, and the young royal and his contingent were escorted to the hotel. It had been rumored about the Corps that there would be a grand celebration ball for all upper classes to honor the prince.

To the Corps' immense disappointment, especially after another supper of mutton, the rumor of the grand ball at the hotel proved false. General Bruce had declared that the prince needed his rest.

An evening that would have been a total loss was softened by an invitation from Custer for Pelham and Rosser to enjoy a fine hash, the aroma of which preceded the invitation. Custer had configured a cooking plate above the gas light in his room, and on the plate was a simmering pot. He was whistling the "Garry Owen" march as Pelham and Rosser arrived.

"Evening, Jim," Pelham greeted James Parker, Custer's roommate. "What's cooking?"

"The king's eggs, some bacon, and a few potatoes."

Parker served up the feast with his usual flair.

Pelham pronounced with full cheeks, "Tom, we're going to miss Fannie's cooking."

"Nope, we're taking him with us." Rosser had already presented Parker with an empty plate and a plea for seconds. "Can you believe the impudence of that royal brat? He could have given us a royal time, and instead we get the royal shaft."

"Don't believe for a minute that it was his doing." Pelham defended the prince. "As a matter of fact, I understand he's quite the social creature. I suspect his nursemaid has instructions from the queen to tone the boy down. Can't have a royal making a spectacle of himself."

"You think?"

"The lad's got fire in his eyes, and is no different from you or me, except for a thousand rules to follow. You think we have it tough? Try being king."

Nate Chambliss appeared in the doorway with an expectant look. "Fannie, I could smell your hash across the area."

Custer returned an apologetic look. "Sorry, Nate, my pot's empty."

"So how is it with you and Jessica Danford?" Pelham asked Chambliss.

"Very well, actually. I'm invited to her house for a day or two over Christmas."

At two o'clock the next day, after meeting with members of the First Class, visiting various academic classes, the riding hall, and the mess hall, and witnessing a second well-attended review, in which Pelham marched as a nondescript with a musket on his shoulder, the prince led his entourage down South Dock Road and departed on the *Harriett Lane*, but not before granting amnesty as a visiting head of state to all those who had tours to walk or confinements to sit, which included Pelham, Rosser, and Custer.

The letter from Clara that arrived on Friday, October 19, contained only good news. Her father admitted to being the force behind her entry into the human anatomy laboratory class, and while she had missed the first month and a half of classes, she had been well received by her male colleagues, who seemed to enjoy her response to a male cadaver. She also reported that she was to visit Geneva Medical College as the guest of Dr. Elizabeth Blackwell the third weekend in November.

The next day, after the midday meal, while Adelbert Ames was visiting Rebecca Astor in New York City, an official piece of mail greeted Rosser upon his return to the barracks. The letter bore the seal of the State of Texas.

"John, it has to be from Governor Houston," Rosser exclaimed with delight. He tore open the letter. But as he read it, the color drained from his face.

"What?" Pelham asked, witnessing the transformation.

Rosser handed him the letter.

Pelham read it and whistled. "Not what I expected."

"Can you believe it? He wants me to stay and graduate."

"And if I'm reading it right, even if Texas secedes."

Rosser was incredulous. "The man is a ... a bleeding Unionist!"

CHAPTER FORTY-THREE

At breakfast, Monday, October 22, Pelham cornered Adelbert Ames with a knowing wink. "So tell me. A great time?"

Ames shook his head. "I now know the meaning of entrapment."

"What?"

"Rebecca is from Concord, Rhode Island, not exactly across the street from New York City. When I get to Clermont, she has a surprise for me. Scarcely have we kissed, and that was one of only two the entire weekend, when she introduces me to her mother, who just happens to be visiting from the city. I have never before been so scrutinized or interrogated in my life. Are your intentions honorable, sir? Do you intend to make the army a career? You wouldn't take my daughter to the frontier, would you? Rebecca won't do well around Indians."

Pelham couldn't stop laughing.

"The old woman had me constantly on the defensive, and Rebecca—she isn't herself around her mother—and I fear her mother will always be around. We had but five minutes to ourselves the whole weekend."

"Your intentions?"

"To flee."

Later, at the midday meal, Charlie Ball asked Walter Kingsbury to announce that he would be taking a straw poll for the presidential election at the supper meal, and that ballots could be picked up on the way out of the mess hall. Kingsbury consented to the announcement, and it roused little discussion in the mess hall.

That afternoon, Colonel Delafield received a lengthy telegram from General Scott, who had returned to New York City, to the effect that matters were rapidly heating up in Charleston, South Carolina. The message read:

> Colonel John Gardner, in charge of federal installations in Charleston Harbor, is grossly undermanned to defend the installations should an initiative be taken by South Carolina to control them.

Scott went on to express frustration with President Buchanan's secretary of war, John Floyd. Floyd had dismissed out of hand the suggestion to reinforce federal forts and arsenals in the South, saying that such moves would send inflammatory signals.

At the supper meal, Charlie Ball hand counted the ballots in the voting box and asked Kingsbury to announce that two hundred and forty-eight votes had been cast in the straw poll, or about 90 percent of the Corps, and that he would have the results in the morning.

"Other than Upton, I'd be surprised if there are a dozen votes for the Republican," Rosser said to Pelham.

Pelham shook his head. "I think there could easily be as many as thirty. Remember, Lincoln is in favor of tariffs, which benefit the North."

"A dollar says you're wrong," Rosser countered. "Twenty-five or less and I win."

The two struck hands.

The next morning, the normally sedate Corps was abuzz in anticipation of the election results. Before the Corps took seats, Pelham was surprised to see Ball heading his direction.

"John, I can't believe it," Ball whispered. "There were sixty-four Republican votes."

Pelham raised an eyebrow. "That is surprising."

"It's absurd."

"Have you told Walter?"

"Not yet."

"You've got to."

"I can't."

"Well, I can." Pelham took Ball's tally and delivered it to Kingsbury.

Kingsbury immediately made the announcement. "The straw poll for the presidency has one hundred and eighty-four votes for the Democrats and sixty-four votes for the Republicans."

Except for an expletive from Rosser, the response from the Corps was passive.

After breakfast, Ball intercepted Pelham. "Sorry, John, I—I just wasn't prepared for the results."

"Don't worry about it."

"John, we're as conservative a group as you'll find in the entire country. Think how the masses will vote."

"You did well to call for the vote. We know Lincoln will win. But you showed me and the rest of the Corps that three out of four of us are not Republican. That is not a bad thing."

CHAPTER FORTY-FOUR

Saturday afternoon, October 27, the air in the over-packed academic building lecture hall was electric with confrontation. The editor of the Cornwall weekly and a reporter from Newburgh were in attendance, and both had sought comment from Colonel Delafield, who respectfully declined.

Taking a position at the lectern, Pelham raised his hand for quiet. The night before, he had slept fitfully, questioning his initiative, but by morning was convinced more than ever of the rightness of what was to take place.

"Thank you all for your attendance today," he began. "The topic for debate is whether a state has the right to secede from the Union, and I know that Mr. Henry du Pont and Mr. Emory Upton have thoroughly prepared themselves to advocate the positions they have been assigned. Henry du Pont will argue that a state has the right, and Emory Upton will argue that it does not. The intent of the debate is to lay the issues before us, not to declare a winner." Pelham resisted the temptation to add that the winner would be decided by others soon enough.

"Before we begin, I would like to acknowledge the presence of Colonel Delafield and his wife, Lieutenant Colonel Reynolds and his wife, the balance of the tactical department, and, it appears, all of the academic department."

Professor Mahan nodded perfunctorily, while Professor Weir offered a genuine smile.

Pelham wasted no time explaining rules specially modified for the debate, which allowed each debater twenty minutes for his primary construction and ten minutes for rebuttal. He made it clear that the scope of the debate was not to be extended, and that no new arguments

255

could be advanced in rebuttal. His remarks concluded, he retrieved a coin from his pocket.

"Mr. du Pont, by academic rank, will call the toss."

Pelham flipped the coin, and du Pont called heads. Pelham opened his fist. "Tails." He turned to the audience. "Mr. Upton will be first to argue the issue."

Upton approached the lectern with his briefcase, from which he retrieved notes and several documents. He glanced at the wall clock, and then at Pelham for the signal to begin.

"I have in my hand a copy of the Constitution of the United States of America," Upton began. "With the signing of this compact, every member state inextricably assigned its right of sovereignty to the resulting Union we call the United States of America. What was previously a confederacy, and which embodied the sovereignty of individual states, ceased to exist."

"The premise for the United States being a perpetual union that cannot be dissolved lies in the process for its ratification. The people of each state accomplished ratification of the Union, not the individual governments of each state. In that one act, 'We the people,' not 'We the states,' became the Union. Governance of geographical boundaries and interests within the Union was rightly assigned to state governments, but only to the extent that such governments abided by and within the constraints of the Constitution and the amendments thereto."

Upton proceeded to support his argument with examples of precedence for the subservience of state governments to the federal government. His chief example was President Andrew Jackson, in 1828, threatening to send troops into South Carolina in response to their threat to nullify a federal tariff law, which they deemed not in the interest of South Carolina.

At Pelham's one-minute signal, Upton summarized his argument, and when his time was up, collected his materials and took his seat.

The lecture hall, respectful throughout Upton's remarks, buzzed in anticipation of what du Pont would say.

"We will now hear the opposing viewpoint from Henry du Pont." Pelham motioned to du Pont, who approached the lectern with his own materials.

"A paradox," du Pont began upon Pelham's signal, "is what we have. For I too hold up a copy of the Constitution, the same one that Mr. Upton showed you. There is nothing in this document that strips a state of its sovereignty in any matter not specifically invested in the federal government. Getting right to the point, neither the Constitution nor its amendments, beginning with what we call the Bill of Rights, give the federal government the power to prevent secession by a state. Further and unequivocally, the Tenth Amendment to the Constitution gives to the states, and the people, all rights not otherwise vested in the federal government. Ergo, a state has the right to secede, because there is no law or provision preventing it." Du Pont paused for effect. "I could stop right there, and probably should. To say more would water down this primal point, which cannot be contested, at least not legally. But I've nineteen minutes to go."

Light laughter erupted across the room.

"We'll have order, please," Pelham said in an even tone.

Du Pont used the rest of his time to defend with historical precedents the rights of individual states, taking head-on President Jackson's actions against South Carolina as unconstitutional, saying that while Jackson got his way, that did not make his actions lawful. He argued that a state had the right to ignore a federal law that went against the laws and interests of the state; and that when the compact between a sovereign state and the federal government was breached, it was null and void unless reparable to both parties. Du Pont then elevated the argument to the "pursuit of happiness" contained in the preamble of the Declaration of Independence, and the "promotion of the general welfare" contained in the preamble to the Constitution. The unhappiness of the people of a state and their view that the welfare they sought had not been promoted by a federal government were legitimate bases for redress. When redress was not satisfactorily served, the extreme measure of secession was a viable remedy.

Pelham kept a close eye on Colonel Delafield throughout the debate, and was relieved to see the superintendent closely following the arguments and not once pulling at his whiskers. Despite his personal leanings, Pelham was impressed by the evenhanded treatment that Upton had given his side of the issue.

On Pelham's signal, du Pont took his seat.

"Mr. Upton will now have ten minutes to rebut Mr. du Pont's argument."

Upton approached the lectern. "Indeed we do have a paradox," he conceded. "The letter of the Constitution and letter of its amendments may appear ambiguous, but their intent is not. The founding fathers envisioned a perpetual union of its member people. Furthermore, Article VI of the Constitution requires by oath or affirmation that federal and state legislators, executive officers, and judicial officers support the Constitution of the United States of America. Ours is the most solemn and permanent of marriages. Support of the Constitution is not an option. It is a sacred trust."

Upton again argued that "the people," not the states, formed the country, that majority rule was the cornerstone of democracy, and that the vast majority of the "the people" comprising the country would entirely oppose any thought of secession.

Upton sat down and du Pont stood up.

In du Pont's rebuttal, he quickly seized upon Upton's metaphor of marriage, remarking that marriages that did not work out resulted in divorces, and that secession was no more, no less, the result of a failed marriage. He then returned to the central issue, the absence of any provision in the Constitution or its amendments that would preclude a state from seceding. Lastly, du Pont built the argument that there was no provision to prevent a state from undoing what it had done to join the Union, suggesting that the people of a state, by public referendum, could decide because of their collective grievances to vote themselves out of the Union.

Du Pont sat down.

The debate was over and Pelham approached the lectern. He eyed the audience, which seemed to him in authentic reflection. He was pleased with what had taken place. Neither debater had made any connection with the divisive issue of slavery. Both had gone to the Constitution and its amendments.

"Let's express our appreciation to Mr. du Pont and Mr. Upton for a fine debate."

A sincere, though muted, round of applause was given both du Pont and Upton by all in attendance.

After the room emptied, du Pont and Upton waited in the hall for Pelham.

"So what do you think?" du Pont asked.

"What do you think?" Pelham countered with a smile.

"I had expected more of a response," Upton said, visibly disappointed.

"Don't confuse what you didn't hear with the import of the message. You both did well. You served up what has frustrated both Unionists and states' rights advocates for eighty years. You presented the paradox."

Pelham and du Pont returned to the barracks together, and during the short walk du Pont made it clear that he wished he'd had no part in the debate, that personally he believed secession was wrong, even unconscionable. Yes, he had voted Democrat in the straw poll, but he abhorred the thought of a divided nation. His remarks stung Pelham, but Pelham only said that he respected du Pont's suppression of personal opinion, that he had well and impartially defended his position in the debate, and that the debate was now history.

Later that afternoon, Pelham reported as ordered to the superintendent's quarters, where Delafield congratulated him on the debate, making the observation that the defensibility of the opposing arguments did not bode well for the country.

When Pelham returned to the barracks, he found a letter from his father on his desk. The letter conveyed the news that Butch Jansonne had been sacked the last week of picking season, when Pelham's brother Charles had found him whipping two of the blacks. The final straw, however, had been a visit the same week by the county sheriff, who delivered a lawsuit brought by the neighboring Watson family. The lawsuit accused Jansonne of destruction of property, to wit the death of the runaway slave Charlie Watson, and named the Pelham family co-defendants by virtue of supervising responsibility. The lawsuit alleged that the slave ran off due to excessive maltreatment, and the Watson overseer swore the idea came from Butch Jansonne. Pelham was relieved to read in the next sentence that the lawsuit had been dismissed less than a week later.

In the balance of the letter, his father provided an update on the family and plantation matters, chief of which was an agreement between himself and Samuel. If Samuel could get the plantation work done without an overseer, he would serve as the new overseer and receive one quarter of the salary paid a white overseer.

CHAPTER FORTY-FIVE

While discussions in the barracks, between classes, and in the mess hall continued to center on the debate and the issue of secession, Henry du Pont and Emory Upton sought cover from the bombardment of supporters and detractors.

The following Monday, with the temperature dipping well below freezing, Pelham went to the library between classes to check out Charles Dickens's *American Notes*, finally giving in to Clara's urging that he read it. He was on his way back to the barracks when du Pont approached him.

"Can we talk, John?" Du Pont's expression suggested a serious matter.

"Sure. What is it?"

"Not here." Du Pont led Pelham around to the side of the barracks. "I need a favor—a big favor."

"Anything, so long as it's not money," Pelham said with a grin.

"I need a second for a pugilistic contest."

"Pugilistic contest? You're fighting someone?"

Du Pont nodded.

"Who?"

Du Pont hesitated. "Upton."

"Emory? Are you kidding me?"

Du Pont shook his head.

"That makes no sense."

"He thinks I called him a liar."

It was Pelham's turn to pause. "Did you?"

"You know better than that. Somebody got to Emory, and Emory won't say who—and obviously believes him."

Pelham couldn't help smiling. "And you two were doing so well."

"For a whole week."

"What was it you were supposed to have lied about?"

"That too is a mystery. He wouldn't tell me."

"Vintage Upton. When is it to be?"

"Day after tomorrow, below Fort Clinton."

"That's quick."

"Anyway, I was hoping you would—"

Pelham interrupted. "You know Emory and I are friends. But if that's what you want, I'll stand by you."

Du Pont grasped Pelham's hand. "I need more than that. I need training. You did a first-rate job on that sadistic First Classman our plebe year. I'll take any tips you can give."

After class, Pelham met du Pont in the fencing gymnasium and fitted him with boxing gloves. He then gave him tips on stance, footwork, balance, breathing, and how to maximize power behind punches. Then he talked about Upton, pointing out the obvious, that Upton had a two-inch longer reach, so there was a zone that he needed to be either inside of or outside of. Otherwise, Upton could pop him at will.

"The important thing," Pelham said, "is to stay centered on your feet, just like in fencing, and parry the incoming blows. Move in only when you see an opening, and then strike and retreat. Breathe regular and often. The less you breathe, the faster you fatigue."

Pelham also donned gloves and demonstrated two combinations of punches: two left jabs and a right cross, and then two left jabs and an uppercut. "Okay, now you try it."

The response from du Pont was less than inspiring.

Pelham forced a straight face. "Not bad. Watch me again."

By supper, everyone in the Corps knew about the fight and few cared why, only that there would be one. Rosser was in that camp, putting his entrepreneurial spirit to good use.

CHAPTER FORTY-SIX

Tuesday, October 30, a letter from Clara brought sunshine to an otherwise gray day. After classes, Pelham reclined on his bed and slit the scented envelope with a penknife. The letter was unlike any of her others, save for the final paragraph in which she again affirmed her willingness to suffer all for the chance to be with him again.

Her focus was on the autobiographical book she had read, *Twelve Years a Slave*, written by Solomon Northup. The author was a free Negro who had been kidnapped, brutalized, and sold into slavery while conducting business in Washington DC, leaving a wife and three children. He was shipped by his captors to Louisiana, where he was purchased by the owner of a cotton plantation. In his twelfth year of captivity, every year seeking an opportunity to escape, Northup finally secreted a letter to a politically connected friend, who launched an investigation that resulted in his rescue.

Clara asked Pelham if he had read the book, and asked if the things described in the book really happened. Pelham wrote back that he had never heard of the book and that he was not personally aware of any free blacks who had been sold into slavery, but that he couldn't deny that such things happened. He again expressed hope that one day she would see Alabama for herself, see how the vast majority of blacks were treated, that humankind, not slavery in and of itself, was the evil.

By supper, Rosser had taken more than fifty bets on the outcome of the du Pont-Upton fight. The vast majority favored Upton, the taller and wirier fighter, who at least had experience dueling with swords. Word of the skewed betting somehow got to du Pont, with predictable effect, and Pelham found himself not only a boxing coach but the steward of du Pont's confidence.

News of the fight had also reached Lieutenant Lee, who chose to keep it to himself, it being common for tactical staff to look the other way when cadets settled disputes.

In the thirty minutes of free time after supper, Pelham and du Pont again met in the basement of the academic building.

"Take your stance," Pelham said, immediately moving parts of du Pont's body. "Left shoulder forward, chin down, hands in front, left hand up and forward, thumbs up, more bend at the waist." Pelham stepped back. "How do you feel?"

"Like a pretzel!"

"The important thing, Henry, is to keep your guard up, keep moving, and bide your time. Don't be in a hurry."

A few minutes after taps, Pelham was still at his desk when he heard a knock at the door. The South Carolinian, Henry Farley, stood in the doorway, a sheepish expression on his face.

"What brings you out risking a skin?" Pelham asked.

Farley motioned for Pelham to come to the door. Rosser was into an engineering problem and paid them no attention.

"What is it, Henry?"

"Du Pont and Upton."

"The fight?"

"It was a joke, John."

They both heard the door open three floors below. Farley peered over the banister. It was a cadet returning from the showers.

"A joke?" Pelham repeated.

"I tried to explain to Henry. I've just come from his room. It was never supposed to get this far."

"What? You're the one who ratted on Henry?"

Farley smiled weakly. "I maybe stretched a point."

"What did you tell Upton?"

"That du Pont thought he wasn't being honest in the debate."

"Honest?"

"It was just a rib, and you and I both know Upton's a flaming abolitionist. If he'd really been honest, he'd have come across much different. Anyway, some of us were talking that it was a shame to see the two of them getting along so well. I suggested it wouldn't last. Paddy

O'Rorke said it would. That led to a bet, and I—I wanted to hedge my bet."

"You dog." Pelham had to repress a smile.

"But du Pont is still going through with it!"

"Why?"

"He said the whole Corps is expecting it, and how would it look if it got out that the two of them had been duped by a sham? Worse… by me."

Pelham smiled. "There is something to that logic."

"He made me promise to keep quiet, to just let it happen."

"Then I suggest you do just that. Bide your tongue and get back to your room."

CHAPTER FORTY-SEVEN

The next day, Delafield was oblivious to the stream of cadets moving across the Plain toward old Fort Clinton. He had just received another telegram from General Scott.

James saw the tension in the colonel's face. "Sir, I made some fresh coffee."

"James," Delafield said. "John Floyd, our slippery secretary of war, has ordered eleven 32-pounders and a hundred and ten Columbiad cannons to be made and sent to Ship Island, Mississippi, and Galveston, Texas. Do you have any idea how much firepower that is?"

"No, sir."

"You know what this is, James?"

"No, sir."

"Treason. That's what it is, boldfaced, served-up-hot treason by a Virginian who's arming the South." Delafield took the offered cup. "Here we are a week short of the election, and the cotton states have declared from the treetops their intention to secede once Lincoln is elected. Why in God's great creation would we invest in fortifying the shores of two states that will no longer belong to us?"

James offered the superintendent a slice of pound cake.

"Buchanan isn't paying attention, James. Three of his cabinet are avowed fire-eaters. Along with Floyd, you have Howell Cobb of Georgia, his secretary of the treasury, and Jacob Thompson of Mississippi, his secretary of interior. Those three won't let the Washington sun set on their traitorous rumps the day their states secede." Delafield looked skyward. "God grant Buchanan some wisdom."

Below and east of old Fort Clinton, the crowd of gray uniforms grew to witness the fight between du Pont and Upton. A number of cadets huddled around Rosser, who was taking last minute bets. Both du Pont and Upton were attired in riding pants and long-sleeved undershirts, and both were fitted with eight-ounce boxing gloves.

Pelham massaged du Pont's shoulders. "How do you feel, champ?"

Du Pont mumbled something unintelligible.

Pelham glanced across the small opening in the crowd at John Rodgers, Upton's roommate and second. The two exchanged nods.

"Let's do this, Henry." Pelham slapped du Pont on the back.

The crowd of nearly a hundred and fifty cheered as Upton and du Pont faced off. Walter Kingsbury stood between them as referee.

"There will be no rounds," Kingsbury announced. "Simply a fight that continues until one of you concedes or is down for the count of ten. There will be no hitting below the waist, no kicking, no biting, and no head butting. Anyone doing so will be declared the loser."

Du Pont and Upton nodded.

"Touch gloves and may the best man win."

"This is stupid, Emory," du Pont whispered as they touched gloves.

"I know. Farley told me everything, and I agree with you—we don't have a choice."

Upton hadn't finished his sentence when he stung du Pont with a left jab to the chin, snapping his head back.

Dazed, du Pont absorbed a second jab, followed by a right to the stomach. Barely ten seconds into the fight, du Pont dropped to one knee, gasping for air and tasting blood.

"You okay, Henry?" Kingsbury stood over him.

Du Pont spat red and got to his feet.

"Give it up, Henry," Upton urged. "You don't need this."

Du Pont took a roundhouse swing at Upton, missing and losing his balance.

Upton answered with another jab, followed by an uppercut, both landing squarely on du Pont's jaw. Du Pont stumbled backward, blood trickling from his mouth. Shaking his head, he lunged at Upton, locking him in a clinch.

The crowd responded with boos, and Kingsbury stepped in. "Break it up, Henry."

Pelham shouted instructions to du Pont. "Guard up, Henry. Keep moving!"

Du Pont was clearly dazed, and the crowd sensed an all too short fight. Some screamed for Upton to finish the job, others urged du Pont to make it a fight.

The two separated, and after absorbing another head shot, du Pont clinched again. The pattern continued, and after two minutes du Pont had yet to land a punch.

"Dammit, Henry, give up," Upton insisted. "I don't want to hurt you."

Du Pont wiped his nose with the back of his glove, and in the process painted his face red.

"It's your choice, Henry," Upton said, and popped the right side of du Pont's head with a hook that rang his ear.

Du Pont clinched again, his upper lip fat and his left eye already swollen. All the while, in du Pont's corner, Pelham coolly repeated the same instructions—again and again, "Guard up. Move around. Breathe, Henry. Back off."

Du Pont finally seemed to hear Pelham, and noticed him moving his hands apart and repeating the gesture. He backed away from Upton and took some deep breaths. He began waving his arms and shuffling his feet just inches beyond Upton's reach.

Upton's next three punches, two jabs and a hook, fell short.

Du Pont began jutting his head like a barnyard chicken, drawing laughter from the crowd.

"Henry, you can't hide and you're hurt. Give it up." Upton lunged at du Pont with a jab, followed by a hook, either of which, had they hit their mark, would have been the talk of the barracks. But neither did, and Upton found himself off balance.

Du Pont didn't hesitate. He pummeled Upton's face and midsection with a series of rights and lefts, the blows more surprising than effective. Before Upton could collect himself, du Pont delivered a punch that audibly popped Upton's jaw, snapping his head back.

The crowd was ecstatic. They had a fight.

For the first time, du Pont was the aggressor, and it was Upton clinching and suffering the boos of the crowd.

The two continued to fight without a break for nearly twenty minutes, the crowd cheering the ebb and flow of fortunes. The longer-armed Upton at one point regained the advantage, putting du Pont down a second and third time. But du Pont kept getting up, and as the battle wore on, exhaustion overtook the abolitionist. The scar from the duel with Gibbes had opened on his right cheek, and each time he attempted to wipe his eyes, du Pont popped him with a jab. Upton's face grew ashen, his breathing irregular. Du Pont, no less exhausted, his lips swollen and one eye swollen shut, at least remained in balance.

A lackluster right hook from du Pont to the side of Upton's nose finally put him down, his face in the dirt. The crowd screamed for him to get up.

"One—two—three—four—five—"

Before Kingsbury reached ten, Upton managed to get to his feet. He swayed on rubbery legs, blood streaming from his nose.

The crowd sensed the end and swung in favor of du Pont, whose right hand was poised behind his ear.

Upton's eyes were glazed. His arms hung listless at his side.

"Put up your guard, Emory!" du Pont shouted.

Upton didn't respond.

Du Pont circled his fist as if to power his punch.

"Now," cried someone in the crowd. "Do it now, Henry!"

Du Pont glanced at Pelham, and then at the crowd, and then at Upton's bloody face. He dropped his right hand.

The crowd stood in shocked silence.

Du Point stared at Upton and attempted a grin. Upton blinked hard and responded with a feeble nod and an even more distorted grin.

When the two touched gloves, Kingsbury stepped in and shouted, "I declare this match a draw!"

CHAPTER FORTY-EIGHT

The day after the fight, the attention of every First Classman was on Professor Mahan's midterm civil engineering exam, to be administered the next day. Rosser, whose grade point in the course had again slipped well under 2.0, didn't know whether to study or pack his bags.

"Think of it this way, Tom," Pelham said after supper, himself immersed in review of the course notes. "You can get it all back on this one."

"And just how am I supposed to suddenly comprehend everything that's flown right over my head? I tell you, you'll be rooming by yourself."

"You could try Henry."

"I don't think so."

"How is Henry not a good idea?"

"He's not … real happy with me."

Pelham glanced up from his notes. "What?"

"He found out I bet on Upton."

Pelham smiled. "Burned the wrong bridge?"

Rosser shrugged.

"Still, talk to him," Pelham pressed. "Plead for mercy, grovel if you must. What do you have to lose?"

Rosser realized that Pelham was right. He gathered up his notes and the course text, and slinked down the stairwell, out the back door, and over to the First Division. He knocked on du Pont's door and without pretense bared his soul.

Du Pont, expressionless, let Rosser ramble on about how sorry he was, that the bet wasn't personal, and how he couldn't face being drummed out of the Corps.

When Rosser had exhausted his plea and there was no reaction from du Pont, he turned to leave.

"Why did you wait until tonight?" Du Pont said. He turned to his Virginian roommate, Llewellyn Hoxton. "Lew, do you mind if I work with Tom a bit?"

Hoxton was already collecting his study materials. "Take my chair, Tom. I'll study in bed."

For five hours, three hours after lights out—Pelham made up a dummy that got Rosser past bed check—Rosser hung on every word du Pont said. Long after Hoxton was asleep, du Pont talked engineering terms, concepts, and formulas, and drilled Rosser on definitions and engineering design procedures, and made him work problem after problem. Together, they reviewed Rosser's answers and the steps he had taken to get them. If Rosser made a mistake, du Pont made him work the same type of problem again until he got the right answer.

When du Pont finally released Rosser, he wondered if the man would make it back to the Eighth Division.

Chapter Forty-Nine

The next morning, Friday, November 2, was cold and wet. Pelham and Rosser hung their long overcoats outside the civil engineering classroom, the last in the section to be seated. Rosser's head was shiny with perspiration, his pallor pasty, and his eyes vacant.

"Section, attention!" Pelham, section leader, commanded, as Professor Mahan entered the room. "Sir, the section is all present!"

Mahan returned Pelham's salute with a wave of the hand. "Take seats." Mahan surveyed the class, his gaze momentarily resting on Rosser, whose head hung so low it nearly touched his desk. "You'll have the rest of the class period to complete the midterm examination, and as usual, the use of any notes or texts is strictly forbidden." He gestured for Pelham to pass out the test papers, and when Pelham was finished, gave the order to commence work.

For nearly an hour and a half, there was stark silence except for the sounds of pencil lead scratching, erasers erasing, and papers shuffling.

Periodically, Mahan glanced over his spectacles about the room.

As time ticked by, one by one the members of the class got up, turned in their tests, and left the room. Fifteen minutes before the end of the class period, Pelham departed, leaving Rosser and one other man still at work.

Ten minutes later, Rosser was on his fourth pencil and his test paper was a smudge of erasures. He had done everything that du Pont had said. He had read every problem before beginning the test, worked the easiest problems first. He had numbered his steps and showed all his work so he could get partial credit if he made a mistake. Du Pont had been right about what would be on the test, but as Rosser worked the problems, he began to question his judgment. Was he using the right formula, had he memorized it correctly, had he made errors with his slide rule? The familiar panic of a brain gone dead returned.

"Cease work," Mahan announced without mercy.

Rosser, the only one in the room besides Mahan, put down his pencil. With hands shaking, he assembled his test papers and placed them on Mahan's desk.

Pelham didn't have a chance to talk to him until at the midday meal. "So—how did it go?"

Rosser casually buttered his bread. "You're gonna miss me."

Nearly three hundred miles to the south of West Point, South Carolina Representative William Porcher Miles followed Texas Senator Louis Trezevant Wigfall and a number of other members of the Senate and House into a seldom used committee room in the United States Capitol Building. Elation and anticipation was on every face as they assembled about the room's large conference table.

"Gentlemen of the South," Wigfall began from one end of the table. "We've the weekend, a Monday, and then election day, and there is more solidarity for our cause now than we could have ever hoped for. May the power of heaven remain on our side."

Miles stood up. "Each state will follow the process we agreed upon. That is, have a public referendum to renounce membership in the Union. A majority vote in that direction then frees them to enter whatever new compact they might view in their best interest."

At a recess later that day, Wigfall asked Miles whether he regretted not being able to make his annual pilgrimage to West Point. Miles surprised him. "On the contrary, Louis, the timing for a trip to West Point could not be better."

CHAPTER FIFTY

On Monday, November 5, West Point was embraced by cold and fog, although the fog lifted mid-morning. After the midday meal, a plebe delivered Pelham another perfumed letter from Clara.

"Have a heart, John," Rosser protested as he entered the room. "I smelled Clara's letter coming up the stairwell."

Pelham ignored Rosser and read the letter in the light of the window. There were four sheets of vellum with Clara's fine handwriting and signature flowers. She reported that life at Clermont was all about the election, and that, with the exception of Carol Hill, all of her friends would vote Republican, had they the right to vote. For the first time, she wrote at great length about what in Lincoln's platform appealed to her, and again asked for his forgiveness that she should think this way. She went on to describe rather graphically an autopsy that her anatomy class had witnessed the day before, observing, "How kind God was to put a layer of skin over all that forms us, that it might be quite hard to love one another otherwise."

But the most surprising news concerned her father. She wrote, "I wanted to tell Father face to face about you and me, how wonderful you are, what a gentleman you are, and how much I dearly love you, but he still hasn't come to visit. In fact, I haven't seen him since mid-summer, the claims of the university so great—he says. Anyway, two weeks ago, I wrote him about us and today received his response."

Pelham felt his heart race.

"I wish I could report that he is thrilled for me, for us, but that would be an untruth. However, he did not contest my love for you, and now I can go to work on him, the way only a daughter can."

Pelham finished the letter, satisfied, as Clara was, that they were no longer in the closet. He almost felt sorry for the man, knowing what

Clara was capable of. He slipped the letter in a drawer nearly full of her letters, and turned to Rosser. "Carol Hill sends her best."

That afternoon after class, Pelham found Rosser stretched out on the bed, staring at the ceiling.

"Have you been to the sally port?" Pelham asked. The midterm test grades had been posted.

"I can't make myself do it." Rosser spoke as one condemned.

"You are pathetic. I'll be right back."

When Pelham returned from the sally port, Rosser hadn't changed position. Pelham stood in front of Rosser with his arms crossed. "Aren't you even going to ask?"

Rosser's eyes were closed.

Pelham kicked the bed. "Tom, your execution is stayed!"

Rosser opened one eye.

"You dog, you got a 2.3! Your new grade point is 2.15."

Rosser fairly levitated from the bed. "The hell you say."

"The hell I say! I only got a 2.2."

"For true?"

"For true, my friend! Apparently Henry knows his stuff."

Rosser let out a holler that could have been heard at the hotel. He hugged Pelham, danced about the room, hugged Pelham again, and then ran as fast as his legs would take him to the First Division.

At supper, in the joy of the moment, Pelham and Rosser determined that they must celebrate. If ever there was reason to visit Benny Havens, they had one. Chas Patterson, nursing a cold, allowed he couldn't join them, and neither Pelham nor Rosser wanted to jeopardize Ned Kirby's position as company commander.

Fifteen minutes after call to quarters and bed check, Pelham and Rosser slipped down the Eighth Division stairwell in their socks, shoes in hand, and out the back door. They sat on the steps to put on their shoes, when a voice came out of the darkness.

"Going somewhere?"

Pelham recognized the voice, as did Rosser. As one, they snapped to attention in socks and saluted Lieutenant Lee, who now stood in the lamplight.

Before either of them could speak, Lee held up a hand. "Not a word. You'll only incriminate yourself, and then I won't have a choice."

Pelham and Rosser dropped their salutes.

"I suggest you return to your room. If you do, this goes no further."

Pelham and Rosser nodded feebly.

"And, Mr. Rosser, nice work on the exam."

Chapter Fifty-One

Tuesday, November 6, Election Day, classes should have been suspended for lack of interest, not only for cadets, but for faculty as well. The previous day, Colonel Delafield had informed the Corps that it would be kept abreast of election results as they came in. As in the election of 1856, telegraph dispatches communicated state results with blinding speed. The election of Abraham Lincoln was decided by early evening.

At the midday meal on Wednesday, the final tallies were in. Lincoln had been elected president with 40 percent of the popular vote and 59 percent of the electoral vote. He had taken every Northern state, and California and Oregon as well. The Northern Democrat, Stephen Douglas, managed a respectable 29.5 percent of the popular vote, but a paltry 4 percent of the electoral vote, comprised of Missouri and three of the seven votes from New Jersey. By contrast, the Southern Democrat, John Breckinridge, garnered only 18 percent of the popular vote, but 24 percent of the electoral vote, including all of the Deep South. John Bell of the Constitutional Union rounded out the election with 12.5 percent of the popular vote and 13 percent of the electoral vote, all from Kentucky, Tennessee, and Virginia.

In the span of one day, the incessant rhetoric of political campaigning was over. The reign of the Democratic Party was over. The Republican Party was in, and would scramble to set its agenda and fill its appointments.

That evening in the First Class Club, Pelham, du Pont, and Upton sat at one of the smaller tables discussing the election.

"It is important that Breckinridge took all of the cotton states," Pelham said, not in the least surprised by the election results.

"What surprised me," du Pont said, "was that he also took my state and Maryland."

Pelham turned to Upton. "Your man is in, Emory."

"And a good one, I assure you. He'll serve us all well, given half a chance."

"But he won't get the chance." The pronouncement was from Charlie Ball, Rosser's guest at the adjacent table. "Not to govern the South, anyway. I'd be surprised if John and I aren't back in Alabama within the month."

"I hope you're wrong, Charlie," Upton replied. "You deserve to graduate."

Upton spoke Pelham's heart and Ball's directness soured him, but Ball was right. If Alabama seceded, they would have no choice.

"And, of course," Ball added, "there will be many on the fence in the border states. If Delaware secedes, I wouldn't think Henry would stay."

"Delaware's not going anywhere," du Pont said emphatically. "And the South shouldn't either."

Ball let it go.

"Still, Charlie's point can't be ignored," Pelham said. "A man's allegiance is to family, home, and state, before country. Besides, once a state secedes, those from it probably won't even be allowed to stay here. I mean, what would be the point?"

"It will be interesting to see what the regular officers do," Ball mused. "Lieutenant Lee is a Virginian; Lieutenant Colonel Hardee is from Georgia. If Virginia and Georgia bolt, I don't see them serving the Union."

Du Pont stood up, his temperature elevated. "It hasn't been twenty-four hours since the election, and neither Breckinridge nor Douglas, and certainly not Bell, have talked secession. Let's not overreact."

"More to the point," Upton said, "it would be lunacy not to give Lincoln a fair chance. Give him time to compromise. He'll do what he has to do to keep the Union whole."

"Trust me, Emory," Ball said, almost under his breath. "It's not up to Lincoln."

CHAPTER FIFTY-TWO

On Thursday, with a night's sleep making little difference, Pelham wrestled with an endless series of outcomes. He believed as Ball and other Southern cadets did, that secessions would come, and there was an undeniable magnetism and energy to the prospect. As a consequence of the distractions, he moved through morning classes unprepared, his recitations weak. That his grades would suffer concerned him little. As soon as it was clear that Alabama would secede, he would write his father and ask permission to resign.

After the midday meal, and upon his return to Central Area, Pelham saw Lieutenant Lee in the company of two gentlemen in three-piece suits and long overcoats. As they walked in his direction, Pelham recognized one of the men. It was the congressman he had met on the train, William Porcher Miles of South Carolina.

Pelham didn't hesitate to approach the man.

Miles immediately recognized Pelham. "Well, well. Lieutenant Lee, this is the young man I traveled the train with back in August." Miles hesitated. "John Pelham, right?"

"Yes, sir. It's kind of you to remember."

"You're a man not easily forgotten, and one with a healthy appetite as I remember." Miles smiled. "Lieutenant Lee, might I have a private word with Mr. Pelham?"

"By all means, sir. I'll wait for you in the commandant's office."

Miles put his arm around Pelham's shoulders. "Let's walk, John. It is indeed good fortune that I run into you. I am here to speak with the South Carolina cadets, something I do every year, but particularly useful this year. This evening, I am hosting a dinner at the hotel, and I would be most pleased if you would join us."

Pelham beamed. "Sir, I'd be honored to join you."

"Excellent. Let's make it seven o'clock, if that's convenient."

"Quite convenient, sir."

That evening at the West Point Hotel, in a room reserved for the South Carolina contingent and closed off except for food service, Pelham found himself seated next to Miles. The others at the table were eight South Carolinian cadets, including Henry Farley from D Company.

Miles wasted no time getting to the point. "Gentlemen, I am here for just the night and will be returning south on tomorrow's boat, and I mean to Charleston, not Washington."

He reached for his wineglass, the only such glass on the table, and raised it. "Gentlemen, I propose a toast to the great State of South Carolina."

The South Carolinians and Pelham raised their water glasses. "To the great State of South Carolina."

Miles nodded at Pelham. "I trust you all know Mr. Pelham."

The question brought cheers from the other cadets, and a catcall from Farley. Pelham waved off the attention.

Miles toasted a second time, to the State of Alabama, and while the main course was being served, engaged Pelham in conversation. "We are in a most interesting time, Mr. Pelham."

"Indeed, sir."

"And you wear the right colors here."

"I'm sorry, sir?"

Miles declined to explain, since the hotel's waiting staff had begun to serve supper. After everyone was served, he asked Farley to close the door.

"Gentlemen, nothing said in this room leaves this room. Are we agreed?"

Everyone, including Pelham, agreed.

Miles drew himself up to the table. "The die is thoroughly cast, my young friends. The Black Republican and his party can have the Union, but not South Carolina. The State of South Carolina will resume her place among the nations of the world, with all the attendant powers and opportunities that have been for so long denied it."

The pronouncement was electric, and the euphoria around the table palpable.

"The experiment of the United States has failed, the result of a Constitution betrayed by states of the North not caring a whit for the states of the South. The basic tenets of the Constitution no longer apply to 'we the people,' but to 'they the people of the North.' And so be it. The construct of the Union has changed so dramatically that its dismemberment or even death will be a blessing to all concerned." Miles eyed each man in the room. "North and South have evolved so differently that they have become two entirely different animals, one preying wantonly upon the other."

Pelham was taken by the effect Miles had on the South Carolinians. Henry Farley's red hair was now no match for his cheeks.

"I am very pleased to hear that the question of secession has already been debated here at the Academy." Miles gave Pelham a knowing wink. "And that convincing argument for the right to secede has already been voiced. I am here to announce that South Carolina will be the first to do so, but also to announce that most assuredly it will not be the last. Soon the states of the South will form a new and glorious union whose values are one."

Farley led a cheer that Pelham feared could be heard throughout the hotel.

"We are all of us cotton states, South Carolina, Alabama, Mississippi, Georgia, and Florida. We are pledged to secede from the Union as soon as public elections can be held. Our hope is that we can accomplish the process before Lincoln takes office. Buchanan is not inclined to interfere with us, and there is time enough." Miles spoke as though he had the keys to heaven, and the sons of his state couldn't wait to get in.

"Mark my words. More than the cotton states will follow. Look for Texas, North Carolina, Virginia, Tennessee, Kentucky, Arkansas, Maryland, Missouri, and Delaware to choose the right way. Ours will be the grandest of nations, exceeding what the United States could ever have hoped for, and we will call ourselves the Confederate States of America."

The loud response raised by so few surprised Pelham, and it was a struggle not to join in the jubilation.

"So, what say you, Mr. Pelham?" Miles asked, while the others cheered.

"Is there no room for compromise, sir?"

Miles gave Pelham a contemplative look. "Compromise has no place in God's chosen course for us."

Farley jumped up on his chair, his eyes wild and his face flushed with passion. "I pledge my sword and my life to South Carolina!"

Pelham saw in Farley unswerving conviction, and one by one, the other South Carolinians pledged the same, their eyes shiny with tears.

Miles put his arm around Pelham's shoulder. "This is just the beginning, John. We will become a country of millions. You are about to witness an incredible chapter in history."

The next day, Congressman Miles departed on the noon steamer. Pelham had briefed Rosser on the evening before, and the Texan's reaction was not his own. Rosser was ready to walk out the gate and not look back. Around campus, wherever two or more cadets were gathered, the topic was secession. How many states would secede? Would the North acquiesce? Would there be compromise—slavery allowed in the new territories? Would Lincoln comprehend the thin thread that held his country together?

That evening, after lights out and bed check, Pelham heard a tap on the door. He slipped from his bed to find Henry Farley in the hall.

"I need to talk with you, John."

Pelham joined Farley in the hall, closing the door behind him.

"I have your confidence?"

"Of course."

"I'm resigning."

The pronouncement caught Pelham by surprise.

"I want to be first, John. South Carolina is holding its convention later this month. Miles said so."

"But why now?"

"Like I said, I want to be first. It's important to me, John. Once it begins, there will be an exodus."

Pelham didn't doubt it. "Your resignation. You should craft it carefully."

Farley nodded. "I know. I've already written it, and have permission from my father. I'm simply saying that I'm needed at home."

"Needed at home." Pelham smiled. "I like that." He put a hand on Farley's shoulder. "You're sure about this?"

"I'm dead sure, John."

CHAPTER FIFTY-THREE

On Saturday, November 10, the South Carolina General Assembly called for a convention to draw up an ordinance of secession. Two days later, Henry Farley submitted his resignation to Lieutenant Lee, despite Lee's attempt to persuade him to delay until South Carolina had actually seceded. Lee submitted Farley's resignation to Lieutenant Colonel Reynolds, who passed it up the chain to Colonel Delafield. Farley informed Pelham and Rosser at the midday meal that he had done the deed, and then informed his fellow South Carolinians.

Farley's resignation took a week to process, and during that time, he settled accounts with the Corps quartermaster, du Pont, who added his own chastisement to that of the others.

On the day of Farley's departure, November 19, South Carolina had still not convened to draw up its ordinance of secession, prompting many to question his decision. But Farley remained resolute, and after the midday meal, his friends bade him farewell. The last to do so was Pelham, who pulled him aside. "You have your wish, Henry. Make the most of it."

"I intend to, John. Bless you and all who follow me."

Farley's departure was a clarion call that had many speculating on who would be next. Sunday evening in the mess hall, a heated exchange broke out between three South Carolinians and half a dozen Northern cadets. Charlie Ball of Alabama quickly sided with the South Carolinians and flicked a spoon of peas at the most vocal Northerner. The volley was incendiary. Before Ball could reload, the dining hall erupted in a food fight. As the battle wore on, none was unmarked, and the most deadly combatant proved to be George Custer, who mastered rapid-fire launching of Brussels sprouts.

Chambliss was everywhere trying to control the Corps.

"Enough, Fannie!" Pelham shouted. "Tom, you too!"

"Just one more." Rosser tossed a water-soaked wad of bread at Emory Upton.

Kirby, Ames, and du Pont joined in the attempt to end the carnage. For the third time Kingsbury hollered, "Battalion, attention!" Finally, the worst of the offenders were collared and a ceasefire achieved. When order was restored, the ravages of war were evident on uniforms, tables, chairs, walls, windows, floor—and even the ceiling.

Rosser glanced at Custer and burst out laughing. Custer's hair was thick with bread pudding.

"Check your dress coat," Custer shot back. Rosser had taken a hit in the chest with gravied mashed potatoes.

Chambliss stood on a table in the center of the dining hall, livid. "Dammit to hell, people, do you understand what you have done! You'll be walking Central Area until graduation." He ordered every man back to the barracks to change into utility uniform and to return for work detail.

If there was ever a time Pelham was glad to be a private, it was then. He knew what Chambliss faced as first captain. He would be held responsible for the entire incident. Yet the flare-up had served a purpose. By the time the Corps had scrubbed every surface of the dining hall and returned to the barracks near midnight, the tension in the air had evaporated, tempers had cooled, and a measure of good humor had been restored.

CHAPTER FIFTY-FOUR

When the United States Congress convened on Monday, December 3, the two senators from South Carolina were absent, having both resigned. However, at the urging of the South Carolina governor, the state representatives, including William Porcher Miles, remain seated, though they would do so only until preparations by the state for its secession convention were finalized. Before Miles headed home, he co-authored and delivered a letter to President Buchanan, the subject of the letter being South Carolina's position on Union forts in Charleston Harbor.

That same Sunday, the Corps awoke to a hard freeze and a long sermon from Reverend French on the perils of trusting in the things of this world.

Late that afternoon at the superintendent's quarters, Colonel Delafield welcomed Lieutenant Colonel Reynolds into his study.

"James, we are not to be disturbed."

The house servant closed the door behind them.

"A brandy, John?"

"No, thank you, sir."

Delafield poured two fingers for himself. "Read this dispatch from Scott." Delafield downed his brandy as Reynolds read.

Reynolds put down the telegram. "Incredibly presumptuous."

"Criminal is the word I would have used. You have a commission from South Carolina acting as if their state no longer belongs to the Union, presenting the president of the United States a letter of truce on Forts Moultrie, Castle Pinckney, and Sumter in Charleston Harbor. The unmitigated gall of South Carolina, saying they intend no action against the installations as long as they are not reinforced, and allowing that they'll pay a fair, but not unreasonable, price for them."

"What about the federal arsenal in Charleston?" Reynolds asked. "The telegram doesn't even speak to it."

"I know. Major Anderson has his hands around a beehive."

"Don't you mean Colonel Gardner, sir? I believe he has charge of Charleston."

Delafield shook his head. "Did. Major Anderson replaced him a few weeks ago. The work of our seditious secretary of war. A month back Gardner attempted to remove arms from the arsenal to better supply his installations. Floyd berated him for the action, and had him reassigned. And the devil knew what he was doing when he brought in Anderson."

"Why would you say that, sir?"

"You trust him?" Delafield asked.

"With my life, sir."

Delafield gave him a jaundiced look. "Anderson is from Kentucky, his wife is from Georgia, and he's pro-slavery. Doesn't that make you a little uncomfortable?"

"Sir, Bob Anderson is a patriot and the finest sort of man. He was my artillery instructor here at the Academy, and we served together in the Mexican War. He served brilliantly for General Scott and was severely wounded at Molino del Rey. The man has fight; he'll do his duty."

Delafield pulled at his whiskers. "Um. Maybe he can walk the fence better than anyone else. Still, this premature cat and mouse game bodes ill. Nothing good will come of it."

"In truth, sir," Reynolds said. "I doubt Anderson has a hundred regulars to man the three forts, let alone the arsenal. He can't initiate a fight, and I suspect that when South Carolina jumps, the Union will take money for the forts and run."

"I suppose. Buchanan is the lamest of ducks. He's all but abdicated being commander in chief."

"Sir, in fairness to him, what would you do in his position? How do you force the South to accept the election?"

"That's just it. They do accept the election! They've taken it as their mandate to form a slave union, and unless Buchanan makes some sort of deal on slavery, we're half the country we were."

"And slavery is only part of it. Still, sir, you're right, we're treading eggshells, and there is likely nothing Buchanan can say or do to appease the South that the Republicans won't unsay or undo."

"The shame of it," Delafield said in a defeated tone. "South Carolina is the one fueling the fire. I say let the brigands go and good riddance."

At supper, Monday, December 10, Chambliss informed Pelham that he and Jessica Danford had called off their relationship. Her father, initially warm to an Academy man, had cooled to the thought of the man being from a secession state, since he believed Tennessee would be just that.

"But she's from Virginia," Pelham said.

"Northwestern Virginia, the Clarksburg area. Her father is a committed Unionist and said he'd move the family across the border if Virginia chose the wrong side."

"I'm sorry, Nate. You two seemed well matched."

"We're not totally done. If Tennessee doesn't secede, we've pledged to pick up where we left off."

"You think they won't?"

"I hope they don't."

"Nate, Tennessee is a slave state."

"But also a border state."

That night, Pelham wrote two letters, neither to Clara. In light of South Carolina's intention to hold a secession convention on December 17, his first letter was to his father asking for immediate permission to resign, especially since Alabama had already declared its intent to secede. He strengthened his argument with the fact that most of the other cotton state men had already written home for permission to resign.

Pelham's other letter was to Judge A. J. Walker. It was short and to the point, requesting guidance on how best to proceed to make himself useful to the state of Alabama once he resigned.

CHAPTER FIFTY-FIVE

Monday, December 18, Pelham nearly ran all the way to the Ordnance Compound for coastal gunnery class. Despite gray skies, the gloom of academics, and the uncertain status of the nation, Clara's letter had him thoroughly in the Christmas spirit. He had read it three times. She was a gifted writer, and her anecdotes were full of wit and mirth. Her description of the seasonal transformation at Clermont was better than a painting, and there was not a negative word or thought expressed in the letter.

She also wrote that she was doing famously in her anatomy course and, per his request, would not provide details. But her most unexpected news concerned her father. The good doctor was finally warming to the notion that a cadet, even from Alabama, was not such a bad thing. She quoted him saying, "I have heard that gentlemen of the South are often beyond reproach, and such a man is my desire for you." That he had also expressed to her the same concern that Jessica Danford's father had about Chambliss, seemed a small thing to Pelham. In his mind, the Confederacy could be fully established in six months; and ties with the United States would be in place for the benefit of both in not many months thereafter. Unquestionably, the North needed the South's cotton, and the South needed the North's textile mills. It would be but a matter of time before her father came around.

At the midday meal on Friday, December 21, the Corps learned that the previous evening South Carolina had formally voted to secede from the United States of America, declaring itself a sovereign commonwealth. Representatives at the South Carolina secession convention had voted one hundred and sixty-nine in favor of session—none opposed. That evening at supper, news of South Carolina's secession spread like an intoxicating mist over the Southern faction of the Corps. Ball caught Pelham's eye across the dining hall, and the two toasted each other with water glasses.

The next afternoon, Delafield called a joint meeting of the Tactical Department and Academic Department. He addressed the realities of what they faced, and delineated the actions that should be taken with respect to the Corps, given that other states would likely follow South Carolina's lead. The discussion that followed anticipated a stream of cadet resignations, as well as circumstances that would undoubtedly have an impact on academic classes and cadet performance. It was also recognized that Southern members of the two departments would likely follow their states. Delafield made it clear that any decisions to leave the Academy or the army would be honored, and requested that Professor Mahan direct his department heads to adjust expectations for cadet performance until such time as normalcy was reestablished.

The last issue discussed was how best to expedite voluntary separations to minimize disruption at the Academy. Lieutenant Colonel Reynolds said he would address the Corps at the supper meal, and asked that his four company tactical officers do the same in meetings with their companies after the meal. Lieutenant Lee was given the First Class Club as the venue for D Company's meeting.

When Walter Kingsbury finished publishing the orders at the supper meal, he introduced Lieutenant Colonel Reynolds.

"Battalion, attention!" boomed Kingsbury.

"Take seats, men." Reynolds's tone was easy and reassuring.

Pelham respected and liked Reynolds. The man had proven the equal of Hardee, and could inspire as easily.

"As you know," Reynolds began, "South Carolina has announced its departure from the Union. And other states have announced similar intentions. Whether they do or not and how this will all play out, we don't know. Regardless, the Academy is faced with the challenge of maintaining order and discipline, and continuing its mission to educate and train the Corps of Cadets.

"We are nearly upon Christmas break," Reynolds continued. "A time to remember and reflect, and to appreciate who we are and the bond we share. As some of us depart and go our separate ways, let those who stay respect the choices that have been made and harbor neither animosity nor disdain, considering that if we were in their shoes, we would likely do the same."

Reynolds talked about the importance of maintaining the daily regimen, focusing on academics, not relaxing order and discipline, and moving through the Christmas holiday with a positive, thankful attitude. He then spoke to the administration of resignations. At this, Pelham noticed du Pont, sitting at the battalion head table, squirm in his chair. It would be du Pont's duty to out-process all such cadets.

"Immediately following supper, your company tactical officer will meet with you," Reynolds said, and then introduced the company tactical officers. Each officer announced where his company meeting would be held.

"Let me conclude," Reynolds said, "by saying that, as in the past, you of the Corps will be informed of all matters that affect your lives. It is no less than you deserve. Either I or your company tactical officers will communicate developments on the national scene as they become known."

Reynolds looked around the room of more than two hundred and seventy sober-faced cadets. "In this uncertain time, may God bless our country and watch over each and every one of you. You are dismissed."

In the First Class Club, chairs were moved to accommodate the whole of D Company. Pelham, Rosser, Kirby, and Custer stood shoulder to shoulder.

At the approach of Lieutenant Lee, Paddy O'Rorke, at the door, stood straight as a pine. "Company, attention!"

"At ease, gentlemen." Lee crossed the room and took a position beneath the window at the end of the conference table.

"I've been thinking of what to say," Lee began, meeting the eye of every man in the room. "How I might soften the harshness of what lies ahead. But I find there is no benefit in sugarcoating the reality of what we face. I will be brief, for there is not much I can add to what the commandant has already said. Suffice to say, we cannot undo what has been done. When you return to your rooms, you must put aside the obvious burden of what you have heard or may hear from this day forward, and how it will play upon you and your families, and even the friendships you've formed here at the Academy. You must do your duty in spite of distractions. As you would on the battlefield, you must accept what is and go on with the business at hand, conducting yourselves as disciplined soldiers and completing your academic assignments to the best of your ability."

Pelham noticed that Lee repeatedly glanced at the Stars and Stripes that hung in the corner of the room.

"I have a concern," Lee continued, "and I will say this only once. Some may have the tendency to see others differently as events unfold. I insist that this not occur in D Company, and I will not stand for it. As the commandant has said, we will treat one another with the respect we ask in return. Certainly, no member of the Corps has wished for what is upon us. Rather it is the doing of political processes over which we have no control. Our lot at West Point is to live in harmony and draw no lines in the sand. I promise to deal harshly with any evidence of dissension or malicious gossip. I trust that I am clear on this point."

The silence in the room attested that he was.

Lee spoke for another five minutes, describing the process by which he would keep them informed, and the procedure for a member of the company to exercise his option to leave the Academy. "Lastly, before any man makes the decision to leave the Academy, I want him to come to talk personally with me."

Rosser raised his hand. "Sir, what will you do if Virginia secedes?"

"No different from you, Mr. Rosser," Lee answered softly. "I will do my duty as I see it best."

Chapter Fifty-Six

Monday, December 24, was the Corps' first day off for the Christmas holiday. By mid-morning, Pelham, Kingsbury, Ames, Rosser, and half a dozen underclassmen, all wearing long overcoats, frolicked on skates on the ice of the Hudson. The wind chill was below freezing, despite a brilliant sun.

"Stay more centered over your feet," Kingsbury shouted to Pelham. His personal goal over the last three years had been to teach the Alabamian how to ice skate, and he was pleased with what he saw.

At noon, Ames and Rosser, the latter happy to be off the ice after a series of falls, headed back to the barracks for the midday meal. Pelham and Kingsbury, in possession of passes to Garrison's Landing across the Hudson, readied for the trip Kingsbury had promised. Pelham's pass was Lieutenant Lee's response to the debate. It would be his first long-range skate, and his first trip to Garrison.

Kingsbury skated up to Pelham. "Ready for this?"

"Don't worry about me." Pelham massaged his gloved hands for warmth. "Just keep looking over your shoulder to see if I'm vertical."

"You'll do fine. Remember, eyes out front, not between your feet. And as an incentive, if you cross the river without a fall, I'll buy the first round."

"'Lay on, MacDuff.'" Pelham jumped out in front of Kingsbury.

The two crossed the Hudson in a matter of minutes, and on the far side removed their skates, slinging them over their shoulders.

"Just up ahead." Kingsbury pointed to a pub with the suggestive name, Van Winkle's.

"Greetings, lads." The man behind the bar flashed a grin. "You can drop your skates by the door."

Pelham and Kingsbury hung their overcoats and forage caps on wall hooks and made for the fireplace. The establishment was empty except for an Irish terrier curled up by the hearth. On the mantle were evergreen clippings arranged with holly that gave off a pleasant scent. All about the room were seasonal decorations.

Kingsbury approached the bar. "Merry Christmas to you, sir."

The bartender extended his hand. "And to you. You can call me Rip, and, no, it's not my real name. You're to be my first customers this fine day before Christmas. What might I serve you?"

"Two pints of ale!" Pelham shouted from across the room. "And put it on his tab."

Van Winkle smiled at Kingsbury. "And something to eat?"

"What have you got?"

"The special, a plate of bratwurst with sauerkraut, mustard, hard rolls, and butter. Quite nice, actually."

"Anything else?" Pelham asked, having never had bratwurst.

"Nope, just the special."

"Then two of your fine specials," Kingsbury declared.

"Anything for two Academy lads who have obviously braved the river. The ice can't be so thick as yet." The bartender gave Kingsbury a concerned look.

"Trust me, sir, it's hard as rock," Pelham said as he took the stool next to Kingsbury.

"Aye, but 'tis good to remember ice is still water."

The door opened, ushering a gust of freezing air and two locals bundled in layers and topped with Dutch hats. Stripping their layers, the two took stools next to Pelham. The one next to Pelham was short, the other stocky and tall. Both were in their late fifties.

"Whatever you're serving for food, Rip, and a pint," the tall man said in a raspy voice.

"You from across the river?" the short man asked Pelham.

"We are, sir, and a Merry Christmas to you."

The tall man eyed Pelham. "From your accent, I take it you're a Southerner?"

Pelham ignored the man's tone and offered his hand. "I am, sir, from Alabama. John Pelham's the name."

The tall man made no move to take Pelham's hand. After an awkward moment, the short man took it. "Please to meet you, John Pelham. Peter Duncan's my name. That's quite a uniform you've got there."

"I suppose you'll be gone soon," the tall man pressed Pelham.

"Sir, if Alabama leaves the Union, I would return home, if that is your question."

"Yeah, sure, after we pay to put you through that nose-in-the-air school."

"It ain't the boy's doing, Jack," the other man said. "Leave him be." Turning to Pelham, he whispered, "Don't mind Jack."

Kingsbury nudged Pelham. "Let's take our meal by the window."

Pelham nodded. "Pleasure, Mr. Duncan."

The short man nodded back respectfully. The tall man growled into his beer.

Pelham and Kingsbury crossed the pub and sat next to a frost-lined window, which framed a Currier and Ives landscape of the Hudson and West Point on the distant bluff. When the meal was served, Pelham found bratwurst very much to his liking. He ordered another round of ale, and it wasn't until three o'clock that the two of them left the pub.

By the time they crossed the river, trekked up the bluff road, and entered Central Area, the highlight of the afternoon was already in progress. The tradition had been started by Superintendent Robert E. Lee, and was likely intended to exhaust cadets to the point that they couldn't pursue unworthy recreation. It was the annual chasing of the greased pig, and a crowd of nearly two hundred formed a tight circle, cheering and laughing at what was happening inside the circle.

"John!" Rosser shouted. "You and Walter are missing a good one."

Pelham pushed his way into the crowd. Inside the circle, Paddy O'Rorke was chasing a pig lathered with axle grease. He would have the allotted one minute to catch the pig. O'Rorke feinted right, feinted left, and deftly maneuvered the pig against the legs of the crowd, where it would have seemed to some a simple matter to reach down and grab the animal, and earn the rights to a fine pork dinner with friends. O'Rorke, indeed, got his hands on the pig, but after a grunt and a squeal, it wriggled free and darted between his legs. His balance upset, he pitched butt first in the quagmire.

"Hail the first sergeant," laughed Pelham.

"This one can't be got!" Rosser insisted, himself covered with mud. "Give him a go, John!"

Pelham might have considered it, were he not in dress uniform. As a Third Classman he had caught the pig, and Rosser had shared in the culinary award.

Another man was in the circle, and after him another, and still another; the Golden Fleece eluding them all.

Then McElheny, the first plebe to give it a go, jumped inside the circle.

Rosser elbowed Pelham. "This should be good."

McElheny was instantly a whir of motion, chasing the pig in a circle at a pace none of the others had. When his time was nearly up, like O'Rorke, he skillfully backed the much fatigued animal against the crowd. Unlike O'Rorke, when he reached down, instead of trying to wrap his hands around the pig, he pushed it down into the mud and sat on it. Despite accusations of cheating and unsportsmanlike conduct, McElheny was declared the winner. With great delight to all the plebes, he selected nine of his classmates to share a Christmas feast at a table that would be reserved for them in the dining hall.

After supper, John French, in his role of spiritual leader, conducted a Christmas Eve service in the chapel. His message was one of peace, tolerance, and dependence upon an all-powerful God to heal all things, including the recent wound to the nation. Pelham left the chapel wondering at the reverend's choice of words. As previously planned, he joined five other cadets in his vocal group at the superintendent's quarters for caroling, singing "It Came Upon a Midnight Clear," "Oh, Little Town of Bethlehem," and "Away in a Manger."

Awaking to the stillness of Christmas Day, Pelham and the rest of the Corps found everything a glorious white. Central Area, the commandant's office, the academic building, the quarters along Jefferson Road, the Plain, the distant West Point Hotel, everything man-made and otherwise was blanketed with six inches of light, dry snow.

There were no formations that day, and at midday, a sumptuous Christmas meal was served in the mess hall. The artfully done menu boasted oysters, roast beef, roasted turnips and potatoes, candied yams, yeast rolls, and mincemeat pie. McElheny and his friends enjoyed these, along with succulent roasted pork.

After the meal, Pelham walked the Plain, enchanted by the white landscape and the thought that he would never again see so much snow. His eyes were alive to everything; his mind was ensconced in memories. As he walked, the largest flakes he had ever seen began to fall. When he returned to the barracks, he bounded up the stairs, intent on penning a thought that had played in his mind during his walk. When he had revised and re-revised what he had written, he put his quill pen in the inkwell and started a letter to Clara, describing the beauty of the snow-clad campus, the joy of the day, and the plans he had for the two of them when sanity was restored to the universe. At the end of the letter, he added, "My lady and love, this is not a perfect world. What we are facing makes me all the more sure of, and thankful for, an all-powerful God who controls all things. I pray you will enjoy the following, which speaks my heart that grace is indeed key." And at this point he wrote what he had drafted earlier and entitled "Grace and Snow."

> Have you ever thought or cared to know
> How grace so much is like the snow
> That swirls and streams from far above
> So white and light, and pure as love
> Covering all that lies below
>
> Or think you this—it isn't so
> That grace so different is from snow
> Which only hides and cannot clean
> The sin of life and all that's mean
> That grace alone defeats the foe.

Pelham sealed the letter and took it to the orderly room. He then went to the library, and for a third time checked out Nolan's book on cavalry tactics and the use of artillery.

CHAPTER FIFTY-SEVEN

December 26 passed with little fanfare, and it was not until the next day that Colonel Delafield received General Scott's telegram relating the events of the night before. Major Anderson, to his credit, had shown his mettle. He had moved his command from Fort Moultrie on the mainland to Fort Sumter, an unfinished fortification situated on a two-hundred-acre island at the mouth of Charleston Harbor. The cannons at Fort Moultrie were spiked and the gun carriages burned. The families of the officers and enlisted men were sent to unfortified Fort Johnson across the harbor. Anderson and his command of nine officers, seventy-four enlisted men, and forty-three civilian construction workers would hold out where the odds favored them most. Captain Abner Doubleday, Anderson's second in command, was instructed to limit construction activities to those that would best enable its defense against bombardment and amphibious assault.

In the same telegram, Scott informed Delafield that he was moving to Washington in order to have immediate access to the president.

Saturday morning, December 29, Charlie Ball intercepted Pelham outside of the mess hall. His face was radiant, his hand extended. "I've done it, John—submitted my resignation. Reynolds should have it this afternoon."

Pelham took Ball's hand. "It doesn't matter that Alabama hasn't seceded?"

"The convention is planned. It will happen."

"Somehow I knew you would be first."

"I tell you, brother, it's exciting—damn exciting. And I know you'll be right behind me."

That afternoon, General Scott reported, in the longest dispatch Delafield had yet received, an unusual exchange. Senator Jefferson Davis of Mississippi, a senator from Virginia, and a former senator from South Carolina, who until South Carolina's secession had been assistant secretary of state for Buchanan, were to meet with the president on December 27 to discuss the gravity of any future federal initiatives in the South. Having been informed by former senator Louis Wigfall of the events the night before in Charleston Harbor, Davis and his associates confronted the president with the Sumter charade. They considered it a breach of the earlier accord made with the three South Carolina commissioners. The meeting concluded amicably enough, with a tentative agreement that the status quo would be maintained until terms could be adopted to turn the federal installations over to South Carolina. However, a day later, the South Carolina commissioners acted independently and precipitously. They declared to the president that the breach in their agreement was irrevocable and demanded that he do the only honorable thing—order Anderson and his troops to leave Charleston immediately. Buchanan was indignant and dismissed their demand.

In the same dispatch, Scott informed Delafield that Secretary Floyd had chosen the Louisianan Pierre Gustave Toutant Beauregard to be the next superintendent of West Point. Scott went on to say that Beauregard had served on his staff during the Mexican War, and had twice been wounded and brevetted for gallantry. He said he was a good man by every measure, and would arrive at West Point in January. While ecstatic over the prospect of turning over the reins, and pleased that his wife was finally taking to the idea, Delafield was struck by the selection.

In the days following Christmas, Pelham and the rest of the Corps were briefed on dispatches received by the leadership of the Academy. On their own, they read newspaper accounts chronicling South Carolina's indignation over Anderson's audacious maneuver, and South Carolina's subsequent bloodless seizure of Forts Moultrie and Castle Pinckney, and the Charleston arsenal.

On the last day of the year, Pelham spent the morning in the library, finding the day's newspaper unusually thick. It contained reprints of two documents prepared by South Carolinian lawmakers. The first was entitled, "Declaration of the Immediate Causes which Induce and Justify the Secession of South Carolina from the Federal Union." The second was entitled, "An Address to the People of the Slave-Holding States of the United States." Pelham read the two documents with a growing sense of frustration. The crafters of the documents had more than achieved their aim. His heart pounded with indignation. No Southerner reading the documents could respond otherwise. For the first time, Pelham was wholly convinced that the intent and benefits of the Constitution no longer served the South.

Returning to the barracks, he wished that the Christmas break was over, that he was again immersed in academics, and that he had no time to stew over the grievances of the South.

That night, in a conciliatory gesture, Lieutenant Colonel Reynolds granted the First Class the privilege of assembling in their club to bring in the New Year. He even authorized the use of tobacco products.

"Can I get you another punch?" Patterson asked Pelham, a thin thread of smoke rising from his pipe.

Pelham exhaled and flicked ashes from his cigar into a tin cup. "Could you make that a flip?"

"Soon enough, John. And I, for one, would like Benny's take on all this."

The evening was alternately gay and solemn, the gaiety a function of bawdy anecdotes, songs, and reminiscences about plebe year; the solemnity a function of political argument and planned departures by Southern classmates once their states seceded.

At ten minutes before midnight, Pelham clapped his hands loudly and stepped up on a chair. He raised his glass. "My friends, in minutes we will enter the year of our class, and in honor of our class and our bond as brothers, I wish to toast West Point!"

All in the room echoed the toast.

Hardly had the toast been made, when Pelham began singing the second verse of "Benny Havens, Oh," in a voice that stilled the air.

To our kind old Alma Mater, our rockbound highland home
We'll cast back many a fond regret, as o'er life's sea we roam
Until on our last battlefield the light of heaven shall glow

We'll never fail to drink to her and Benny Havens, Oh!

Oh! Benny Havens, Oh!—Oh! Benny Havens, Oh!
We'll sing our reminiscences of Benny Havens, Oh!

Pelham's perfect pitch gripped the heart of every man present. He had expected the others to join him, but instead was given the floor. When he finished, the room erupted with bravos and the stomping of feet. Pelham returned a weak smile and gestured toward Chambliss, who now stood on a chair.

"In less than a minute, brothers, we'll ring in our last New Year as cadets and clearly the most uncertain year of our lives." Chambliss raised his glass. "Let us bring it in loud and strong!"

When the minute hand struck midnight, the response was strident.

Should auld acquaintance be forgot
And never brought to mind?
Should auld acquaintance be forgot
And auld lang syne?
For auld lang syne, my dear,
For auld lang syne.
We'll take a cup o' kindness yet,
For auld lang syne.

CHAPTER FIFTY-EIGHT

After leaving Piedmont Station and stopping for a few hours of sleep around midnight, Pelham and the Alburtis battery arrived at Manassas Junction mid-morning, July 20. He was surprised, traveling within earshot of the railroad, not to have heard a passing train. Later he learned that railroad engineers and crews had refused to operate the trains the previous evening, complaining they had been without sleep for twenty-four hours. Confederate commanders were beside themselves, but the railroad men did not return to work until daybreak.

Pelham was greeted near Manassas by one of Beauregard's general staff officers and a sergeant.

"Alburtis battery?" the officer asked.

"Yes, sir. Lieutenant Pelham, battery commander."

"You made exceptional time, Lieutenant. The entire column did. I'm Major Whitman, and this is Sergeant Cramer. He'll see to your men and horses."

Pelham shook the dust from his scarf. "Where do you want my guns, sir?"

"Just pull them off the road for now. Except for harassing artillery and picket fire, the Union hasn't tried anything since Blackburn's Ford, which is odd, but answered prayer."

The officer motioned for Pelham to follow him. "I'll take you to headquarters."

"Lieutenant Findley!" Pelham shouted to the rear of the battery. "Do whatever the sergeant tells you."

Minutes later, Pelham was ushered into a marquee tent filled with generals and those of near rank. He recognized Beauregard and Johnston leaning over a map table. The officers surrounding them included Jackson and Johnston's other brigade commanders, except for General Kirby Smith, whose brigade was still at Piedmont Station. Jackson took notice of Pelham and gave him a faint smile.

Pelham felt a hand on his shoulder, and turned to see Tom Rosser with nearly a full beard. "Brother Tom." Pelham hugged the man. "Damn, if you don't look the soldier. And what's this?" Pelham fingered the epaulet of a captain on Rosser's shoulder.

"Just got 'em, roommate."

Pelham gave him a warm smile. "They look good on you, but don't expect a salute."

Rosser returned a smile, but the strain of the past few days was etched on his face.

"You look like you've been at it."

"We've all but melted our barrels. We're trying to make the Yankees think we've got twice the artillery."

Pelham nodded. "I bring more. With Johnston's other batteries, we bring twenty-four guns."

A man approached them. "Well, if it isn't my two nemeses!"

Pelham and Rosser recognized the voice immediately, and turned to see Fitzhugh Lee in a major's uniform.

"It is good to see the two of you together again," Lee said. "I'm just jealous you'll be commanding guns tomorrow, while I run around as a staffer."

"For General Ewell," Rosser said. "And don't kid yourself, sir. You'll have a brigade of cavalry within a month."

"I would just as soon the war not last that long."

A plumed hat approached from the other side of the tent. "Fitz Lee?" Jeb Stuart wrapped his arms around the smaller man. "How long has it been, Fitz?" Stuart cocked his head. "I thought you'd been killed by Indians."

They all enjoyed a laugh.

"If we can make it happen," Stuart said, "let's the four of us get together tonight. I'll try to come by Ewell's headquarters after dark."

An aide to General Johnston suddenly shouted above the din of the tent. "Attention! Gentlemen, your attention, please!"

Johnston, senior to Beauregard, stood beside him in front of the war map, which was now held aloft by two orderlies. "Gentlemen, lest there be any confusion, I have given General Beauregard, who fully understands the situation and lay of the land, command of the field and the authority to implement his operational plan. So please give the general your undivided attention."

Beauregard nodded to Johnston and scanned the faces of Johnston's brigade commanders. "I cannot thank the Army of the Shenandoah enough for coming so quickly to our aide."

The commanders in Beauregard's Army of the Potomac gave a rousing cheer.

"We now have parity," Beauregard continued, "and unless my classmate, Irvin McDowell, preempts us, we are going to take the battle to him in the morning, turn his left flank at Centreville, and cut his line of communication and supply to Alexandria. We'll make Professor Mahan proud."

Most in the tent well understood his meaning.

"In our distinct favor is the circus that is forming about the Union forces. Spectators by the hundreds from Washington and surroundings are quite literally gumming up the roads. All coming, I suppose, to witness the demise of the Union Army."

Laughter filled the tent.

"If we succeed, my friends, we can hope to end the North's aggression, for we will have their capital in our sights, and I suspect a rather large number of prisoners with which to bargain."

Beauregard proceeded to describe the locations and strengths of the Union forces and the Confederate forces, and to lay out his plan for Longstreet's and Early's divisions to lead the morning attack from Blackburn's Ford and Mitchell's Ford.

Later that evening, Pelham, whose battery was being held in reserve, as was much of Johnston's army, found Lee and Rosser in Ewell's camp, seated on a log by a fire. Rosser offered him a cigar and some burnt coffee.

Pelham tasted the coffee and dumped it on the ground. "Think of it, Tom, three months ago we were at Benny's."

Lee surprised them both by saying, "You know, I would enjoy a flip about now."

Rosser's face was animated in the fire. "And strike me dead if I wouldn't take the worst of the mess hall food with no complaint."

Pelham glanced east across Bull Run at the countless fires on the Union side. "I wonder if we'll see some of our own."

"I pray not," Rosser said. "I'd hate to make that decision. Yet you know they're there, every one of them. The class was graduated a month early in May, and Custer's class made such a stink, they were graduated in June. Both classes were sent straight to Washington. That was all in a letter I got from Lew Hoxton, du Pont's roommate. Poor Lew. Henry mentally beat him into graduating, but when Lew put on the blue uniform, he realized his mistake. He resigned his commission and is now somewhere out west commanding a battery for our old commandant, Hardee—now a major general."

"Hoxton's a good man," Lee said. "The decision was tough for many Virginians."

After thirty minutes, Stuart had not made an appearance. Pelham stood up and stretched. "I've got to get back." He clasped hands with Lee and Rosser. "May we celebrate a glorious victory tomorrow."

Rosser grinned. "And toast with some good Kentucky bourbon."

Late that night, after two trains returned to Piedmont Station to load General Kirby Smith's troops, an incident occurred. On the trip back to Manassas Junction, one of the trains derailed, resulting in a delay of many hours. A summary investigation suggested that the problem was caused by either poor tracks, a collision with something on the track, or an outright act of sabotage. Strong suspicion of the latter and extremely hot tempers resulted in a swift trial and execution of the train's conductor.

Chapter Fifty-Nine

Seven Months Earlier
West Point, New York
Second Semester, 1861

The first days of the New Year were a tonic to the Corps, with perspectives narrowed from what would happen to the country to what would happen in Professor Mahan's class. By the close of Friday, Rosser despaired that he had lost his entire cushion of "tenths."

On Thursday, January 3, Nate Chambliss invited Charlie Ball to address the Corps at the end of the supper meal. The dining hall was uncharacteristically silent in anticipation of the popular Alabamian.

Ball, the man who would have been first captain of his class, stood at the lectern. "My friends—and you are my friends, whether of Northern or Southern persuasion. Tomorrow, I depart for home. To my classmates, I say that we have come a long way since our first days as plebes. Along that way, you have helped make me the man I otherwise would never have been, and for this I thank you. I count the past three and half years as the best years of my life. What a privilege to have been a part of the Corps, and for the Corps to have been a part of me." Ball fought for composure. "I am indeed blessed and bid you farewell."

The dining hall erupted in cheers that shook the building's windows. As Pelham applauded, he found himself envious of the man who would be able to pick any position he wanted with the Alabama militia.

The next morning, Ball stood in Central Area ready to leave, with his classmates and others enshrouding him in a gray cocoon. He was not a little surprised, given it was an academic day. A lesser number escorted him to the South Dock, where he boarded the ferry to Garrison, and waved a final time to those on the dock, which included Pelham and Rosser.

The following day, Saturday, began as a cold, gray day, but by early afternoon was transformed by sun, blue sky, and rising temperatures. After the midday meal, Pelham and Rosser returned to their room, Rosser picking up a novel and Pelham starting a letter to Clara. Suddenly, the door to the room burst open, and Dan McElheny appeared with a silly grin on his face.

"What's got you so happy?" Pelham asked.

"I have a note from the author of your letters."

Pelham stared at McElheny, and Rosser spun around in his chair.

McElheny went on. "Joseph, who works summers and holidays at the hotel—he said you would remember him—he delivered it. It's definitely from Miss Bolton. I know her handwriting and perfume better than you do."

Pelham looked at Rosser, who shrugged ignorance, and then back at McElheny. "Dan, don't you play games with me."

"I wouldn't!" McElheny was grinning ear to ear as he handed Pelham the note.

It consisted of one line: "Dear knight, I am at the hotel. Your lady."

"Let me see it," demanded Rosser. After he had, he jumped to his feet, dragging Pelham from his chair. "Damn, if this ain't a come-lately Christmas present! Take his other hand, Dan."

Rosser proceeded to lead the three of them around the room in an awful jig. "I suppose you'll be breaking some rules?"

"Every one," Pelham promised.

He reached for his long overcoat, squeezed the breath from McElheny, and plunged down the stairwell.

Daring anyone to stop him, but encountering no one, Pelham ran to the hotel. When he reached it, he saw Clara waving in the parlor window. He sped past the desk clerk and found her still at the window. She was dressed in red and green velvet, her shoulders covered with a white wool shawl. Her face was radiant. But even at a distance, he could tell she had been crying. He moved towards her, and she him, and they met in the middle of the room. For a long moment they were unable to do more than gaze into each other's eyes. He retrieved a handkerchief and dabbed her cheeks, and then drew her to him, her body one with his. He framed her face in his hands and kissed her softly, and then long and hard.

When they separated, he whispered, "This isn't a dream?"

Her eyes closed, she whispered back, "No, it's not."

He led her to a love seat, and after a great deal more kissing apologized. "I should have shaved this morning."

She ran her fingers across his stubble. "I don't mind." She settled against his shoulder.

"How did you …?" Pelham wasn't sure where to start.

Clara reached across him and took two mints from a glass jar on the coffee table and offered him one. "My dear knight, this is such an awful world. I had to do something." She peppered him with airy kisses, and in a giddy tone announced, "You can thank Ellie that I'm here. In fact, she almost joined me."

"I thought she and Henry were over."

"They are, not that she's found someone else. It's just the separation—and she still has feelings for him." She cast her gaze to the floor. "What's going to happen to us, John?"

"Only good, I promise."

"John, I love you so very much. Too much, I think. But I know God has a plan for us, and I know that I have never been happier in my life."

Pelham wanted to respond with something romantic, something clever, but could only manage, "Me too."

"Let's go to Canada, John."

For a moment, he thought her serious. "Let me just look at you."

"Not here." She lowered her eyes. "I'm in room 208 at the end of the hall. It's an incredible view of the river. Give me five minutes. I'll leave the door unlocked."

"Are you sure?"

She smiled and was gone.

Five minutes later, after pacing the hall and passing again and again the same etchings of the Hudson Valley, the Academy, and cadets and soldiers in various uniforms, Pelham knocked softly on the door to room 208, turned the knob, and entered.

Clara was in bed under a comforter drawn up to her chin. A blaze crackled in the room's small fireplace, and the smell of lilac was in the air.

Pelham tossed his overcoat on the vanity chair and stood awkwardly. "You, my lady, are the most precious of imps. Why didn't you tell me you were coming?"

"I wanted to surprise you. And I didn't finally decide until the day before yesterday, when Ellie said, just do it, Clara." She pointed to the window. "Look outside. It's so beautiful."

"Maybe later."

She extended her hand and patted the bed. "I do love you, John Pelham."

"I believe you do." He sat next to her on the bed.

"Hold me."

He circled his arms around her bare shoulders and kissed her. "You are warm as toast."

"Hmm. I wonder why?" Her eyes were closed.

He explored and caressed her through the comforter. "You're naked, aren't you?"

She opened her eyes. "Maybe."

Passion denied for five months surged through him, and he slipped his hand beneath the comforter.

"Oh," she exclaimed. "You are cold as ice."

Pelham stripped himself of shoes, dress coat, and trousers, and slipped under the covers.

"Damn, this room is cold," he said.

She giggled as he fumbled beneath the comforter with his long underwear. "Aren't we in a hurry!"

When he finally pressed against her, she made a squeaking sound.

"You're sure?" he asked.

She nodded.

What followed was more than Pelham had dreamed of, and there had been many dreams. He and Clara kissed, explored, and loved deeply and completely, and after they were wet from perspiration and exhausted, they lay beside each other.

"Did I hurt you?" Pelham asked with concern in his voice.

Clara rose up and gazed down at him. "You truly are my sensitive knight, aren't you? No, you didn't hurt me. It's just that …"

"What?"

She shrugged.

"Are you a—?"

She put a finger to his lips. "Not anymore."

He grinned with pleasure and glanced at the vanity clock. "It's barely three o'clock. Next time will be better."

"I'm sure it will." Her smile lit up the room.

"We just need to talk a while."

"And kiss?" She wrapped her arms around his neck. "John, we are going to survive this, I know it."

"We are, my lady, but we must be as wise as serpents. Let me tell you what I was writing when blessed McElheny delivered your note."

She beamed. "Yes, do."

"We just need patience. The country is split, and I feel certain it will become two nations. Until that happens, there will be a time—possibly months, but more likely a year or more—when we'll have to suffer the counsel of fathers, family, and friends that we forget each other and move on. If we are strong and can bide our time, meet as often as we can, as deliciously as we are now, the world will regain its axis and we will survive. But to be clear, my lady, you must know that our future will be in Alabama, with you the mistress of a plantation."

"You'll not be a soldier?"

"I pray not," he said, sitting up with his back against the headboard.

Clara sat up beside him, pulling the comforter across her chest.

"This very day," he went on, "Alabama is having a referendum to decide the question of secession. The majority of the people will vote for it, and within the week we'll separate from the Union."

"I've been praying against it," Clara admitted. "But it is all over the papers. So many states say they are leaving."

"Don't despair, for it will be a good thing, and feathers ruffled will be unruffled soon enough."

She nestled in the crook of his shoulder. "So you will leave the Academy?"

Pelham said that he had yet to receive his father's permission, but that it would come, and when it did, he would resign. "If Alabama does not need my services in the militia, I hope to help Pa with the cotton. Anyway, I think you would very much like your new home in Alabama, and I know with certainty that the Pelham family would adore you."

"John, I love all you've told me about your home, about Alabama, and especially your family. I'll love everything, even the summers, for I can learn to perspire."

"And with dignity. But there is the dream of your being a doctor. If you think the North unaccepting, you'll find the South even more close minded."

She kissed him. "Right now, I'm thinking only about you being my husband, about having your babies, and you being their father." She kissed him again. "I was crazy to think of being a doctor."

"Don't say that. Times change and you should be a part of it, and you are gifted the way a doctor should be. You don't have to abandon your dream—not until our second child."

She kissed him for saying it. "There actually is a medical school considering me, but that is far from settled. Anyway, about your slaves, I will trust you to show me how it is not a bad thing, that your Negroes are God's creatures like you and me and are treated well."

"You will see for yourself. Now tell me about life at Clermont."

"I wish you hadn't asked. Carol Hill's gone back to Mississippi after her father ordered her home. She left after Christmas and I do dearly miss her. We all do."

"I assure you the exodus is in full vigor here as well."

"Can I ask you a question?"

"Anything."

"Your slave friend, Samuel. What is it that you haven't told me?"

"You want to know it all, do you?" He obliged her curiosity with as much detail as he could remember about the day in the cotton field, about the game he had forced Samuel to play, about his father, about Willie's salt and pepper talk, and how something remained unresolved with Samuel.

"That must have been so hard losing your best friend, and then growing up so fast."

He shrugged. "It was a lesson I had to learn."

"But what is it that isn't resolved between you and Samuel?"

"I can see I'll have to watch my tongue." He told her about the year before he came to West Point, about getting the acreage from his father to clear and plant, and about Samuel and the other blacks who worked for him, how they had been on their own for almost nine months and had gotten a crop in. "And through it all, Samuel worked the hardest. And we were together again, almost like before. And he was such a thinker. He would come to me, not as a friend, but as someone who saw a problem and knew how to solve it and suggest this or that. I would see right away that he was right, and we'd do it, whatever it was, his way."

"Sounds like a wonderful man."

"He is, and that is the problem. After we broke the land and before I left for West Point, I promised that I would set him free when I had the power to do so. I wanted him to have what I had."

Clara beamed, "You are a truly good man, John Pelham."

He shook his head. "You don't understand. I can't free Samuel."

"Of course you can't, you're here at West Point."

"No, I mean, even if I was back home."

"Why not?"

"It's complicated."

"Tell me," she insisted, raising her arms and locking her hands behind her head, and in the process exposing one of her breasts.

"Maybe later."

CHAPTER SIXTY

That evening, Pelham arrived at the barracks just as the Corps was returning from supper. The look on Rosser's face told Pelham all he needed to know. He would pay for his pudding. That night, he told Rosser about Carol Hill's return to Mississippi, and Rosser said she had made the right decision, that someday he might try to revive the relationship.

The next morning, Kirby informed Pelham that Lieutenant Lee wanted to see him immediately.

Pelham made his way across Central Area and climbed the stairs to the suite of offices on the second floor reserved for company tactical officers.

He knocked on Lee's door. "You wanted to see me, sir?"

"Dammit, Pelham, I hope it was worth it." Lee didn't hide his frustration.

"I'm sorry, sir."

"How do you miss not only supper formation, but the entire meal?"

Pelham stared hard at the painting over Lee's desk, a western scene of a remnant of cavalry crouched behind dead horses in the face of an Indian charge. "No excuse, sir."

"Do you think I like coming in on Sunday?"

"No, sir."

"Mr. Pelham, how does someone with your potential so often put his brain on leave?"

"Yes, sir."

"I had every intention of making you a lieutenant for the second semester."

Pelham remained motionless.

"But you give me no choice."

Pelham's gaze dropped to the floor. "Yes, sir."

"You'll walk the area for the next month, since confinement obviously makes no impression on you. And I'm letting you off easy. You could easily be walking the area until graduation."

That afternoon, after chapel and the midday meal, Pelham fell into formation in full dress uniform under arms with seven underclassmen to stand inspection by the officer of the guard. Three demerits later, he began his three-hour tour of walking back and forth across Central Area.

Wednesday, January 9, Colonel Delafield received a telegram from General Scott, informing him that the Union merchant ship *Star of the West* had been fired upon as it approached Charleston Harbor to land supplies and reinforcements at Fort Sumter. Fortunately, a subsequent telegram stated that there had been no injury to persons or damage to the ship. Despite pressuring by Governor Francis Pickens of South Carolina for immediate surrender of Fort Sumter, the uneasy truce held. As a concession by the self-proclaimed Commonwealth of South Carolina, Major Anderson would be permitted to provision his men with vegetables and meat from the Charleston markets, with the clear understanding that the garrison of Fort Sumter would not be reinforced. Additionally, the women and children of the garrison currently at Fort Johnson would be afforded passage to New York City.

At the supper meal, the Corps was informed by Lieutenant Colonel Reynolds that Mississippi had seceded from the Union. On January 10, Florida was the next domino to fall. The next day Alabama seceded, and all eyes fell on Pelham, who did nothing. He had not received permission from his father to resign. On January 19, Georgia seceded, uniting the Cotton Belt. In the mess hall that evening, news of Georgia's departure had the Corps speculating on whether the former commandant Hardee had resigned. Two days later, it was confirmed that he had.

On Monday, January 21, a flustered Delafield ushered Reynolds into his office. "I'm again inclined to a shot of whiskey. The country's unraveled, John."

"Only if we recognize secession, sir."

Delafield shook his head. "We, the Union, can do or not do whatever the hell we want, but the simple fact of the matter is that Buchanan hasn't raised a finger to stop a single state from announcing it and doing it. Until he does, there will be no stopping those that have the notion."

"In fairness to him, sir, he's struggling with the Constitution, whether he has the legal right to take action, let alone forceful action."

"I know, and I find it ridiculous. In one breath he says unequivocally that a state cannot secede, and in the next says that the federal government is powerless to prevent it. It just doesn't make sense!"

"No, sir."

"By my count, the seceded states have taken three more arsenals, Augusta, Baton Rouge, and Mount Vernon, and nearly a dozen forts along the Southern coast. Hell, with the exception of Fort Sumter and Fort Pickens off Pensacola, the South controls everything."

"There is still Texas, sir."

"For how long?"

Reynolds shrugged.

"Not a day goes by, I don't hear from Scott," Delafield continued. "Today, he says he's never seen Lincoln so riled over Buchanan's inaction. That once he's in office, he'll be out-the-gate bold to undo what's been done. He told Scott to ready for action—that any surrendered federal installations will be retaken, and any installations still garrisoned will be reinforced."

"That will bring conflict, sir."

"Indeed. But Lincoln's a shrewd one. He knows he cannot be the aggressor, that federal installations in the South are his ace in the hole. South Carolina is not about to hand over the forts in Charleston harbor, let alone the arsenal."

"Pandora's box."

"Yes. Still, even with Lincoln ready to fall on his sword to preserve the Union, something sane might happen before the inauguration."

"In any event, sir, the Corps handles the chaos better than I expected."

"Which is a true blessing. Where do we stand now?"

Reynolds drew a folder from his briefcase. "Fewer than forty have resigned for state affiliation reasons."

"There will be more. Not all of the states have jumped." Delafield then muttered under his breath, "Just two more days and this will be Beauregard's problem."

That same morning, in the chambers of the United States Senate, two weeks after his home state of Mississippi had seceded, an emotional Jefferson Davis bid farewell to his colleagues. Later in the day, before Beauregard made his initial appearance at West Point, Delafield defended Davis to Reynolds.

"You don't know the man," he said. "Jeff Davis is a states' rights man, not a secessionist, but what was he to do? Mississippi has already made him a major general, in charge of their militia, and I pray it stops there. I would hate to see him commanding an army of Southerners."

"He won't hesitate to fight, sir, if ordered to," Reynolds argued. "And the man can rally the dead."

"He'll do his duty, no doubt, and be a worthy foe if it comes to that. But he wants peace as much as we do. He's seen enough of war."

That evening, at the encouragement of his wife, Delafield asked James to join him on the veranda. They both stood in the darkness of a day that had been wet, cold, and gray.

"James, I expect you've had as much of West Point winters as I have," Delafield said as he looked across the Plain.

"A warm coat fixes that, sir."

"You can come with us, James," Delafield said, his tone hopeful. "My position in charge of New York Harbor provides for paid house service, and, of course, that would include room and board. Mrs. Delafield and I are much attached to you."

The black man also gazed across the Plain. "You are kind to offer, sir."

"We would be in your debt if you came with us, James."

"I thank you, sir. Your offer is most gracious, but the healing in my life has been here. The strange thing, sir, when I leave, even for a holiday—go to the city—the past comes back to me ..."

Delafield put a hand on the man's arm.

On Wednesday, January 23, Colonel Pierre Beauregard assumed command of West Point—its twelfth superintendent. A parade review scheduled for that afternoon to honor the occasion was canceled due to rain, the announcement bringing a thunderous roar from the barracks. The next day, Delafield and his wife, having shipped their household goods to quarters on Governors Island, departed the Academy without fanfare.

That evening, Colonel Beauregard addressed the Corps at the supper meal, his words stirring and void of politics. The fit and impeccably dressed man, fully twenty years younger than his predecessor, impressed all in attendance, including Pelham.

On the way back to the barracks, Pelham and du Pont walked together. "How long before he leaves?" du Pont asked.

"Not long. His being here makes no sense."

"Pity. I like him."

On Friday, January 25, Lieutenant Charles Fields, tactical officer for C Company, submitted his resignation, the first regular army officer stationed at West Point to do so. News of the resignation was a great disappointment to a company composed predominately of Northern cadets. That evening, in the First Class Club, Pelham learned from Emory Upton that Reynolds wasn't going to give Fields the opportunity to say farewell to his company.

"Things have changed," Upton said. "There is a possibility, though I think it a small one, of armed conflict. That changes the map."

On Monday, five days after assuming the superintendency, Colonel Beauregard sent for Reynolds. Upon Reynolds's arrival, Beauregard closed the door behind him.

"Is there a problem, sir?"

Beauregard handed Reynolds the telegram. "I just received it."

"Louisiana has seceded?"

"By the end of the day, it will be official."

"Your intentions, sir?"

"Do I have choice?"

Chapter Sixty-One

Before supper Monday evening, du Pont bounded up the Eighth Division stairwell to the fourth floor, finding Pelham and Rosser at their desk. "Old Bory's gone—left on the afternoon steamer!"

Rosser glanced over his shoulder. "Barely time to change the sheets."

"The three Louisiana boys are leaving too."

Pelham slammed his fist on the desk, almost knocking over the inkwell.

"Damn, roommate, what's in your craw?"

"It's not right me being here. I should be gone too!"

"I don't understand your hurry, John," du Pont said. "What's so urgent in Alabama?"

Rosser got up from his chair and yawned. "Well, I don't need permission. I can leave any damn time I want, and now is as good a time as any. Mahan can shove this text up his ass!"

"You stupid rock!" Du Pont exclaimed. "Texas hasn't seceded."

"You forget, I'm from Virginia too."

"So? Virginia hasn't seceded."

"It will," Rosser countered. "They both will."

"I don't understand you, Henry." Pelham confronted du Pont. "Delaware is a slave state, no different from ours. Why are you in our face?"

"I'm not in your face, and go for all I care, but Delaware is no cotton state. We'll never leave the Union. Not over slavery or anything else."

During the supper meal, the dining hall was a hive of thread-worn rhetoric and voices that had begun to take on belligerent tones. The

316

mess officer alerted the waiters to remove food platters at the first signs of a food fight.

But there wasn't another scene. Before the meal was over, Walter Kingsbury called the Corps to attention, and Nate Chambliss rapped the lectern with a gavel. At the same time, Lieutenant Colonel Reynolds, Lieutenant Lee, and the remaining two tactical officers appeared from the faculty mess at the opposite end of the dining hall.

The dining hall was silent as Reynolds made his way to the lectern. Lee and the other two officers spaced themselves around the perimeter of the dining hall.

Reynolds gestured for Chambliss and Kingsbury to take their seats.

"What more can the man say?" Rosser whispered to Pelham.

"I suppose more damage control." Pelham sat with his arms crossed.

"Gentlemen, please continue eating." Reynolds fixed his hands on the corners of the lectern and managed a smile. "It seems that hardly a day passes that we aren't served up a major development, and today has been no different, has it?" His words were measured. "Yet our response, even to this development, should be no different than we've talked about before. We are an institution funded federally and by individual states. We cannot contest a student's right to leave or stay in light of his motivations, political or otherwise, and we can't contest the decision made by those in the regular army faced with similar choices. That Colonel Beauregard has seen fit to return to his home state of Louisiana is neither surprising nor wrong. It just is. Life here at the Academy need not, and will not, change because of it. Tomorrow, Colonel Delafield will return as acting superintendent, to serve until a successor is chosen."

Reynolds paused.

"The conclusion to what is happening is far from predictable, and there are many initiatives being tried to resolve differences at the national level and to achieve a peaceful end. My counsel to each of you is that you do your duty in the classroom to the best of your ability. Let's allow others in Washington, knowing circumstances and facts we cannot know, to pursue what is best for the nation. Finally ..." Pelham sensed that Reynolds was looking directly at him. "There are some in this room from states that have already seceded. Most are awaiting permission from families to leave, and that is their desire and right. I adjure all of you to respect and honor these men, who must be in the most uncomfortable of positions."

Reynolds's words achieved their aim of calming the Corps. That evening, even Rosser backed off from his commitment to resign, saying he would wait for Texas to announce its independence. But regardless of the commandant's remarks, Beauregard's departure solidified Pelham's and Rosser's commitment to leave as soon as it made sense. Knowing this could be any time, they busied themselves on the way back from the mess hall with soliciting interest for a final trip to visit Benny Havens.

The next morning, Tuesday, January 29, both Pelham and Rosser were summoned to Lieutenant Lee's office.

"Have a seat," Lee said, closing the door behind them. "I won't take much of your time, but given your circumstances, I wanted you to know that I am very close to making my own decision." He lowered his voice. "I will very likely resign my commission and offer my sword to Virginia. Unless I see real evidence that Virginia will not secede, that will be my decision. My hope was to finish out the academic year, so that D Company wouldn't suffer unneeded transition. But that's four months down the road, and I don't know that it is possible."

"What are the odds, sir, that Virginia will stay with the Union?" Pelham asked.

Lee stroked his beard. "I should think nil, and I say that for the simple reason that we border two sides of the nation's capital. Any Union movement against the South, South Carolina in particular, will cross Virginia's soil, and Virginia won't abide it. At best, we would be neutral on secession, but our hand would be forced if the Union intended harm to a Southern neighbor."

"Is there any realistic chance of reconciliation, sir?" Rosser asked.

"Between the South and the North?"

"Yes, sir."

Lee gave an equivocal gesture. "Neither wants war, I'm certain of that. The rub is that neither is willing to concede nor compromise. It's a rather irrational game we're playing."

"Do you see the Union taking unilateral action, sir?" Pelham asked.

"Even with the seizure of federal installations in the South, no. Not on Buchanan's watch." Lee glanced out the window. "I'm convinced that the worst is down the road. Do yourselves and your states a favor and hang in here as long as you can. There is much in the second semester that might benefit you later, if you understand my meaning."

Chapter Sixty-Two

Tuesday night, a snowstorm pounded the Hudson Valley and sorely tested all who went to Benny Havens' Landing. When Rosser, Kirby, and Patterson finally arrived, with Chambliss and du Pont in tow, they were surprised to find Custer already sitting at the hearth sipping an ale and smoking a cigar, his feet propped up on a chair.

"Dicey night," Havens boomed from behind the bar. "I'll fix you boys right up!"

Custer tipped his tankard at Rosser. "About time."

"How the hell did you beat us, Fannie?" Rosser demanded. "We left the barracks the same time you did, and wasted no time in coming."

Custer nodded toward a pair of skates hanging on the wall.

"You didn't!"

"Why not?"

"You're not sane, Fannie!"

"Nothing to it. From the South Dock, head south, and it's the first tavern on your right."

"You're worse than Pelham," Chambliss said, looking around for the man.

Custer anticipated him. "Not here yet."

"Needn't any of us worry about John," Patterson said, shedding his overcoat and gloves. "He'll appear when the flip does."

"Chas is right, lads." Havens placed a tray of ales on the table. After eyeing Chambliss and du Pont, he extended a hand. "Don't believe I've had the pleasure."

Patterson made the introductions. "Nate Chambliss is first captain of the Corps, Benny, and Henry du Pont is our class president. You are in august company."

The others snickered.

"Nate will have a flip, Benny, but I'm not sure about Henry. He's more into sherry."

Rosser nearly choked on his ale.

"There is nothing wrong with sherry," du Pont said indignantly. "But these are unusual times, and maybe I will try what you've talked about all these years."

"Just so," Havens said with a generous smile. "I'll get straight to it."

Pelham's cloaked figure moved through the dark shadows of the snowstorm, the odor of wet wool pungent in his nose. He was beyond the South Gate and less than a half mile from the landing. He chastised himself for finishing a letter to Clara that could easily have waited until morning. The short delay had allowed the storm to fully wax.

At the approach of a wagon, he ducked behind a frozen elm, drawing his overcoat tighter and leaning into the blowing snow. His shoes and socks were soaked and his feet numb. Only a sixth sense guided him past the granite precipice that had cost Jefferson Davis a fractured leg.

Then, as quickly as it had blown in, the storm slacked, as though God had said, "Enough!" A half moon soon appeared in a patch of starry sky, casting shadows on the fresh snow. Pelham saw the faint glow of the landing below and began his descent, slipping on the icy steps, clutching tree trunks and rock with deadened fingers.

Finally, he pounded on the tavern door. When it opened, Rosser seemed to sway from side to side.

"Damn, roommate, looks like you got the whole of it!" Rosser caught Pelham before he fell.

Custer stripped Pelham of his overcoat, gloves, and hat, and helped him to the fireplace. "Let's have your shoes, John. You're a drowned rat."

"About time, Master Pelham," Havens bellowed from the bar. "These friends of yours were about to run it back to the barracks."

The others laughed.

"You'll be wanting the usual?"

Pelham shuddered, his face colorless. "If not, Benny, I die from exposure."

"Can't be having that. No, sir. Nobody dies in my tavern."

The conviviality of the gathering was a stimulant to each one present, and instantly the celebration of brotherhood was taken to another level, when Benny rang the bell and delivered seven steaming tankards of flip.

"Here you go, boys."

"Y-you're a G-godsend … Benny," Pelham stuttered, wrapping partially thawed fingers around the hot tankard. After a couple of swallows, he began to breathe easier, and for the first time noticed du Pont. "Do my eyes deceive me, Henry?"

Du Pont nodded, almost sheepishly, the tankard of flip untouched in front of him.

"Damn, Henry," Pelham exclaimed, "just look at you. You're at Benny Havens' Landing and haven't gone straight to hell."

Du Pont ignored the remark. "I have yet to imbibe."

"Then imbibe, Henry. Your salvation is not at stake."

"You all seem to worship what I can take or leave."

"Don't be a prude, Henry," teased Kirby. "Take it."

"A prude, am I?" Du Pont sniffed the tankard and took a sip. Then he took another sip and smacked his lips, eyeing the beverage with curiosity.

"Careful, Henry, flip can sneak up on you," Pelham warned, and then stood up. "To Henry and Nate's first visit!"

Rosser seconded the toast.

Pelham winked at Custer. "Fannie's been here a few times."

"You could have picked a better night," du Pont observed after another sip.

"True enough, Henry."

The seven friends caught up on the day and the latest mental flogging administered by Professor Mahan to poor Rosser, who once again hung tenuously to the bottom rung. No one broached the subject of parting, preferring topics of merry making, until Pelham drew himself up in front of the hearth. "My friends, Tom and I thank you for coming, an expression of no mean account, especially in this weather." He forced a smile.

"So this is it," Patterson said, refilling his pipe. "You and Tom are next?"

Pelham eyed Patterson and the others who had fought the storm, and then stepped forward, offering his hand to Kirby, who took it and shook it firmly.

"We are friends, aren't we, Ned?" Pelham blinked back the moisture in his eyes. "And our souls are forever bound in God's grace."

Now it was Kirby's eyes that shined.

Pelham turned to du Pont. "Henry, same question."

"Of course, John. Since plebe year. Best friends."

"Hear, hear." Chambliss raised his tankard, as did the others.

Pelham's face was red from the heat of the fire. "Where do you see this going, Henry?" he asked.

"Now that's a broad question," du Pont said, not altogether distinctly. "I admit we are in a sad state. But some hope remains that we can work something out. We always have." He took another sip of his flip.

"You think so, Henry?"

Du Pont shook his head. "No. Not really."

"My friends," Pelham continued, "despite what you've seen and heard from me since Alabama made its decision, I've had a real time of it. This is a foul business, me being here when I should be home with Charlie Ball."

"Not your doing," Custer protested. "We all know it."

"You'll get your permission," Kirby said.

"Permission or not," Pelham continued, "how do I just hang around as if nothing is happening, when I know full well what I might be called to do?"

"And pray tell, what is that?" Du Pont stood up, his face flushed with flip. "I suppose if we met on the field of battle, you'd just run me through?"

The remark tickled Pelham. "Henry, haven't I done just that in every fencing class?"

The tavern filled with laughter.

"John," said Patterson, "'brevity is the soul of wit,' and you are the soul of brevity."

Chambliss took the floor. "John, you take yourself too seriously. No one doubts your motives, least of all me, and you know how we feel about you. While I may be leading the Corps, you, my friend, are its favorite and always have been."

"True words," said Kirby.

"Face it, John," Chambliss continued. "You could be first captain, if you cared a whit for playing the game."

"I think not," Pelham said. "But, clearly, I'm now on the outside, both Tom and me, where we breathe in order and exhale chaos—"

Du Pont interrupted. "What the hell does that mean?" Without waiting for an answer, he burped, smiled, and suggested another round of flip.

Pelham chuckled. "I'll join Henry, but someone has to help me carry him home!"

"I'm fine. Really ... fine." Du Pont nodded, a pasty grin on his face.

The order was placed, setting Havens back to work, and the men passed the evening recounting anecdotes that defined nearly five years of shared experience. Fifteen minutes before midnight, Havens, who had been unusually quiet all evening, announced, "Boys, 'tis time you were getting back."

"Benny's right." Pelham was already on his feet. "My friends, the six of us have been through the best and worst of times, and we've always been there for each other. Tonight you are here for Tom and me, and have helped me make sense of something."

A blurry-eyed du Pont looked at Pelham. "Huh?"

"Honor, Henry. Honor."

"Honor?" du Pont repeated.

"I felt I was betraying it. That being here, I was unfaithful to Alabama—and unfaithful to the Union."

Rosser was suddenly on his feet. "Now hold on a damn minute. What the blazes does honor have to do with it? What's wrong with finishing what we started? I for one have invested too much of my body and soul in this place to quit on conscience."

With a finger on Rosser's chest, du Pont reminded him that he had been ready to resign a week before.

"That was ... then," Rosser declared awkwardly.

Kirby stood up. "Here it is, John. You, Tom, and all our Southern mates have been put squarely in a place not of your choosing, and the rest of us know it. In your place, I would think and feel the same. But the fact is that you and Tom have the same rights as the rest of us. You were picked to be here the same as Nate, Henry, Chas, Fannie, and me. So long as we're not in armed conflict, I see no problem with you staying all the way through. I would—and see no taint on my honor."

"There it is," Rosser said, as if he had said it himself.

"Besides," Kirby smiled, "if you do stay, you just might see the light."

"You bastard!" Rosser exclaimed, his response smothered by laughter.

"Although," Kirby added, eyeing Chambliss, "maybe we should secure their weapons."

"Wait ... a minute." Du Pont attempted to put a right-handed glove on his left hand, and spoke as though he had borrowed his lips from someone else. "We get rings—class rings in two weeks. John, you and Tom—you still want your rings?"

Rosser was first to respond. "Hell, yes, after what I've been through!"

"And you, John?"

Mention of the ring caught Pelham off guard. "You would want us to wear the ring?"

"Of course," Kirby exclaimed, slapping him on the back. "We're brothers. You're as much a part of the class as I am, and always will be."

Chapter Sixty-Three

Saturday, February 2, Pelham was sitting at his desk when Rosser's size thirteen shoes pounded up the stairs. He turned to see the grin on Rosser's face.

"Professor Mahan's dead?"

"Better!" Rosser exclaimed. "Texas has joined the Confederacy. The delegates voted yesterday, one hundred and sixty-six to eight."

"So you're gone?"

"It has to be ratified by public referendum on the twenty-third. But it will happen, and when it does, I'm gone."

Pelham embraced Rosser's jubilance for his own. "We'll go arm in arm, for I'm certain to have permission by then."

"Let's do it, John. You and me on the ferry, waving at our Yankee friends."

The next Friday, Pelham received two letters: the permission he had expected from his father, and a letter from Judge Walker. The letter from his father contained a separate sheet of vellum with the precise wording Pelham needed to resign. But his exhilaration was short-lived. The judge, who had earlier insisted he catch the next train home, now admonished him to stay put, to finish the course of instruction, and in so doing best equip himself to serve the new country. Pelham wanted desperately to argue the point in a return letter, but the strength of the judge's advice was doubled by a clause in his letter: "And this is not only my opinion, but that of Jefferson Davis." Additionally, Pelham couldn't deny the value of what he would learn in the balance of military art, engineering, ordnance, and artillery and cavalry tactics. The judge's advice also took seed with Rosser, who resolved to stay, despite the intense desire to distance himself from Mahan.

Delafield had come to the point where the sight of a telegram from Scott made him physically ill, and that was the effect of the most recent dispatch dated February 17. The telegram communicated that seventy-year-old Brigadier General Twiggs, commander of the Texas Department of the Army, had surrendered his command to the new Confederate State of Texas without a fight, and thereafter resigned his commission to serve the Confederacy. In his place, Colonel Robert E. Lee took command of the Texas department, and he and twenty-six hundred federal troops who had garrisoned forts along the Texas frontier were allowed to leave the state, but only with individual weapons, personal effects, and limited supplies.

After sharing the telegram with Reynolds, Delafield lamented Governor Houston's predicament. The governor had advocated strongly for the Union, and in the process had alienated all of the state's fire-eaters, vehemently led by the ex-senator Louis Wigfall.

On Tuesday, February 19, Lieutenant Colonel Reynolds strode at an accelerated pace across Central Area, the courier having made it clear that the superintendent needed to see him right away.

Delafield handed Reynolds the briefest of Scott's more recent telegrams. It read, "Jeff Davis took oath of office yesterday. He is now provisional president of the Confederate States of America."

"But Davis didn't want the job," Reynolds said.

"Of course he didn't. He's a soldier first, better suited for command. But he had no choice. They elected him in absentia. Still, it's to our gain—as I think he still remains hopeful for peace." Delafield held up another dispatch. "Scott says that Davis is sending a formal commission to meet with Buchanan, and if need be, Lincoln. However, Davis has made it clear to the commission that their authority is limited to paying for federal installations on Southern soil, including Sumter and Pickens, and paying the Southern share of the Union national debt. Under no circumstances are they to discuss terms for reuniting with the Union."

"That Davis is president, and not one of the fire-eaters, gives me hope," Reynolds said.

"Yes, but I fear Lincoln is not averse to the use of force," Delafield countered. "Not if it will keep the Union whole."

Reynolds slowly nodded, "Then Davis must make his deal on Buchanan's watch."

That evening in the mess hall, what Pelham had dreaded finally surfaced. Two classmates confronted him and Rosser in rather harsh terms, one holding a newspaper article that specifically named them as having been conferred appointments as first lieutenants in the Confederate Army.

Rosser's response was one of indignation. Pelham took a softer approach.

"The both of you know us well enough. We would never accept a position in the Confederacy while in the employ of the Union, which we are as cadets. You can believe what you want, but neither of us has been contacted by anyone about any such commission, and neither of us has initiated anything from our end."

The issue was finally resolved when du Pont and Upton came to their defense.

Friday night, after the Corps had entered the mess hall, news came that Cozzen's Hotel in Buttermilk Falls was on fire. Chambliss immediately formed the four cadet companies and led them to the scene. Flames, whipped by strong winds, spewed from the main building. There was no saving the building or some of the nearby cottages, but before the roof of the main building collapsed, the Corps managed to recover most of the hotel's furniture and furnishings. On the march back, Custer observed ruefully that the loss of the hotel meant fewer ladies for the summer hops.

On Saturday, the six guns of the West Point battery were sent to Washington DC, and Delafield communicated to Reynolds a thwarted plot to assassinate Lincoln in Baltimore. The next day, a one-line dispatch from Washington reported that Texas, by public referendum, had voted forty-four thousand in favor of secession; thirteen thousand opposed.

On Wednesday, February 27, outside the mess hall, Pelham again had to defend his presence at the Academy. When he returned to the barracks, he vented on Rosser.

"It's your call, John," Rosser said. "I'm only too ready to leave."

Pelham shook his head. "President Davis should make the call. I should write him now."

"It will be two weeks before we hear back. Hell, if we time this wrong, we might end up incarcerated."

It took Pelham less than fifteen minutes to pen an explanation of their dilemma to the head of their future country.

The next day, Pelham and the rest of the class received class rings, at a cost of twenty-five dollars a ring. Pelham read the inscription inside his ring, *John Pelham, Graduating Class of 1861.* The ring's gold setting contained on one side the insignias of the Corps of Engineers, Cavalry, and Ordnance Corps; and on the other side the insignias of the Infantry, Artillery, and Judge Advocate General's Office. The polished signet stone was engraved with the class crest, a sword behind a shield, and with the class motto: "Faithful to Death."

At the supper meal, the First Classmen were obnoxious with their rings, passing them around tables for underclassmen to covet.

"I'm using my seal tonight," Patterson told Pelham as they left the mess hall.

"Anyone in particular?"

Patterson smiled. "A girl I met before you returned from furlough. She has potential."

Pelham intended to use his seal as well, responding to a letter he had just received from Clara.

After a feeble attempt at studying, Pelham reread Clara's last letter, the eighth since their intimacy, the memory of which had not faded. Pelham dipped his pen in the inkwell and began, "My lady, the seal on the envelope was made with my class ring, received this very day, which I shall wear and use for the rest of my life."

The letter finished, Pelham heated and dripped sealing wax across the flap of the envelope, let it cool slightly, and applied his signet ring.

CHAPTER SIXTY-FOUR

On Friday, March 1, Colonel Delafield once again said good-bye to James and the other house servants and made his way to South Dock to catch the steamer to New York City and his wife. The day previous, the sky a brilliant blue, the Corps had conducted a grand review honoring his departure and the arrival of his replacement, Colonel Alexander Bowman, Class of 1825.

Friday afternoon, Colonel Bowman's enlisted aide entered the superintendent's office. "Sir, would the Colonel care for some coffee?"

"Make that two, please—Lieutenant Colonel Reynolds will be joining me."

Minutes later, Reynolds was seated in Bowman's office.

"Let's pick up where we left off, John," Bowman said, referring to the briefing that Reynolds had started the day before on what Bowman needed to know regarding the tactical department and Corps of Cadets. Earlier in the day, Professor Mahan had briefed him on the academic program. The whole sequence of being selected superintendent, transferring to someone else the duties of his prior assignment, and moving to West Point had taken less than a week, and Bowman was scrambling to catch up.

When Reynolds finished, Bowman asked, "The Southern cadets from seceded states, they are all gone?"

"We still have a few, sir. In the First Class, only two, John Pelham of Alabama, and Thomas Rosser of Texas."

"They intend to stay with the Union?"

"I wish, sir. Actually, short of hostilities, they have expressed a desire to graduate. They are both good men, certainly not troublemakers, and the Corps seems amenable to their presence."

"I suppose five years is a long time to come up empty."

"Colonel Delafield briefed you on how General Scott keeps us informed, sir?"

"He did, and I've already received and responded to the first of his dispatches. Additionally, I have heard from William Seward, a good friend. He'll soon be Lincoln's secretary of state. I visited with him before coming here. He told me that on February 25, Jefferson Davis sent a three-man Confederate commission to negotiate surrender of the two still-occupied federal installations in the South."

"Colonel Delafield told me about that, sir."

"Excellent, but did you know that because the Union doesn't recognize the existence of the Confederacy, the commissioners have no direct access. They are communicating with Seward through Justice John Campbell."

"That I did not know. And, sir, I see that as a problem, both in lost time and meaning lost in translation."

"Seward is an honorable man, but I think he has climbed too far out on a limb. He is allowing the commissioners to think what they want, believing he can work out the details. The problem is that while Seward has the president's ear, he is not the president, and Lincoln has proven to be his own man. I don't see him giving up his kindling."

On Saturday, March 2, Texas formally joined the Confederacy. On March 4, Abraham Lincoln and James Buchanan left the Willard Hotel, near the White House, for the east portico of the unfinished capitol building, where Chief Justice Roger Taney swore in Lincoln as the sixteenth president of the United States.

The following day, a synopsis of Lincoln's acceptance speech was printed and distributed to the Corps. In the synopsis, Pelham saw an impassioned appeal by Lincoln to preserve the Union and for compromises that would heal strife between North and South. He handed the flyer to Rosser, who, upon reading it, expressed surprise that Lincoln promised not to use force to maintain the Union or to interfere with slavery where it existed. If true, he told Pelham, a shooting war might be avoided. Pelham was more pessimistic, certain that Lincoln would not give up Fort Sumter and Fort Pickens.

In the days and weeks that followed, Pelham and Rosser pursued their studies as though the inauguration and attendant events pertained to another country, as though they were exchange students finishing a semester abroad. With so few Southerners remaining, the mess hall, First Class Club, and barracks were forums for discussing Republican agendas and saving the Union. However, if Pelham or Rosser were in the mix, such topics were avoided. The need for such concession was minimal, since Pelham and Rosser generally kept to themselves, self-exiled in their room.

During this time, Pelham witnessed considerable change in his friends. Those who had articulated and defended the rights of individual states and the basic themes of the Democratic Party, most notably Henry du Pont, were now ardent for the Union and its perpetuation. Even the lighthearted Custer was prone to defend Lincoln. Yet, Pelham asked himself, how could he begrudge them or anyone else their political stance? A person deciding the issue of secession would naturally gravitate from the fence to one extreme or the other. He certainly had. Wasn't he more convinced than ever of the rightness of Southern states to form a new union of like-minded people, with like-minded interests?

After chapel on Sunday, March 17, Pelham sat at a desk in the library reading the March 16 edition of *Harpers Weekly*. It contained the full text of President Lincoln's inauguration speech. A deeper interest in the man who might be his enemy spurred Pelham to read the entire speech. After doing so, he saw the man differently, though no more favorably. Lincoln was not the man painted by Judge Walker, Senator Wigfall, or Congressman Miles—and he was no Buchanan. There was backbone and fight in him, an eloquence that would draw respect, and an appearance of selflessness that would command blind allegiance.

Pelham reread parts of Lincoln's speech and reflected on the issues debated by Upton and du Pont. Lincoln maintained that perpetuity, as applied to the Union, was implied in the fundamental law of national governments. Accordingly, no state could lawfully secede on its own volition. The Union must be maintained, unless by due process and by the people it was dissolved. The majority must rule in a democracy. But hadn't public referendums in states of the South done just that—voted overwhelmingly to dissolve ties with the Union? How was due process somehow lacking? In his mind, he judged Lincoln guilty of double-talk.

Yet, as Rosser observed, Lincoln had made it clear that the issue of civil war rested entirely in the hands of the South, that the North would not be the aggressor. If Lincoln's word was his bond, why couldn't the Confederacy have its way? What did it matter that the Union didn't recognize it? And if Sumter and Pickens remained in federal hands, couldn't the Confederacy abide the insult, at least long enough to gain strength?

That evening, Pelham lay in bed unable to sleep. A statement by Lincoln in his speech kept rolling about in his head—"Plainly, the central idea of secession is the essence of anarchy." It made no sense to him. Hadn't the thirteen colonies seceded from Great Britain? Hadn't history been nothing, if not a continuum of seceding factions and succeeding governments?

CHAPTER SIXTY-FIVE

Monday, March 18, Lieutenant Colonel Reynolds joined Colonel Bowman for breakfast on the veranda of the superintendent's quarters. James appeared with a pot of steaming coffee, a platter of scrambled eggs, ham, and fried potatoes, and a basket of hot biscuits.

"Will there be anything else, sir?"

"No thank you, James."

When they were alone, Bowman said matter-of-factly, "We nearly had us an incident." He then informed Reynolds that the day before, one of General Beauregard's cannons had nicked a corner of the Fort Sumter parapet with a training round.

"It may have been tit for tat, sir," Reynolds replied, "in response to one of Anderson's crews nearly lobbing a training round in downtown Charleston."

"Both accidents, and both suggesting that neither side is quite ready for war."

Reynolds smiled at the observation.

"Thank goodness for no injuries," Bowman added. "Makes white flags, inquiries, and apologies all the easier."

"Gives me the shivers to think what Bob Anderson is up against," Reynolds said. "He is quite literally sitting on a powder keg. Any word on the Confederate commission, sir?"

"They are still in Washington. Seward's last telegram indicated that the potential still remains for Sumter and Pickens to be handed over to the Confederates. Now that he's in office, Lincoln's under great pressure from moderates not to antagonize the Confederates. Although there are as many who would decry him treasonous if he turned over the forts. Still, the president isn't one for backing down, and I am convinced he can shovel this crap."

"I understand General Scott insists on reinforcing Pickens and Sumter." Reynolds buttered a biscuit.

"More accurately, I think, his position is that if we intend to defend them, then we should be serious about it. He says that Anderson is wholly dependent upon Charleston for food, and has been denied permission to release construction workers who consume nearly half his food supply."

"Interesting, Scott's position—given he's Virginian," Reynolds said.

"But staunch against slavery," Bowman replied. "Which, I suppose, is what cost him the presidency against Fillmore."

"No question he's a brilliant military mind, but at seventy-three and the size of both of us, he's barely able to cross the street. We need a true field general."

"And Scott knows it," Bowman said. "I understand he's keen on Bob Lee."

Reynolds's countenance brightened. "Aren't we all?"

That afternoon after class, Pelham found three letters in his room: two on his side of the desk and one on Rosser's. He opened the letter from Clara first. It was short and expressed growing anticipation over graduation, just three months away. She surprised him with the news that her father thought he might attend graduation, having never seen West Point.

The second letter, from his father, expressed surprise that he hadn't returned home, but supported his decision to finish as much of the course as possible. "All we hear at the courthouse," his father wrote, "is the call for militia to defend ourselves against Northern aggression. Some anticipate pillaging, which I find patently absurd. Your mother and I pray there is no substance to the possibility of actual war—that men of reason can arrive at a peaceful compromise." His father went on to praise Samuel's initiative in planting and weeding early; and then relayed the sad, but not unexpected, news that Reverend Smith had gone to be with the Lord, and that Reverend Knox had delivered an inspiring eulogy.

Rosser's letter was his second from Sam Houston, an impassioned plea that Rosser not follow, as one of many sheep, the pathway to destruction adopted by the state he had so long served, but which had now fallen headlong into the mire of rebellion and a dire fate. Houston speculated that by the time Rosser received his letter, he would have been stripped of his office.

The next day, checking the news dispatches that were kept by the Academy librarian, Pelham learned that Edward Clark had been named the new governor of the Confederate State of Texas. Houston, the multi-term congressman from Tennessee, seventh governor of Tennessee, first and third president of the Republic of Texas, multi-term senator from Texas, and seventh governor of the state of Texas was out—*persona non grata*.

On April 4, Colonel Bowman received a decoded telegram from General Scott—all official dispatches were now encrypted. After reading the message, Bowman sent a runner for Reynolds. Five minutes later, the two were behind closed doors. Reynolds read the deciphered message: "President has directed Sumter be resupplied, by force if necessary."

Reynolds shook his head. "His line in the sand."

Bowman nodded. "Yesterday, the schooner *Boston* waltzes by mistake into Charleston Harbor and takes a round through the mainsail. The damn thing was carrying ice, for God's sake! There's no telling what will happen to a resupply ship."

"Everyone's on edge, sir."

"Don't tell me. I just bit Professor Mahan's head off. He tells me this morning that cadet grades are falling, and I tell him, to hell with grades—these kids are going to war!"

Scott continued to feed Bowman coded telegrams twice daily about Fort Sumter and the resupply effort. Over the next seven days, the telegrams described a scenario of Lincoln's own design. He would resupply the fort with bread and salt pork. Additional troops would not be landed unless the resupply effort was opposed. It would be the Confederacy and not the Union to cast the first stone.

On April 5, Lincoln selected Captain Gustavus Fox, an Annapolis graduate turned merchantman, to resupply Fort Sumter. Governor Pickens of South Carolina was informed of the resupply effort, and that no troops would be landed if the provisions were delivered unopposed. He was also informed that three Union warships and a revenue cutter would be posted off the sandbar in front of Charleston Harbor to escort the resupply ship, should it come under fire.

As late as April 7, Seward, through Justice Campbell, was still assuring the Confederate commissioners in Washington that Fort Sumter could be surrendered. For his part, Seward was not intentionally misleading the commissioners, as Lincoln had indicated that he was agreeable to exchanging Sumter for the allegiance of Virginia to the Union. However, during the afternoon of April 7, that prospect dissolved when Lincoln learned that Virginia was in session to consider an ordinance of secession.

Captain Fox sailed south from New York Harbor on April 9, and on April 10, President Davis directed General Beauregard, the former Academy superintendent, to demand surrender of Fort Sumter. If it was not surrendered, General Beauregard was to reduce it as he saw fit.

On April 11, as Captain Fox steamed south through rough seas, Beauregard prepared a formal demand for the surrender of Fort Sumter. Shortly after noon, three military aides under white flag carried the demand to Major Anderson. Anderson received the demand and requested time to converse with his staff. After an hour's deliberation, Anderson returned with a written response to his former West Point artillery student—that he could not and would not surrender the federal installation. He did, however, add orally that in a few days he would be starved out and forced to surrender. Both the written and oral responses were communicated to Beauregard, and in turn to President Davis. Davis instructed Beauregard to obtain written confirmation of Anderson's oral response, expressing distrust not of Anderson, but for the Union in general, given perceived fabrications by Seward and others.

At midnight, the Confederate aides returned to Fort Sumter with the demand that Anderson put in writing what he had said aloud. Anderson did so, saying that he would evacuate the fort at noon on April 15. However, he added a caveat—unless his government resupplied him before then. The senior Confederate aide, knowing of the approach of the Union resupply ship and its escorts, and also understanding Beauregard's position, penned a short response to Anderson, writing that Confederate batteries would open fire in one hour. Anderson accepted the reply and shook hands with the Confederate aides, saying that if they never met in this world again, he prayed they would meet in the next. It was 3:20 AM, April 12, 1861.

CHAPTER SIXTY-SIX

At 4:30 AM, April 12, when John Pelham and Tom Rosser had been asleep for six hours, Confederate Lieutenant Henry Farley pulled the lanyard that fired the first shot of the American Civil War, a signal shot over Fort Sumter. Colonel Bowman learned of the bombardment of the fort at 7:00 AM. He summoned Reynolds, and they decided it was best not to inform the Corps until they received further word from General Scott. Neither was convinced that the firing on Sumter would be the catalyst for war, but rather an incident calling for measured response.

After thirty-four hours of bombardment and the miracle of no casualties, a Confederate shell started a fire, threatening Sumter's main magazine. Major Anderson agreed then to surrender Fort Sumter, provided that he could conduct a one-hundred gun salute to the Union flag before it was taken down. Shortly after noon on April 14, the surrender ceremony took place. During the artillery salute, a pile of cartridges was sparked, exploding and killing one man and mortally wounding a second. After the ceremony, Anderson and his command boarded a Union vessel and steamed north.

After Bowman received Scott's telegram the afternoon of April 14, he addressed the Corps. At the supper meal, his remarks about the incident were brief and factual.

After the meal, Pelham joined Kirby, Upton, and others who regularly attended the bi-weekly prayer meetings held in front of the altar in the cadet chapel. Lieutenant Oliver Howard was more than a little surprised to see Tom Rosser accompanying Pelham.

"Good of you to join us, Mr. Rosser." Howard extended his hand.

"I'm not sure I had a choice, sir."

"That may be, but this is indeed a time for prayer."

"Yes, sir."

"Tom, come sit by me," Emory Upton said.

When all were seated, Lieutenant Howard bowed his head. "Father God, we come before you with humble and heavy hearts and a desire to know your will. As our nation faces its gravest hour, we pray wisdom and grace for our leaders, both Union and Confederate. We do not know what the future holds, except that soon most of us will leave this place to do our duty in the light of serving you. We pray for strength, compassion, and honorable conduct. We pray that we might do our duty well. Father, we know that in all things, through the worst that this world has to offer, you intend good to those who know and love you. Bless our time together and our fellowship. In Christ's name, Amen."

In a departure from his biblically-based message, which would be followed by discussion and prayer, Howard began with a question. "What is on your heart right now?"

A long silence greeted the question. It was broken by Rosser. He stood and made eye contact with each man in the group. "Except for John, the rest of you will be fighting for the North, if it comes to that, and I want you to know that I have no desire to harm you, let alone kill you. And I hope that you have no desire to kill me."

Rosser's remark not only eased the tension in the chapel, but started a dialogue that ranged from confusion to frustration over how men of faith lived out war, and more pointedly, a war between brothers.

Howard read scripture that encouraged prayer for one's enemies, and offered interpretation without reference to the current situation. Finally, he gave his concluding prayer, thanking God for the survival of those at Fort Sumter, and asking for divine blessing upon all in attendance and upon a divided Union.

After the prayer meeting, Howard asked Pelham if he might have a word with him.

"Am I going to see you at our next prayer meeting?"

"Sir, I think I will be a great distance from the Academy by then."

"I understand. I will pray for you, John. I know you are a praying man. It is essential that we remain so."

This was the first time Howard had addressed him by his first name. "Yes, sir, and thank you for tonight. Your message was clear and needed. Something much larger than us is at work here."

At the supper meal on Monday, April 15, Lieutenant Colonel Reynolds approached the lectern, his face drained of color. "Men, this has been a day that will change history as we might have seen it or wanted it. It is my sad duty to inform you that a state of war now exists between the United States of America and the Confederate States of America."

The response of silence in the dining hall was numbing.

"President Lincoln has called for the conscription of seventy-five thousand militia from states loyal to the Union to repress what he has termed the Southern Rebellion."

Pelham looked down at his plate.

"In light of the circumstances, it is unlikely that the Class of 1861 will have its one month of graduation leave. I will have more on the disposition of the class in the days to come."

Without looking at Pelham or Rosser, Reynolds continued. "There are those of the South still with us. They are to be afforded every courtesy. They are not to be confronted with what others have done. They are still your brothers."

That night Pelham and Rosser resolved to submit their resignations the next day, and Rosser paced the floor as Pelham finished his letter of resignation and blew on the ink. He handed it to Rosser, who read it.

> West Point, N.Y., April 15, 1861.
> Sir, I have the honor to tender the resignation of my appointment as cadet in the service of the United States. I have accepted no place or appointment from any state or government.
> I am, sir, very respectfully your obedient servant, John Pelham, Cadet, USMA.

Rosser nodded his approval and returned the letter to Pelham who inserted the letter, along with his father's permission, in an envelope.

On Tuesday, April 16, Pelham and Rosser submitted their resignations to Lieutenant Lee after breakfast. Lee read them without comment, except to say he would forward them through channels.

"What about you, sir?" Rosser asked.

"I too will be leaving."

"Sir, I don't know that it's possible," Pelham said, "but I would be honored to serve under your command if there is a way you can make that happen."

"Me too, sir," Rosser said.

Lee did not respond to their request, but only wished them the best of luck.

Together, Pelham and Rosser visited Henry du Pont, informed him of their decision, and asked that he expedite the process. His demeanor distant, du Pont said that he would.

Late in the morning, Colonel Bowman received a dispatch from General Scott, stating that President Lincoln would be offering command of the Union army to Robert E. Lee, now residing at his home in Virginia.

At the midday meal, Pelham and Rosser informed their friends that they would be gone within the week. As with du Pont, their responses were generally cool. Numbed by so many perceived defections, Pelham accepted that even close friends like Ames and Hazlett would greet their departure with diffidence. What surprised him was Emory Upton, who exhibited the most warmth.

The next day, Scott telegraphed Bowman that Colonel Lee had declined command of the Union Army, citing his reluctance to take part in an invasion of the Southern states. A second dispatch, late that afternoon, reported that Virginia had seceded and that Lee had resigned from the army.

On Thursday, Pelham returned to his room after the last academic class to find a letter from his father. The letter expressed heartfelt regret over the demise of the Union, ardent concern for the future of Alabama, and the strongest desire that Alabama distant itself from South Carolina, whose actions, he believed, had precipitated the war. It was apparent to him that President Davis would not have ordered Beauregard to bombard Fort Sumter, had he not known that South Carolina would have done so on its own.

"We are elated," his father wrote on a positive note, "that you will be returning home very soon, and will have fatted calf and anything else you desire awaiting you." But it was what followed that gave Pelham the greatest joy. "While I'm at a loss to what he means, Samuel wanted me to relay that he no longer wants what you promised him. He offered no explanation, so I leave it up to you to interpret his meaning. Anyway, I am glad to report that he and young Ora are just married and she expecting. Samuel says he would like a large family and Ora will be a wonderful mother."

Pelham couldn't wait to share the news with Clara.

"You will also want to know," his father continued, "that Samuel has done a great service to the family and the plantation, and I have no reservations about his overseeing the planting and harvesting. Moreover, he commands the respect of blacks as has our dear Willie. Lastly, regarding Willie, I must report that he has finally slowed, and has the cough I so greatly dread. That he spends most evenings with Samuel, wanting to leave things in good order, is a true blessing. We shall all dearly miss him."

In the days that followed, Pelham made a point of being the last to enter a classroom and the first to leave. He wanted to avoid contact with everyone but Rosser. Rosser, on the other hand, had for all purposes ceased to be a cadet. He attended no formations or classes, and arrived on his own recognizance at the mess hall to take his meals with Pelham.

Saturday's mail call included a letter from Clara, and Pelham opened it with trepidation, not knowing if it had been written pre-Sumter or post-Sumter. By its date, it was post-Sumter, yet no reference was made to the conflict or to Lincoln's declaration of war. Rather, Clara wrote of things pleasant and of their life together when all the craziness was over.

Saturday afternoon after classes, Pelham heard a knock on the door.

Ned Kirby poked his head inside. "So—how is it going?"

"I won't lie. It's been tough, Ned."

"Where's Tom?"

"Selling uniforms. You know him—never misses a trick."

Kirby smiled. "John, I'm here because some of the boys ... we want to give you a proper send-off."

Pelham put down his book. "Send-off?"

"We were thinking a final run to Benny's—tomorrow night."

For the first time in weeks, Pelham smiled. "Now that would indeed be a proper send-off. Who's coming?"

"You'll see."

CHAPTER SIXTY-SEVEN

Sunday night, those running it to Benny Havens' Landing slinked away from the barracks under moonlight in twos and threes, and most made their way in silence. Passing Cozzen's Hotel, Pelham was surprised to see a new roof on the main structure, and large piles and stacks of construction materials about the grounds. He followed Rosser for the last time down the stone steps to the landing, his thoughts a thousand miles away. He had learned from the *Charleston Mercury* sent by Henry Farley that it was the senator he had met on the train, Louis Wigfall, now a Confederate colonel, who had rowed to Fort Sumter during the bombardment to convince Major Anderson to surrender.

Inside the tavern, Havens greeted more cadets than he had seen in many years, and Letitia was fully employed taking orders and preparing flip. "We need more rum, husband," she shouted, as she disappeared up the stairs to the locker where the liquors were kept.

When Pelham and Rosser arrived, Havens bore a panicked expression. "Tell me there are no more."

Pelham surveyed the room. At one table sat du Pont, Chambliss, Patterson, Kirby, and Ames, and at another table were Kingsbury, Custer, Upton, and O'Rorke.

"No, Benny, I think we are the last."

"Beloved God, thank you. Not that I'm beyond the company. It's just that if we're raided, the country will be out half its officer corps."

Haven's wit lightened the mood in the tavern.

"A flip for me, Benny," Rosser said.

"You have to tell me that?" Havens said, as though offended. "And it's on your friends for the both of you."

343

Pelham and Rosser surveyed the room full of friends, and visited personally with each one. Presently all save Upton, who would sooner dance with the devil, had a hand on a steaming tankard of flip.

Pelham stood by his chair. "Thank you for this night," he said to them all. "And Walter, Emory, and Paddy—you do Tom and me great honor by your coming." He held his tankard high. "To the dearest of friends."

"Hear, hear," du Pont exclaimed, beneath a mustache of flip.

Rosser claimed the floor. "Let those of the North take no offense that those of the South have no desire for marriage, and let those of the South take no offence that Lincoln has no desire for divorce."

"And would that the war could be settled in like fashion in court," Kirby said.

"And without blood," Ames added.

Upton stood up, unbearably sober, a tin of black coffee in his hand. "God ordains governments to rule, and those in authority to exercise power, which is what separates us from monkeys, but authority granted or taken comes with its peril—"

To the delight of the others, Rosser pushed Upton back down in his chair and took his place. "On behalf of whatever Upton just said, I propose a toast to the Class of 1861!"

Hurrahs filled the tavern.

Patterson, who had been pensively stirring his flip, took the floor. "In the words of the Bard, 'Double, double toil and trouble; fire burn, and cauldron bubble. When shall we ...'" He paused to count noses. "Eleven 'meet again? In thunder, lightning, or in rain?'"

"Clever man," said Kingsbury. "How about when North and South are done and one?"

The others laughed heartily, Rosser biting his tongue in the presence of so vast an enemy. As a diversion, Pelham suggested another round of flip.

"If you gentlemen will excuse me." Letitia Havens bowed with her hands in a prayerful pose. "You have worn out this old lady, and I'll be wishing you all a good evening. But before I do—" She crossed the room and hugged the necks of Pelham and Rosser, fighting back tears.

As the woman started up the staircase, Rosser shouted, "To Mrs. H!" All rose to their feet and cheered the woman until she disappeared from view.

"She's a good woman, her," Benny said. "Sometimes a little emotional."

"How many years, Benny?" Patterson asked.

"Joined at the hip these forty-five years, we are. Each year better than the last."

"We see it, Benny," Pelham said. "May we be so lucky."

For the next two hours, emboldened by elixir, the gray-clad friends made light of things others wouldn't have voiced, until, to the surprise of all, Benny Havens shouted, "Lads! If you will pardon me—and it's not my place …"

Rosser looked at Havens, who was standing in front of the hearth. "What is it, Benny?"

"Master Tom, I struggle to keep my peace …"

Havens looked warmer than Pelham had ever seen him, and he was quick to his feet. "Why should you keep your peace, Benny? If anyone has a right to speak, it is you."

The old man wrung his hands. "Yes, well. First, thanks to all of you for coming, for filling my coffers—but what is undoing me is the business that brings you here. You men—and I call you men, for you are—but when I first laid eyes on you, some of you anyway, you were boys. Just boys." He slapped his thigh, a thing he did when he was about to ask a question. "Do any of you come from families that didn't fight in the Revolution?"

The silence in the room suggested otherwise.

"No, of course not. Your families, as did mine, shed blood—British blood if they could, but likely their own as well, and because of it, because of their sacrifice, you and me are heirs of something no people in history have ever had. Sweet liberty, blessed freedom, each man the equal of the next."

Rosser shifted in his chair.

"The country may not be perfect." Havens's eyes sparkled. "I'll grant you that, and things are crazy mixed up now, but I'm telling you—it's a damn sight better place to live than any other on this big ball of dirt."

Upton raised his coffee tin. "Amen, Mr. Havens."

"Tell me," Havens continued, his eyes on Pelham and Rosser, "how a South Carolina, or an Alabama, or a Texas, or any other state, is going to be better off as its own little kingdom, or holding hands with other such kingdoms, than it is right now? The Union works because we are different, and contribute different. It works because we have sound government, and not too much of it, and because we have a leader whose tenure is short and at the will of the people." He wrung his hands again. "I say again the country's not perfect, and we don't always see eye to eye, or love the man on top. I for one didn't vote for Lincoln. But he's my president, and for the next four years, I'll get through it, and don't know why we all can't."

Pelham had slipped to the bar to pour Havens a glass of ale.

"Thank you, Master Pelham." Havens took a long draft, and then reached in his pocket. He extracted a pouch of pipe tobacco, making a show of sniffing it. "Don't you see how we need each other? This here tobacco, of which I am quite fond, comes from North Carolina, which I'm told is likely to flee the nest. But, dang, if it ain't the best tobacco I ever piped. But do you know those big Baldwin locomotives that move trade throughout the Southland?" Havens stared directly at Pelham. "Where do they come from? Why from Philadelphia—that's where."

"Don't think just because I fix your drink and cook your meal that I'm not aware of what goes on. And don't think I don't have a stand on it, because I do. But it's not political, lads. It's heartbreaking personal. All these years, I've watched you, and those who came before you. Some of you make it, some of you don't. But damn, if I'm not proud of every one of you!"

Havens' countenance turned morose. "I see something ugly, fully brewed, and boiling over. I see my lads pitted against each other, facing off in the hell of battle, friend against friend—and it is madness!"

He hung his head.

"There, I'm sorry. I've said too much. You'll decide your own minds, as rightly you should. It's just that—"

"Just what, Benny?" Pelham joined the tavern keeper at the hearth.

"It's just that I hate to see the dream end."

Pelham put his arm around Havens. "Benny, you are truly the dearest, kindest soul on earth, and you must never think that we don't understand your meaning. You express it only too well. But what is to be done about it?"

Pelham glanced at his friends, and then back at Benny.

"Benny, can you not see the thing from our side—for Tom and me? It is not a matter of issues, of rightness or wrongness. We're sons and brothers of families that love us and that we love. We left homes to come here, go to school, and become soldiers. But isn't it natural that we go home? Would it be natural if we didn't? We can no more separate ourselves from what makes us who we are, than change the color of our skin."

Pelham's eyes darted around the room.

"I know you can't see it, Benny, but perhaps—just maybe—the dream you speak of isn't gone. Maybe it isn't over. Maybe it's just changed, evolved differently than you expected."

He put a hand on Havens' shoulder and turned to the others. "Brothers, shall I surprise you?" He retrieved a piece of paper from his dress coat. "Benny, our class has yet to pen a verse to you, to add to all those that have come before, and our time is almost done. With the permission of my classmates ..."

"Yes, John, let us hear it," Chambliss exclaimed. Kirby, du Point, and the others said the same.

Pelham sang the refrain to "Benny Havens, Oh," and then words that none of them had heard before.

Go we now our separate way, boys, fate's not to us been just
We know not what the future holds, the lifeblood poured from us
But when all is done and all is past, we pray God heals our pain
And brings us back to Benny's place, to toast our bond again.

Custer leaped to his feet, joined by the others, all of them singing:

Oh! Benny Havens, Oh!—Oh! Benny Havens, Oh!
We'll sing our reminiscences of Benny Havens, Oh!

Chambliss slipped the handwritten stanza from Pelham's fingers and led the group a second time through the new verse, as Pelham looked on in silence.

347

When they finished, there was not a dry eye in the tavern.

"Bravo, John," Rosser shouted, his voice cracking. "Bravo, my dear, best friend!"

Du Pont blew his nose and hollered, "A cheer for Alabama!"

Havens's hand was suddenly in the air, and Rosser bellowed, "A word from Benny!"

"Master Pelham, Master Rosser—I am so proud of you, so proud of all of you. You are truly without choice, but you're a testament to all that is noble. Forgive a foolish old man for saying what he ought not. Further, I am so sorry, lads, for the hand you've been dealt. 'Tis the devil's work, but you'll play it your best, I know you will, and you'll make me proud."

Pelham embraced the old man. "Thank you, Benny. God bless you and your family."

"To Benny Havens," Rosser shouted.

"To Benny Havens," echoed the others.

Pelham bounded to the front door. "Away boys, tomorrow is here."

As his friends filed out singing yet another verse to the tavern keeper, Pelham nodded at the legend, flashed a smile, and entered the night.

Chapter Sixty-Eight

Two hours later, on April 22, the charge-of-quarters cracked the door to Pelham's room and found him at his desk, the gas lamp still on. Returning at 3:00 AM, he found the same. While duty bound to report a man out of bed after taps, a two-demerit offense for each infraction, what was the point? "Try and get some sleep, John."

Pelham turned, his face drawn and colorless. "Thanks, I need it." A nest of wadded vellum had formed around his chair. He leaned back, stretched his arms, and read his last effort.

April 22, 1861, West Point, New York
My dearest Clara,
When you receive this, I will be several days gone from the Academy. Forgive me, my lady, for not writing sooner, an unpardonable sin against my true love, for which my only excuse is the realization that the dream we have fought so hard to preserve cannot be. It is fantasy for us to think we can survive the war and that you can be happy in Alabama for the rest of your life.

That we should not come together as one, not raise a family of the most beautiful children, and not grow old and more deeply in love with each season, is more than my heart can bear or my pen admit. But I am not God and am powerless to affect what charts our course. Yet I do love you, my lady, and always will, and on another canvas our love would have been a masterpiece, a story for the ages.

Therefore, my lady, I reluctantly return to you your heart, which I have cherished more than my own for these eight glorious months. I free you to give it to another with my blessing and the full blessing of almighty God.

With this parting, my lady, I ask that you pray for me as I will for you, and know that as I leave West Point this very morning, and henceforth attempt to do my duty as God grants me vision and strength, that if the worst befall me, I shall await you in heaven.

Your faithful knight,
John

He was no more pleased with this than his earlier drafts, but he ached for sleep. He folded and inserted the two sheets into an envelope, waxed, and sealed it, and then crawled into bed. He slept fitfully for a short time, until Bentz and his drummers did their worst. For the last time, he played the game, standing reveille formation as though nothing had changed.

When he returned to the room, Rosser was sitting on the edge of his bed. "We're the last to leave, John. How do you think it will go?"

Pelham shrugged and headed down to the orderly room, but when faced with the drop slot in the mail box, he could not bring himself to insert the letter.

Breakfast was as solemn a time as Pelham had experienced, but passed without incident. He ate little and declined Kingsbury's invitation to address the Corps. He felt that enough had been heard from departing Southerners. Rosser similarly refused the offer.

After the meal, Chambliss surprised Pelham outside the mess hall, the look on his face grave. "I didn't say anything last night because I hope it comes to nothing, but I heard from my brother in Nashville yesterday."

"Oh?"

"He thinks Tennessee will secede—that the federal response to Fort Sumter was too much."

Pelham nodded. "On the way back from Benny's, Chas told me Arkansas was likely to leave, though he thinks he can still graduate." He put a hand on Chambliss's shoulder. "For one of us, yours is good news. I'd rather have you with me than against me."

"John, my heart is not with the Confederacy."

"Fair enough, Nate. But you'll go home if Tennessee secedes."

"I won't have a choice."

"None of us do."

After breakfast, the barracks divisions were quiet and Central Area was deserted, with everyone but Pelham and Rosser in class.

"We've three hours before we leave," Rosser said. "I'm taking a nap."

Pelham decided on a walk, his first in civilian clothes. The sky was clear and the campus renewed by spring. Crossing Jefferson Road, he walked the perimeter of the Plain past the library, and then north along the river bluff. The green of spring was in the grass of the Plain, and would remain so until the tramplings of summer encampment. Near Fort Clinton, he sat for nearly two hours beside Kosciusko's monument, gazing across the river at the distant hills. When he walked past the hotel, gardeners were busy weeding and planting, and on the path to the summer encampment, men distributed cinders from a large horse-drawn wagon.

The familiar scent of spring was strong in the air, the temperature mild. The elms and maples of Trophy Point were in full leaf, and the shadblow and dogwoods in brilliant bloom.

He was drawn down to North Dock and Flirtation Walk, which he followed as far as Kissing Rock. Then he retraced his steps to the Plain, past the commandant's quarters and the superintendent's quarters to the barracks.

It was nearly twelve o'clock when he returned to Central Area, and a quartermaster wagon was in front of the Eighth Division stoops. Rosser was talking with a young enlisted man, his effects already in the wagon. The prospect of an immediate departure lifted Pelham's spirits.

"Give me a minute," he shouted to the driver.

The driver jumped down from his seat. "Sir, let me help you. I'm Private Bowers, sir. I'm new here and work the stables. I've heard a lot about you and Mr. Rosser. You're legends, sir."

Pelham smiled. On the fourth floor, he picked up his valise and pointed to a steamer trunk.

Bowers struggled, but he hoisted the trunk onto his back. After loading the wagon, he climbed up to the driver's seat. "You both can ride up here with me, if you like."

"I'd rather walk, thank you," Pelham said.

Rosser said the same.

The private made a clucking sound, and the team lurched forward, crossing Central Area past the commandant's office. As the team rounded the First Division, Pelham and Rosser were stunned to see what appeared to be the entire Corps blocking their way. At the front was Nate Chambliss, and behind him, Henry du Pont, Ned Kirby, Walter Kingsbury, Emory Upton, Adelbert Ames, Chas Patterson, Charlie Hazlett, George Custer, and Paddy O'Rorke. Chambliss stepped forward and shouted over his shoulder, "How is it we say good-bye to a brother?"

The throng erupted in hurrahs and whistles, and swiftly descended upon Pelham and Rosser, hoisting them on their shoulders.

Pelham was speechless.

"You don't deserve this," Custer shouted with a grin. "You damn traitors. I'll be keeping an eye on you."

"You do that, Fannie," Rosser shouted back. "And you won't have to look far, because we'll be at the front of it."

Du Pont pointed an accusing finger at Rosser. "So fast to slit throats?"

"You Northerners can surrender anytime you want—no hard feelings." Rosser's words drew a raucous response.

"Good luck, boys," Kirby shouted. "Trust your flip to me!"

"A low blow, Ned," Pelham yelled back.

"Tom, now you can grow a beard," Patterson bellowed. "For 'He that hath a beard is more than a youth, and he that hath no beard is less than a man.'"

"Where do you get that stuff?" Rosser shouted back to Patterson.

Upton extended a hand to Pelham. "May God protect you from all the flaming arrows. And you too, Tom."

The formation for the midday meal being half an hour off, the banter and cries did not diminish as the Corps carried the two Southerners past the chapel, the library and post headquarters, and down South Dock Road to catch the Garrison ferry.

At the dock, Pelham and Rosser embraced their friends, shook hands, and shed tears. And after last farewells they boarded the ferry, where Pelham finally sensed the peace he had been seeking.

Chambliss ordered the Corps back to the barracks, and as the ferry sounded its horn to depart, from the mass of gray moving up the road, a single figure ran at breakneck speed back toward the dock.

Rosser squinted. "Who is that?"

Pelham cupped his eyes. "I'd swear it's Dan McElheny, and he's waving something."

By the time McElheny reached the dock, the ferry had pulled away. Pelham could see that McElheny had a letter, which he stuffed inside the band of his forage cap and sailed onto the ferry deck.

"For you, John!" he shouted over the noise of the steam engine.

Rosser grabbed the cap, removed the letter, and winged the cap back at the dock. McElheny grabbed it midair and raced back up the boardwalk.

"I believe this is yours." Rosser handed Pelham the letter, which Pelham quickly opened.

"That's not Clara's handwriting," Rosser observed as Pelham read.

"No. It's from Kingsbury's fiancée, Eva Taylor." Pelham handed Rosser the crumpled photograph of a very attractive woman. On its back was the name Sallie Dandridge.

Chapter Sixty-Nine

It was on the ferry to Garrison, before catching the train to New York City, that Pelham informed Rosser he was going to visit Clara at Clermont College before heading south. Rosser's protestations were to no avail, and he acceded to the detour.

Late in the afternoon, Pelham found the Clermont campus exactly as Clara had described it, rays of a falling sun highlighting a tranquil quadrangle of three-story redbrick buildings trimmed in white, with intervening trellis-covered crosswalks and meticulously landscaped grounds.

Having learned from Miss Frampton where Clara would be, and satisfying the woman that he was only going to simplify Clara's life, Pelham surprised Clara as she emerged from her advanced French class. When she saw him, she flew into his arms.

"This time you're the little sneak," she exclaimed, kissing him full on the lips in front of all the other girls.

Pelham grinned. "Discretion, my lady."

"Hang discretion. You don't know any of these girls." Clara pulled him back into the classroom.

Now Pelham was the aggressor, embracing, kissing, and caressing until they finally came up for air. "God, I have missed you!"

She nuzzled his chin. "I can't believe you're here."

"Didn't I say that in January?"

"You are so clever to find me."

"Our friend, the troll."

"You're—not in uniform."

"Tom and I are headed home, Clara." Pelham started to tell her what he had come to say, but found himself saying meaningless, safe things, holding and kissing her as if nothing had changed. But after a few minutes, he nerved himself. "My lady, can you bear hearing what I must say?"

Her eyes glistened immediately with tears, and she nearly collapsed in his arms. "Dear God, why us?"

He stroked her hair and rocked her in his arms.

"It's—it's not fair, John."

He gave her his handkerchief, and she blew her nose. After a time she managed a smile. "I guess we're not going to Canada."

He smiled weakly.

"I'll never see you again, will I?"

He drew her tight, overcome with emotion. "My lady, I wish with every part of me that I could say that you will. But the conflict that is coming will be more than you or I could ever imagine. It will be ugly beyond what we could ever conceive. The South, for its part, will fight to the last, for we have everything at stake. And whatever the outcome, I fear you and I will be in such different places. You'll be a doctor—I'll be a farmer."

"A plantation owner," she corrected him, fresh tears streaming down her cheeks. "John, you will forever be my knight."

Pelham could no longer hold back his tears, and together they wept freely. When there were no more tears to shed, he kissed her once on each cheek.

"You, dearest love, will always be my lady, and I will say to you now what you have so longed to hear, and what has been true since first we met. I love you, Clara Bolton. I love you with all my heart."

When Pelham and Rosser left Clermont, Pelham tore up the letter he had written. As best they could, they avoided New York City, where talk of the city seceding from the state had authorities throwing anyone suspicious into overfilled jails. In like fashion, they avoided Baltimore, where mobs controlled the streets. At Pelham's insistence, they headed west and eventually crossed the Ohio River at Maysville, Kentucky. The superintendent of Maysville College informed Pelham that his sister, Bettie, had departed three weeks earlier.

CHAPTER SEVENTY

THE FIRST BATTLE OF BULL RUN
SUNDAY, JULY 21, 1861

The Confederate attack on McDowell's left flank planned by Beauregard, approved by Johnston, and anticipated by Pelham and every commander west of Bull Run, did not take place. The previous afternoon, after two days of reconnoitering Confederate positions and points to cross Bull Run, and reprovisioning troops, McDowell directed his aide, Lieutenant Walter Kingsbury, to assemble the division commanders. At First Division headquarters, he exchanged a warm handshake with one of the commander's two aide-de-camps, Lieutenant Paddy O'Rorke. The other aide, Lieutenant Emory Upton, had directed Union artillery fire across Blackburn's Ford on the eighteenth and was otherwise engaged.

When the division commanders were assembled, McDowell got straight to the point. "Gentlemen, we launch the main attack at two-thirty in the morning." He pointed to the battle map prepared by his chief engineer. "Confederate strength is well south of Stone Bridge, still centered on Blackburn's Ford and Mitchell's Ford, and we've seen no evidence of significant redeployment. Bory's stretched himself thin over eight miles of Bull Run, and our intelligence is that his left flank is anchored with no more than two regiments at Stone Bridge. The opening is clear—"

There was commotion at the entrance to the tent, and Kingsbury turned around to see Lieutenant George Custer, covered with dust and heading his direction.

Kingsbury smiled. "What do you have?"

Custer shook the dust from his forage cap. "Frankly, General Scott is at a loss why you haven't attacked the Rebs yet. He's getting political heat, and doesn't like the fact that half of Washington is coming out to see the show. He insists McDowell get on with it before the Confederates gain more advantage."

"You're going to tell him this?"

"No. I'm going to give him this sealed letter that says the same thing."

Kingsbury grinned and shook his head. "General Winfield Scott's courier. Fannie, how is it you always land on your feet? I heard you were about to be court-martialed at the Academy until your class was graduated early and you were sprung free and clear."

Custer smiled. "It's all about destiny, my friend."

At two-thirty Sunday morning, July 21, McDowell set his plan in motion, which from the beginning suffered setbacks. The two divisions that were to make the main attack by flanking Stone Bridge to the north "bottlenecked" in Centreville, and then had to wait on the Warrenton Turnpike for repair of a bridge east of Bull Run. However, of greatest impact to the battle plan was the miscalculation of the distance to be covered by the flanking divisions. Instead of seven miles, they would have to cover thirteen miles.

At five o'clock, Pelham heard Union artillery open fire in earnest to the north of his location around Stone Bridge. Then there was more artillery fire to the south at Blackburn's Ford. He scrambled the battery, ordering his troops to eat something and prepare for a long day. Throughout the early morning hours he was in meetings with Colonel Bartow, General Jackson, and General Bee, awaiting orders.

Shortly after eight o'clock, Colonel Bartow informed Pelham that the brigade and General Bee's brigade were ordered to move posthaste to reinforce the Confederate left flank—that the Union was moving a large number of troops to the north. General Jackson's brigade was to follow in reserve.

The battle that would unfold centered on an intersection a mile west of Stone Bridge, formed by the Warrenton Turnpike—oriented roughly east-west—and Sudley Springs Road—oriented roughly north-south. Key terrain features were Matthews Hill to the northeast, Dogan Ridge to the northwest, Chinn Ridge to the southwest, and Henry House Hill to the southeast. Young's Branch, a steeply sloped, narrow tributary to Bull Run, meandered south of Dogan Ridge and Matthews Hill, and north of Chinn Ridge and Henry House Hill.

The landscape was a patchwork of farmland, pasture, and meadow, with scattered pines and patchy, dense forests of oak. Tall grass, chest high corn, and a scattering of wooden fences finished the landscape, and everywhere dips and depressions would later offer fleeting haven to infantry.

On the upslope of Matthews Hill, just shy of its crest, the original force of nine hundred Confederates and two light cannons first encountered the Union flanking force, which would eventually number twenty thousand. Incredibly, the Confederates resisted the onslaught for nearly an hour, before being reinforced by the brigades of Bartow and Bee.

Pelham's Alburtis battery and the battery attached to Bee's brigade unlimbered behind a natural parapet on the crest of Henry House Hill, and fed a furious shelling on the Union advance along Sudley Springs Road.

By mid-morning, six senators, at least ten congressmen, and hundreds of civilian notables, oblivious to what was to unfold, appeared on the east side of Bull Run, fully expecting to witness the end of Southern foolishness. However, what they did was add confusion to the movement of the green Union troops, who were puzzled by the presence of women in Victorian attire, spreading picnic blankets and arraying them with victuals and drink, while they went into battle, to kill or be killed.

Soon the Union attack was bolstered by two regular army artillery batteries on Dogan Ridge, boasting heavier guns than those of the Confederate batteries. The batteries were commanded by Captain Charles Griffin and Captain James Ricketts. Commanding two-gun sections in Griffin's battery were Lieutenants Adelbert Ames and Charlie Hazlett. In Ricketts's battery, Lieutenant Ned Kirby commanded two guns.

By eleven o'clock, the brigades of Bartow and Bee, and the original Confederate force on Matthews Hill, were vastly outnumbered and forced to retreat a mile, across the turnpike and Young's Branch to

Henry House Hill. Pelham's battery and the other batteries covered the Confederate retreat and pounded the Union troops as they overran the abandoned Confederate positions.

An hour later, General Jackson deployed his nearly three thousand Virginians along a broad front on the southeast side of Henry House Hill, just below the crest. On his right flank were South Carolinian troops and on his left, Jeb Stuart's Black Horse Cavalry. The exhausted and wounded troops who had been on Matthews Hill congregated at the rear of Jackson's brigade.

Jackson ordered Pelham's battery and two other batteries to fall back under the fusillade of the Union's longer range rifled-guns on Dogan Ridge. As Pelham limbered his guns to fall back, his horse was hit by a minie ball, but managed to keep its footing. The last battery to withdraw, Pelham spotted a mass of blue uniforms appearing from the wood line along Bull Run, in position to roll up Jackson's right flank. Instinctively, he unlimbered his guns and fired deadly canister, until the blue troops disappeared back into the woods. Relimbering his guns, he deployed them in a slight depression immediately in front of Jackson's defenses.

For the next two hours, Jackson and the other units on Henry House Hill withstood withering fire from Union guns, and the torrid pressure of repeated infantry assaults. All the while, Generals Johnston and Beauregard exhorted unengaged brigades to advance with all speed to the sound of the guns. Colonel Bartow, attempting to rally his beleaguered troops, was mortally wounded by a Union sniper. General Bee was likewise felled, but not before exclaiming to his men, "Look at Jackson standing there like a stone wall! Rally behind the Virginians!"

On the Union side, regiment after regiment fed the Union line, threatening the Confederate left flank, outnumbering the Confederates almost three to one. However, McDowell failed to mass his ground attack, choosing instead to attack piecemeal, one regiment after another, while his artillery attempted to soften Confederate positions.

Shortly after one o'clock, McDowell sent Lieutenant Kingsbury to Captains Griffin and Ricketts with orders that they move their batteries to the crest of Henry House Hill. Both commanders questioned the order of advancing artillery in front of heavy infantry. Nevertheless, they limbered their guns and proceeded forward, reaching the crest of

Henry House Hill at about two o'clock. They unlimbered their guns just south and east of what was known as the Widow Henry's house.

A thundering duel ensued with the Confederate batteries three hundred yards across the plateau. Opposing infantry hugged the earth as jets of flame poked holes through wreaths of smoke. The smoothbore Confederate guns proved deadly accurate, and Confederate sharpshooters took their toll. In Griffin's battery, Adelbert Ames was lifted off his feet and spun around by a minie ball in the thigh. Ordered to the rear by Griffin, he wouldn't hear of it, instead directing that a tourniquet be tied above the wound and that he be positioned on a rock, so he could direct his guns.

In the haze of black smoke, Griffin informed Lieutenant Hazlett that he was taking two guns to the south of Ricketts battery to pour enfilade fire on the Rebel guns. Griffin succeeded in moving his guns, and almost immediately was faced with a large number of blue-uniformed soldiers in an open field on his right flank. He loaded canister and was about to eliminate the rows of humanity, when the Union chief of artillery ordered him not to fire, declaring, "They are friendly troops, just look at the uniforms." Griffin argued vehemently, "They are not friendly! How could they be, coming from that direction?"

An instant later, the argument was settled. Jackson's blue-uniformed 33rd Virginia Regiment charged the Union guns. Their barrage dropped most of the gun crews and all of the horse teams in Griffin's battery. Ricketts's battery faired worse. Ricketts himself was felled by four minie balls, and his second in command was killed instantly. Ricketts's battery suffered twenty-seven killed or wounded, and Lieutenant Ned Kirby found himself in command of a battery that could not move.

Seeing the exposed guns, Jeb Stuart charged the Union batteries from the southwest, scattering the remaining gunners and supporting Union infantry. Another of Jackson's regiments joined the charge and, despite a furious barrage from Union troops, overran and captured the Union guns. However, possession of the prize was short-lived, as the Union counterattacked and retook the guns.

During the whole, Pelham had his spyglass to his eye. Across the plateau, in the remnants of what remained of the two Union batteries, he spied a man looking in his direction. The man's face was sooted and wholly unrecognizable. He suddenly bent down and helped a second man to his feet, and turned for the Union lines.

For the next hour, the battle seesawed, the Union guns changing hands several times. More fresh Union troops, including the light brigade of Colonel Oliver Howard, extended the Union right flank over Chinn Ridge. Sixteen hours earlier, at the conclusion of McDowell's battle briefing, Howard had offered prayer for the Union army.

Just before four o'clock, McDowell ordered an all-out assault on Jackson's brigade. Expecting the attack, Jackson directed Pelham and the other Confederate battery commanders to load canister and to wilt the barrels if need be. As Jackson trooped the line, Pelham heard him calmly encouraging the men. "Wait until they are fifty yards, then fire, give them the bayonet, and yell like furies."

The Union attack began, pressing the Confederate line again and again, but the line held. Shortly after four o'clock, the Union found its own right flank exposed. General Kirby Smith of Johnston's army had finally arrived by rail. It fell in quickly to extend the Confederate left flank, joined by Jubal Early's brigade and other Confederate regiments. In mass, they initiated the turning movement that began rolling up the Union right flank.

The scent of victory was strong in the Confederate nose. Beauregard ordered a general advance along the entire Confederate line; and within minutes, Union troops fell back, withdrawing to the turnpike. The Union retreat remained orderly across Stone Bridge, with some Union troops crossing at fords to the north. However, the withdrawal soon turned into a rout, when retreating troops found the turnpike blocked with supply wagons waiting to cross Bull Run. Advancing Confederate artillery fired on a second turnpike bridge, capsizing a haul wagon and preventing all but foot traffic. Confederate cavalry, led by Stuart, stung the flanks of the retreating column all the way to Centreville. Artillery, individual weapons, supply wagons, and horses were abandoned in the panic. A thousand Union soldiers were captured.

The battle was over.

On Henry House Hill, convinced that the Union had abandoned its guns for good, Pelham directed a dozen of his men to follow him with all of their six-horse teams and three additional wagons.

In the midst of the Union dead and wounded, the broken wagons, the upturned cannons, and scattered munitions, Pelham shouted, "Boys, would you look at this!"

"What's that, Lieutenant?" Sergeant Miles asked, his tone animated with victory.

Pelham ran a reverential hand over a tarnished brass barrel. "I trained with these for almost five years. We've just captured the West Point battery."

Pelham was about to order a check for survivors, when he heard a noise. "You hear that, Miles?"

"What's that, sir?"

Pelham cocked his head. "There it is again."

"Sir, I'm about deef with all this shootin'."

Pelham stepped around two mangled bodies and squatted beneath a gun barrel. Half buried in the dirt was a man, his blue uniform soaked with blood.

"Somebody give me a canteen," Pelham shouted as he bent over the man, who wore the epaulets of a captain. Pelham put an ear to the man's mouth. "Can you hear me, sir?"

The man managed a low moan.

"Here you go, Lieutenant." One of Pelham's cannoneers handed him a Union canteen.

Pelham soaked his bandana with hot water from the canteen and swabbed the man's forehead. As he did, he noticed the man's Academy ring.

"Sergeant Miles, get me medical supplies and a doc if you can find one. Do it quick. I mean now!"

Pelham leaned down and whispered in the man's ear, "Sir, I'm going to poke around a bit. You let me know if anything hurts."

Pelham made a cursory inspection, feeling around several gaping wounds. Eliciting no response, he deduced that the man was in shock.

"You've got some holes in you, sir. In fact, you're mighty lucky to be alive. Can you tell me your name?"

The man moved his lips, but there was no sound.

"Here, take some water. It's okay. You're not gut shot."

Pelham raised the man's head, and the man took water, one slow gulp at a time.

"Sir, your name?" Pelham asked.

The man took a deep breath. "Ricketts—"

"Easy, sir. You're in good hands."

"Obliged ..." The man's breathing was slow and heavy.

"Sir, if I may, a question. Did you have a man in your battery by the name of Kirby?"

The man opened his eyes and stared at Pelham, and after a long silence nodded his head.

EPILOGUE

FORTIETH REUNION, CLASSES OF MAY AND JUNE *1861*
NOVEMBER *1901*
WEST POINT, NEW YORK

What started as a beautiful Saturday morning with a full dress parade by the four hundred and eighty member Corps of Cadets; a West Point victory over Annapolis, 11 to 5, in the seventh year of Army-Navy football; and a trip to the West Point cemetery had been reduced to an overcast afternoon, everything taking on a shade of gray. The May and June Classes of 1861 were celebrating their fortieth year. Fewer than twenty members and former members of the two classes sat on folding chairs for the ceremony in a clearing west of the ivy-covered West Point Hotel, which was celebrating its seventy-fifth anniversary. A number of wives and other family members were also present, sitting in chairs set apart from the class members. The remembrance ceremony was for the most part somber, but seasoned by Henry du Pont with enough mirth to achieve a good end.

"Good words, Henry," Tom Rosser said, putting his arm around du Pont's shoulders as he sat down.

Rosser's own remarks had preceded du Pont's, and had opened the program; a gesture of good will from his Union classmates. Rosser's wife, she seeing West Point for the first time, sat with Libbie Custer, the widow of Rosser's dear friend and Civil War nemesis. The Texan had weathered well enough over the years, but carried a lean in his posture. Having been wounded seriously three times in the war, he should have shown more evidence of infirmity. That Rosser had finished the war a major general, would have amazed his former taskmaster, Professor

Mahan. Devoted to the girl he met in the war, and whom he married just hours before he and all of the male wedding guests rode off for Gettysburg, Rosser had struggled for purpose and identity after the war, as had many Confederates. He served as chief engineer for a railroad, and in the Spanish-American War was made a brigadier general for the country he had once fought against. Early in their marriage, his wife had given him seven children. They had named one of the sons John Pelham.

Henry du Pont had also fared well, receiving the Congressional Medal of Honor, and concluding the war as chief of artillery for the Department of West Virginia. He too had married and fathered seven children, though only two lived to adulthood. For many years, he was president of the Wilmington and Northern Railroad. He was also instrumental in the family business, which he incorporated as E. I. du Pont de Nemours and Company. Earlier in the reunion, du Pont had informed Rosser that he was now inclined toward politics.

Rosser and du Pont waited for the remarks of Adelbert Ames. Like Rosser during the war, he had attained the rank of major general; and like du Pont, he had received the Congressional Medal of Honor. After the war, he had resigned his commission to enter politics, serving as U.S. senator from Mississippi, and then as Mississippi's governor. Later, he had the distinction of being the last "carpetbag" governor of the South; and like Rosser, was commissioned a brigadier general in the Spanish-American War. He and his wife had six children, one of whom graduated from West Point in the Class of 1894. Ames too was little changed, except for whiteness of hair and a goatee.

"My beloved friends," he began. "The visit to the cemetery is a clear reminder that we've not much longer here to stay."

Several of the assembled found the remark amusing, though at the cemetery there had not been a dry eye when du Pont read the roll call of deceased classmates.

Ames acknowledged the attendees and family members, and the remarks made by Rosser and du Pont, and suggested that it might be pleasant to review what had happened to those who had played such an important or amusing role in their lives as cadets.

"The bane of our existence, Old Bentz," he began, "continued to bugle for another fifteen years until forced to retire. He died in 1878, offering his horn to St. Gabriel, and, as we saw in the cemetery, received a very fine marker from the Corps of Cadets.

"Also buried at West Point is General Winfield Scott, who in 1863, after fifty years of remarkable service to the nation, retired to West Point. Here he witnessed the end of the war, before passing into paradise in 1866 at the age of seventy-nine.

"And what about our superintendents? Colonel Delafield was promoted to major general, became chief of the Corps of Engineers, and after retiring from the army, served as regent for the Smithsonian Institute. Old Del died in 1873. Our last superintendent, Alexander Bowman, passed early in 1865—I'm not sure what got him."

"Our shortest-tenured superintendent, Beauregard ..." Ames glanced at Rosser. "Old Bory commanded Confederate armies throughout the war, and afterwards ran two railroad companies and became an inventor of some renown, with several patents to his name. It was in 1893 that he entered eternity.

"As for our commandants, William Hardee commanded Confederate corps throughout the war and survived to run a cotton plantation in Selma, Alabama. This being insufficient diversion, he also operated a warehouse, an insurance business, and presided over the Selma & Meridian Railroad. Hardee passed in 1873.

"John Reynolds, God rest his soul, was the Union's best corps commander. I personally know he was seriously considered by Lincoln to command the Army of the Potomac. Reynolds, of course, fell at Gettysburg, but we all know that—" Ames had to dry his eye on that one.

"After surviving Fort Sumter, Major Robert Anderson was promoted to major general, was a driving force in creating our Association of Graduates, and by and by picked Nice, France, as the place to depart the earth, which he did in 1871. As we saw, he too is interred in the West Point cemetery.

"After the war, Jeff Davis was charged but never convicted of treason, though he did spend two years in prison before Northern and Southern notables posted his bail. He was elected to the U.S. Senate again, but not allowed to serve, and completed two fine literary works on the Confederacy before he passed in 1889.

"And what of our lieutenants? Oliver Howard, our Bible-preaching math teacher?" Ames couldn't resist a laugh. "Hell, he goes straight to the top, wearing all the stars allowed, commanding Union armies, and receiving the Congressional Medal of Honor in exchange for a right arm. But even with one arm he continued to soldier on the frontier, and in the early eighties returned to West Point as superintendent. To his considerable credit after the war, he was a co-founder of Howard University in Washington DC, a nonsectarian institution for men and women, with no regard for race. And, of course, other institutions bear his mark. As far as I know, the man remains on this side of the grass." Ames smiled again. "It appears to pay well to be in the Lord's camp.

"Fitzhugh Lee, one of my favorites—and Rosser's too—did what we would have expected. Made major general early in the war and commanded cavalry units throughout, and at the end—after Jeb Stuart was killed—very ably supported his uncle, Robert E. Lee. Following the war and after a hand at growing cotton and a family—he and his wife had five children—he served four years as governor of Virginia. After that, like Rosser, he was a brigadier general in the Spanish-American War. Last I heard, he too is still kicking.

"Finally, what of our professors, those demigods who held our fates in their stoic little hands? They, of course, are all lecturing in heaven now. Professors Mahan and Agnel died in office in 1871. Professor Church died on his mathematics throne in 1878. Professor Weir not only lived to retire in 1876, after forty-two years at West Point, but lived to the ripe age of eighty-five, giving up the ghost in 1889. Professor Kendrick—I for one will never forget his peach brandy—retired in 1880 and departed for glory in 1891. He was eighty, and I understand there was quite a turnout for his funeral. Old Bartlett, he outlasted them all. After forty years, he retired in 1871 and passed in 1893 at the age of eighty-eight.

"As for the Warner sisters, those dear angels of God. Some of us knelt this morning at Susan's grave, the plot donated by the Academy. And I daresay one day the earthly remains of her sister, Anna, will reside beside her."

As Ames continued, Rosser reflected on the roll call at the cemetery. He thought of Chas Patterson, Shakespeare incarnate, and the first to die in the war. He had been a lieutenant colonel, leading his infantry regiment at Shiloh in April 1862. Walter Kingsbury, whose voice ruled the Plain and the mess hall, was next in September 1862—leading his regiment into the hell storm of Antietam Creek near Sharpsburg on the bloodiest day of the war. When they carried his body away, it bore eight musket balls. In tragic irony, he was killed by men in the division commanded by his brother-in-law, Major General David Jones. Five months later, his beloved Eva delivered a son, Walter Kingsbury, Jr. Rosser understood that Eva never really recovered from Walter's death.

Rosser had to blink hard, thinking of Ned Kirby at Chancellorsville. He'd been seriously wounded, his leg shattered, but he wouldn't allow himself to be taken from the battlefield. He continued to inspire his men until he collapsed from loss of blood. After the battle, his leg was amputated, and for a time there was hope he would survive. But when gangrene developed, senior officers in the Army of the Potomac approached President Lincoln on Kirby's behalf. Lincoln immediately came to Kirby's bedside and promoted him to brigadier general an hour before he breathed his last.

Rosser's thoughts turned to Gettysburg, where for him and so many, the war had been lost. On the Union side, Paddy O'Rorke, first captain and favorite of the Class of June 1861, was killed rushing his regiment to the defense of Little Round Top. Hours later, Charlie Hazlett fell next to his guns on the same piece of smoking earth.

But for Rosser, he had a hard time remembering these and other things. The war was a lifetime ago. His reflections turned instead to George Custer, last in his class but its highest ranking and most decorated member during the war. He and Fannie, both commanding cavalry brigades, had chased each other up and down the Shenandoah Valley the last two years of the war, Fannie proving as tough a foe as he had been a faithful friend. They had renewed their friendship after the war. But he was gone now, and had been for many years. Thinking of the Little Big Horn, he glanced over at Libbie Custer. The little woman, still pretty as a picture, would never remarry. She would be brave and proud for her man until the day she joined him.

He thought of Nate Chambliss, who had managed to graduate with the class. But when Tennessee announced secession and Chambliss submitted his resignation, rather than being allowed to resign like others of the South, he was dismissed for refusing to do battle with the Confederacy. Chas Patterson shared the same fate two weeks later, when Arkansas seceded. In any event, Chambliss survived the war to marry the youngest daughter of former commandant William Hardee, and to run a cotton plantation, edit a newspaper, and teach mathematics at the University of Alabama. Much to his credit, Chambliss had been one of the first Confederates to renew ties with West Point and to join the post-war Association of Graduates. He had been a key planner for the fortieth reunion before dying at the age of sixty-two, missing the reunion by two years.

Ames concluded his remarks. "I am deeply honored to be a member of our class, and even more so to be a member of the Long Gray Line. God bless you all—and may God grant us safe passage into his peace."

Ames received a standing ovation. As he returned to his seat, du Pont announced that everyone was on his own until supper, which would be in a hotel dining room reserved for them.

"Let's the three of us walk," Ames said to Rosser and du Pont. "The cold has got to my bones. If I don't keep moving, I seize up in my thigh."

"I don't expect any of us is without an extra hole in him," Rosser observed.

The three walked the short distance to the newly constructed Battle Monument, the most impressive edifice on the West Point campus. Upon the broad circular terrace, a five-foot diameter Roman Doric column of granite rose forty-six feet, supporting a winged statue of victory. Positioned at octagonal points around the terrace were eight square pedestals topped by large bronze-banded granite spheres, which were flanked by small cannons. The monument had been designed to memorialize the officers and men of the regular army who had died in the Civil War, and its dedication four years earlier had been attended by du Pont, Ames, and Chambliss. The bronze bands around the granite spheres bore the names of two thousand and forty-two enlisted men. The base of the granite column bore the names of one hundred and eighty-eight officers. The three of them silently read the names at the base of the column.

Rosser suddenly fell to his knees and wept openly.

Ames put a hand on his shoulder.

Rosser's finger was still on the name—Daniel McElheny.

"I know, Tom. I know." Ames was no less affected.

Du Pont placed a hand on Rosser's other shoulder. "Damn, he could make us laugh."

Rosser struggled to his feet, and the three of them stood side by side, silent, staring at the names on the column.

Turning toward the Plain, Rosser swept a hand across the horizon and the distant structures. A behemoth stood a hundred yards north of the library and overlooking the Hudson. The structure was named for General George Cullum, and boasted a huge ballroom beneath a ceiling of three hundred and forty lights. "Except for Cullum Hall, where the likes of us could have had some fine parties, nothing's changed."

"Forty years," Ames said, as if not believing it.

"Yet there have been changes," du Pont said thoughtfully, "and Emory Upton must have enjoyed one of them a great deal."

"Emory?" Rosser expressed surprise.

"Henry Flipper, Class of 1877. He was our first Negro graduate, and was a cadet while Emory was commandant."

"Wasn't he ... silenced by the Corps?" Ames asked, almost apologetically, referring to the practice of members of the Corps not talking to one of their own except on official business.

"Yes, all four years, and not surprising, I suppose, given the times. But the incredible thing is that Flipper took it all in stride, and upon graduation, to a man, the Corps roundly cheered him and took his hand in friendship. I'm told it was a very moving scene."

"Indeed," Ames said. "For myself, I always thought Emory a different duck, but he was more man than most of us."

"And not so different, really," du Pont said. "Emory and I became close after the war, both of us in a position to assist West Point. A remarkable man, and no more honorable and serving a heart has ever beat." Du Pont paused. "He certainly did not deserve his end."

Rosser and Ames nodded. They all knew the story, that after the war, in which he attained the rank of major general, Upton had fallen hard for a young and very beautiful woman, who deeply loved him. Her effect upon him had been transforming. But just two years into the marriage she died, at about the time he learned he was to be commandant at West

Point. A few years later, at the age of forty-two, the class abolitionist put a gun to his head. Some speculated it was continued grief over the loss of his wife, but du Pont and others knew he also suffered from intense headaches and the sensation of blood surging through his head. Toward the end, he thought he might be going insane. And indeed, after his death, an autopsy revealed that he had suffered a brain aneurysm and a probable brain tumor.

The three fell into a silence, which Ames finally broke, looking off across the Hudson. "How is it none of us has mentioned John?"

Du Pont, who until then had been a rock, could not hold back the tears. "John," he choked, "was our best."

Rosser, out of tears at the time, drew the two of them to himself and forced a laugh. "You know, I envy the boy. Think of it—he'll never grow old." He pinched his cheeks. "Me. I'm so wrinkled, I can't find my face."

Du Pont and Ames, whose cheeks were also deeply lined, welcomed the humor.

"Tell us, Tom," du Pont said. "Tell us about John."

"Okay, but let's start moving again. I've got the same problem Adelbert has."

As they walked in slow circles around the monument, Rosser related the events as best he could recall them, from the time he and Pelham had boarded the steamer in April 1861.

"I saw a lot of John during the war, both of us serving in Virginia and in Jackson's army. Jeb Stuart loved him like a brother and kept him close by. He wanted John's input on everything." Rosser paused, as though reflecting. "Remember the girl I snuck into camp for Pelham?"

Ames smiled. "Clara Bolton?"

"How could we forget?" du Pont grinned.

"Good memories. The sweetest gal, and obviously over the edge with our John. Anyway, the two of them survived that year on letters and her trip after Christmas."

Du Pont put a hand on Rosser's arm. "She came back to West Point?"

"John never told you?"

Ames shook his head. "Not a peep."

"I suppose I was the only one who knew—me and Dan McElheny." Rosser had to clear his throat again. "Anyway, after Sumter, they agreed to end it, not that they had a choice." Rosser felt no need to go into the trip to Clermont. "But on the boat from West Point, John showed me a letter from Eva Taylor, who, of course, married our Walter. In the letter she said that a Miss Sallie Dandridge was no longer seeing anyone and would be pleased to have him call upon her in Virginia, at a place called the Bowery, near Martinsburg."

"And?" du Pont pressed.

"He did. Before Manassas, the Army of Virginia trained near where her family lived. I met her a few times—quite a looker—and she and Pelham hit if off from the start. They saw a lot of each other between campaigns, for that was where the army rested and wintered as much as it could."

Rosser paused and adjusted his scarf against the chill wind.

"The last we talked, John announced that he was going to marry her once there was time to do the deed. This was about the time he received a final letter from Clara Bolton. She was attending Smithfield Medical College and had a proposal of marriage from a recently graduated doctor, the two of them having courted for a time. She wanted John to know and to have his blessing, which he freely gave her. He was genuinely happy for her."

Rosser hesitated, as if catching his breath. "As for John the soldier, from the very beginning, at First Manassas, he proved himself the shining star of the South, all action and humble as dirt. He just had a knack for artillery, how to do battle, and getting his guns in and out of the most god-awful places. His men would do anything for him. Audacious—that's what he was. Damn, he was audacious!" Rosser waged a finger at Ames. "After Manassas and what Pelham did there, Jeb Stuart says, 'I want horse artillery,' and tells Pelham to make it happen and be its chief. He wanted guns moving like the wind across the battlefields, and John delivered. It wasn't long before he had five batteries under him, and not a few times the artillery of other divisions. I daresay Pelham's horse artillery was one of the most unnerving weapons we had against you boys."

"Easily," Ames admitted, remembering too well.

"Yes, Pelham's guns were everywhere at once," Rosser mused. "He would move, shoot, move, shoot, and never be in a place long enough for you guys to get a bead on him. Audacious!"

Ames laughed. "Sharpsburg and Fredericksburg, that's where I remember him best—I mean, worst."

Rosser smiled. "Damn right. Especially Fredericksburg, and that would have been December 1862. You bluecoats outmatched us in numbers—more than usual—and we were in a pinch. That's when John told Jeb Stuart he could take two guns and get some enfilade fire on you bluecoats. A damn scary sight. Your front stretching three miles, three rows of infantry, fifty-five thousand strong, bayonets gleaming, coming straight at us. Anyway, what he did with those two artillery pieces was nothing short of a miracle." Rosser shook his head. "For hours, he pinned your left flank, the sixteen thousand troops of John Reynolds, our old commandant. And how does he do it? By moving his guns after every shot—that's how! There was no give-up in the man. After an hour, you guys got lucky and took out one of his guns." Rosser put a finger on du Pont's chest. "So then, what does he do? For another hour, he hops around with just the one gun, blazing away—Reynolds slowed down—a hundred of your guns trying to nail him." Rosser took a deep breath. "That was my roommate. That was a good day—damn, that was a good day. All of us, from Lee down, knew what Pelham had done. That's when General Lee singled him out, called him, 'the gallant Pelham,' said, 'It is glorious to see such courage in one so young.'"

Ames and du Pont shared Rosser's pride.

"What you say is true, Tom," du Pont said. "John would never retreat."

"Amen to that." Ames nodded.

Rosser drew himself up. "Did you know that John was in every engagement he could possibly have been in? More than sixty, and through them all, he lived the charmed life, never sick, not even a scratch—though it didn't pay to be his horse."

Ames and du Pont appreciated the humor.

Rosser glanced up the Hudson. "Our own Fannie, God rest his soul, in the middle of the war sends John a telegram of congratulations!"

"Just what he'd do." There was affection in Ames' voice.

"It was Kelly's Ford where John went down, wasn't it, Tom?" du Pont said almost in a whisper.

Rosser's gaze dropped to the pavers around the monument. "It was—it was March 1863."

Du Pont put a hand on Rosser's shoulder.

"The morning of Kelly's Ford, John was breakfasting with Stuart, when a courier nearly ran his horse into the fire with news that large Union cavalry had engaged Fitz Lee's cavalry pickets. I'm told Pelham didn't say a word—just borrowed a horse and rode to the call of the guns. He was everywhere in the early stage of the fight, exhorting the troops, the consummate officer high on his horse." Rosser's voice quavered. "I talked to a man who was there, who witnessed it. There was an airburst, and John just fell from his horse. When they got to him, he was unconscious. At first they couldn't see a wound, but then they found where a small splinter of shrapnel had pierced the back of his skull. He never regained consciousness. Our John—who had not suffered a scratch—died the next morning."

Ames and du Pont had to turn their heads.

"Stuart, of course, was heartbroken. In John, he'd lost his right arm. Sallie Dandridge was devastated. Clara Bolton, thank God, she never knew. John's body lay in state in Richmond for three days—thousands paid their respects." Rosser's eyes glistened. "Our dear friend was mourned throughout the South and eventually taken home to Jacksonville."

Du Pont wiped his cheeks with the back of his hand. "I can just see him now—that grin of his."

"The irony," Rosser said. "I went down at Kelly's Ford too, not a quarter mile from John. Think of it. I survive and live out my life, and he dies thinking the South is winning its independence."

The wind blew leaves across the terrace of the monument and between their feet.

Two cadets in dress gray, who had been watching the three alumni at a respectful distance, now approached the monument. From the two chevrons at the cuff of their dress coats, Rosser recognized them as Second Classmen.

One of the two addressed him. "Sir, I see from your arm band that you are Class of May 1861." The cadet extended his hand. "We couldn't help noticing your connection with the monument."

"Indeed." Rosser forced a grin and shook the cadet's hand. "The name is Tom Rosser, and don't be taking pity on us. I'll have you know we were once as young as you. What's your name, son?"

"MacArthur, sir, Douglas MacArthur. And this is my classmate, Ulysses Grant."

Rosser cocked his head. "Any kin …?"

"My grandfather, sir."

Rosser managed a smile. "You know, your grandfather made life very unpleasant for us." He introduced Ames and du Pont.

"Sirs," MacArthur said, "I'm sure we'll come across your names next year when we study the Civil War."

"That would be The War between the States, young man," Rosser said.

"Had you won the war …" Ames observed politely.

"I'm from Arkansas," MacArthur said, as if to make amends. "Ulysses is from Illinois."

"Sir." Grant's tone held deep respect as he addressed Rosser. "To my mind, this monument is as much yours. I can't imagine what your class went through."

"We all have our challenges," Rosser answered evenly. "And I daresay yours will too."

The three veterans were held captive by the two cadets, answering endless questions about what it was like to be a First Classman on the eve of the war, to serve in the war itself, to face friends in war, to learn of their deaths, and to reconcile after so much had been at stake. They particularly grilled Rosser as one who had been on the losing side.

"Now, I think it is my turn," Rosser said when he had been picked clean. "Tell me, do you play everything by the book here?" He was remembering the old days, the things he, Pelham, and Custer had done.

"Actually, sir." Grant turned to MacArthur. "Can I tell him, Doug?"

"He might appreciate it more than you think," MacArthur said with a straight face.

"Sir, you see the reveille cannon over there?" Grant pointed to the cannon next to the post flagpole. It was fixed with bolts to a concrete pad.

"I do."

"One night last month, Doug, with very little help, put that cannon on top of the clock tower in Central Area! His plan—pure genius. No one has a clue how it was done or who did it." Grant beamed with pride.

Rosser glanced at MacArthur, whose face bore a wide grin. "What say you, Henry, Adelbert? Does that qualify for the large testicle award?"

They all laughed.

"Sir," MacArthur said, "we've badgered you enough, but I've one last question—which you might think strange."

"Shoot." Rosser stood, arms crossed.

"Sir, next year we celebrate the centennial of the Academy. As you know, we have many traditions here, and some of us wonder how much is fact and how much is fiction. For instance, we sing 'Benny Havens, Oh.' All those verses."

"Yes." Rosser smiled. "There are a lot of verses."

"Sir, my question—did the man really exist?"

Rosser's response was a long laugh. Prior to the reunion, he and Ames had visited Havens' gravesite in the Highland Union Cemetery south of Buttermilk Falls, though the town now went by the name Highland Falls. Buried beside him were Letitia and their three children. They had learned over a pint in a local pub that Havens had tired of the tavern business in the early years of the war, and had begun to spend time in New York City, though he still considered the Landing his home. After his death in 1877, at the age of ninety, the tavern and home were razed to make way for a new railroad, the same railroad whose trains now rumbled beneath the Plain.

"Young man, would you like to see where his tavern used to be?"

IT IS FINISHED

While serving as the postmaster of Charlottesville, Virginia, Thomas Lafayette Rosser died on March 29, 1910, at the age of seventy-three, his wife at his side.

Having served two terms as United States senator for the State of Delaware, and having proved himself a lifelong advocate of West Point, Henry Algernon du Pont died peacefully at his Delaware home (Winterthur) on December 31, 1926, at the age of eighty-eight.

A close friend and golfing partner of John D. Rockefeller, the last surviving member of the Class of May 1861, and the oldest living graduate of the Academy, Adelbert Ames died at his summer home in Ormond Beach, Florida, on April 13, 1933, at the age of ninety-seven.

ACKNOWLEDGEMENTS

The Parting could not have been written without continual reference to the nonfiction works of Mary Elizabeth (Betty) Sergent (1919-2005), *They Lie Forgotten* and *An Unremaining Glory*; and her fictional work *Growing up in Alabama*. In aggregate, they chronicle the West Point Classes of May and June 1861 and the life of John Pelham. I am truly blessed to have known Mary Betty—a wonderful woman of faith and a friend of West Point—and to have accepted her challenge to write this story.

I am most grateful to Elaine McConnell, Suzanne Christoff, Susan Lintelmann, Alicia Mauldin-Ware, Valerie Dutdut, and the many other extremely helpful members of the West Point library, special collections and archives staffs, who suffered me to nest in their quiet space, and who provided the photograph of Edmund (Ned) Kirby, the sketch map of West Point, and the photograph of cadets conducting artillery drill on the Plain. Similarly, my thanks to Brett Bradshaw, president of the John Pelham Historical Association, for permission to use the photograph of John Pelham taken in his furlough uniform, and thanks as well to the association's treasurer, Bill Gilmore.

A very special thanks to Tom Petrie, my friend, classmate, and renowned collector of American art, for his permission to adapt the painting "Encampment on the Plain," by William Guy Wall, 1862, for inclusion in this book. As a member of the Gettysburg Foundation's board of directors and a man with a thorough knowledge of the Civil War and American history, his insights were most helpful to me.

Thanks also to Jon Malinowski, professor of geography, United States Military Academy, classmate Freed Lowrey, and Rich Barbuto (Class of 1971) for their review of period-specific descriptions of West Point and the times; to classmate Paul Haseman for his unwavering support; to Anne McNeil for her "horse sense;" and to the *many, many* friends who read the various editions of my manuscript and gave the feedback needed to make the story better.

Thanks also to the Squaw Valley Community of Writers family, who encouraged me and prodded my writing craft in a better direction, and to Elizabeth L. Barrett for her line editing.

A very special thanks, also, to the West Point Class of 1961, who conceived, funded, and continue to maintain Reconciliation Plaza; and to its member, Colonel (Ret.) Ed Brown, who has been a true ally throughout the writing of this story.

Finally, immeasurable gratitude to my loving family, to the Class of 1967, and to every man and woman of the Long Gray Line that for more than two centuries has stood in the gap for a thankful nation and after the Civil War played such an important role in its healing.

AUTHOR'S NOTE

Much of *The Parting* is based on facts derived from archival research and nonfiction publications; and seasoned by my experiences as a West Point cadet and graduate, and later, as an Academy adjunct assistant professor. Such form the basis for the story's period portrayal of West Point, the cadet class system, the regimen of summer encampment, the hops at the West Point Hotel, meals in the mess hall, the routine of barracks life, the regimen of academics, the extracurricular activities of cadets, and the inexorable unraveling of the country.

The reader may wonder at the truth of whether Jefferson Davis actually chaired a federal commission to evaluate West Point in the summer of 1860, and whether Major Robert Anderson (who later commanded federal forces at Fort Sumter) was part of that commission; whether John Pelham was president of the Dialectic Society and could have encouraged the society to debate the right of a state to secede; whether Flirtation Walk was truly the venue for intimacy portrayed in the story; whether the first-ever visit by British royalty to North America included a stop at West Point; whether Benny Havens ever existed, with his lure of hot flip; whether a straw poll was taken within the Corps before the election of 1860; whether Henry du Pont actually fought a pugilistic contest with John Pelham as his second; whether cadets really skated across the Hudson to Garrison, and at Christmastime chased a greased pig for the right to a feast; whether the antics of cadets (those future defenders of American and world liberty) could be as inane as portrayed in the story; whether academic life was as rigorous as described; whether Henry Farley of South Carolina, the first Southern cadet to resign in the face of secession, later pulled the lanyard that started the Civil War; and whether Douglas MacArthur and Ulysses S. Grant III were actually cadets in 1901. The reader may take heart that all these things and more are based in fact or the documented memory of those alive at the time. Additionally, the reader may take comfort that most of the characters in the story (cadets, Academy military and academic leadership, and others) are real, and that their relationships to one another and their actions within the story are, with few exceptions, authentic.

Whether John Pelham actually had a love affair with Clara Bolton, I leave to the reader, but not the reality that he was caught by Lieutenant Colonel Hardee displaying his affection to a girl while attending a hop at the West Point Hotel, and for that offense was confined to quarters for the balance of summer encampment. That Pelham met and fell in love with Sallie Dandridge in the fall of 1861, and that they were engaged to be married, is also much more fact than fiction.

The events of the three days leading up to and including the First Battle of Bull Run are similarly based in fact; and the likelihood is great that John Pelham and Ned Kirby indeed peered at each other across the crest of Henry House Hill during the decisive encounter that gave the Confederacy the first major victory of the Civil War.

The story's epilogue, the fortieth reunion, while apocryphal, could easily have taken place, and the fates of the story characters presented in the epilogue are true.

To my readers, I cannot urge strongly enough that if you have never visited West Point, that you do so; and that among all of the historical attractions you see, you allot sufficient time to experience the emotion and relevance of Reconciliation Plaza.

Lastly, I wrote the poem on the following page to capture the emotion associated with graduates of West Point returning to the Academy every five years for their fall and spring class reunions. The poem is about reminiscences on the Plain Saturday morning before the alumni parade, when the Corps of Cadets marches to martial music score before a large crowd and passes in review along the extended line of assembled alumni classes, often spanning a timeframe of more than sixty years . . . men and women of *The Long Gray Line.*

IN THEIR EYES

Ere cloaking Hudson mist gave birth to pensive early dawn
And warming sun imbued the day with color's magic wand
Some walked the quiet of that time recalling what had been
When younger then, they too were called, a country to defend

So much the same, the sight and sound and scent upon the wind
Roused memory of former times, sweet chapters deep within
When first the Corps assembled there, uncertain what to be
Til men of worth and men of faith saw clear its destiny

Three hallowed words would cross their lips, a motto ever be
The first was **DUTY**, selfless love, to serve a nation free
Then **HONOR** next, a guarding shield against the tempter's sting
And **COUNTRY** followed, sacred trust, of which they'd often sing

The river's might, the circling hills, beneath God's brilliant arch
Called forth to mind those harried times when they, too, formed to march
When shoes and brass were made to shine, and belts the purest white
Were donned on black trimmed coats of gray, beneath a dress hat bright

Behind them lay so much of life since first they wore the gray
When light their step and clear their eye, they savored each new day
Those happy times of West Point years, when bonds for life were made
Til oaths were sworn and forth they went, their mettle to be weighed

Still on they walk on legs grown old, with eyes that strain to see
But gaining strength with every step, infused by history
By classmates gone whose deeds on earth live on in mind and heart
Remembered friends in marbled stone who bravely did their part

What's that they hear upon the Plain, but sound of fife and drum
As turn they all to join a class whose time to march has come
And march they do with heads held high before the grateful throng
And with them wait for freedom's band to call the new guard on

The granite walls release their hold and free the waiting Corps
Young men and women marching forth to martial music score
They pass the Line, their span of years, as eyes look right to see
And in their eyes catch full a glimpse of who they'll one day be

All sense a spirit in the air, a bond across the stage
As eyes grow moist and hearts beat fast, uniting all in age
The young march off and leave the plain, the stirring music dies
But those who stay, inspired so, renew their lifelong ties

God grant them mercy in your will, the Black and Gold and Gray
To find a servant's resting place, when comes the final day
With family, friends, The Long Gray Line, eternity to share
Immortal life by heaven's grace with all who gather there

© Richard Barlow Adams, 2005

383

ABOUT THE AUTHOR

Richard Barlow (Rich) Adams, born to Colonel and Mrs. Ernest C. Adams, was the first of three sons to graduate from West Point. He received his appointment to join the Class of 1967 from Representative Homer Thornberry of the 10th Congressional District of Texas. Six months after graduation, he deployed to Vietnam as an artillery forward observer for D Company, 1/506th Infantry, 3rd Brigade, 101st Airborne Division. Upon returning to the States, he became a fixed-wing aviator and transferred to the Army Corps of Engineers. After seven years in the military, he and his family returned to Austin, Texas, where he began a career as a consulting civil/environmental engineer. Eventually moving to Baton Rouge, Louisiana, he formed and later sold an engineering company. He is active in West Point alumni affairs and the many activities of his class, and has served as an adjunct professor in the School of Engineering and Applied Science, Southern Methodist University, and as adjunct assistant professor in the West Point Department of Geography and Environmental Engineering. He and his wife have two married children, several grandchildren, reside in Miramar Beach, Florida, and are members of the Destin United Methodist Church.

As Adams pursues his writing, he continues to serve as a consulting forensic engineer, and enjoys speaking engagements, traveling, golfing, skiing (in the past, as Vail Resorts ski instructor), and sharing his faith. Adams is also the author of *Eben Kruge: How "A Christmas Carol" Came to be Written* (Clarion ForeWord five-star review), a story about Charles Dickens and what inspired him to write the Christmas classic.

The Author
(Green Apple Photography
www.greenapplephotos.com)

Richard Barlow Adams as a cadet, Class of 1967

CPSIA information can be obtained at www.ICGtesting.com
Printed in the USA
LVOW12*0818311014

411351LV00002B/5/P